I LOVE A GOOD CHALLENGE

I LOVE a Good Challenge

BY SARA NORTH

Story Boréale

Identifiers:
Library of Congress Control Number: 2024912341
ISBN: 979-8-9892125-2-1 (paperback)
ISBN: 979-8-9892125-3-8 (ebook)

First edition June 2024

Cover Illustration: Alyssa Miles
Cover Design: Taylor Waldron
Editing: Brittany Howard
Proofreading: Jenn Lockwood
Formatting: Erica Dansereau

Published in the United States by Story Boréale
www.authorsaranorth.com
@authorsaranorth

To everyone waiting to be someone's first choice: You're worth fighting for.

This ring on my finger
Is running away with me
And I'll smile each time
I hear you say you love me
'Cause loving you is so easy
It's better than the best dream I have known
And holding you is so freeing
I feel the chains of day fall to my feet
And I can breathe

"Loving You" by Sara North

Chapter One

Lily

My mouth tastes like chocolate. Dark chocolate—bitter and in need of some sweetness to make it a bit more palatable—much like my current scenario. It's fitting because when you work with chocolate and other baked goods all day, every day, you learn to draw parallels between them and your life. Making beautiful things with your hands from flour, sugar, and pure magic is a comfort because they tangibly remind you that what starts as a mess can become a sort of miracle. When you're as romantically challenged as I am, that's a relief.

I've saved up for a year to be in LA for the next six weeks. I don't think I fit into the city, but it is a nice distraction. The great love of my life is chocolate, so when a spot on a chocolatier-intensive course I've had my eye on for years opened, I couldn't pass it up. Becoming more excellent at my craft is an added win.

I rarely take a vacation from Sparrow's Beret, the bakery and café I co-own with my best friend in Birch Borough. After all, if I'm not there, who will keep our town on its toes and constantly evaluating whether or not it should apply to be on a reality TV show? I didn't take into account how lonely it would be across the country from the place I call home, though. I've spent seven nights in a short-term apartment rental, and I'm starting to wonder if maybe the few crummy people in my life who have led me to believe that I'm "too much" are right.

Despite the lingering smear of chocolate on my pants from today's session, I've made my way to a movie for some comfort and a distraction from my intrusive thoughts. It's Valentine's Day, for crying out loud. Nothing good comes from Valentine's Day. I learned a long time ago that love can be . . . fragile. It breaks easily, even when you aggressively attempt to keep it whole. Much like the tiny shavings of chocolate I sprinkle over our pots de crème, which melt as soon as you take a bite, affection seems to melt at the first sign of heat.

If I were home, I'd be bundled up with hot cocoa and multiple layers to keep myself from turning into ice in the still-frigid New England winter air. But here I am, in a t-shirt and high tops. What a life.

The smell of old movie theater mixed with the different stages of buttered popcorn—from stale to freshly popped—hovers in the air. I'm holding the biggest soda I can manage and a tub of popcorn. Yes, a whole tub. A sense in my bones tells me I will need it today. The theater is featuring a special showing of *Pride & Prejudice* (the 2005 version with the iconic hand flex). I knew I had to do everything I could to see it again on the big screen, so here I am.

Just as the lights begin to dim, movement to my right

distracts me. A figure walks down the row in the direction of my seat. It's a man—an alarmingly attractive man. Even in a room full of shadows, I can tell. I'm not sure how science explains our ability to sense that someone is attractive before we even fully see them, but maybe I should study the phenomenon.

"Excuse me." His voice breaks through the ambiance of movie theater sounds.

It's only us in the section, plus a few teenagers to the left. They're giggling, and it's clear they weren't even born when this movie came out (which is depressing). A few senior citizens sit toward the lower rows and are, without doubt, here to see the men in great coats at a weekday matinee show. They're my heroes.

I turn toward the newcomer, my eyes catching on suit pants paired with a button-up dress shirt, which is tucked in and peeking out behind a lightweight trench coat. I lift my eyes enough to see half of his face illuminated by the larger-than-life screen. His eyes are light, his hair perfectly styled, and he is wearing one of those leather-banded watches that make a man infinitely more intriguing.

"Are you British?" I mutter, the butter from the popcorn still sticking to my lips. There's no way this man can be American when he looks like someone my Regency-loving heart would find casually crossing the English countryside and not sitting in a movie theater.

"I'm sorry?"

He's definitely not British. He shrugs out of the trench coat. I'm rarely embarrassed, but I feel myself sinking a little lower in my seat. My jeans shift awkwardly on the leathery seat cushion as he sits in the seat beside me.

"No, not British," he continues with a laugh, discarding his coat on a nearby empty seat.

I don't know what show I've landed on, but I just know I'm being punked. If I had to guess a culprit, Gladys—the simultaneously endearing and frustrating busybody from my small New England hometown—has hired someone to mess with me even though I'm three thousand miles away. I don't know how she knows I'm here, but it feels like the most reasonable explanation that someone who looks like this man has chosen to sit next to me in a nearly empty theater. His level of blatant desirability alone makes me feel like I've landed on a movie set. I don't think they cast men like him to appear out in public where I'm from.

"Ashton?" I whisper expectantly into the air, waiting for a camera crew or a certain celebrity host from the early 2000s to pop out from behind the big red curtains up front.

"What was that?" the man says. He is not affected in the least by my obvious malfunction.

"What are you doing here?" I demand because he couldn't possibly be here to watch a movie.

"Seeing a movie," he says with a grin that flashes even in the dim light.

Instantly, I am riled up by the fact that his voice is exactly like I imagine melted chocolate would sound. I growl a bit. His eyes light up with amusement.

"Did you just growl?" he asks in a delighted tone.

I scrunch my nose. "It's just . . ." I am waving my hand in the air as if I'm about to land a plane (or half a plane since the other is still wrist-deep in the popcorn tub) when his shoulder brushes against my hand. I feel chills run down the back of my spine. His eyes—which I now realize are blue—take on a darker hue as if they're in the process of turning from daylight into a starry night.

"It's just, what?" His voice is suddenly a bit strained.

I'm delighted that he is as affected by me as I am by him. I probably smeared butter on his dress shirt, but I'm slightly satisfied that, even within this brief interaction, I've left my mark on him.

"May I sit here?" His tone shifts back to earnest. He sounds sincere. I'm good at calling people on their crap, and so far, this man isn't reeking of any of it.

"Are you a creeper?"

Immediately, he arches back in his seat. Adjusting his shirt collar, he shakes his head. "What? No."

"Well, then why does a man who looks like you come to a matinee showing of a movie that causes women to forget the world for a couple of hours and makes them dream of men wearing high-waisted pants?"

"Looks like me . . ." he mumbles to himself. I expect him to ask what I mean. Instead, he faces me with a furrowed brow, and I know he's about to throw a curveball. "Why do you love this movie?"

"Are you kidding me?" My popcorn-filled hand, now shooting kernels like tiny cannonballs in front of us, moves toward the screen as if I'm summoning the sun. "The hand flex moment. The dancing. The boiled potatoes line. The rain scene!"

"Interesting. Have you read *Pride & Prejudice*?"

"Of course I have."

"How many times?"

I blink. This man doesn't know how many times I've hidden away with a book in my hand and a dream in my heart just to feel like I belong in a story that's not mine. In books, there can always be a happy ending. In life, not so much. I try to keep my feelings on love as far under the surface as possible, which is surprising, given my tendency to freely express my emotions and opinions. But my love for books and movies set in other times stems from the fragments in my soul murmuring that the timing of my existence is all off. If I had been born in another period, perhaps I would feel as if I fit within my own life. And maybe somewhere else, instead of always wanting to fight with others, I'd feel like I'm the one worth fighting for.

I rally my thoughts to reply. "Dozens. How about you, Mr. Regency? How many times have you read the book?"

He has the audacity to smirk while adjusting his well-fitting designer shirt collar. It is only fair that this aggravating man pays exquisite attention to his attire. I try to focus on his words.

"Sixteen times. I read it every year. When I was fourteen, my mother sat me down and handed me the novel. She told me to read it once a year for the rest of my life. She said it would make me a better man."

My mouth hangs open while he casually sips the soft drink I didn't even notice until now. Because of course he can sip elegantly from a concession cup while I wonder how long my hand is going to smell like butter. It's a good thing there aren't many people in the theater, or we'd be kicked out for talking. It's not like that hasn't happened to me before.

"You're lying," I say with conviction.

"I never lie. And I'm a lawyer." He winks, but his tone and body language tell me it's true. There's something so open and honest about him. Something that I want to explore.

"Fine. You can sit next to me. Especially since you're doing it already."

"Thank you."

"But what are you doing *here?*"

"I'm about to watch Mr. Darcy be broody and awkward and still win the woman of his dreams."

He turns his face toward the screen. His profile is something an artist would swoon over. I now notice his neatly kept beard—more than stubble but less than completely full—that carries a scent of delicious-smelling beard oil. I take a deeper breath and shiver. It's definite. I've never had such a visceral reaction to a man, and I'm so aware of it.

"Infuriating," I grumble.

"Endearing," he counters. "So, um . . ." He gestures in a (dare I say) adorable way to encourage me to tell him who I am.

I lift my chin a little higher and shove a fistful of popcorn into my mouth but regret it immediately when I nearly choke.

"Are you okay?" He pats my back. The spot where his hand gently tries to keep this movie from being my last is now on fire. Forget the iconic hand. I think my spine is flexing.

"Stop it!" I cough. "I'm fine, George."

"It's Graham, actually."

I'm still clearing my throat. "Okay." Cough. "George."

He furrows his brow. "As in Wickham . . .?"

I shake my head and nod toward the screen as the

promotion for the movie theater company begins. It's the reminder to silence your mobile phones, and it's weirdly comforting that I feel unhinged by the sight of it. Still, I want to get right to the movie to avoid thinking about the unusual rhythm my heart has begun to follow. My once dark-chocolate mood is turning sweeter by the moment as I silently beg us to get lost in the familiar film.

"It's possible you'll never know," I retort. By how much I'm already feeling a gravitational pull toward him, I decide it's best to leave a bit of mystery hovering between us.

"Ah, a challenge," Graham muses, his voice rich, beckoning me to angle myself closer to him.

As if on cue, the theater darkens until it's just the runner lights on the carpeted stairs fencing us in as the movie screen lights the way. I don't know what ride I'm on, but I have an intense feeling I'm not leaving this movie theater the same way I walked in.

"Trust me," I hear him continue as the distinctive piano intro begins to play. "I'm definitely not the Wickham of this story."

Chapter Two

Lily

A fter you." The credits roll as Graham stands and motions for me to leave the row first.

But my knees are about to give out. I feel like I've just run a marathon I didn't train for. Sure, I've watched this movie hundreds of times and can quote it in my sleep, but no one prepared me for watching it next to Graham. I wasn't ready for the sight of his forearms as he reached for the drink cup between us. They peeked at me from under his sleeves after he rolled them up during Elizabeth and Darcy's first dance. Those are forearms worth remembering.

Watching the movie next to him brought up memories of sitting on the couch with my mom. I would wait for her to focus on me long enough to tell her how much I always hoped I'd have my own romance story to tell. The dream that, one day, I'd find my own version of Darcy.

And, oh, how I've tried to make room for love. But it's been a bust every time. It started with the punks in high school who liked to joke that I was too weird to be anyone's girl, and the story continued down to the last guy who told me that he was only dating me to see how far I would let him get. I'm a mystery. I'm a conundrum. I'm a fighter. And no man yet has seemed to know what to do with me.

We walk out of the auditorium side by side, and my mind races with questions on how this could turn out any differently. I throw away my popcorn bucket before we reach the fresh air outside. For a moment, my eyes rudely struggle to adjust to the natural light. I stare up at Graham, who waits patiently.

"Okay, well, I'm just gonna wait for my ride." I motion toward an ambiguous destination to try to throw him off my scent. At this point in the movie of my life, when I'm out on a date with the trolls that seem to populate the apps, I'm usually just hoping to make it across the bridge before they try to touch me. This time, I'm wondering what divine event happened in my life that I get to be near him without trying. And I feel a pull to stay. It's terrifying and exhilarating.

He nods, studying my face. He seems oblivious to the fact that we're standing outside the theater and about to be pelted with leftover gummy candy from the group of kids and their tired moms who no doubt just got out of some animated film. They're eyeing us like they are the Lost Boys, and Graham is Peter.

"Why did you walk over to sit with *me* in the middle of the movie theater?" I blurt the words into the air while motioning for us to start walking in a direction that is very much not where any sane driver would pick someone up. My mission is to find chocolate, but I guess I can handle company along the way if he follows.

He falls into step beside me. When I steal an expectant glance at him, he scrunches his nose a little before making a twirling motion with his finger near the top of his head.

"It was your ponytail. Your hair."

"My hair?" I grab the end of my ponytail to try to hide as much of it as possible, suddenly unsure of what to do with this information. "What about it? It's up. That's common."

"The light from the screen on it. Even when it was dim inside, it was . . ." He looks uncomfortable. "Glowing."

I let out a laugh and pause my stride. "Glowing? Did you actually just say that to me?"

"Would you rather I said something like 'it was incandescent'?"

Honestly, by the drop in my stomach at hearing him say the words, I may have preferred that. "I'm not from here," I blurt out.

His eyebrows lift and then furrow. "That's a shame. I'm not from here, either, if that helps. I mean, I do live here, but I also own a home in Boston."

My sharp inhale is audible. There's no arrogance in his statement, just fact. The knowledge that he owns a place a train ride away from my apartment in Birch Borough is too enticing to dismiss.

"I'm from New England too."

His eyes warm. "I knew I liked you."

At this, I grin. "You're wicked *smaht* for doing so." I don't have a Boston accent at all. When I first moved to the land known for acts of revolt against England as a five-year-old, I tried to adopt one and failed. But I force it this time to replace "smart" with something that reminds us both of a place that isn't this Hollywood life.

I continue without pause. "I haven't been to many

places in the world yet, but I'd say that if you're ever heartbroken, Birch Borough is the place to go."

I know I'm right. And even if I never see Graham again, it feels like a universal truth he needs to know. I'm convinced my town is the antidote to everything wrong with the world. It's the only place I've ever felt the closest to belonging, even if it hasn't been in all the ways I have hoped.

"Good to know." His eyes sparkle. "I realize we just met . . ."

Again, he's searching for a name, but I resume walking. Giving him my name feels so personal. It feels like a commitment. Like, somehow, if he has it, he'll never let it go. And if there's one thing I'm sure about, as much as I've dreamed of it, I'm terrified to let a man love me. Truth be told, I'm worried the parts that are uniquely me will die and disappear if I allow a man fully into my life. Will I adapt to make myself more palatable? Or will the thought that not all of me is lovable prove to be true? To get to the bottom of my fear, I'd have to sit with it, and I'm not sure I'd win that battle.

Graham shifts his weight, keeping stride with me, his posture delightfully proper with a hint of nervousness in his tone.

"But . . ." he continues with a smile I imagine is rare greeting me, "when I'm back East, maybe we could go to a Red Sox game sometime?"

I've loved Red Sox games since I was a little girl, but I haven't been to one in years. The memory takes me back to simpler times when my family was in one place. I hadn't yet felt the strain of being overlooked by them, and my way of viewing the world felt like a superpower. "Why would you say that?"

He shifts his shoulder slightly in a way that tells me that he's not only got good plans but that he'll also follow through with them. "Seems like a place for fun and dreams."

I laugh lightly. "Honestly, who are you? You know the works of Austen . . ." I hold off in case the only thing he's read of her work includes Pemberley, but he gives a boyish smile.

"And others."

"And how do you feel about strong women?" I counter quickly, my hand flying to my hip, unable to hold back from spouting out the thoughts springing into my mind. I'm good at that. A little too good. And, for some reason, the idea of him already retreating from me based on my personality makes me regret the tub of popcorn (just a little).

"Are there women who aren't strong? If so, I haven't met one," he replies solemnly.

My mouth falls open.

Graham continues, "Now, if you're talking about having a feisty quality, I like a woman with some fire. Call me an arsonist, but I like seeing how much I can light a spark in her until something between us starts to burn."

His ears tinge a little pink at the same time heat flushes my face. His response shows he intended it to be PG, but now that they're in the air, we also know the words could mean so much more in other circumstances.

I huff, but it's more out of annoyance than frustration. I'm beginning to think there's no way this man could ever be real. I never hold back from honest commentary, so I try to give him all I can to see if he can handle my greatest weapon: my mouth. "Honestly? I don't know whether to love you or take up boxing . . ."

"I hope it's the first one." His response is immediate. No hesitancy.

A blush creeps up my cheeks, irritating me further. It also ignites something in me that's new—perhaps how a butterfly might feel to suddenly find it is not what it once was. Graham laughs, and the sound warms me even more, the sincerity of it disarming me.

"But there's something I need to know if you'll be kind enough to tell me."

The way he's looking at me, I already feel some of my defenses slipping. "Yes?" I ask, holding my breath.

The palm trees towering over us sway in the wind, seemingly unaware of gravity, rooted resiliently to the earth as they stretch toward the sky. The jarring sounds of LA traffic punctuate our conversation while unaffected locals eat an early dinner on the patios of the cafés lining the street. Tourists with large cameras meander down the sidewalk, taking dozens of pictures of the sidewalks and signs they must think are famous landmarks. Meanwhile, they just missed the A-list celebrity disguised in a baseball cap who just walked by.

I find it all amusing. It's amazing what we can be distracted by while missing what's right in front of us.

Graham stops on the sidewalk with a hum, his eyes assessing my face as if I'm a puzzle and he's looking for clues. "What's your dream?"

"What? Why would you ask me that? People don't just

go around asking people about their dreams. We're not living in a musical."

Graham shakes his head. "Agree to disagree. I can't sing, but I do love music."

"Of course you do," I say under my breath.

"Well?"

"Well, what?"

Emotion clogs my throat, but I know nothing will clear it out. If this is what it means to truly be seen by someone, I don't know how to feel about it. "You're a stranger."

"I hardly think anyone who enjoys *that* movie together could be considered a stranger." He gestures back toward the theater, which is fading in the distance behind us. "Fine, I'll tell you mine. My dream is to be a good man."

"You aren't already?"

He shrugs in my peripheral vision, the warmth of him simultaneously calming and yet so brutally exposing all the things I've talked myself out of.

"I hope so. But I'm not sure I would know. Didn't have much of an example except what not to be."

His honesty startles me. And something in me wants to tell him. To let out the words that have been clawing at my mind. The thing I've wanted so badly for so long that I almost forgot it was there. Who knew Austen movies could bring out confessions of my own? Still, something about the softness in his eyes gives me courage. Besides, it's not like I'll ever see him again.

"Fine. The thing that I want . . . I mean, my dream . . ."

He nods for me to continue, though the surprise on his face strikes me as even more endearing. He's not taking it for granted that I'm answering his question.

As I try to collect my thoughts, I think of my parents, who love me but decided to move overseas to help others. I think of how they've always put their work in medicine and helping people at the forefront of their minds and their lives. Somehow, they believed I was strong enough to handle life on my own. If not for my small town, I would believe that love looks like doctors' offices and eating dinner by myself. They tried on weekends to make up for it, but still. People seem to assume that because I'm strong-willed, I'm not soft. But I've been inwardly begging for someone to try to understand who I am. I protect others but don't always know how to protect myself. I need banter to feel like I'm heard. I need wit woven with kindness to feel like I'm seen. The veiled urgency of it makes me want to weep, and I'm nearly desperate to feel understood.

"I want to be someone's first choice." The words burn in my throat but feel strangely liberating. It's one truth from a sea of hidden secrets that cling to the bottom of my soul like barnacles on a boat.

He smiles, a hint of empathy at the corners of his mouth. "I think that's a worthy dream to have."

I nod. My breath hitches. If he hears, he doesn't make me feel bad about it.

"Side note: Why would you take up boxing?" His head tips in an adorable way. It's a charming hint of a man letting himself play.

"As an alternative to loving you, of course."

Graham's eyes glimmer with what can only be described as pure delight.

"Okay, Mystery Woman," he says with a grin. I don't hate it. "Aside from the potential awkwardness of meeting on Valentine's Day, the truth is I don't have a valentine, and I'm in the mood for coffee. Would you happen to be in the mood for some too?"

I most definitely am, but I act like I'm thinking about it. He already has possession of a secret I've never told anyone. At this point, surely coffee won't harm this version of "LA Lily." She feels like a version of myself I've never met before. I have a sense of wanting to verbally spar with him, and it's like seeing tiny buds on once-barren trees. It's exhilarating and feels a bit like nothing could go wrong. What a rare hope. I want to capture it in a mason jar and see if it glows.

"As long as we get chocolate first," I demand. And then, fueled by boldness and a desperate need for him not to turn out like my parents or like all the men who haven't been honest with their intentions, I issue a challenge. "Oh, and George? Don't ever lie to me."

He stops, hands shoved in his pockets and an intensity radiating from his features. "I told you I never lie."

As we continue to walk, insecurity starts to creep in. It's a shadow of that ugly beast I've been trying to beat. If there's any sense in this man, he'll realize that no man has lasted beside me for long. It's only a matter of time before he splits like a chocolate candy shell when I've poured it into the mold, and it's too thin. Still, I have this unprecedented urge to give him the pieces of myself I've pulled behind a curtain ever since I learned how to sew one across the confines of my heart.

"You should know I'm a lot." I break our comfortable silence. "I rarely hold my tongue, and I take getting used to. If you decide that I'm too much at any point, please be gentle. Got it?"

He pauses on the sidewalk again. When I turn to see his face, I almost immediately wish I hadn't. Instantly, I realize that this smile he's giving me—a full one that crinkles the sides of his eyes and reveals the dimples placed close to his neatly trimmed beard—will stay with me for years to come.

"Well, good thing I'm a gentleman." It's the kindness of his tone that sticks to me like honey and loosens my tongue.

"I'm Lily," I say without overthinking. After a smile like the one he just gave me and the honesty between us, it feels only right to give him something he can hold onto now too.

"Lily," he repeats, his voice laced with—if I had to guess—a bit of something like wonder.

He leans toward me. Just when I've convinced myself to breathe normally despite the nearness of him, he holds out his arm for me to take. I may have joked about musicals, but the moment does feel a bit as if a song could break out like a darling Old Hollywood film—one of those that my best friend back home has made me watch dozens of times over the years. Maybe it's the proximity to Hollywood that has me finally understanding what all the fuss is about. There is a lightness in the not-frigid air that fills my senses, the sound of fresh birdsongs in the wind, and the sensation that I need the courage to believe my heart when it urges me to do whatever it takes to fight for this brand-new feeling.

Over the next month, I feel like I'm flying. The sweetness Graham adds to my life feels addicting. We hardly spend a day without each other. And for a while, my fears are quieted. There are moments of intensity, a tug of war between two people, ignited by attraction but grounded by care. He tells me he loves me. I tell him I know.

We adventure together all around the city. I keep him a secret, even from my best friend. I regret it, even though I think the more we can shield what we have, the longer we'll last.

Everything else feels perfect. After long days of being covered in chocolate and thrilled with the progress I'm making, we collapse into each other with the best hugs of my life and hold on tight. We watch *Pride & Prejudice* a few more times, including the one from the 90s. I commit to memory the feeling of his fingers in my hair and his hands around my waist. I become undone by the aftermath of his kisses, knowing my lips have never been so thoroughly adored, and by the intensity with which he cares for me and keeps me close. He does everything he can to make me believe he finds me beautiful. That I *am* beautiful. How? He tells me. He shows me in both mundane and tangible ways how much he values me. How much he chooses me.

We talk about our plans. We make plans. I tell him I can't wait to discover all the ways I can drive him wild and learn all the pieces of the story that have made him who he is.

My time in LA starts to run out. Knowing that I must leave Graham soon, even if only temporarily, makes me feel so lost that I don't know which parts of me are breaking or mending. In a new take on the fears that continuously plague me, I begin to doubt my ability to love him as much as he loves me. I wonder when he'll realize he has had enough of me.

Even though I told him not to lie to me, I feel the lie I tell myself gripping my mind as the weeks progress. It's the lie that says I have to push him away before he does it for the both of us. I will myself to make him the exception to my dysfunctional views on love and my own self-worth.

On the night before my return flight home, when my defenses are shattered, and my entire soul is on high alert, we grab takeout and sit on the front end of his car. We watch the ocean together, the sound of the waves breaking around us. I drop a mini chocolate bar to the ground, and as he hops down to grab it, I see a ring box peeking out of the pocket of his suit jacket.

And then I break Graham's heart.

Chapter Three

Lily

SIXTEEN MONTHS LATER - SUMMER

The rush of the water below feels like a balm to my soul as I lean on one of the bridges that span the river in my small town of Birch Borough. I'm out on my daily walk, and as usual, I've instinctively turned toward the water. The river that runs through the center of town has always been a grounding place for me. The stone arch of the bridge beneath my forearms is cool, a dichotomy to the warmth of the sun on my face. The heat in the air sticks to my skin and reminds me that I'm alive.

Maybe it's the wildness of it all as the water crashes over the rocks and still makes it to the other side. Or how the thunderous sound quiets my thoughts and fears and reminds me that life keeps moving, even when we feel stuck.

I feel in extra need of the reminder today. Even though it's been over a year without him, I feel Graham's absence in every cell of my being. With every breath, I want to tell him how I feel, yet he's not here for me to do it.

During our too-brief romance, I got used to having someone besides my best friend to talk to. Sparrow (or Rory, as I call her) is the most incredible listener, but there is something different when it's a man you trust with your innermost thoughts and not another woman. Knowing the difference now, it seems that both are necessary. I've been effectively cut off from one. And I know it's my fault.

Swallowing back my emotion, I direct my attention toward the shops lining this section of the river. They are quaint and idyllic in the afternoon light, the back of each positioned against the riverbank. If I turn around to the other side, I'll see clusters of birch trees (the origin story of our town's namesake) and the herons that hang out there. It's a wonderfully familiar sight after so much of my life has changed.

Just before my brief chapter in LA, my parents sat me down and told me they had sold our family home. Not as if it was a future event, but that it had already happened. I didn't even have a chance to attempt to talk them out of it. I had always dreamed of taking over my childhood home if I could ever afford it. When I asked them, weeks earlier, why they were "spring cleaning" after noticing some things being driven to the local donation center, they told me they were simply decluttering. *Yeah, decluttering to another time zone.*

And while I know my parents love me, their way of showing it is mostly through financial provision and doesn't have much to do with my heart. As a child, they constantly tried to get me to be more well-behaved, to be more proper, and to live the kind of life that seeks to help others. They just didn't always know how to help me. I know I embarrassed them with my antics. I remember the tension in their voices when they tried to explain to my teachers (more than once) how they planned to work on my behavior. I was never actually violent, but I was good at making threats. I've always been good at speaking my mind and letting people think I don't care. Except, I do care—possibly more than anyone can know.

I try to be grateful and remember that some families are found rather than made. Sparrow's dad was always more of a father figure to me than my own dad, anyway. He taught me how to make croissants at Sparrow's Beret, the French American bakery and café I now co-own with Sparrow. He took me under his wing and gave me the attention I needed. He always knew when I was having a hard time at school. Whether it was allowing me to make the *pains au chocolat* to let out my frustration or putting music on to help calm my nerves, he always did it with a sense of calm care. His little glasses perched on the end of his nose, and his smile was warm.

Sparrow's mother, who was French, passed away when Sparrow was a little girl. It happened before we even met. Looking back, I see how grief frayed her father's edges. Still, he somehow knew that I needed them. And, for as long as he was with us, I felt how deeply I belonged.

I wander farther across the bridge, the sunlight sparkling off the water, still calming me after all this time. As much as I love this place, believing that I belong has always felt just out of reach. So, I hold fiercely to the friends who feel like home. Sometimes, though, it feels like I'll never leave the wounded parts of me behind.

I was the one the boys liked to tease. They would try to recruit me to enact revenge on their nemeses. I'm the girl a high school jock teased with a fake prom proposal only to add, "As if anyone could be with Lily and not be crushed to pieces." Call it a self-fulfilling prophecy, but those words haven't been wrong yet.

I'm still the girl with the quick wit who mainly dresses in black. I'm the unexpected one. The wild one. The woman who speaks her mind and says whatever outlandish thing she wants. I call people on their crap and love to push people's buttons. Men seem to have a hard time realizing I'm a complex human and not a board game.

Have I had some good guy friends? Yes. But I haven't been so lucky with love—until Graham.

Sixteen months ago, I was careless with Graham. He moved through my defenses before I realized what was happening. I craved him. I needed him. And when I saw the ring tucked into his pocket, a whisper in my heart said it would shatter for good if he ever left me. I knew then what I had to do: Make a clean break. I had to be the one to end it before he did.

"Honey, did the river finally hypnotize you, or are you really that lost?"

I snap out of my thoughts, hearing Gladys' voice before her warm arm comes to rest around my waist. If Sparrow's dad was a father figure, Gladys is my eccentric aunt. The aunt you admire yet understand that if you give her free rein in your life, you'll either end up with stories worthy of winning an award or being arrested. There's no in-between with Gladys. If there's an art to speaking your mind, I've learned from the best by her example.

"I'm not lost," I counter, except she knows I am.

"You keep telling yourself that, honey."

I bristle, but there's no point in correcting her.

Her arm remains around my waist. "Now, about that strapping young man you were seeing . . . the tall, dark, and handsome one . . ."

"Edgar." I cringe. He's the latest casualty in the list of men I've dated this year in an attempt to forget Graham, even though I just . . . can't. After months of sulking, I thought maybe, if I couldn't have Graham, I'd try to move on. It might not be the dream, but maybe I could get close to something like happiness. After a series of tragic experiences on dating apps, I took a chance on someone who works in Birch Borough but doesn't live here. My odds felt safer that way. I genuinely like Edgar too. I'd say we made the friend category.

After about a year of acknowledging each other at his boxing studio, we went out for nearly three months before he sensed I was holding back and asked me if there was someone else—to which I replied, "No." But it turns out I would've failed a lie detector test yet again. Because ever since meeting Graham, there has always been someone else, even if it's only a ghost made of memories.

"Yes. Edgar," Gladys says with a hint of sadness. "Poor dear didn't know what hit him after you. And that new haircut he just got isn't doing him any favors now either. Looks like he got into a fight with a Weedwacker."

I laugh lightly, even though the truth of what she's saying stings. "You have no idea."

Gladys shrugs. "Hmm, well, maybe the new man in town will be more promising."

I turn to face her, taking in the way her eyes dance with mirth and a bit of conniving. "Gladys," I warn.

"What? I know this town like the back of my hand. And someone needs to keep an eye out for all the eligible men. Besides your, albeit brief, stint with Edgar—a fine contender despite his unfortunate hair—you've been wilted for months. Lately, that sharpness in you has more bite, and that laughter of yours is harder to come by."

She's not wrong. I am trying to think of a dismissal of the truth when I feel my hand lovingly captured between her own. "You've been different since LA, darling. Since your parents left. Since Rory's dad passed. And I know you've got more spunk and fight in you than you know what to do with, but I miss the girl who had more hope about her."

"Me too," is all I manage to get out.

"Okay, well, I'm off to bring Edgar a coffee at his store. I'm going to see if I can sign up for boxing lessons." She raises her brows at my glare, a wry grin painting her face. "Just because you don't want him doesn't mean other women don't need his expertise—for fitness reasons, of course." She winks, and I let myself laugh. Gladys is ridiculous.

She steps away but looks back at me over her shoulder. "Oh, and take a walk around Founding Street today. I hear it's lovely this time of year."

I shake my head at her antics, but part of me is curious to find out who this mystery man is she's trying to direct my attention to. It's not as if I believe anyone could or would take Graham's place, but it's been long enough that I need to do something to fill the void. At the very least, I have to try.

I want the steady kind of love. The gritty kind that can handle fire and failure and isn't lost along the way. The kind of love that can be tested and tried and stretched to the edge of itself without shattering. The kind I know I can trust even when I don't always trust myself.

From the moment Graham held my hand, I knew I'd been hit by lightning. It altered my life forever as our connection traveled faster than the speed of light. I want to stop the madness.

When I first returned home from LA, I waited by my phone for weeks. I slept with it and even kept it on the counter near the shower with the ringer on high volume, hoping Graham would reach out. He didn't. I can't say I blame him. If he had told me our relationship was one-sided (even though it was a lie) and freaked out at any indication of marriage, I wouldn't have stayed either.

Gladys mentioned hope, and the truth is, I've always hoped I would see him again. But it's a delusional hope where you believe a chance meeting would change everything. Perhaps we'd run into each other on the train to Boston. Or perhaps I'd return to LA, feeling sorry for myself, and find him again at an afternoon matinee.

Instead of turning toward my apartment, I walk the other way, along a not-as-familiar path toward Founding Street. It's off Main Street and quiet when I arrive. I don't come down this road often, sticking closer to the streets with shops, not having much reason to venture down surrounding residential streets. Here, there are rows of vintage houses turned into quaint apartments. It's a street filled with neatly cut grass and iconic architecture that looks so historic and yet homey.

I love my small town, even though I'm vocal about my view of the insanity and frequency of our themed events.

And I'm not merely talking about Christmas or Easter festivities. I'm talking about parades for pets, a chowder festival, and even a Bake Fest and a Regency Ball that will happen next spring (I'm proud to say that's my doing).

People can assume you're boring when you live in a small town—as if you aren't adventurous. But I've learned to find adventure in the cobblestone streets and in the way this town wrestles with my patience. There's fun to be found when Angie from the pie shop always wants to give me an extra slice. I even find pleasure in the changing of seasons here. I think adventure is in the way you live your life, not in where you happen to wander.

As I turn onto the street, I catch sight of a moving truck four houses down. My heart picks up speed. It's always like this when new people move to our tight-knit community. You don't know how their dynamic will change the state of things or what it will mean to have them invade all the spaces that have become your staples. You wonder if there's room enough for another person in your tight-knit community and then find yourself acclimating to them like they've always been there. It's one of my favorite things about Birch Borough.

The large truck commands my attention, and as my feet pick up speed, I look at the license plate. California. My brow furrows, the memories of my time in LA instantly halting my ability to take a deep breath.

Hearing movement near the truck and spotting a pair of men's trousers peeking from behind the rear wheels, I paste a smile onto my face. I'm ready to see what character has just been added to our community when the man rounds the corner. He steps into full view, a cardboard box in his hands.

Spotting me, he freezes. The box falls to the pavement with the sound of glass breaking.

I would normally move to help or find the whole scene amusing. Instead, I'm frozen in place.

Crystal-blue eyes meet mine, familiar and yet haunted. His hands hang limply at his sides, the shift of his hair in the breeze the only movement between us.

"Graham," I breathe reverently and honestly. I recognize the affection in my voice. It's been so long that I almost forgot I was capable of it.

A dangerous hope begins to creep up my spine. Millions of moments between us flood my senses. I remember the sound of his laugh, the scent of his beard oil, and the feeling of his mouth on mine. This version of him before me is so different, yet it's similar enough to wreck me. I swallow, tears already burning the edges of my eyes.

If this is what it means to dream and have it fulfilled, then I'm all in. The expression of shock on his face hasn't shifted, and I'm sure it mirrors my own. If I'm questioning if the man before me is a hallucination, he's surely doing the same.

It's right that Graham shouldn't have expected to see me here. He had mentioned in LA that he wanted to find a new home outside of Boston. I had sworn to him that I was going to go on adventures. The usual . . . work in a few chocolate shops across Europe and do my best to give American tourists a better reputation. I was about to shake the dust of Birch Borough off my high tops, ready to add some international excitement to my life. But I couldn't bring myself to leave after all.

And suddenly, here he is, the embodiment of long-term plans and life-changing love. The sight of him is a shock to my system, not only because of the incredible odds but because how I feel for him has intensified over the time we've been apart. The relief of seeing him is tangible, streaming from the top of my head to my toes. I don't know what I did to manifest a second chance, but this is my opportunity to come clean. To tell him the truth that's been raging in my heart.

I open my mouth. The courage to finally speak the words brewing in my heart is gathering when his eyes close tightly. In the bright sunlight, I think it's a drop of sweat from his brow I see falling down his face. It takes me a moment to realize it's a tear.

I'm waiting for him to give me any sign to rush toward him. My arms already ache to hold him. I want to bury my face in his neck and tell him I'm so sorry for making him believe he was less than everything to me. Taking a deep breath, I step forward as his eyes flash open. The emptiness behind them stops me in my tracks.

"Graham," I plead.

But he shakes his head. So defiant. So assured. And the words that I've waited for die between us.

"I can't do this again." His voice is gritty and unsteady, the edges of it rich with grief.

The disappointment startles me. I feel hot tears pouring down my face, the nightmare of this reunion more than I can physically handle. Disappointment turns to shame, shame to red-hot frustration. And frustration turns to fury. I recognize that I blew it, but the fact that we're here together and he won't give me a chance to make it right hits me harder than if we had never seen each other again at all. I know that now.

The only thing I can do from this moment on is what I've become an expert at doing throughout my life: turning disappointment into self-preservation. Wildly, my eyes dart until I spot a to-go cup on the back of the truck. The telltale sparrow of our familiar logo tells me he's already been to Sparrow's Beret. Rage pours through me because I missed him being there, and now I know he's already entered yet another sacred space in my life.

"Sparrow's Beret," I grind out through gritted teeth. "Don't ever set foot in it again."

I turn on my heels. My vision blurs as I rush down an alley and back toward Main Street. I'm practically running—anything to get away from him as quickly as possible. Ignoring the looks of people I know I'll have to explain myself to later, I rush up to my apartment. Throwing open the front door of the house, I trip on my way up the stairs before reaching my apartment on the top floor. My knee is scratched, my heart throbbing. I barely make it into my home before I hit the floor, my sobs echoing throughout the antiquated space. And as much as I think I could cry until I'm empty, something in me tells me it still won't be enough.

Chapter Four

Lily

EIGHT MONTHS LATER - SPRING

ily, you're my heart. You've become all of it," he says in a low voice, the rumble of it pulsing through my hand on his chest. I feel his heart beating beneath his button-up shirt. My hand drops to my side as I slowly back away, the pain I'm feeling reflected in the look of confusion and heartache on his face.

"I'm going home," I murmur into the air between us. My body wants to lean into his warmth, but the weight of my pain constricts my lungs. The outline of a ring presses through the pocket of his coat. I try my best to pretend I haven't seen it, that I don't know the question he is about to ask. My heart screams and revolts, and I nearly jolt when I feel the fear win. It's the only way I'm able to say the words that are pure poison.

"Graham, this has been a great distraction. But the level you love me . . . it's one-sided."

He winces, and I know he notices the way my hands are shaking. "You don't mean that," he pleads.

"I do."

But instead of calling me on my lie, he reaches toward me, his arms outstretched. Despite my declaration, he is still waiting for me to walk right into them . . .

"Ahh!" I yell, catapulting from my mattress. I stare up at my comfy bed through sleepy eyes as I am sprawled on the floor like a starfish. The sad part is this has happened more than once. The scene is always the same. Except, in my dreams, instead of LA, we are in front of a castle, and instead of his suit and my high-top sneakers, we're wearing clothes from another era. My brain loves to reenact the night I crushed Graham's heart, and I hate it. I hate it so much.

I groan and roll to my side. I'm a roadblock in the middle of the bedroom-slash-living-room floor of my studio apartment and nothing more. To accommodate the weird layout of my apartment, I put my bed in the "living room," which is separated by a hallway and wall from the kitchen and bathroom. I made a makeshift dining and living space in what I think would've been a dining room and pantry. The birds chirp their tunes through the window, and while I know that Sparrow would be smiling at the sight of them, I want to throw a rock out the window (not to hurt them, of course . . . just to startle them enough to sing on someone else's tree branches). I love birds, but I'm not in the mood for a princess-and-her-animal-sidekick kind of morning.

"I need coffee," I mumble to no one but myself. "And chocolate."

I push myself up to a seated position and pull my hair into a high ponytail with a hair tie abandoned under my bed, which I've only now seen because of my position on the floor. I feel like it's a metaphor for something . . . I'm just not sure I like what it means.

"Ugh! Graham. Winnings. Why?" I yell toward the ceiling. Mr. Crumbs (yes, that's really his name) is the landlord of this building. He responds by tapping what I can only imagine is a broom handle on the floor beneath me.

"It's too early for your shenanigans, young lady!" I hear him yell through the wooden floor. "And Graham is a lovely man!"

I manage to stifle an eye roll that I feel from my soul. Of all the men who have come through my life, Graham *was* the loveliest. He even beats Sparrow's fiancé, Rafe, when it comes to swoon-worthy men (not that I could ever tell her that). But Graham is also more frustrating because he never leaves me, even when I'm nowhere near him. And I don't know whether I'm angrier at myself for letting him go or at the fact that I have to constantly be reminded of my mistake with every day that passes.

Unfortunately, we've been thrown together a lot lately because of Sparrow and Rafe's epic love fest, and each time, I've spent every moment trying to pretend that I'm not affected by him, that he doesn't shake me like an earthquake in my soul. Most women would faint if they knew they could have had not only Graham's affection but his commitment as well.

Even now, considering that I once held his love, instead of being angry or yelling at me or telling me off, he's done the most devastating thing he could do to me by being polite but distant. He's a shadow of the man I once knew, and it makes me so angry I can't see straight. And now, we both live in the same small town, and I'm learning some top-tier avoidance skills to cope with potential *Graham sightings*.

I'm not like Sparrow. Before Graham, I didn't believe in the love-at-first-sight-and-till-death-do-us-part type of relationship. Even now, after my horrific reunion with him, I'm dating on the level of purgatory that is modern dating apps. I'm still trying to forget him. (Spoiler alert: It doesn't work.) I know I destroyed Graham's love for me that day nearly two years ago when I rejected his almost-proposal.

The whole town has felt our animosity since he arrived in Birch Borough last summer when the air was sticky with humidity and the need for the sweet relief of ice cream was high. It seems like the world has me stuck on the bottom of its shoe lately because *my* Graham decided to move to *my* small town, and even after our encounter, he decided to *stay*. And what's worse—if one really wants their idea of fated connections to explode—it turns out that he is the best friend of my best friend's (now) fiancé. When Rafe took a break from living in LA and came to stay at Graham's place here in town, Sparrow and Rafe fell in love (because of course they did). Rafe is Graham's best friend. Graham and Rafe met in LA. Graham and I met in LA. It's a whole freaking party of people who were fated to cross paths.

They say the world is small, but I say it's downright claustrophobic. It seems I had talked up my hometown enough that it made quite the impression on Graham. Telling him it's the place to go when you're heartbroken probably didn't help. After watching Rafe break through the castle Sparrow had built around her heart, I've now made sure to bury my own heart and pour piles of dirt over it. Mud, if you will.

The birds continue singing as I roll across the floor, closer to my bed. I think back to seeing Graham on the street earlier this week. To my surprise, he waved at me, but I pretended I didn't see. Oh, I saw, though. And I know if I'm ever going to forget the man who now lives three-and-a-half streets away from me (again, I have only myself to blame for painting Birch Borough as the darling town it is), who has robbed me of my beauty sleep for the past twenty-four months, I'm going to have to do my best to continue avoiding him. Oh, I'll be civil (possibly), but I'm not going to be happy about it. Especially because he still haunts my dreams.

Graham is one of those people I immediately knew I wouldn't be able to forget. There's nothing about him that's ordinary. It's as if everything I've ever thought a man should be is found in him. During our brief time together, he never intentionally said anything off-color. He always made me feel important, was ever the gentleman, and, in the end, told me clearly that he wanted us to last. My experience in LA felt like an anomaly, light years away from the person who has a track record of ghastly dating. Going back home seemed like the perfect excuse to end what was surely bound to fail. But that's what it was—an excuse. Months later, I've learned that it doesn't matter if he lives in the same town or across the world. My heart still wants him.

I take a deep breath and shake out the tension from my neck. My eyes catch on a picture of my parents and me on my bookshelf from an Easter production when I was nine. I'm wearing a ridiculous bunny costume, my blonde hair piled high on my head, and my nose painted pink with face paint. Sparrow (not pictured) was the carrot.

Planting my elbows on the bed for leverage, I catch a

glimpse of myself in the vanity mirror on top of my dresser. The image I see is a mess. I'm exhausted from the façade I'm desperately holding onto.

When I look in the mirror, I see a woman who let the love of her life think he meant less to her than she ever did to him. A woman who told him, to his face, that she wanted nothing to do with him. A woman who has regretted those words ever since.

I wipe rogue *pain au chocolat* crumbs from the large, handmade, soft white counter in Sparrow's Beret, which is Sparrow's namesake boulangerie. We've been besties since the first grade. Her mother was French, and her father was American, and the result of their meeting was an epic love story and a local favorite. Sparrow and I have owned it together ever since her father died a couple of years ago. I've never held another job. We both worked in the boulangerie after school growing up, mostly so I could hang out with her and feel a sense of belonging, but also because I adore the work.

There may be traces of Sparrow everywhere, from the sparrows on the plates to the very name of our shop, but this place also now has my presence ingrained into every nook and cranny. It's how Sparrow wanted it, especially after she was left alone in this world. And I think we've built something to be proud of, even when the realities of owning a business set in.

While we'll always be a single-location bakery (at least, I think so), we did start to expand to online orders. Sparrow is also working on a book to honor her mother with stories and recipes. I think, someday soon, even accounting for the help of the pastry assistants we've hired, we'll need more space to accommodate it all. But everything about our future plans both excites and grounds me.

The shop is my haven, the place I fight with all things chocolate and chat with everyone in town. It's the place where I first learned that chocolate and I have a love-hate relationship (I love it; it hates me). Here, I learned the meaning of being a sister and family to people who choose you and are not genetically related to you at all. Sparrow and I have tattoos on our wrists—hers of a lily and mine of a sparrow. We're bonded for life. She's the one person who has never made me question if I'm worthy of her love.

I was having an existential crisis when I flopped down on a beanbag in our elementary school over twenty years ago after Tommy, an obnoxious troublemaker at that time in my life, pulled my ponytail and ran. It'd been a rough time for me. My snarky manner and my spunkiness haven't always been welcome everywhere. As I retreated to a corner of a classroom, I came across Sparrow, reading a book with a picture of the Eiffel Tower on it. She asked me if I wanted her to read aloud, and I did. At home, my parents were focused on planning their trips abroad, already gearing up to be the humanitarian workers they now are. I wanted to know if I could create my own adventure, even if only through a book in a corner that overwhelmingly smelled like Play-Doh.

The year before I went to LA, Sparrow's father received a diagnosis that meant he wouldn't be with us much longer. After he passed that fall, she fell deeply into grief. Looking back, I realize we both did, and when she insisted that I move forward with my plans to attend the chocolatier-intensive course, falling in love with Graham was healing. When I returned home, Sparrow was still moving through her valley of grief, and I didn't want to add to it. My red-stained eyes were for her as much as they were for the loss of Graham's love. Taking over the shop after her father's passing amidst the aftermath of Graham, I chose to stay close to Sparrow rather than flit off to Europe. I haven't regretted that decision in the least.

There has always been a fire in me—something deep in my bones that feels like if I don't get it out, it may burn me alive. Dramatic? Possibly, but that fire has served me well most days. Occasionally, it overrides my sense of worry— the deep dread that sometimes pulls at my sleep and disintegrates my ability to see clearly. One of those days it took over was the day I met Graham. But then the worry comes back. That was the day I left Graham.

As I scrub the espresso machine, I let my mind wander. It's a dangerous game. The thing about messing up in love is that my mind races with what could have been. Why do the good memories seem to filter through our minds unless we strategically hold onto them, yet the mistakes we make seem to stick to our minds like super glue? We can't seem to scrub them away, no matter how hard we try. Graham annoys me because I can't get him out. And I try to be as prickly as I can to keep him from seeing that my heart has been bleeding out since I hurt him. Since I hurt us. Since he hurt me.

I pick up a ceramic cup and steam milk for my second latte of the day. I'm going to need it. Maybe I need my head examined for revisiting the places in my mind where Graham lives rent-free, but I often feel like an investigator.

I have to take out all of the pieces of our relationship, spread them out, walk through the memories, and try to see if I missed something. I look for anything to make me feel better about the choices I've made.

Watching *Pride & Prejudice* without ugly crying is impossible still. Sparrow thinks it's because I love Mr. Darcy so much. Oh, because that's the other thing: I've never told Sparrow how I first met Graham. Every time I want to, I can't bring it up. My pride won't let me. After I returned from LA and invested everything I had into supporting her with the bakery, months went by. By the time I saw her emerging from her cloud of despair, I didn't want to weigh her down again.

I didn't think I'd have a reason to bring him up, believing that my brief romance in LA was a time capsule I would politely try to forget. But Sparrow is now getting married to Rafe. Since Graham ironically (or tragically) is Rafe's best friend, the man is not only back in my life, but he's also front and center. I'm seeing him around town more and more. I have it on good authority from Rafe that Graham used to travel more. As Sparrow and Rafe's wedding approaches, he's been more visible.

While I love my friends (yes, I include Rafe now), I don't think they can ever understand my troubled history with Graham. Best-case scenario, they will look at me with pity. Worst-case scenario, they choose Graham over me. He is the nicest one of the two of us. Since this wedding will inevitably throw us together, I plan to let them think he just annoys me and not that I fire him up to keep him distracted from my true feelings for him.

The more I act like I detest him, the more Graham will

realize he's better off without me. Maybe it will blur the lines of his own memories of me—of that brief time when I freely shared my affection with him. I plan to continue until all he remembers is this version—the woman who harbors what once felt like love in the vault of my heart. It's my secret. It's *our* secret. He doesn't want to do this again. So, we won't. Case closed.

Chapter Five

Graham

If you ever meet a woman named Lily, run. That's it. That's my advice. After thirty-two years of life, this is the greatest lesson I've learned. If your name is Lily or you know a Lily who doesn't live in Birch Borough or visit LA for a chocolatier-intensive course, fine. I'm sure she is fantastic. But this Lily, *the* Lily who lives in Birch Borough, has ruined my life.

The stool I'm sitting on shifts uncomfortably as I look out into the street. I rest my elbows on the high-top counter, the glass in front of it giving me a clear view of the edge of town closest to the post office. It's not the busiest section, but it's not the outskirts either.

A barely touched cappuccino sits in front of me. It looks deflated, the bitterness of the brew a reminder of the best cup of coffee I've had in this town and which I haven't tasted since I first arrived. As if on cue, a couple walks past the window with to-go cups and pastry bags, unknowingly taunting me as I sit in a coffee shop that *isn't* Sparrow's Beret. The signature sparrow logo on the cups and small white bags mocks me, especially since I was told never to enter the bakery again by Lily herself.

I used to feel like I could succeed at love. But falling in love with her, much like the sub-par coffee I've been consuming, nearly crushed me. I can still smell her perfume and hear her laugh in my dreams. It's nestled between my mind and ribs (however that science works) and has almost made me forget who I am. Because no matter how hard I've tried, no matter how many times I've told myself to move on, she's still stuck in my system. And there's nothing I've been able to do to get her out.

Is she the reason I decided to leave my home in Boston and make the move to Birch Borough? Possibly (that's a "yes"). During our weeks together in LA, Lily described her small, quiet hometown. It was obvious she loved it, but she also thought the sheer number of town events and how everyone was in everyone else's business was pure insanity. I knew she co-owned a café called Sparrow's Beret. According to Lily, they made the best maple croissants in New England. When she repeatedly mentioned her best friend and another woman named Lucy, who gave her extra ice cream at some local diner, I heard the affection in her voice. She made it all sound so . . . charming.

Oh, and Lily's declaration that her town was the place to go if I was ever heartbroken? Yeah, that stuck.

After Lily left (for grand adventures around the world, she said), her words stayed on repeat in my mind, especially when I felt burned out with work, or during a late-night commute from Boston to New York, or over a long flight back to LA. There came a day when, suddenly, after months of thinking about Lily every day, small-town life seemed like the cure for me too.

It may have been a poor decision, but after one particularly long week in court on too many cases, I sold both of my homes in Boston and LA. On a whim, I found an apartment in the town I remembered her speaking so fondly of, which conveniently runs daily trains to Boston. I was looking forward to the slower pace of life, the peace. Everything was working out perfectly. Until . . . I saw her again.

I never thought Lily would be in Birch Borough. Adjacent? Possibly. She had to have family nearby. But living *here*? Lily told me at least a dozen times that we were going to travel the world for the next five years. She would make all the chocolate things. We would see the world together. We'd go on safari to see "real life" elephants, visit Buckingham Palace to harass the palace guards, and eat Thai food in Thailand just to say we did. Oh, yeah, just so it's clear, I was included in those plans.

Soon after I moved to town, my best friend, Rafe, arrived to stay while I traveled on business. By the time my head cleared and I realized I still had feelings for Lily, it was too late. Rafe was in love, and I had already messed up any chance of reconciling with Lily.

It happened just after I landed from LA. I was waiting for the moving truck and wandering through town to kill time. I stumbled across Sparrow's Beret. By some twist of fate, I was helped by someone named Anna, with neither Sparrow nor Lily at the register when I went in. So, there I was, outside my new apartment, full of the best French croissants of my life and buzzing with coffee. I was unloading items from the back of the moving truck, and then

I saw her standing in front of me like I had wished so many times. The burning in my limbs and chest told me that nothing had changed. I was still in love with her—maybe more than ever.

When she opened her mouth, the words that crept out of mine were to tell her I couldn't do it again. In reality, I was talking to my own heart. If she tried to explain, it might have destroyed me. When it came to Lily, the only thing I could control was refusing to hear another word about us. Lord knows I had already thought through every scenario for her reasoning for breaking up with me. None of it could be good.

Her response was anger and a warning to never step foot in her shop again. And so, as the months have passed, I haven't, no matter how much I've wanted another croissant.

Now, our best friends are getting married. My duties as best man must be my priority, even if I've managed to land in the middle of wedding planning with the bride's maid of honor . . . Lily. Tonight is the first time we'll be near each other for any length of time without something else going on as a distraction. It's the future bride and groom and us— there won't be many places for our attention to go.

I wander toward the tiny stone church where Rafe and Sparrow wait. The church is at least three hundred years old and is where I'm meeting the people (besides my mother) that I hold most dear. As I walk up the mossy stone steps, I ask myself how I've managed to get into the mess that putting myself within Lily's orbit again will create. My eyes catch on her immediately when I enter the nave of the church, the back of her high blonde ponytail hanging over the wooden pew toward the front. The sight of it nearly crushes my resolve.

I lean against the stone wall at the back of the church, preferring to stay out of sight for now. Lily and I seem to be the only ones from our party present and accounted for.

You wouldn't know the strength of my feelings for her from the way things are now. It once only took a week of being hypnotized by her otherworldly grey eyes and the sway of her ponytail as she walked, moved, laughed, or fought. In the right light, her eyes take on a subtle hint of dried lavender. I was quickly on board with trying to love her for the rest of my life. Was it fast? Very. Stupid? In my case, also, very.

I'm not an impulsive man. I make careful, calculated decisions. And though I can see in hindsight that we moved quickly, I can also see evidence that she felt the same. I bought a ring. A vintage one with light purple stones around the diamond because the color reminded me of the shade that I used to see when the sun hit her eyes just right. I still see her face when she spotted the jewelry box in my pocket.

I lost my best friend and the love of my life in a single night. And my soul knows there is nothing in me that is over her or ever could be.

It also doesn't help that I tossed the ring box toward the ocean and have tried to forget it exists. I wouldn't return it. I couldn't keep it. And she didn't want it. It's probably drifted far out into the ocean by now and is friends with a sea turtle at this point. I hope they're happy.

Suddenly, my mouth tastes bitter, even though I'm only drinking water. A choir is rehearsing on the stage of this admittedly charming setting. I'm guessing Liam is somewhere nearby. He owns The Music Shop and is good friends with Rafe and now me as well. I'm thankful to have another friend in town. It was a rough start when I landed here. I'm still being vetted by the townspeople. While I've got the best job in the world now that I'm managing Rafe's music career (which is going splendidly, if I do say so myself), and I have an apartment that's not in the city, in a town that is perfect for adopting a big dog when I find the right house, it's clear that everyone in Birch Borough loves Lily. (They also seem to fear her.)

While no one knows the full story between us—shockingly, not even Sparrow or Rafe, for that matter—I'm the odd one out. The tension between us is palpable. As a result, people are staying at a distance. Everyone is nice but cautious. They clearly don't know what to do with me. And since we reunited in the oddest of circumstances, I don't know what to do with myself either.

I didn't expect to move here and have to prove I'm a good man. I somehow always thought that if I was a good man—if I could make the world better—the gnawing in my gut that tells me I need to try harder would quit. I didn't anticipate feeling an even stronger desire to prove myself— to prove that I'm nothing like my father, who tended to live on the wrong side of the law. Becoming a lawyer was supposed to tip the scales, balance the books, and help people in as many ways as my father wronged them. My mom raised me to be a man I'd be proud of. I've tried to honor her. And while my father's choices still keep me up at night, now they are accompanied by the reflection of animosity in Lily's eyes.

But I'm here to stay. I like the quiet pace of this town. I want people to get to know me. I'm ready to plant some roots here. I'm less than an hour's drive from my mom, and the train runs into the city. Even if I feel like my soul is limping every time I see that blonde ponytail in my peripheral vision, I plan to make Birch Borough my home.

Besides, I'm rooming with my best friend, Rafe, until the wedding. We're living the life. Just two early thirty-somethings, one heartbroken and one ready to take on the world. How could moving here have been a mistake when he found everything he ever wanted?

I finally catch sight of Sparrow and Rafe in a dimly lit corner of the old church. They must be waiting for the choir to finish rehearsals. Even from afar, they look more in love than ever as they sit next to each other. Rafe holds a guitar on his lap. He's singing softly to Sparrow, who is looking at him like he's her whole world. I remember that feeling. I want that feeling again. I'd give anything to know what it is like to have someone look at me with eyes that see beyond the collected persona I present on the surface. While I dated plenty of women before I met Lily, no one made me want to give up everything to love them. Women tend to quickly get bored when they realize how reserved I am, or they ghost me for someone a little less analytical.

Or they reject me because I'm not a Frenchman. I peek over at Sparrow and Rafe again and can't help but grin. Once, a few months after moving here, after seeing Sparrow occasionally on my previous morning commute, I decided to try to kick off my dating life again. I approached Sparrow on a train platform in Boston. I asked her out and tried to sell her on all my good qualities. She rejected me because, as she declared, "You're not French." Ironically, she found her Frenchman in Rafe. Surely, if my friend found that kind of love, I can find it too, right?

The first time I noticed the lily tattooed on Sparrow's wrist, I realized how deeply Lily had dug herself into the soil of my heart. Because she is in everything I see now. Everything I feel and every dream I have, she's stamped her name on. If they could ever sell a stain remover pen for the stains that plague our minds, I would invest immediately.

I knew I needed Lily in my life from the afternoon we met, but she must not have felt the same. While I immediately valued her independent spirit, it ended up being the very thing that tapped into one of my biggest fears— being useless to those I love. I'd hoped she would need me as much as I needed her, but alas, it wasn't meant to be.

The worst thing that has happened isn't Lily breaking up with me. It's knowing in my bones that no woman will ever live up to her in my heart. She pushed me away, and I shouldn't want her—need her—and yet every part of me knows that I do.

The cold from the stone wall starts to sink through my suit as I wait. Participating in a wedding when you're single and looking for love is already its own kind of challenge. Being in a wedding with the woman who rejected you while you wished she would love you back is a nightmare.

"Okay," Sparrow says from her little perch on the stone stairs leading up to the altar where she and Rafe will exchange their vows in a few months. "We just wanted to gather the two of you here to see where we're getting married, of course . . ." she continues.

I glance over my shoulder toward Lily in the row behind

me. She hasn't spoken to me yet. Her presence feels like a necktie that needs loosening. My fists clench at my sides for the effect she still has on me. Her hair is pulled up in her signature ponytail, a sight that makes my heart beat faster and drives me nuts. The way her grey eyes catch the soft light filtering in through the windows of the church is enough to drive a man wild. Forget the dimple that always plays at the corner of her mouth. I see it, even though I know she's doing her best to avoid acknowledging me.

"And that's why you two will be the glue that holds this wedding together."

I startle, suddenly aware that I've just missed key information. Distracted by Lily, I don't know what Sparrow just said. I'm trained to be on the case, to remember everything said in the court of law. But right now, I've got nothing.

"Are you okay, Graham?" Sparrow asks.

"Yeah, George," Lily adds with a hint of mischief in her tone. She stands and moves to my row, the hair on my arms rising in response to her nearness. My attraction to her hasn't dimmed, even in the heartache. She knows me enough to know I wasn't fully present a moment ago, which means the dimple sighting was because she knew I was about to choke—a rookie move on my part.

"I'm . . . fine, Sparrow." I'm proud that my voice doesn't waver but less proud that I've made Rafe raise his eyebrows with a knowing look directed my way.

"I know it's a lot," Sparrow continues softly. "But we just can't think of two people we'd want to be a part of our day more than you two."

I feel sweat breaking out on my forehead. I have no idea

what she means, but for this couple, I know I'm all in.

I don't feel I'm familiar enough with Sparrow to call her by her nickname, Rory, like almost everyone else. I notice she strictly calls me Graham, though, unlike Rafe, who has his own private nickname for me. Once, he and I were in line for some overpriced tacos at a restaurant in LA. An actress from a Hallmark movie was in line as well. (I didn't know it at the time, but I looked her up later that night.) She told me I was handsome enough to be a lead in the movies. In fact, she wanted me to act with her during her next leading role. While flattering, I know my face showed my level of alarm. There was no way that I wanted to be the poor guy in the city who got dissed for the girl who ended up realizing she belonged back in a small town with a man who wore flannel.

Rafe thought it was hilarious, though. Ever since, he has called me *Hallmark Hot G* on his phone, caller ID, everything. One of these days, I will snatch his cell and change it back.

I don't really mind. Rafe and I are like brothers. In the past, I've always felt like the odd man out in my friend group. I couldn't explain why. Rafe is the steady person in my life. He pushes me away from getting stuck in my holding patterns, which typically involve isolating myself. We may know how to push each other's buttons, but I'd do anything for him, including being in a wedding with *the* Lily, the woman who blew up my idea of love. By now, I know he knows that, although I had once asked Sparrow out, someone else has stolen my heart.

I just wish I hadn't lost it in the first place.

I pull myself back into the present moment. As I look

between Sparrow and Rafe, I feel Lily's heavy gaze on the side of my face. I swear she mouths, "Can't be you. Anyone but you."

If I look her way, she'll pretend there is nothing between us. How she can ignore our history so well should send me reeling. We bantered while we—or I—fell in love, but this is different. It's like she's channeled any hint of affection for me into pure animosity, and I'm over here trying to behave like her hostility doesn't crush my heart a little more every time.

My usually level head is spinning.

"And, Lily," Sparrow continues, "you'll be helping even more at the café since it's wedding season."

"Of course, my people," Lily grits out.

"Okay, well, Graham, I just wanted to make sure you are okay with helping us with some of the extra details for our wedding preparations. Since Rafe has to be in Nashville soon, as you know, having you here to handle it alongside Lily will be perfect!"

Rafe grins as Sparrow's eyes move between Lily and me. It feels like a trap. I've walked into the lion's den. The sense that spring is a time of renewal just got shot to pieces. But I can't crack. I can't give Lily another reason to feel like she has the upper hand. From the corner of my eye, I see her tap her foot. I feel her willing me to say no to whatever we've been circling, but I decide to hold my ground. I raise my chin and set my jaw. The transformation from amusement to concern etched on Rafe's face should be enough to give me pause, but it only makes me more determined to solve this problem. While I knew I'd be the best man (I may have teared up when Rafe asked me, while blaming the cold air, of course), this sounds like I'll be filling in for Rafe's duties occasionally while Lily fills in for Sparrow's. This will force a new proximity with Lily that I haven't dared to let myself comprehend. I've heard that the only way out is through. So, I will myself to move forward.

"Sparrow, I'm more than okay. Whatever you two need from Lily and me, you've got it."

Sparrow's smile assures me I've made the right decision. I ignore the look of shock on Rafe's face and the sound of Lily's growl.

What have I done?

We're only hours into gathering to plan the wedding wildness, and I'm ready to throw things. Sure, I've been known to chuck a baked good or chocolate bar toward unsuspecting loved ones in the past. This time, though, I want to throw something of significance. Maybe I'll search for one of those rage room things in the area when we're through with today's meeting. That has got to work off some steam, right?

It has to be better than walking toward the diner—appropriately called Train Car Diner since it's an actual train car converted into a restaurant and where I'm heading to meet with Sparrow and Rafe for an extension of kicking off the official start of the wedding festivities—and seeing Graham through the window. He's sitting like the perfect model of a man that he is. Sparrow has never thought of him as more than undeniably handsome, but I still think he is the most stunning man I've ever seen. His light blue eyes are something I would write songs about if I had any of Rafe's talent. Graham always smells like fresh air in the middle of how I imagine an English countryside smells. Darn all the romance novels I've read for making me wax poetic about the delicious manly scent that radiates from him.

I pause just before walking into the diner to sneak a second look at Graham. It looks like I'm the second to arrive, even after trying to time it so that Rafe and Sparrow arrive ahead of me.

His hair is light brown with natural highlights. They make him look like he just happened to be out in the sun, and it marked him from the rest of the world. I've always known he has money, but I also know how hard he works for every single cent. He's the type of man who is so good you almost think he can't be real. And when you do realize his polite and elegant mannerisms are genuine, it scares you to think that you could be the one to cause him pain. (Having already been the one to cause him pain, I know all too well that I'm right to be afraid of myself.)

All I know is that as I pull open the door and walk toward the table where he sits, his eyes flicker up to meet mine. And I think to myself that he shouldn't be allowed to still look at me like I once lit up his world, even if the warm expression in his eyes fades moments later. Not when I've treated him the way that I have. I know what I am.

A long time ago, I learned it's best to say what I am thinking. I don't hesitate to poke buttons. After all, why are buttons there if not to be pushed? My theory is that you have to make sure they're working now and then. Barring potential proposals, I always say what I mean because what's the point in filtering myself? We're all a bit of a mess because we're human. I just happen to embrace it a little more than others.

I drag my feet as I approach the booth. When I get stuck behind a waiter delivering plates of burgers, fries, and a mountain disguising itself as a slice of lemon meringue pie, the delay gives me time to think about how I'm going to pull myself together.

Finally, the obstacle in the aisle clears, and I walk toward the man I'm doing my best to forget. Immediately, Graham slides over, making room for me to sit beside him in the booth. All I can manage to give is a slight, awkward nod in return, my words uncharacteristically lost.

At the church tonight, I nearly combusted. Graham's willingness to help with the wedding while Rafe and Sparrow handle Rafe's growing music career as I cover the bakery and my maid of honor duties was wild. I could feel him trying to avoid looking at me, and I nearly cracked. His mannerisms don't just unsettle my mind; they unsettle my heart. Except for the time he cut me off before I could apologize for what happened between us, he is always the perfect gentleman.

I'm trying to think of how to break the awkward silence when Sparrow rushes in, her arm around Rafe. She looks up at him like he's a living answered prayer, and I know he is that for her. Rafe has his arm wrapped around her shoulders. He kisses the top of her head so gently that something tugs within my chest. They slide into the seat across from us, faces beaming.

Happiness is all I want for Sparrow. However, I know things are about to change drastically between us as Rafe is now her "person." I'll always be the best friend, her *ride or die* when it matters most, but it's shifting. I see it happening before my eyes. She's becoming his, and he's becoming hers. They're about to make this "until death do us part" vow to each other, and it just aches a little. I feel as if the best I can hope for at this point is to volunteer myself as an apprentice under Gladys for Birch Borough's resident busybody and wildcard commentator, who will end up with stories to be told to Sparrow and Rafe's grandchildren.

Unwillingly, my eyes roam over to Graham. He is now leaning toward our friends. The hand closest to me is nearly clenching in a fist while the farther hand waves animatedly as he tells them a story. I'm only half-listening, which stands in sharp contrast to Graham, who is engaged in the conversation. He laughs when needed, giving frequent smiles of encouragement to Rafe and Sparrow, and is the perfect embodiment of a supportive friend. No wonder he's the best man.

I take advantage of the privacy of the moment, however. I know he's so focused on them he won't notice my almost physical reaction to his nearness. I let myself bring our memories to the surface to inspect them once again. It's a crime scene, and I make sure I don't miss a clue or leave something behind that would unravel my alibi. Soon, I find myself focusing on the way he's filled out his suit jacket since the last time I saw him, the taut muscles underneath telling me he's been working out more. I catch a few new lines added to the sides of his eyes when he smiles, although the way they etch his face tells me he's going to age really well (figures). And I'm struck by the thought that I could've had the privilege to see it up close.

My skin flushes with an unexpected heat. The diner is now too warm, the lights are now too bright, and the flowers in little vases on the tables are too . . . flowery. More people have entered. They chat with Lucy, the waitress who has worked at this diner since Sparrow and I were in high school. She appreciates my vegetarian self's need for a veggie burger, and somehow, she once found a way to ask Jerry, the cook in the back, how to make the best barbecue veggie burger possible. I'm forever indebted to her for that kindness, among many others.

"Hi, darlings," Lucy greets us. If she's here, there's no way that anyone else is serving us.

"Oh!" Rafe exclaims, rhythmically drumming on the table. "Lily, I was once told to ask you . . . why do you appreciate the name *Lucy* so much?"

"*While You Were Sleeping*," Graham answers before thinking better of it. And my ears burn that he remembered such a detail and so quickly.

"That's right!" Lucy grins. "It's Lily's favorite rom-com. When she learned my name, I immediately became her favorite waitress in this town."

I give her a grin.

"Am I wrong?"

"No." I shake my head, finally finding my voice after feeling like it dropped to the floor under the booth along with Graham's two cents.

"What'll it be?" Lucy lifts her order pad, pulling a pencil from behind her ear.

We give our orders. When she leaves, I start to bite my nails. My foot taps furiously (it's doing that a lot tonight) as I wait for my friends to take a breath. Cautiously, I look toward Graham, and our eyes lock. In what I once declared a dead zone, I feel a fire reigniting. His proximity is going to be my undoing. If I can't have him, then I have to banish him far, far away. Neverland is still too close.

Or . . .

"Let's pick a song!" I yell like a madwoman, pointing to the jukebox in the corner.

Without looking at Graham, I grab the sleeve of his jacket and pull him out of the booth. Like the decent human he is, he apologizes for us both. I don't know if it's more annoying or comforting that I know he's probably politely smiling as I drag him toward the opposite side of the diner.

"Excuse us," he says pleasantly to the people mid-bite in their meals as we rush past. He acts as if I didn't just attack him without warning, as if this was the plan all along. As soon as we get past the edge of the booth section, I whip around to face him. I focus on his throat and not his eyes.

"I know you can't do *this* again, but just let me talk. Please," I fiercely whisper (yes, it's a term). Pushing my finger into Graham's very defined and very broad chest, I try to commit the feeling to memory. Maybe tonight, before I fall asleep, my brain will catch up and tell me if it feels the same as a couple of years ago. I continue without pause. "I'm not sure what you're *really* doing in this town or what stunt you're pulling by agreeing to help with this wedding. I know you don't want to be near me, but it's tough cookies, buddy, because I'm not going anywhere."

"I never said I didn't want to be near you," he counters.

I try to ignore his words because they instantly warm my insides like a hot chai latte. "Even so, we're barely civil to each other."

"That's your doing," he says.

"And yet, you're the one who said you didn't want to do *this* again." My breathing is labored, my rib cage rising and falling a little too quickly. My body is on sensory overload.

For too long, my heart has been boarded up like an abandoned, haunted house when it comes to men—specifically, *this* man. By not loving him, I've turned into someone I don't fully recognize. I need him to know how things have changed.

"A weird twist of fate has thrown us together," I begin again. "But Rafe and Sparrow's happiness is more important to me than anything. So, let's set a few things straight and establish how the next few months are going to go since we have to work with each other. First of all, there will be no touching."

He shakes his head without much of an expression.

"What do you mean *no*?" I demand.

Graham shrugs. "You just grabbed my jacket. I'm walking you down the aisle. At that point, I'll have to hook your hand through my arm." He says the words like they don't make me weak in the knees. Like I don't instantly imagine the photos that will be printed and posted online of the two of us in a chummy setting with love all around, forever immortalized. Like I won't print a copy to hide in my dresser drawer for the nights when I feel sorry for myself.

"Then that's it. That's the only time." When he shakes his head again, I make a low growling sound in my throat.

"Rehearsal," he reminds me quietly. I see him look around, probably making sure no one is observing me start to overheat.

"George."

"Still Graham."

I sigh. "No touching. Except for the wedding and the rehearsal." I wave my hand in the air frantically. "You get it?"

"Is there anything else you want?" The look in his eyes and the faint test in his tone takes me back to a night we got ice cream together. With sand between my toes, we sat on the beach to watch the waves rolling in on a spring night. Graham asked if there was anything else I wanted out of life besides gloriously immersing myself in chocolate decadence and travel. At the time, I said *him*.

"You're not playing fair." My voice is soft and hesitant.

He sighs, shifting his weight so he is leaning slightly away from me. "Fine, any other rules, then?"

But I don't feel like setting up any others. I know if he doesn't touch me (other than those few moments in the wedding and rehearsal, which I may be able to convince Sparrow to let me wear gloves to block out the feeling of his touch), I might be okay. Clearly, I'm struggling with even being near him, but I will myself to believe I can manage. I'll behave in a civilized manner, except for saying his name. Before, I only called him Graham after he kissed me—and the one time I had hope after he arrived. But if we're not kissing, he's back to George in my book. He must be. I can't handle letting him get any closer to me than that.

And I need to get him out of Birch Borough for my future sanity. A manic plan starts to form within my mind, and since I'm known for being impulsive, I follow it. "Change of plans. No rules," I say.

His eyes widen. "No . . .?"

"I propose a game instead."

The faint tick in his jaw tells me he's intrigued. "What kind of game?"

I stand a little taller and try not to notice the way his expensive cologne is searing my senses. "Eh, not a game, exactly. A challenge. A series of them." I can feel the sudden grin playing at the corner of my mouth. I have to applaud Graham for maintaining eye contact throughout this conversation while I keep trying to look everywhere else to hide what I'm feeling. He must have learned how to beat any rogue thoughts out of him when he became a lawyer.

"Challenges. Plural?" he replies matter-of-factly.

I nod.

"Proceed."

"I will issue you a series of challenges leading up to the wedding. You can take them or leave them, but if you leave them, you automatically lose."

"What sort of challenges?"

"They will be designed at my discretion with the intention of pushing you outside of your comfort zone." *And hopefully, drive you so crazy you leave voluntarily.* I'm already thinking of how to involve Gladys.

"Will I be publicly humiliated?"

"Depends on how you respond. I won't humiliate you on purpose, if that's what you're getting at."

"Will each one be with you?"

"What?"

"Will you be present for each challenge?"

Doubt suddenly kicks in to the rational part of my brain. I look over and see Rafe and Sparrow watching us discreetly. I don't like where this is going, but I'm too far in now. Graham is right. Turning this into a game will require seeing even more of each other than I had planned. As it is, I'm pretty sure he thinks I've blocked his number (I haven't). Still, I nod with a noncommittal shrug, and he relaxes a bit.

"Well, what's at stake? What do I win? What do you gain?"

This, I can answer. I breathe in deeply before replying. "If I win, you rent out your fresh-off-the-market apartment to anyone who wants to experience the cozy New England life. I'll only see you if you drive through town to meet up with Rafe. You can move to the next town over, or Boston, or back to LA. Maybe try out Nashville. I don't care."

He stiffens. I totally do care, but I'm not about to admit it. "So, losing to you also means I lose my home and get kicked out of town?

"Don't worry about winning . . . because you won't." I know what I'm asking is absurd.

His eyes shutter a bit, the playfulness disappearing, only his iron will remaining between us. "But *if* I win?" he counters.

I bite the inside of my cheek. I'm playing to win, but an alternative future flashes before me—one where Graham and I aren't at odds, and I finally get to explain myself. His nearness makes me wish for things I'm not sure are possible. There's an absurd hope brewing that makes me willing to see if maybe there can at least be forgiveness, even if I'm unsuccessful in my mission to remove Graham's presence here. I want it too much. I hear myself reply, "Then you stay in Birch Borough, and I don't say another word about it."

"You don't have a right to tell me where to live, regardless," he says, his arms crossing with a bit more confidence, revealing a flash of the man I remember handling difficult legal cases with unshakeable poise. "Yes, I moved here, but I didn't think . . . you said . . ." He trails off, vulnerability visible on his face. "You have no reason to fear me, Lily."

"Of course not. I've never thought I did." And I don't. Not one bit. If anything, my only fear is him seeing how much I still want him.

His instant relief is palpable but quickly reverts to detachment. His eyes scan my face with robotic precision instead of hunger. I hate the unexplainable urge to sob suddenly creeping into my consciousness.

"We've got to find a way to work together for Rory and Rafe," I clarify. "Because if we don't figure this out, it will destroy their wedding day. I won't be responsible for bringing a whole vibe to their wedding that is honestly depressing."

"Of course," he affirms quickly. Neither of us would do anything to intentionally hurt our friends, even though I'm sure our mysteriously hostile dynamic is already a heavy thing for them to carry. Knowing this fiasco with Graham is temporary is the only thing keeping my voice from shaking.

"Do we have a deal?" I ask. My whole body wills him to agree. I need a sense of possibility that, even though I'll inevitably see him because of our friends, he isn't going to suddenly be in every area of my life. If I can't have him and there *isn't* forgiveness between us, I don't want to run into him in town every single day for the foreseeable future.

Just have to get through the wedding.

Shifting his weight, he reaches into his pocket and pulls out a few quarters. They clink and land with a sharp thud in the machine as he presses the button for the song on C18. "This Will Be" by Natalie Cole begins to play. Graham leans against the jukebox. His breathing is steady, but his body language is intentional. I feel the pinch on my spine from wearing higher wedges today than usual.

"Counter deal," he finally says through gritted teeth. Standing up straight, his blue eyes are cool as he stares down at me.

I squint my eyes to see if I can break his concentration. No dice. I can see why people in the courtroom used to crack under his gaze. The man gives back nothing. But I know him more than I've let on to everyone else, so I step a little closer and watch as his calm façade starts to crumble. The energy between us pulses with our proximity. I see it in the light tap of his right foot, the soft clearing of his throat, the almost imperceptible shift of his shoulders.

"My final offer," he says.

Instinctively, I know he's not just talking about some challenge. He's talking about us. My heart rate picks up, and I take a step back.

"Proceed," I choke out, stealing a word from his own playbook.

"I will go with your deal. It's unhinged, but I'll go with it. And I issue a counter challenge of my own."

He looks around the diner once more, and I follow suit. Rafe and Sparrow are absorbed in each other, their faces all smiles. Lucy approaches them, and I note our food arriving at our table. As she walks away, they look around the diner for the two of us. It's time to get back. Graham nods toward the little alcove to the side of the jukebox. I angle toward it as he protects me with his frame from the view of the rest of the restaurant. Whatever he's about to say must be good. Really good.

Emotion creeps up my throat because he's done this

before. Covered me. Hid me. Made sure I felt safe and protected. Whatever he's about to say, he doesn't want anyone else to hear.

His right hand lands on the wall to the left of my face, and I try not to notice the lightening of his hair, where it might start to turn grey. I ignore the way his forehead casts a shadow over his pale blue eyes, enhancing their intensity. To anyone observing, I know his posture looks like Bill Pullman dreamily leaning toward Sandra Bullock. No one would ever know how it feels to have him so close without being able to call him mine.

"Throughout your challenges . . ." he begins. My heart beats so loudly it pulses in my ears. "I'll challenge you back, twofold. First, I challenge you—" his voice catches like the needle on a record player before beginning again, "to never lie to me."

I nod, even though I know this gives him the power to ask me anything, and I'll have to respond with truth. When we first met, I demanded that he always tell me the truth, and I'm the one who lied. I don't have it in me to ever tell him another one.

"And I challenge you not to fall in love with me. Again."

I inhale sharply. My stomach feels like it drops to the floor. I search his features and realize he's serious. He's really challenging me to do this.

I swallow but can't get the words out. The energy between us hums. I meet his gaze with as much intensity as I can muster. The flood of memories of moments just like this consumes my mind, but I push them back. One day, I'll release all the emotion. But today is not that day.

So, I rise to my full height. My dress catches on one of

the picture frames on the wall behind me. It shifts back into place as I stare into the eyes that I could draw in my dreams. With my back (literally) against the wall, I know I'm fighting for more than peace during this wedding. I'm fighting for my chance to finally move forward.

"Game. On."

My whisper sparks something in his eyes, and I catch a hint of his relief. Does he truly think he will win this one? It's too bad he doesn't realize he's already partly lost. Because to fall in love with him again requires me to have fallen out of love with him—which I haven't.

He holds out his hand to seal our deal. I know I can't touch his skin, though. It would release a torrential flood of emotions I can't handle yet. It's clearer than ever that I have to get him out of town because I can't go back to what we were.

Sensing the war within me, he drops his hand and clasps it around the lapel of his jacket. I focus on it to displace my discomfort and have to suppress the smile that wants to creep onto my lips. Graham's default outfit always has been a perfectly tailored suit and tie. Once, he shared some of the challenges he faced as a boy growing up with a single mother. After college, when success started coming his way, he developed his style sense as a way to leave behind the days of wearing holey shoes and hand-me-downs. The image of a young Graham dreaming of a better future has never left me.

I don't make eye contact again as I turn away from him, not trusting myself to avoid doing something stupid like adjusting his tie or his pocket square just to feel like I've played a part in his dashing, well-groomed look. Thankfully, Sparrow waves us over, a French fry wedged between her fingers. She's staring at me as if to telepathically let me know she's worried for me. I'm worried for myself.

Pushing from the wall, I step around him. I have nearly left Graham in the dust when I hear him clear his throat behind me. I freeze, glancing over my shoulder as he takes a step toward me, the inexplicable pull between us still alive and well.

"And, Lily," he says softly, his fingers clenching the lapels of his jacket. "For the record, nothing about this is fair."

L ils, do you actually get coffee here?"

I smile at Sparrow's nickname for me but cringe a bit at her tone. She's not wrong to be surprised that I would venture away from the gourmet espresso and French pastries at our shop. Sometimes, though, when I need a break from the boulangerie—simply because I live and breathe it—I sneak away to the trendy coffeehouse located at the far end of the downtown shops in Birch Borough for a cup of brewed coffee that at least enthusiastically tries to compete for a coffee snob's attention, albeit with more frills and wild caffeine concoctions than I know what to do with. The coffeehouse is far enough away that no one can see me entering or leaving from Sparrow's Beret but close enough that I can run back and join the fray whenever new drama strikes in town.

In the past, I've considered running for some leadership position in Birch Borough. I feel as if this corner of New England was specifically made for my personality to exert maximum impact. Then again, I also recognize my persuasive qualities might be best utilized outside the office.

I'm glad to have the chance for a little one-on-one time with Sparrow, away from the hustle and bustle of the bakery. I have no problem being on my own. Okay, maybe I have a little problem. But watching my best friend prepare to get married is making me feel all the things. I usually wear my independence with pride, a badge of honor. I do my own thing. I go my own way. But I also didn't realize how much I depend on the security of always having my best friend around and how much Sparrow's presence has given me the courage to be on my own.

Sparrow and Rafe's love was a whirlwind romance that I don't think either of them could've fought even if they wanted to. They're so mad for each other now that it would cause anyone to consider the idea of fated mates. While their attraction was instantaneous and they slow-danced into love, Graham and I were a lightning storm—a wild explosion of light, charged particles, and moments that felt like magic. After only a few weeks together, I couldn't tell where I ended and he began. It was exhilarating and mesmerizing all at once.

"Lils, is there something going on? Why are we here?" Sparrow asks.

She sits across from me, her brown hair tied back with a ribbon today, fringe casually falling across her forehead. Ever since she's been with Rafe, she's been embracing more and more of her French side, and it's working for her. Meanwhile, I'm trying not to unload all my worries in one single outburst.

"There's nothing going on," I reply. "I come here to get

away from it all and remind myself that I may be aging, but I'm still relevant." I look around at all the Gen-Zers. I want to explain to them how I'm the definition of vintage. I wore butterfly clips and iridescent nail polish before we had cell phones.

A young woman walks by. She takes one look at my shoes with an expression I don't appreciate before walking on.

"Hey, at least I know what it means to page somebody!" I yell.

Sparrow chokes back a laugh as I sink into my seat again. Sure, my parents had the pager, but a reference is a reference.

"How likely do you think it is that she had no clue what I meant and thought I was just saying something dirty?" I smirk.

Sparrow pretends to think about it. "I'd say one hundred percent."

"That's what I thought."

The music blaring in this place is not comforting. It's got me a little on edge with lyrics I can't understand and music that is no doubt trending.

"So, how's it going on the dating apps?" Sparrow is looking at me, but her eyes are a touch too wide, her smile a bit too forced. I know she knows something is up, especially after my little chat with Graham at the diner.

I sigh and shrug. "The usual. Horrible. Lots of men holding fish. Or photos with children who aren't theirs. Or sitting on a weight bench facing the mirror, and I am left questioning their confidence to take a picture like that in a crowded gym. Honestly, I don't know if it's more acceptable in a crowded place or not."

Sparrow is feigning interest, though I see she is trying to hold back her laughter, so I continue my tirade.

"Or they'll upload bathroom mirror selfies—fully clothed—with gross bathroom sinks that they don't crop out. I honestly don't know how these men expect to win anyone over. It's unnerving, at best. And don't even get me started on car selfies. If I see one more man in his car with a cell phone reflecting in his aviator-style sunglasses, I think I may spontaneously combust."

I release a breath and observe the people at the next table looking at each other as if they're regretting their seat choice. I don't blame them.

"That's a lot," Sparrow says politely. A to-go drink is placed on the table in front of her, and I see her immediate smile. "You ordered for me?"

I nod. She goes to lift it and nearly knocks the cup over. I smirk inside. I love her, but Sparrow hasn't lost any of her clumsiness by getting engaged. I guess love doesn't remove all our quirks.

We pick up our drinks and take our time walking through town back to our shop. Easter is this weekend, and it's our unspoken understanding that we'll be working more than usual to fulfill all the orders. Maple croissants, macarons, and chocolate bunnies are in the queue for the day. All the other shop owners around town are no doubt stuffing plastic eggs to the brim with candy and treats for the egg hunt. Shirley, the owner of the dress shop and tailoring service, All Sewn Up, is probably making a new bowtie for this year's Easter Bunny costume. I'm pretty sure I even spotted a hand pie from Angie's Pies in the shape of a carrot as we passed her storefront. Along with the other locals busily getting festive in this town, Sparrow and I have been preparing our whole lives for moments like this.

As we walk in silence, my confidence wanes. I know I need to tell Sparrow the truth about me and Graham. I must tell her. The expiration date for this conversation is so far past due I should be evicted from our friendship. When we walk past the little blue house on the corner—the one that was my childhood home and hasn't seen my family gather in several years—a sense of longing overtakes me. It frustrates me more than anything.

How can we know deep in our hearts that we have nothing to complain about, nothing to be ungrateful for, and yet still feel at war with ourselves? How can there be an inexplicable weight of the world on our shoulders that we can't seem to shake, even if it doesn't make sense to our rational minds?

My parents call me only every few months, even when they're halfway across the world. I feel their absence. I still get jealous now and then of all the people who get to see them every day in real life while I settle for a screen. And I can tell you all the reasons technology is wonderful and how I utilize it and won't grumble about it, and yet I'm still wishing there was a way technology would advance enough so a screen still doesn't feel like a wall I can't climb between us.

I understand their motivation and their choice to live and work overseas. I admire and respect them for it. Yet I still miss them so much that I sometimes find myself crying when I wake up alone in my apartment, wishing for the days I didn't know how painful their emotional distance was, when I could walk downstairs to the sight of my dad making pancakes on Saturday morning, my mom exasperated at the sound of the whistling tea kettle she forgot to turn off for the thousandth time. I wish I could call them and tell them to meet me at Train Car Diner for a piece of pie and believe that they'd accept the invitation just because we can.

Trivial moments. Wonderfully unimportant. Everything to me.

It's only when we're back in the café twenty minutes later, and I'm surrounded by our familiar pastries and the well-worn details of the bakery that I love, that I feel a sense of peace click into place.

Not even five minutes later, that peace is interrupted.

"Okay, spill," a soft voice says.

I whip around from the stove where I'm tempering chocolate. It flings off my spatula and hits the wall with exaggerated flair. I grumble, knowing it will take me a good ten minutes to scrub that melted goodness off the tile.

Sparrow is staring at me a few feet away. Her arms are crossed, her feet in a relaxed ballet position she often holds while standing.

"Whatever do you mean?" I attempt. But it's no use. My moment of reckoning is finally upon me. "Fine." I sigh, abandoning the chocolate that's now seizing behind me. "Let's do this."

My heart wasn't in the moment anyway.

Sparrow narrows her eyes. "I know something is going on with you. And I've been trying to give you space. But, Lils . . . " she begins, pulling out her nickname for me again in the hope of breaking me, no doubt.

"This is about him," I begin.

She nods. "Is it awkward that Graham asked me out on

that train platform, and I told him I would only date a Frenchman? Yes. Have I reconciled the fact that he's best friends with my fiancé? Also, yes. So, if I can power through, I need to know why you can't."

"Maybe I just don't like him," I mumble, the lie bitter on my tongue.

"Eh!" Sparrow makes an obnoxious noise that honestly resembles a sound I would make, a challenge in her eyes. "I'm not leaving until you tell me. And I'm only going to pretend for a minute that I'm not hurt because you haven't told me what's going on with you two."

"With . . . Graham and me?" This innocent act is making even me cringe.

"Lily," Sparrow warns. She grabs a bag of chocolate and sticks it in the microwave, her finger hovering over the quick start button, a daring expression on her face.

"You wouldn't," I mutter.

It seems Rafe has brought out her playful and terrifying side. Does she really plan to ruin chocolate just to get me to crack? When she hits the button, my mouth goes slack. I race to the microwave, nearly crashing into the counter between us.

"No!" I yell as Sparrow steps aside and lets me rescue the chocolate from the microwave. I cradle it like a baby before setting it back on the counter. "I wouldn't hurt you like that," I whisper to it.

Chocolate may hate me, but I've always tried to be true to it. And while I've seen the microwave utilized for chocolate, I made a vow not to. I have enough trouble with the stuff without adding radioactive waves.

"I'm going to crush D'Artagnan for teaching you his

ways," I reply without spite, utilizing the nickname I gave Rafe when he first arrived in town last fall before I even knew he is actually French. I amaze myself with my perceptiveness at times. Still, my effort to deflect the conversation is waning.

And suddenly, I'm tired. "Okay," I relent. "What do you want to know?"

Sparrow's eyes widen like she can't believe I'm suddenly willing to get it off my chest. The truth is, I know telling her will be a relief.

"All of it." She pulls a stool out from under the counter and sits, crossing her legs and leaning in as if she has all the time in the world.

"Who's watching the front?" I peek through the window on the kitchen door and spot Anna. Thank goodness we've hired more people to help us at the bakery.

"Now, Lily," Sparrow sings.

"Graham and I met . . . over two years ago," I blurt out.

She nearly falls off the stool before righting herself. "Two years ago? But that's—"

"Right after your father died, yes. We met in LA while I was at the chocolatier-intensive course." Her mouth drops open. I choose to power through. "We dated."

"You . . . *dated?*" Sparrow yells, grabbing onto the counter.

"You may want to sit on the floor before you hurt yourself," I deadpan. "Because there's more."

"More?" Sparrow reaches for a coffee croissant from the baking racks nearby and takes the largest bite she can manage.

I use the opportunity to reveal the rest. "The first day

we met, I challenged him not to lie to me. In reality, he should've gotten *me* to sign something. Anyway, we kissed . . . a lot and had a mad few weeks of being everything to each other."

At this point, Sparrow is sputtering and coughing so much it's enough for Anna to peek into the back kitchen to find us, my face blushing and red and Sparrow choking on stray pastry flakes.

"Are you okay?" she asks with concern.

Sparrow nods. She clears her throat and chucks the half-eaten croissant over her shoulder, where it lands on the counter with a satisfying thud. Anna takes this as a cue to retreat.

"You mean to tell me . . . you . . . Graham . . . *kissed?*"

I nod.

"Wait. I remember telling you how radiant you looked on our video calls. You told me it was all the chocolate and sun!" Sparrow exclaims. A look of understanding crosses her face. "*That's* why he was looking at you like you were a ghost at Rafe's birthday party! There is some serious chemistry between you two. Almost like . . ."

"Lightning?" I ask softly.

"I was going to say love."

I fight the burn behind my eyes. "He loved me once."

I know Sparrow enough to realize that she's agitated and heartbroken. She's so sweet and has the best heart. She can't help but feel fire and pain for those she loves.

"There was a ring," I confess.

"A ring?" Sparrow reaches for the abandoned croissant and takes another bite, the café crème filling spilling onto her fingers. She lifts her hand. "Wait, wait, wait . . . if he had a ring . . . he didn't hurt you, did he? Because Rafe seems to think that *Graham* has been hurt, and I . . ." She trails off, a question in her eyes. "I'm just wrapping my mind around this," she says somewhat unintelligibly as she stands and begins pacing back and forth.

"I hurt him," I admit. "Shattered him, really."

Sparrow studies my face, and I fight the emotion of it all. It's rough when friends who know you so well can read you better than a meteorologist reporting the weather (thankfully).

My best friend slumps visibly. Her brow furrows. "So, you're acting like you hate him because . . . you're mad at him for being here?"

I shake my head. "I'm mad at myself."

"Oh, Lils." She moves toward me. I know she wants to hug me, but I just can't handle kindness right now. When it comes to Graham, I don't deserve it.

Pivoting quickly and walking to the front of the store, I make a beeline for the pastry case. Our spring pastries are on display, and the lavender-and-honey macarons alone are enough to keep us in business this time of year, never mind our lemon crème-filled croissants.

"Lily Anne Thomas, don't you run from me!" Sparrow appears beside me. A few customers look up from their once peaceful moment in our store to get in on the commotion.

"Don't mind her." I try to keep my voice cheerful while (lovingly) shoving Sparrow back toward the kitchen. She holds her ground, though. We're in a weird standoff as she pushes me toward the registers, and I grip the counter in resistance. We're grunting from the exertion of a tug of war with no rope. Suddenly, her hand slips over my eyes, and I squeal as she gains the advantage.

"Let me go!"

"No!" she insists. "Not until you tell me the rest. You're just going to act like you hate him forever? You're going to ignore him when you see him on the sidewalk?"

Drat. I should've known Graham would tell Rafe and that little sneak would tell my friend.

"Abandon ship!" I fiercely whisper while thinking again that there really should be better words for that level of volume.

"So, my best friend and Rafe's best friend are just going to pretend they're what . . . enemies?"

I lift my eyes toward the ceiling. Sparrow may have a few inches on me, but I'm scrappier. I untie the bow of her apron and hear her grumble of frustration as I wrap it around one of the cabinet handles. She releases me for only a second. Swiftly, I turn around to grasp the counter near the coffee station and pull myself away from her. I'm out of breath.

We look at each other for about three seconds before we burst into laughter. It's loud, unrestrained amusement for how utterly ridiculous we are. And it feels good, even though I know I'm raw from vulnerability.

Sparrow wipes her eyes with her hand, and a flash of the lily tattoo on her wrist reminds me that she's conducting this intervention for me. I peek toward the seating area, noticing Mrs. Kipper, one of our former schoolteachers, glaring at me over her coffee cup in the corner of the bakery. She points to the *Quiet. Coffee is a private conversation.* sign over one of the windows. It takes everything in me not to roll my eyes. The sign was a joke put there by Sparrow's father, but Mrs.

Kipper is clearly determined to ruin any sort of fun.

"We're not in school," I mutter. I stare down at the tattoo on my wrist of a sparrow in flight. Sparrow and I got them because of our bond. And it's essential I remember that right now. "Are you mad?" I say in an undertone to my friend.

Sparrow's eyes lock with mine, tears from our laugh fest still lingering at the corners of her eyes as she unwraps her apron string from the cabinet handle. "I'm not now."

I nod, a bit relieved.

"I'm . . . concerned, though."

She nods toward the back of the store. Anna has the good sense to start handing out samples, no doubt trying to cover for the little show we just gave our customers. Two friends attempting to get to the truth in a bizarre act of affection.

Back in the safety of the kitchen, I gather the ingredients I need to restart the chocolate I was tempering earlier. We have about a million (okay, that may be a bit of an exaggeration) chocolate bunnies to create this year for the egg hunt and Easter festivities, and I'm already behind. I can't seem to work as fast with Graham in town.

Sparrow lingers near my station. "Lily, I love you. And I feel like I should've been a better friend and gotten to the bottom of what I was observing between you and Graham a lot sooner."

I shrug. "We both know I wouldn't have let you."

Sparrow nods, her elegant frame going still. "Can you . . . are you still okay with being in my wedding?"

The hesitation in her voice guts me. I drop the ingredients on the counter, reach over, and pull her into a hug. I'm not an overly affectionate person with others, but there's no way I will let her think she's alone as she prepares for one of the most important days of her life. Besides Rafe and our crazy town, I know we're the closest thing to family each other has. We are both only children, and my parents were always the more absent type. Sparrow and I see each other nearly every day—well, except for when I went off to LA, and we can see how that turned out with Graham and me.

Leaning back with my hands on her shoulders, I look her in the eyes. "Sparrow, I wouldn't miss being a part of it for the world."

Her eyes fill with tears. "Good. Rafe would've been devastated anyway." She attempts a wink, but we both know she is incapable of winking, so it just looks like she's having some sort of fit with one eye. Still, her attempt is admirable. "Will you behave?"

I laugh. "Oh, we both know that's not possible."

"Seriously, Lils, are you going to . . . what? Not be okay . . . but be able to make it through this? Really?"

I shrug and start melting the chocolate for the second time. "I'll manage. We made an agreement, and I plan to drive him out of this town."

"Lily," Sparrow warns.

"It's fine. I won't physically harm him—intentionally. But having him constantly nearby is just burning me up inside. I can't take it. I'm not sleeping." I say the last point with a bit more inflection so she gets just how upsetting that part is. I need my sleep.

Sparrow shakes her head. "Where would you even send him? What do you mean *drive* him out of town? For the millionth time, we're not in England, Lily. We may be a small town, but I swear you revert to olden days, like it's perfectly acceptable to talk about ousting someone like this."

It's becoming clear that I need to make Sparrow understand what I'm going through. "I know Rafe will be upset when he loses his buddy, but they'll see each other elsewhere. Technology is a miracle, you know. Besides, he can just move to the next town over. He's welcome to still have a home in New England and get his fill of clam chowder and lobster rolls. Just not . . . here."

I take a breath. With everything in me, I want to make sure I don't hurt her or give any cause to worry as I hasten to reassure her. "Your wedding will be gorgeous. We love you both too much for anything to get in the way of that. But after? My heart can't take seeing him around much longer."

The glimmer of hope I still hold for a potential reconciliation rises in my mind, but I quickly crush it. The more I ponder what happened between us, the more it doesn't seem like a viable option. Graham will always be kind and polite, but until he can trust me again, he won't be my person.

Sparrow nods in understanding. She opens her mouth then closes it. I lift my brow, and she begins again. "And there's no chance?"

I know she's asking about Graham and me. While I appreciate her optimism, I also know it's a waste of time. My head feels heavy as I muster the strength to move it side to side.

"Oh." Sparrow exhales with obvious disappointment. "I've seen the way he looks at you, Lils."

I clear my throat, making an extra effort to let the utensils and bowls I'm using beat aggressively on the counter. My frustration has to go somewhere.

I have no right to be angry over Graham. We could've been everything to each other, and we're just . . . not. There are pieces of his life that I know nothing about. I want to fill in those spaces. I want to know what he has loved and lost these past few years. I want to do a time-lapse of his face to make sure I've recorded all the changes to it. I want to inspect his life and figure out if he's really happy now. Did my decision free him, or does he still dream of me too?

Sparrow tries one more time. "And you won't fight for it—to get it back? Whatever you two had."

I turn to meet her eyes, hoping she recognizes the flash of pain in them enough not to speak of this again. "There's nothing left for us to fight for."

Chapter Eight

Graham

"Do you want to tell me what we're doing here?" I lower my voice.

Rafe is holding his guitar case in one hand. He flashes me a stupid grin as we approach the gazebo in the middle of town. "Oh, you know . . . we're just two fairly young men who used to live in big cities but have now fallen in love with being part of a small town. Kind of like those Hallmark movies you've been told to star in."

I give him an unamused stare.

"So, if we're invited to an event here," he continues, "we show up to that event, my friend."

A chuckle escapes me. He is giddy with joy over the next few hours. I'm sure today will include something we'll one day need pictures of to prove it happened. I look away, hiding the grin on my face as I focus on the glimpses of water visible between a few shops across the way.

Birch Borough is known for the sound of the rushing river that runs through town. It can be heard in the distance, carried across the slightly chilly air that reminds me of the new things starting to unfold all around us.

Breaking up the roar of the water are the squeals of children—at least a hundred—jumping up and down as they walk toward the trail to the pavilion that hovers at the end of the shops a few streets down. An Easter egg hunt is happening in less than an hour, and the town is literally hopping with excitement. I cringe that I thought of something so Easter-related.

"Now, dear . . ."

I turn toward the woman's voice that suddenly speaks at our side, immediately recognizing Gladys, the town busybody and motherly figure who also "knows how to appreciate a fine-looking man" (not my words). My memory recalls quite a few instances of Lily mentioning the reels Gladys kept sending her featuring handsome chocolatiers around the world.

Thankfully, she's looking at Rafe, a hint of mischief in her voice. "What do you think about putting on an Easter bunny costume?" Her voice is on the edge of elation.

I choke back a laugh and clear my throat. Her eyes break contact with Rafe's long enough to give me a once-over and then return to see Rafe's response. Sometimes, there are advantages in the delay of gaining the town's favor, particularly during moments like this. Rafe is muttering in French, as he does when he's overwhelmed or excited (in this case, he's definitely overwhelmed).

"I already have your sweatshirt on under this, Gladys," Rafe replies smoothly, opening a bit of his bomber jacket to reveal it, the image of Gladys and Rafe together staring back at us. He received the sweatshirt as his Christmas gift from her. Smart man to wear it today. At this, I can't help but let out a laugh.

"Quiet, Wickham," Gladys says to me, her eyes lighting up with a blaze I want to immediately quench.

"How did you . . .?" My thoughts race. It would be my guess that Gladys is trying to get a rise out of me. While it's irritating that this is the nickname she's given me, something straightens in my spine when I realize that Lily has been talking about me. *Lily has mentioned me to her, huh?*

She raises her pointer finger and brings it a little too close to my chest for my liking. "I have pictures of you around town, so don't even think about crossing me."

"Ma'am . . ." I begin.

"Gladys," she corrects, and I feel like a schoolboy about to get . . . well, schooled. She elaborates without hesitation. "You were in the general store yesterday and had to bend over to grab something on the bottom shelf. I just couldn't help myself. I mean, you could be studied for the way your pants are tailored. Have you ever considered modeling for one of the art classes at It's Art, the shop just down the way?"

My mouth is hanging open, and my cheeks are burning.

"You were in public! If you didn't want to be noticed, you shouldn't have been bending over . . ." She trails off, pointing at Rafe. "I got photos of him unloading instruments last year and sent them to Rory, and we all see how she felt about those benefits."

Rafe clears his throat and shakes out his hands in a French-turned-American way, as if he's willing all of this to be a memory—quickly.

Gladys continues to protest. "I don't post them. I just

send them to people who may appreciate the views. I'm an artist myself, you know. And if you're embarrassed about the human form, talk to God about it." She quirks her eyebrows, and I'm beginning to wonder how much influence she's had on Lily's mannerisms.

This conversation is quickly moving in a direction I hadn't anticipated. I choke on the air and start to pace, a hand moving through my hair.

"Gladys, let's go get a coffee. Lord knows I could use it. *C'est parti!*" Rafe mercifully interrupts and directs her toward Sparrow's Beret just down the street.

I'm left standing on the sidewalk, mortified. Something in me hopes there will be a glitch, and the photo she captured will just happen to disappear from Gladys' photo library. But I suspect the damage has already been done. I'll probably see her collection pop up in a town calendar to raise money for some bridge repair or something soon. *How did I end up here again?*

All I know is that ever since Lily's little dare at the diner the other night, my insides feel like they're on fire. The way she challenged me and the memory of her nearness makes me think I'll be lucky not to have permanent dark spots under my eyes. The fact that she would even dare try running me out of this town is so frustrating that I feel like my hair could stand up on its own without any product.

She's the woman who told me everything we used to have was one-sided. The sound of her voice still keeps me up at night. Her eyes have branded me. I'm undone in her presence, and I wonder if she realizes the effect she continues to exert over me. Lily has "bewitched me, body and soul," and I know there's nothing I can do about it.

She's also the woman currently walking across the street with a basket full of chocolate bunnies (handmade by her, no doubt) like she's an Easter fairy and not the woman who shattered my heart and let the pieces blow away in the wind. I still haven't found all of them.

The moment she spots me—looking like a crazed man as I stare at her, I'm sure—feels like a punch in the ribs. She pauses then closes her eyes. The sharp rise and fall of her chest is obvious as she takes a deep breath. When she opens her eyes again, a newfound determination is in her step.

I rise a little taller and wait for the impact when she's within a few feet of me. There's an otherworldly pull between us, and the closer she gets, the more I feel my temperature rising—once caused by love, now by the devastation of what I lost.

"George," she says crisply.

"Lily."

She's wearing a black boatneck striped shirt beneath a charcoal cardigan, the tops of her shoulders peeking out and tormenting me as her creamy skin begs to be touched, the spot where her neck and shoulder meet taunting me thoroughly. A frigid breeze moves around us, and for the first time in my life, as I watch it circle through the ends of her hair, shifting it to the front and then to the sides, I'm jealous of the wind.

"Gladys was here," I say. She tenses, and I know she's already heard all about it.

"Yes, she was . . . that is, I saw her. I think you should expect to be asked to feature in her town calendar for the new year."

Ah, so there is a calendar. I'm satisfied that I was right.

The delicate shade of pink on Lily's cheeks is also very satisfying.

"If I'm here in the new year, of course," I add. I have no intention of losing Lily's challenges, but the reality is that it's too much fun not to give her back a bit of fire for all the sparks she sends me.

"Be lucky you dodged a bullet, then. Edgar still hasn't recovered from Gladys trying to make him take his shirt off for last year's calendar. Raising money for charity never looked so good—or scared." She grins.

Everything in me is begging me not to ask, but I know we can't move on from this without clarification. "Edgar?" I ask, but her pleased squint into the air tells me I didn't keep it as cool as I had hoped.

"He owns the boxing studio, In the Ring, down the way."

I nod and look away casually, determined not to look at her, even though I want to analyze every aspect of this conversation into next week. Something in her tone tells me there's more to their story, and it may fuel a future bout of insomnia. But I can't help turning back to her a moment later, mouth already open for a follow-up question.

Lily must sense this as she tilts her chin up, a look I don't like in her eyes. "I challenge you not to ask me about him."

She's keeping me from information, and as someone with an investigative personality, she knows I'll press for the details. Not willing to give in to my curiosity no matter how much it's grating on me, I decide to stick with a potentially safer question. "You . . . box?"

Lily turns toward me, a hand on her hip. A chocolate bunny almost catapults from the basket with the force of her pivot. Whispers of a conversation we once had invade my brain, but with her so near, I can't recall the details. Somehow, it feels important that she started boxing.

"Yes, I box. I could take you, that's for sure."

I scoff a bit, more to irritate her, but I'm also instantly frustrated by what the image of her and me in a boxing ring is doing to my insides. Another thing to haunt me. "We'll see."

"We'll see? I'll take you here and now if you want me to prove it."

"Is this one of your challenges?" I counter.

Her chest is rising and falling in such a quick rhythm that I almost want to check her pulse, but I know if I touch her right now, it will hurt me more than it would ever hurt her.

"Bunnies!"

A squeal from across the street causes both of us to turn our heads. We catch sight of a little girl with a white dress, face paint of a nose and whiskers swept across her face. She is nothing less than adorable. Her hair is blonde, almost the color of Lily's, and something in my heart tugs at me.

Lily shakes her head slowly. She softens, bending to eye level with the little girl, who nearly collides with her, a big smile on her face.

"Hey, darlin'!" Lily says. I'm caught off guard by the easy way she seems to soften.

"Bunny!" the child declares again.

Lily laughs and waves at someone who must be the girl's mother. The woman is slowly walking toward us with one hand on her growing stomach and another little boy holding tightly to her other hand.

"As a vegetarian, chocolate bunnies feel as though they

should be against my moral code, but I can't deny the people what they want. I think we've got some bunnies that need a good home, Leisel," Lily says to her as she closes the distance.

I see that Lily's eyes are unnaturally bright. And maybe she's great at faking with everyone else, but I notice the way her expression, while friendly, is tight. It's as if her own mask of face paint has been applied, pretending her smile is her real one and not her polite one.

Because Lily has at least eight different smiles. One for when she's embarrassed. One for when she's amused by something. One for when she's holding back a laugh. One for when something is actually funny to her. One for her friends. One for when she's playing. One for when she's polite. And one for when she used to look at me.

The woman I now know is Leisel raises her free arm and gives a huge sigh. Her eyes widen as she looks between Lily and me, another grin tipping her mouth up.

"Oh, Leisel, this is . . ."

I know it's killing her to have to say my name. To be honest, I don't think I could handle hearing it on her tongue, so I rush in, stretching out my hand. "Graham. I'm Graham."

"Leisel," she says, a brightness in her tired eyes despite clearly being dragged around town by small, enthusiastic feet for today's event. "And, yes, as in *The Sound of Music*."

"Ah, I always did like that one." I give her a wink and get some satisfaction as Lily starts chucking bunnies at kids who are starting to gather all around her. I'd help her pass out the candy, but I know she wouldn't accept my offer if it meant her having to admit she couldn't keep up on her own.

Leisel and I take a step back. Her children are now tucked behind her like little ducks. We stand and enjoy watching the chocolate bunny massacre of the year. Ears are bitten off, eyes are gone, feet are missing, and melted chocolate covers the mouths of many delighted faces.

Lily hovers in the middle of it all, looking like an angel and not like the woman who just told me she could take me in a boxing match.

"She's all bark and no bite," Leisel says with amusement. I let out a scoff. Her eyes widen. "Okay, so a bit of a bite."

"How long have you known her?" I question without taking my eyes off the woman before us.

"Oh, ages. My husband went to school with the four of them—Sparrow, Lily, Ivy, and Grey."

It's not the first time I've heard about the four friends of Birch Borough, although it does strike me that I have yet to see many sightings of Ivy and Grey.

Leisel continues, "The four used to be inseparable, and you'll still see them around each other quite a bit. But circumstances and life kind of paired them off. With Sparrow—or *Rory,* as Lily calls her—and Lily working together at the bakery so much, their families became more intertwined."

I nod as if all this information is common to me, mainly to see if she'll keep giving me the insider scoop.

"It was hard on Lily, you know, when her parents left. They're such great people, but I think she's felt the pressure to be perfect or to find her own adventure in life."

While I know her parents now do humanitarian work overseas, I didn't know their absence had been tough on Lily. Now, her past comments about needing to make her mark on the world make a bit more sense.

"Do you know anything about Edgar?" I barely manage to get out the words before we're interrupted by the arrival of more screaming children.

Lily tenses as she registers more children approaching and turns to us. "George! Let's go!"

With a quick apology as I wish Leisel and her kids a nice day, I jog to keep up with Lily's retreating form.

"More bunnies," she gasps into the fresh air.

"I don't think this is part of my wedding duties," I rebut.

Lily grunts. "Your wedding duties include easing the burden off Rory and Rafe. Right now, with Rory trying to hold down the café and me redirecting these young little heathens to eat their chocolates outside rather than inside our place, I'm doing us all a favor."

She pauses briefly to look over her shoulder. Her eyes focus on my throat and not my eyes. I've noticed that's been her thing since I moved to Birch Borough—she barely makes eye contact with me. It drives me mad. I feel as though she doesn't see me anymore because she never really looks at me. But I also know that to have any hope of getting over her, I need to learn how to avoid letting her actions affect me.

"Oh, by the way, are you bringing a plus-one?" she asks casually.

That stops me in my tracks.

"What?" I sputter. Amidst all the wedding thoughts and plans, I didn't even think or ask whether I should find a date. "Are you?" is my brilliant response back. It feels like the outdoor thermostat just got kicked up one hundred degrees.

"I was . . . thinking about it," she replies, acting as though her words didn't just punch me in the gut. It hurts because this is all we are to each other now: slightly hostile, barely speaking, not friends, and two people who could've been in love. Instead, it feels like we have both been thrown into an arena, trying to see who will survive.

"Who are you bringing?" I ask as casually as I can, as if the mere idea of Lily with someone else isn't causing a train wreck of emotions in my mind.

"I might ask Edgar . . . We used to . . . He kind of . . . The person who—" She stops and starts a few times.

"Owns the boxing place, yes," I finish for her, my heart humming to a different beat than usual. My worst fears are confirmed. The only reason I don't start dry heaving is the words *used to*.

I've seen Edgar around town. I knew who he was when Lily mentioned him. Tall with dark hair and eyes and a strength that is clear in every step he takes. He has tattoos on his forearms and a necklace that I haven't seen a man brave enough to wear since the early 2000s. I may hate the choice, but I respect it. At least I know he'll get some of Lily's random pop culture references.

When we reach the café, I break my stride, pausing to hover outside of the door.

"What are you doing?" Lily hisses.

"I'm not allowed in here." It feels ridiculous to say, but she knows I've always respected the boundaries she put in place.

"Oh." She peeks up at the sign and then at the door, seeming to come quickly to a resolution. "I need help. *You* can help. It's fine."

"So, does that mean I can get coffee here now?" A grin

escapes me because I know that as we're figuring out how to be near each other again, this is her safe space. And her letting me in—and thus, letting me back in, in a way—is a big deal.

"Don't push it." Lily throws the door open, and I catch it before it shuts in my face.

As we enter the bakery, Lily rushes to the back counter, opens a cabinet, chucks her basket at me, and hastily begins to throw more chocolate bunnies toward it. By the time I reach her side, I immediately recognize the mayhem. Inside the cabinet are beautiful, handcrafted chocolates thrown over, under, and tossed aside haphazardly.

Lightly, I laugh as Lily tosses them over her shoulders, clearly expecting me to catch them without even making eye contact. I'm in the zone of catching them and storing them safely in the basket, so it takes me a minute to realize that the atmosphere in the bakery has shifted and what must be the normal hustle and bustle has quieted.

I look around while Lily mumbles under her breath and the espresso machine hums. I catch Sparrow's wide eyes staring in our direction. I think I detect a bit of hope in her gaze, but it must be because she still doesn't know what Lily and I once had is now only a relic of heartache. I scratch the back of my neck and meet the eyes of several customers. Everyone has stopped enjoying their croissants and coffees to take in the sight of Lily and me, as if the sight of us together is something to get used to.

While my fragile hope feels foolish now, I once wished this was a sight Birch Borough would see all the time. And the reality that she's been seen with another man, even for a short time, hits me in my gut. We've both tried to move on.

However, I never lasted more than a few dates, while Lily may have had a whole other fulfilling relationship between now and the last time I saw her. Even if she isn't with someone presently, I realize I'm standing in the space where she has, no doubt, had crushes throughout the years. Other guys have taken her on dates on these very streets. Birch Borough is the very place where she has been hurt by immature boys, but it's also where she has dreamed of settling down.

I knew I wasn't the first guy in her life, but I wanted to be the last. The thought of letting that dream go again is harder to fathom now that I'm in her hometown.

Embarrassment creeps in at the idea that people may think I'm the one to blame for this scenario. All at once, I know what I have to do. I don't know if it's her challenge to me or the feeling of knowing I'm finally standing in the place that Lily calls her second home, but I'm done.

In the middle of the café, with townspeople listening all around, I do something that is the painful equivalent of kicking myself where it hurts. "Lily, it's a challenge," I say, determination in my voice.

"What?" she says over her shoulder in an exasperated tone. She turns to face me, suddenly recognizing how quiet the shop has become.

I do not doubt that my jaw is set like iron. "I'm adding another challenge. You seem to like those."

Her eyes, once disarmed, now flash. She is annoyed, and I'm the cause. Again.

"You can't do that. But if you're going to insist, George, just spit it out. Or let's go because I don't have time for this. I have bunnies to throw at kids, for crying out loud. Easter is upon us!" She motions impatiently for me to continue.

"Bring a plus-one."

Her hands grip the counter behind her tightly. She narrows her eyes and takes a deep breath. "Fine."

"Fine," I reply.

"All of this is fine!" Sparrow says lightly. We turn toward her, the sounds of a café coming back to life reverberating around us as if all is normal with the world. To be honest, her tone sounds terrified, but I'm trying to be positive.

It's clear to me now that Lily has the right idea in trying to drive me out of this town for her own self-preservation. And I was right to tell her we can't do this again. One of us is staying in this town, and one of us is leaving. But if I play my cards right, in an alternate twist of fate, maybe we can both stay here together. I want the last version so much I can feel it humming between my ribs.

At that moment, in Sparrow's Beret, the place I was once banned from and now find myself standing in, I decide to show Lily that I'll always be the man she found in the movie theater. This stubborn, gorgeous woman needs to know that while I didn't go after her the first time, if she lashes out again, I'm responding in kindness. If she's out for blood, I'll bring the bandages. She might want to fight, but I will come in peace. I'm rewriting the narrative. And I know where to start.

Chapter Nine

Lily

It's been three days since Graham told me—challenged me, rather—to bring a plus-one to Sparrow and Rafe's wedding. My stomach is in knots. I've eaten two croissants this morning and five macarons but drank only one cup of coffee. In short, I'm clearly ill. Even my *"pain of chocolate"* apron (a snarky spin on *pain au chocolat*) isn't motivating me to work.

I don't want to ask anyone to go with me to the wedding. I don't need anyone. They're my best friends, for crying out loud. I'm irritated by his challenge and irate that I'll have to see him with someone else. While we satiated the wild children in this town by handing out chocolate bunnies, I thought for a moment that we might be able to work side by side. Surely, we could form a type of truce, if you will. But his challenge has completely wiped me of any hope for reconciliation. He clearly wants us to move on. He's probably trying to get me to go out with someone else so that I drop my crusade to run him out of town. I should've expected it, prepared for it.

Wrist-deep in my last batch of *pains au chocolat* for the day, I'm taking all my frustration out on this dough, and I know it. My apron is plastered with chocolate from the day's work, accompanied by sugar and flour smeared across it as well. While I'm typically covered in chocolate, spring is the time I'm bathed in it. At Christmas, there's an uptick, but it's just the prelude to the season. From Christmas onward, I spend hours and hours making chocolate hearts, boxes, and roses. Then, I'm hit with Easter and spring wedding orders. Plus, ever since I was a teenager, I have made chocolate treats to give to some of my favorite people in town. At Easter, I'll usually donate a bunch of my handmade creations to surrounding homes and pretend that the Easter Bunny brought them.

After everything that happened with Graham during my brief stint in LA, you'd think I would be a little opposed to chocolate, but I crave it even more now. Graham used to watch me practice melting and making decadent chocolate creations in his gorgeous LA kitchen. He'd sit on a stool and watch me, a comforting presence, even if he was working on a case. Though we've been apart a long time, there have been moments when I'm melting chocolate, and I can almost hear his steady encouragement. Now, the scent of warm chocolate unlocks memories of laughter and love. If I loved chocolate before, he made me love it more. And I think, in my mind, I've been trying to transport my way back to those moments ever since.

Hence, why I've been spending even more time locked away in the bakery's kitchen, making every chocolate delight I've ever learned—except for the one I've pretended hasn't existed for the past couple of years. No matter how much I longed to recreate it again, I wouldn't let myself. Now, at Sparrow's request, today is the day I have to put my emotions aside and try to convince myself it's "just cake," even though, to me, it's anything but.

Despite how much I work with it, the running joke is that chocolate hates me. I must admit, it does seem that way. But I don't let it win (except when it does). I have a huge passion for utilizing the potential of chocolate to create the most delectable baked goods and sweets possible. I may not have ended up traveling around the world, making things out of chocolate, but I'm doing my darndest to be the greatest chocolatier Birch Borough has ever heard of. I expect my mastery of the chocolate arts to take me years, but I've already invested so much. Leaning into my passion is what this town, Sparrow's family legacy, and, quite frankly, I deserve.

The swinging door whines. I look up to find Sparrow standing just inside the doorway with a flush on her cheeks—and not the kind she has when she's seen Rafe.

"Um . . . Graham is here," she says quietly, as if she didn't just gut me with this announcement.

I'm still not used to him coming into the bakery. It's enough to deal with him in town, let alone having to see him in my space too. This is my chocolate cave, and I am the clever troll who guards its entrance. Despite my internal protests, though, in some small and hidden way, I want him to witness this special part of my life that he missed by not being part of it. He has been in possession of every other area of my heart before now. Might as well let him see this part too, on his farewell tour.

"Send him back here," I finally manage to say.

"Are you going to be nice?"

I barely hold back the roll of my eyes and focus intently on whisking chocolate and cream for a silky-smooth ganache. I made and frosted a cake earlier this morning. I have been waiting until this moment to pour the final drips of chocolate goodness over the top as the finishing touch.

After the heavy cream and chocolate melt together in a pan on the stove, I stir and stir. My thoughts swirl like the mixture coming together before me. This ganache has to be the best one I've ever made. It just has to be. With a final flick of my wrist, I shut off the stove and set the pot on the industrial counter to cool before turning back to Sparrow.

"I'm not going to commit a crime. Don't worry. I like Rafe too much for that. Plus, can you imagine me in a jumpsuit? No, thank you." I give her a grin, but my heart isn't in it. Instead, I'm thinking of all the ways I'm going to attempt to hide Graham's effect on me and still avoid touching him. I'm thinking of how my heart and my hope are about to collide because of a cake. My "famous" chocolate cake, which is waiting in the blast chiller behind me for its final cascade of rich ganache.

And before you question whether it's worthy of the title, trust me, it is. I came up with this recipe when I was a teenager. Sparrow has asked me to make and sell them in the shop, but I haven't been able to bring myself to do it quite yet. Making this monumental cake when I feel like it is one thing; having to make it on the regular is another. I want it to be special and something people look forward to seeing when I can't resist the urge to make it.

There aren't many things I can confidently make on my own without the recipes Sparrow's parents left behind, but my chocolate cake is one of them. Sparrow insists this is the cake she wants to serve at her wedding. She doesn't want a fancy cake made by a stranger or even another bakery in town. She has been determined from the beginning to have her wedding cake made by me. And because I'll do anything for her, I agreed.

"I just want today to be a happy day." My friend looks at me with expectation written across her face.

"I'll attempt to behave. Scout's honor." I smirk in her direction.

"You were never a scout, Lils."

I grab a stray piece of chocolate and chuck it in her direction without a word. Sparrow simply laughs and ducks as the flying candy whizzes past her head.

Today, Graham is under the impression that he is just here for a cake tasting. It's a common enough duty when you're part of a wedding, albeit it is a little strange for the best man to tag along. Rafe hasn't ever experienced my cake yet, so Sparrow and I asked him to stop by and taste it to make sure he's on board. Since she is so nice, the bride-to-be invited Graham too. Little does she know he's already tasted it.

Over two years ago, I made it for him. When he took the first bite, I thought he was going to cry. He was in love with it. I'm not sure if it was the chocolatey goodness or that we were so lost in each other, but I haven't been able to make the cake since. I remember too clearly the smudge of chocolate on the corner of his mouth, a hint sticking to his upper lip in a way that should be illegal. I remember his eyes widening and then closing when I told him I made it from scratch. And I remember the way he bit his lip before asking if he could have more.

At that time, we had been seeing each other for about a week when I decided to make my famous chocolate cake to impress him. Looking back, I recognize it as a sign from early on that I would dream of being with him for the rest of my life. Some men might have been intimidated by such a gesture. Graham, however, was immediately smitten.

Sparrow doesn't realize what asking me to make this cake again means. Graham doesn't know what he's walking into today. If there's any trace left of the man who used to watch me practice my chocolate-tempering skill, telling me that I melted him too, then I know the memories will hit him. The good ones. Memories you want to live in and still miss because they are so beautiful. I just hope I haven't done so much harm that they've been wiped away too.

"Where's Rafe?" I continue, noticing that I don't hear his laugh or the strumming of a guitar anywhere—the usual signs of his presence.

"He's on his way," Sparrow replies with a lovesick smile.

It's a good thing she is distracted by love. I'm praying neither Rafe nor Sparrow notice how trapped I feel from the choice I made. I'd give anything to be back in Graham's LA kitchen just to experience those days again. Sparrow disappears through the swinging door and is back within seconds, no doubt with Graham in tow.

I hear him before I see him. The timbre of his voice carries through the air and hits me right in the heart, like my ribs are a dartboard, and my heart is the bullseye.

"Thanks, Sparrow. I haven't been back here yet."

Refusing to turn around, I keep busy washing dishes, doing my best to ignore the scent of his cologne creeping into my space. It mixes with the aromas of chocolate and melted butter and is enough to make anyone swoon on the spot. I grit my teeth and keep scrubbing.

"Lily."

I hear Graham's voice behind me. I know he nodded in my direction like the gentleman he is. But I can't look at him yet. Not when I know what's coming. "George," I reply sharply.

Sparrow launches into small talk, and they discuss Liam's newest video of his cat, which has already gotten over 1.5 million views on social media. They chatter about how Rafe is feeling since he is heading to Nashville next week to co-write with a well-known French singer who is trying to break into the music industry in the US.

In my peripheral vision, I follow Graham as he walks toward me and sets a to-go beverage cup on the counter. I turn my head a little to see what it says, and my heart flips over in my chest. The side of the cup reads: "Vanilla Chai—Almond Milk—Lily."

He remembered.

It takes a superhuman effort to will myself to keep my emotions in check. Did the man I secretly still love not only bring me something but my-favorite-warm-drink kind of something? I barely manage to get out a squeaky, "Thank you."

Graham nods in acknowledgment, never breaking the flow of his conversation with Sparrow. Seeing him with my friend in our kitchen makes me want to curl up like a cat by a warm fire and purr with contentment before the reality of how far Graham and I are from where we started sets in. Knowing I must move to keep the emotion at bay, I walk to the other side of the work area.

I sense Graham tracking my movements as I pull out the cake from the blast chiller and gingerly bring it toward them. Despite how many times I've rehearsed this scene in my mind all morning (hence, the many apologies I made to the croissant dough), my hands are trembling. I set it on the counter in front of them, focusing on every detail of the frosting, the cake board, the tick of the clock in the corner, and wait for the moment he recognizes what I've made.

"Absolutely. I know this will be good for him . . ." He pauses and stares at the cake. "Is that what I think it is?" The force of his question proves that any previous attempts I've made to put a chink in his armor have boomeranged back to me.

"It's chocolate cake." My voice is small and distant.

"Your chocolate cake?" he asks, a hint of something in his voice I haven't heard since those moments in his LA kitchen.

"Yes, I made it."

Sparrow clears her throat to stop me from staring, and I remember I must stir the ganache or pour it before it cools too much. I manage to hold the saucepan steady, willing my hands to stop shaking as the melted goodness coats the cake and drips down the sides in the most satisfying way.

Nobody says a word. I know Graham and I are silently somewhere else right now. We're caught up in countless unspoken memories. When I sneak a glance in his direction, he gives me a resolute nod. I may try to put up a good front, and I may be an expert at holding my ground, but from the beginning, Graham has always been able to see me to my core.

Sparrow has every right to ask for this cake, yet briefly, I almost apologize for taking us back to the moment I first made it for him. It was a good one. He ate a generous slice of cake, and then we shared a kiss so intense it would melt glaciers. He tasted of chocolate and a hint of the latte he sipped while enjoying it. He tasted of mocha and . . . Graham. To be honest, that is the most potent and visceral memory of them all. It was then he told me he loved me for the first time. And I knew that he meant it.

I clear my throat and watch the ganache set as it meets the coolness of the air and the cake.

"Rory, would you do the honors?" I turn to Sparrow. I don't trust myself to hold out a serving knife without my nerves revealing themselves, so I nod toward the utensil, grabbing some of our pastry bags to use as makeshift cake plates.

She cuts into the layers, making a sound of delight as the cake proves to be soft inside, the buttercream and freshly poured ganache stretching a bit and swirling with the cake crumbs. I absolutely hate the *M* word when it comes to describing cakes, so I can't even think of it, but if any cake matches the word, this one is it. It's so soft and fudgy inside that it shines.

Graham takes a fork from the pile on the counter and stretches his neck side to side like he's about to go to war and not dig into a baked good.

Sparrow is already two bites in, her eyes wide with appreciation, and I can't help but laugh. The joy of her delight overtakes some of the pain that pulses through my fingers from clenching them so tightly.

"You really want this as your wedding cake?" I ask her.

I still can't believe, out of every single French patisserie item and baked good we could make, this is what she wants.

"One thousand percent. No question. This is it." Her mouth is still full of cake as she nods enthusiastically. She's almost done with her piece, while Graham has yet to take a bite.

"And do you want cupcakes, small cakes, or a big one to cut into?" I'm speaking way too quickly, and Sparrow catches it, her eyebrows rising as she looks between Graham and me. I don't slow down, continuing without pause. "I'm going to make you a small one too, and I'll frost it with vanilla meringue icing so it looks like a wedding cake. You can keep it for your first anniversary and cut into it . . ." Finally, I trail off.

"Yes, all the things. Yes."

I flash a genuine grin before allowing myself to look at Graham. He is still staring at the cake like it personally offends him. I think, in a way, it does.

"Oh, Graham—I'm so sorry. Do you not like chocolate?" Sparrow asks.

He lifts his head, a polite smile creeping over his lips.

"Oh gosh, are you allergic? I didn't even ask!" she continues, and I'm just waiting to see what he'll admit to in this conversation.

"No, and no," he replies. His eyes lift slowly from the slice of cake, trailing over the counter and up, up, up, until they laser into my own. "I love it."

Heat crawls up my neck from the admission and, no doubt, from the reference to our shared memory. I don't know whether to give myself an award for knowing him this well or to cry at the smoldering gaze he is serving me. Even though I know it's against his will, it is mixed with enough tension and heat that I could've baked this cake without an oven.

The bell over the front door rings. Sparrow rushes through the swinging doors to greet whoever just stepped in, leaving Graham and me to each other.

"Do you remember?" he asks as soon as it's just us.

I nod.

"And you made it anyway?"

"Sparrow asked me to."

He clears his throat lightly and looks toward the counters full of chocolate-covered pots and utensils.

"It was a challenge to bring myself to do it," I admit because I can't seem to ever fully shut him out.

"I love a good challenge," he says with a hint of authority in his voice that grips my attention. He leans over the counter toward me for the last part of the sentence, close enough that the edges of his beard brush against my cheek before he straightens back to his side. Graham has several inches on me, even when I wear high wedges, so I know his move is on purpose. And I remember, on one of our last nights together in LA, when I confessed feeling like a challenge to most people, leaning in close and murmuring sweet things in my ear as his beard brushed my cheek had been his response. I open my mouth to say something—anything—but can't find my voice.

With an intensity only he can pull off as effortless, he scoops up a huge bite of cake and slowly puts it into his mouth, never breaking eye contact with me. My stomach swoops low, and my lungs constrict when I spot it—the same dab of chocolate that once graced the edge of his perfect mouth is there again. Chocolate from the same cake that got me a declaration of love the first time he tasted it. And he's not moving to wipe it off.

"What is it?" Graham says with a deep, gravelly tone in his voice that I shouldn't like so much. "Something on my face?" Instead of using a napkin, he has the audacity to stare at me while he brushes the back of his hand across the side of his mouth. It does nothing but smear the chocolate, though he even pulls his lips with his teeth to ensure he got it all. I can't speak. The man who knows how to use every single piece of silverware on a fancy table and has a whole drawer full of pocket squares (he told me once) just used his hand instead of a napkin, and darn it, if it's not one of the most attractive things I've seen him do. *One point: Graham.*

"Hallmark Hot G!"

I glance away from Graham quickly, torn by wanting to continue watching him eat but also grateful for the interruption. Rafe rushes in, calling out the ridiculous nickname he has given Graham, a huge smile on his face and his fingers entwined with Sparrow's. Someone once thought Graham could be in a Hallmark movie as the lead (he totally could), and Rafe won't let him hear the end of it. Frankly, I find the nickname downright delightful. And even though my heartbeat still feels like it's ricocheting throughout my body, it's for reasons like this that the Frenchman has worked his way into my heart as a dear friend. He's just kooky enough to keep up with me.

Sparrow follows behind her fiancé, free hand over her lips, telling me that they must've snuck a kiss before they made their appearance.

"Yes! I can't wait to try this!" Rafe yells, a forkful of cake appearing in his hand. The man has a sweet tooth that is at my level. His taste is more to just eat all the things instead of ninety-nine percent chocolate, which is my ratio.

"*Ouais, ouais, ouais,*" Rafe says, and I can't help but laugh. The word sounds like "way" but is the French equivalent of "yeah" in English. And darn it again, if Rafe doesn't keep doing things to make me like him while also making me grateful for the hint of levity he adds to the moment.

"C'mon, darling." Sparrow nestles under his shoulder. His arm wraps around her effortlessly while he continues to shovel cake into his mouth.

"So. Good," Rafe murmurs.

"Yes, I know." Sparrow laughs and gives me a wink. "This is the cake!"

I smile and try to be happy. I get to make a wedding cake for my best friends, and it should have me over the moon. Instead, all I can focus on is the feeling of Graham looking at me, a faint smear of chocolate still near his top lip, and the way I hear him say, "It certainly is."

Chapter Ten

Graham

Honestly, I think I know how to get a suit tailored." My tone is a bit salty, and immediately, I wince. We just finished an early dinner at Train Car Diner, and Rafe asked to tag along to see my suit for the wedding. *"To make sure I fit the look for Hallmark's casting department."* He threatened to send them a headshot (which I don't have) if I went alone.

I'm about to suggest he take acting lessons since he isn't fooling me at all.

"Affected by a certain blonde woman much?" Rafe replies with an easy grin.

While I genuinely care for him, I feel the need to smack it off his face. I think being around Lily again is infiltrating my thoughts with more aggression than usual. I don't know what to think about it because everything in me seems to be reverting to an unfamiliar primal response. I release a grunt and keep walking down the street, the warmth of the early evening sun shining on my face reminding me of a certain hike Lily and I took in the foothills of LA long ago. I swear my shoulders have been hunching lately, like the earth is dragging me downward, though that's not the look I would ever go for. I've worked hard for my good posture.

My mother's best friends knew how to ballroom dance. I have vivid memories of Donna and John telling me to hold my shoulders back, soften my hands, and move to the music as I pretended to lead a girl when I was only twelve.

With my self-taught sense of style, I recognize that I look more like I belong in a city and not in a small town, but I'm not letting go of my fashion sense. My teenage years were spent working a job after school to help pay our rent, always trying to hide the holes in the bottoms of my shoes from my mom. I still tighten my feet in my loafers when it rains.

As soon as I could afford it, I made sure that no one had any reason to suspect that I used to live on fluffernutter sandwiches (a New England thing with peanut butter and marshmallow crème taking the place of jelly) or used to study by candlelight like characters from a Dickens' novel to save money on the utility bills. Those days are over, and I've never looked back. Now, I almost only ever wear suits, donning shorts or sneakers only to work out or on special occasions. It's odd how we can be so far removed from what we once were, but one tangible reminder or piece of clothing can make us feel pulled into the past.

I shake my head to free my mind of the memories and try to focus on what I'm about to get into. Rafe may think he's clever, but based on the looks he keeps throwing my way, I know Sparrow must be waiting for us at All Sewn Up, the dress shop and tailoring service here in Birch Borough.

If Sparrow is there, a certain blonde woman who floated through my dreams last night isn't far away. Rafe's hand lands on my arm. We pause, and I see the sign for the store glowing like a beacon in the distance.

"Hey, wait up, Graham." His insistent tone makes me turn to him. Rafe's face is serious. "I'm sorry," he continues. "I shouldn't have joked about her."

As the courage I've built up suddenly starts to wane, I give him a quick nod. I know I need to get used to Lily's presence circling me again. But my tense mood isn't just because of my constant awareness of her. This town is sinking into my soul in the best of ways. In addition to living near my best friend, Rafe, I can see Sparrow becoming a dearer friend too. She's not just my best friend's girl. I need to get this right. I'm ready to put down roots, build a home, and start a family. But the more often I see Lily, the more unsure I become that my dreams are ever going to be possible.

I wince again and will my face not to freeze that way. Rafe pulls me toward an alcove as a family passes us on the sidewalk. The sight of their happy faces makes my heart clench a bit.

"Please tell me what happened between you two," he says.

He doesn't even have to say her name. We both know whom he is referring to. Even though I knew this day was coming, I feel the embarrassment and shame creeping up my neck. A flush overtakes my face, as it always does when I think of Lily rejecting me on the beach that night. While I war with myself on where to begin, Rafe's gentle nature and patience assure me that it's time to tell the truth.

"Um, so . . . " I say as a stellar beginning to this cautionary tale, "Lily and I knew each other before I moved to Birch Borough."

He nods for me to continue.

"We saw each other for a while."

Rafe's eyes widen. "Wait—as in . . . Lily went out with you on purpose? Like it wasn't some sort of fake-dating scenario?"

I rear back. "What? No!"

Suddenly, it strikes me how weird it probably is to see two grown men having a deep chat near Bette's Ice Cream with families and high schoolers moving in and out. I direct us toward a store that is already closed for the day. Even though it is only early evening, in a small town, you learn that you're no longer in the city rather quickly when you want a coffee at 5:00 p.m., and everything is already closed.

"Okay, so, you went out with Lily . . ." Rafe muses. "*When?*"

"LA."

"When was she in LA?"

"A couple of years ago . . . for a chocolatier-intensive course."

"Wait. Is this when you ignored my calls for weeks and had that goofy grin on your face when I showed up at your house before you kicked me out and told me you were on a quest to find yourself? I thought you had lost it. You were just . . . with Lily? I mean, we met in LA, so it's not too far off . . . wait—did you follow her here?" Rafe's voice has risen an octave since the last question.

"No," I protest immediately. "I mean, she mentioned this place, but I thought for sure she'd be gone when I moved here."

Rafe's eyes narrow. "Did you hurt her?" His unusually gruff tone sends me rearing back again. "After observing your obvious tension around each other, I've been wanting to ask. And if you did, so help me . . . she is what I imagine a sister would be. I love you, man, but this is—"

"Will you quit with that? I . . ." I trail off because the words are just so hard to get out.

"You what?" Rafe asks the question softly, but I hear the anxiety in his tone.

We're treading into dangerous territory since Lily is Sparrow's best friend, and we both know it. What I am going to say might change his opinion of the situation—maybe even of Lily. I don't know how to feel about it. I don't want to misrepresent what happened. Silently, I remind myself that it is best to just keep to the facts, and maybe the truth will surface.

"I told her I loved her," I say the words bluntly.

Rafe blinks. Once. Twice. He furrows his brow. "I need to sit down."

I follow him to a bench a few storefronts away, and we sit.

"You . . . Lily . . . *love?*" He hunches over, his forearms resting on his knees. A sense of dread fills my gut. I nod as I feel Rafe look toward me. "Did she know how you felt about her?"

I nod again.

"Did . . . she love you back?" Rafe continues, his voice incredulous.

If I thought I was right in trying to avoid this conversation before, my instinct proves correct when I realize it's hitting rock bottom for him to question it. "I thought she did."

Rafe's hand brushes through his hair. I hear him speak in French under his breath. He stares across the street. My friend seems beside himself. I think of suggesting we drop the conversation and just continue to the tailor's shop. Discreetly, I check my watch. In four minutes, we'll be late, and even more alarms will go off between the four of us.

Before I can speak, Rafe turns to me. "*Dit moi*. Tell me."

Scratching the back of my neck, I release a sigh. "There's nothing to tell. I had a ring in my jacket pocket; she saw it and went home. Back here. She said what I thought were mutual feelings were one-sided. I never heard from her again."

"A *ring? C'est impossible!* You wanted to marry her?" Rafe hops up like he just can't help himself. His fingers move as if simultaneously playing an invisible piano near his legs while also strumming an air guitar.

I count nearly to twenty by the time he settles beside me again, his face lined with distress. Because of course he is—just as I was for him when he wasn't sure how things would turn out with Sparrow. Except, now Rafe is about to get married, while I've felt the sting of what happens when things don't work out. When no one fights for you. When there's no forgiveness to be found.

My eyes burn, and I want so badly to clear my throat. I wanted to marry Lily so much that it made me sick when I realized it couldn't happen. I feel his hand rest on my shoulder. I look around the little streets of Birch Borough, a far cry from the city, but they are still places in which I have found refuge.

"Graham, I'm sorry. I really am."

And I know he means it. Giving a slight nod, I make eye contact and try my best to grin. I know it looks forced, but I try.

"So . . . you . . . moved *here* despite everything? I mean, I can't say I'm unhappy you did because, wow, it's changed my life. But this just feels like torture for you." Rafe's eyes widen, and I see the reality of my situation sinking into his brain.

I know how to put it into perspective for him. "Wouldn't you have done the same if Sparrow was torn from your life, and this was all you had left of her?"

He doesn't have to answer me.

"I know it seems ridiculous, but I didn't think she'd be here. I had *reasons* to think she wouldn't be here." I sigh. "Still, I should've told you sooner. I'm sorry I didn't. But when I realized she was still here, and you had already met Sparrow . . . I just couldn't . . . I . . ." There's no need to finish my train of thought. Rafe gets it.

"What are you going to do?" His words echo throughout the approaching evening. The weather is causing me to shiver a bit as it wrestles with the lingering chill of winter to allow it to turn fully into spring.

"I'm going to get fitted for a new suit—even though I already have a closetful. I'm going to stand beside you and be happy for you. Then I'm going to leave town if Lily wins the bet she dared me to. Considering my counter challenge is for her to keep herself from falling in love with me again, there's no hope for winning. Don't worry. I'll make sure you're married and safely tucked away in your new home first. Not ever kicking you to the curb, man."

I stand and am a bit relieved when Rafe steps in line beside me. A warm glow from the shop's interior is within reach when Rafe tugs on my arm. "Graham, I'm not one to give you false hope. I hope you know that."

My jaw clenches, and I nod, expecting the worst.

"But I've seen the way Lily looks at you. And I think what may feel like scorn is, instead, proof of how much she cares."

Before I can respond or process the monumental words Rafe just dropped into the air between us, his focus shifts to the smiling woman waving through the shop window.

"Go on," I tell him.

He bounds up the steps and into the shop like a man in love. Through the glass, I watch his reaction. His expression is in awe of Sparrow. He grabs her hand and twirls her around in a dress (not a wedding gown), laughing as he pulls her close. He whispers something in her ear just as Lily emerges from behind a curtain in the back that must serve as a dressing room. Rafe and Sparrow react to her arrival with obvious enthusiasm. Instead of turning to them, she looks around the shop. Her hesitant expression seems almost as if she's looking for someone. A level of vulnerability flashes across her face. I see a flash of the woman I once knew so well, and my heart immediately clenches.

Could she be looking for me?

Cracking my neck, I walk up the steps and open the door. Immediately, I am hit with the force of Lily's stare.

Knowing I am about to be near her again has me so on edge that I just now catch sight of what she's wearing. She is so beautiful that I can't even speak. On Lily's slender form is draped a black satin gown, halter-style, with a sort of collar around the top that resembles a large choker. Even though the fabric circles her neck, the deep V mesmerizes me. Before I can think better of it, my greedy mind takes in the rest of the gown. It molds perfectly to her waist, showing off the curve of her hips before it flares out and down. The hem hovers just off the floor. Her toes peek out with a light blue nail color that I know I'll try to find in the sky tomorrow.

Must get a grip.

Heat creeps through my hand with an intense flash. I want to reach out and touch the curve of her waist to see if the feeling is different from when she's worn clothes in another material.

"George." She states the word as a fact more than a greeting. Her tone shakes the rogue thought from my mind.

"Lily." My voice doesn't crack, and I take that for the win that it is.

"I thought you'd have enough suits by now that you wouldn't need this appointment." She lifts her brow.

"I don't."

"Then what are you doing here?" Her arms are crossed, her posture guarded in every way. Sparrow and Rafe are watching us, and I hate that nothing I can do will erase the history between Lily and me. It hovers in the air between us, a hunter that we can't ever outrun.

"My friends asked me to be here. So, I am." So simple but true. She doesn't need to know what it took from me to walk through the door. What it takes from me every time I'm around her and trying to pretend that my smile hasn't changed.

"Okay, well, we're heading out," Sparrow says so quickly that I know something is off. I narrow my eyes, trying my best to suss out an ulterior motive, when Rafe gives me a grimace. He mouths that he's sorry. I stuff my hands into my pockets to keep the frustration from pouring over.

Lily appears beside me, encroaching into my space. "You're leaving?" she asks them.

The faintly shrill quality in her tone reveals just how on edge she is right now. I used to think I brought her peace, and the change in knowing how nervous she is to be alone with me—even in a public place—sends me reeling. It's a sucker punch to my ribs.

"Rory, I can't— I need help with the dress," she continues shakily. Her nerves make her voice louder than I think she intends.

"Oh, well, have Graham help you," Sparrow replies with a smile that is a little too wide to be considered normal. "Oh, and Graham, you know what? I think a black suit you already have in your closet will work just fine!" She moves quickly to the door and is on the sidewalk without looking back.

"No problem," I call after her stiffly, now fully aware that I was never getting a new suit for the wedding in the first place.

"Good luck!" Rafe is pulled through the door behind her. I see him glance through the window with a shrug and a *sorry* gesture before he's gone. So much for being my best friend. I may have to rethink who is suitable for that role in my life if I make it out of here in one piece.

I clear my throat and turn to the wide-eyed woman beside me. "You need . . . help?" My words sound forced, but I'm doing my best not to look like a complete fool. It's not working.

Lily bites her lip, frustration written all over her. I assess the situation as discreetly as I can. I'm trying my best to figure out why she won't be able to get out of this dress alone while simultaneously willing myself to look away and not think about her stepping out of it. It's a conundrum.

She stirs, and the dress rustles. I look up to find Lily standing in such a way that the mirror in the main room gives me a clear glimpse of the back of the dress. My mouth goes dry. Her whole back is exposed, except for the choker piece, which has tiny buttons running down the length of it—lots of them. And it hits me why she would struggle to get out of the dress. Someone has to assist her with the dozens of buttons.

"Isn't there someone else who . . .?" I trail off.

"Normally, yes," she affirms. "But it's bingo night at Gladys', and Shirley told us to lock up." She points to a set of keys on the counter across the room.

"And you can't take this home?" I immediately cringe.

"To sleep in it, George? No, I can't." She turns toward the mirror and reaches behind her neck to fiddle with the buttons. I hear her say under her breath something to the effect of, "Should've worn the blue one," and, "Last time I try vintage," and, "Let's see her try to make maple croissants without sugar."

I'm a little afraid of the threats pouring out of her mouth and am about to call it a night and let her fend for herself when I catch the shakiness in her hands.

If Lily is my nemesis these days, I've caught her in the most vulnerable moment. I debate just letting her figure it out because as much as I want to show her that I'm still here—still wanting to be beside her—I also think she's wrestling with wanting to love me back. She told me she wanted to be someone's first choice but didn't believe me when she became mine. And seeing her like this leaves me feeling more raw than I care to admit.

I back toward the door to allow my lungs the space they need. It only seems possible to breathe when I'm farther away from her. But my heart has a different mission. I remind myself to let her know I'm not the enemy.

"Challenge me," I blurt out suddenly.

"What?"

"With anything. Challenge me. Please." Hesitantly, I move closer, willing my hands not to reach for her.

"You don't need to do this, George."

With what can only be described as a growl, I close the distance between us.

"What are you doing?" she exclaims, her eyes catching mine in the mirror. She sees me backing up and then coming forward again. Not my proudest moment.

"I'm helping you."

"Why?" The question hovers, her eyes never leaving mine. It's the hottest form of tension, watching each other in the mirror. It creates a level of removal that allows us not to feel as if we're purposefully staring. Except, the moment proves even more intense because I can see myself too. I see the thin veil of sheer attraction in my eyes, my clenched jaw, and the way I'm leaning toward her more as the seconds pass. There has always been a transparent tie between us. Now I have proof of our connection. We don't often get the gift of seeing what we're really like in a situation and realizing it is not what we imagine.

"Why, George?" Lily pleads.

"Because you need help."

We still haven't broken eye contact, and my hands hover just above her shoulders. "I'm going to need to touch your neck to get at the buttons. I won't touch you more than I have to. Is that okay?"

At this, she looks at the carpet, her bottom lip caught between her teeth. I wait for her answer. More than just the opportunity to touch her again, this moment is the chance to know, on some level, she still trusts me enough to let me.

In the mirror, she meets my eyes once more and nods. The lighting in the room makes her eyes look greyer with hardly a trace of the lavender color that only seems to appear like a solar eclipse—rare but sightworthy when it does.

Slowly and carefully, I press my fingers to the tiny buttons, more than a half dozen of them mocking me. My fingers tense, begging me to commit to memory every detail of this moment. As I struggle to undo one of the elastics caught around a satin button, my thumb slips and taps the bare top of her back. Lily sucks in a breath, and I immediately drop my hands.

"I'm sorry—I didn't mean to . . ." I begin. I'm cut off by Lily's hand reaching for my own. The ends of her fingers wrap around mine. Our gaze connects in the mirror, and I spot the glisten in her eyes.

"I know." She takes a deep breath. "I know."

I shake my head and try again. I notice details I never noticed before. I marvel at the tiny pieces of her hair that have fallen from her ponytail, the edges tracing the curve of her neck. The hair on her arms is standing at attention. Her spine shivers when I make it to the bottom of the row, and my fingers release the fabric.

"All set. You're free." I try to flash her a grin in the mirror, anything to lighten the moment.

Lily turns toward me, one hand holding the now open collar so it doesn't fall forward. The other hangs loosely at her side. "Thank you," she says.

I severely dislike how small she sounds. I want to tell her I would still be more than kind to her if she'd let me.

"No problem," I reply, even though we both know it's not true. Being near her is a problem. For both of our hearts.

She walks toward the dressing area. I turn to leave when I hear her footsteps stall. Looking back to make sure she's okay, I see we've struck the same pose but mirror each other. Her chin is over her shoulder, eyes heavy.

"You were kind to me just now"—a long pause—"and I know I don't deserve it." She says it so matter-of-factly, but I don't miss the sincerity in her tone. And then she's gone, the swish of the fabric of her dress fading as my heartbeat rings in my ears.

Chapter Eleven

Graham

"Ordinance number one," Clark speaks toward the crowd assembled in the Town Hall meeting room.

Though Clark is the owner of Aesop's Tavern, he is presiding over this eccentric town meeting. I was strongly advised by Rafe to put in an appearance at tonight's event.

"You won't regret it," he informed me with a wink and a few more French sayings thrown in that I still don't understand. "Plus, it's good to show your face around town. Become part of the culture here so they don't think you are a stuck-up city boy."

So here I am. Clark stands at the front of the room behind a folding card table over which a crooked plastic tablecloth is thrown. The scene is a bit informal. He does have an official name plaque, though, and a gavel. So, color me impressed. If I hadn't had the experience of living in a small town, I'm not sure I would believe these types of meetings actually exist in real life. Of course, I am familiar with the premise because of *Gilmore Girls*—which Lily made me promise I would watch (and I did).

Right off the bat, I can see that, instead of a Taylor, this corner of New England has a Clark, who wears vests instead of sweaters and owns a tavern instead of a grocery store. He must be good at keeping his cool, though, because everyone keeps voting him in to the position of moderator.

Currently, I find myself squished beside Lily, who seems to have decided to torment me by plopping down on the empty chair to my right. The old part of me is delighted to be this close to her, while the new one is screaming to be cautious and back away as quickly as possible. The little wooden seats I worry might buckle under my weight aren't helping my comfort levels either. Sparrow and Rafe are sitting together to my left.

I'm doing my best to concentrate on Clark's booming voice. Meanwhile, I'm distracted by a game of bingo being played a few rows and diagonally ahead of us by a group of four seniors who have set up shop, complete with clipboards and dabbers. I'm trying to figure out how this isn't being shut down immediately. They're trying to quietly call out the letters and numbers, and it's distracting.

"B12!" whispers an older woman I've never seen before. "D42."

"That's how you do it!" I catch an old-school cabbage patch move while I attempt to tune them out and listen in to the main event.

Clark's voice carries loudly into the crowd. "An anonymous Birch Borough resident proposes that Liam should not be able to use the lookout point near the bridge to film videos of his cat, A-cat-pella."

"Hey! That's his favorite spot!" Liam leaps up, his fist in the air. A hushed murmur passes over the room. The dramatic scene would be very inspiring if I didn't know it was all for a cat.

"You should be in one of his videos," Lily deadpans beside me.

"Is that a challenge?" I grit out with a grin despite my horror. No part of me wants to be in a video with a cat, but this woman isn't shy about pushing my limits. She's brilliant but brutal in the best of ways, and I know she'd relish watching me suffer on any social media platform with a feline, especially since she knows I love dogs.

"Oh, you bet your bottom dollar it's a challenge," Lily practically squeals with restrained delight.

I shake my head, but before I can get out a protest, Clark lifts his hand.

"All in favor," he says.

No one raises a hand. In the brief time I've lived here, it is clear this town loves Liam and his cat too much to do anything that would hinder him from making the supposedly viral videos I have yet to see. I'm intrigued, though, and make a mental note to look up his account, especially since I'm going to need to ask him if I can guest star in one of his posts. Gladys told me that he might be starting a merch line soon.

"Next order of business," Clark continues. "We've spotted a seal lingering near the river's edge for the past week. The rescue station for marine animals has been called. They are happy to report they believe the little one is doing well. Now, all we need to do is name her."

"I'm sorry, what? How did we end up here from LA?" I mumble the words just loud enough for the seats around me to hear.

From beside me, Rafe just grins at my question and tips his shoulder as if to ask if I can believe how great this scene is. I feel as if I've entered a portal to another world. The individual with the gavel should definitely be examined—and the rest of the town too, for going along with it.

"All in favor of Carol?" Clark suggests.

A few hands lift about the space. I don't know whether to be horrified or impressed that not only are people voting, but they already know the meeting agenda enough to have an opinion on the name they're voting for.

"All in favor of Louise?"

A flurry of hands fly up, with the exception of mine. Before I can register what's happening, Lily's arm wraps around my sleeve. She lifts my hand high in the air.

"If you're here, you have to vote," she demands.

I refrain from rolling my eyes, but only just barely. Between the effect of her proximity on my head and the fact that I can now add voting for a wild seal's name to my life experience, I'm waiting for a UFO sighting to be reported next.

Clark lifts both palms in the air in a swaying, conductor-of-a-symphony-orchestra motion. "Louise, it is! Oh, Louise and Clark, how grand!" he yells to the accompaniment of a few laughs and a whooping noise in the corner as he writes the name on a rolling chalkboard beside him. The chalk piece taps a staccato rhythm. I'm picturing all the ways this town would go viral if word of this got out. Birch Borough could pen a TV show with the cast of characters around me. I would make sure I managed the contract somehow, of course.

"It's Lewis and Clark," I reply under my breath. As I say

the words, I lean back in the chair. My movement causes the seat piece to fly up, nearly knocking me backward. The pitch in the back has me at a strange angle that my spine is having a hard time adjusting to. That's what I get for letting my all-too-literal side out in public.

"He should go exploring to find out," Lily mouths in return. She takes a satisfying bite from a chocolate cupcake that she somehow snuck into Town Hall. She pulls a second one from a to-go box tucked beneath my seat and passes it to Grey from the bookstore, who is sitting in the row behind us.

"Honestly." Clark directs the word sharply toward us, his alarmingly bushy eyebrows lifting at the horror that people are eating during his town meeting. Lily takes an extra-large bite of the cupcake just to throw him off and grins when he shifts his attention to me.

It's ironic how deeply I fell for Lily, considering she is the opposite of me—usually slightly disheveled, always speaking her mind, fiery in the best of ways. She's wild and free and always wears black.

I'm analytical, an overthinker, value my alone time (though Lily is welcome to intrude), and keep my true feelings close to my chest. But from the day we met in the movie theater, and she asked if I was British because I looked to her like a man she'd find walking across the English countryside, I knew it was love. As much as she used to drive me crazy, I know Lily saw me. As much as she teased me, she also grounded me. As much as she used her wit against my defenses, she helped me view the world differently. She made me a better man.

She's still making me a better man, even though she

doesn't know she still affects me now. I may have been successful at my previous job in corporate law, but it wasn't fulfilling. Before moving to Birch Borough, I knew a change was needed. While I won't say my encounter with Lily was entirely to blame, I will say that I started to lose my passion for my work around the time we met. After our version of a meet-cute in LA, I realized I wasn't living. I was getting a paycheck and beating my own record of winning cases and making investments, but I was alone. Everything felt . . . empty.

When I met Lily, that all shifted. A greater sense of purpose entered my life. I knew then the "why" behind all my decisions to be a better man than my father. It wasn't only for me; it was so I could be the man she needed. The man she could depend on. Suddenly, the accolades and security associated with my job didn't matter as much if I wasn't happy. I felt like there had to be a way to make the world better while also improving the state of my inner world.

Even surrounded as I am now by this quirky town that makes my head spin, I wouldn't trade that truth for anything.

Clark finally stops glaring at us and resumes the meeting. "Next up! Mrs. Fiore's flowerbeds extend two feet too close to the public park, creeping beyond her property line. The powers that be are concerned that if we don't address it immediately, others will begin to take advantage of violating our town's bylaws. However, if we get rid of the flowers, that's not only wasteful but is also downright irresponsible." His bushy eyebrows lift in thought. "So, all in favor of keeping the flowerbeds in the event Mrs. Fiore continues to care for them, raise your hands."

The vast majority raise their hands. Again, I'm wondering if the next order of business is going to be about the price of canned goods going up ten cents at the store or the flag outside of the burger place blowing in people's faces as they walk past.

"Now, let's see, let's see," Clark continues, bending and staring intently at the notes before him on the folding card table. He doesn't have a podium, which is making this judicial procession even more of a puzzle.

"I—for one—would like to have them vote on the lawnmower that starts every Saturday morning at eight o'clock," I admit under my breath.

"Oh, quiet, you," Lily hisses beside me in a muffled tone. A crinkling noise and the smell of chocolate tell me without looking at her that she's not only opened a chocolate bar, but she's also thoroughly enjoying it. "But you're right. That is annoying," she concedes.

I'm waiting for the next topic, unnerved by how quickly I have become riveted at the events unfolding tonight, when I see Clark's eyes searching the room. They land on me.

"Ah, what a shame," he says. "With Sparrow and Rafe's wedding coming up," he begins with a smile that doesn't quite reach his eyes, "another issue has come to light."

I look at Rafe and Sparrow. Their brows are furrowed. I turn to Lily. Her mouth is hanging open, with her teeth marks evident in the mini candy bar hovering in front of her face.

"What in the . . ." she begins.

"He is looking at me, yes?" I mumble. I'm afraid to break eye contact with Clark's stare. His head is bent forward, his eyes peeking over tiny metal-rimmed glasses.

"This is a bit delicate," he says slowly, releasing a long sigh. "Our next order of business—submitted anonymously—is to vote on whether or not we'll be enforcing *Operation Run Mr. Winnings Out of Town*."

"What?" I ask in a tone louder than usual and stand to my feet.

Out of my peripheral vision, I see the chocolate bar drop to the floor, an indication of Lily's highest level of shock.

I turn to her, my face angling downward. "Did you do this?"

Her eyes lift slowly to mine with a vacant look.

"Lily, did you do this?" I repeat in a rush when she doesn't answer.

"I didn't," she protests, shaking her head vehemently.

"Bingo!" the little group I almost forgot about yells without looking up.

Rafe is standing beside me now, energy crackling off him. He raises his voice. "Listen, I love this town, but what are you even talking about right now? Graham is one of us."

"He is not one of us!" an older woman I barely remember seeing once at the small grocery store—or was it wandering through the bookstore?—shouts behind me. I'm so flustered I can't even place her.

"Sorry, dearie," she continues. "But you don't hurt our girl and then expect us to rally around you. It's just not possible, no matter how handsome you are."

"Hurt your . . .?" I say, the words barely making a sound. Suddenly, I'm back in the courtroom, witnessing people taking the stand and becoming so overcome or shocked at what they were asked that the words wouldn't come out.

"We've all seen the tension between you both. It's

shocking," interjects a woman I know to be Mrs. Kipper, a former schoolteacher I met at the library while I was picking up a fresh stack of books for the month.

"I propose that he stays!" To my shock, Gladys yells her support for me, her voice ricocheting off the walls of the hall.

I'm certain that people who have made important decisions regarding this town and the nation's history have met in this space. This is not one of those moments. I slump back into my seat, the shock settling in my limbs. It won't matter if I complete all her challenges and win the bet with Lily if the town doesn't support me being here. It hits me between the eyes—the reason it's been harder to fit in despite how much I've wanted to . . . they think I broke her heart. They have no idea it was the other way around.

"It's true that we've seen the tension between you two . . ." Clark says with a hint of disbelief.

Without a word, as if it's supposed to magically solve my problems, Lily hands me a chocolate-caramel cupcake from the tiny box, pulling it from within in a way that is becoming very *Mary Poppins*-like. I take a bite, the sweet cake getting stuck at the back of my throat. It's not *the* famous chocolate cake, but it's close enough. If I'm getting run out of town, at least I can enjoy Lily's baking skills one last time to soften the blow.

"He's not leaving, Gladys," Lily states.

I would've loved a more convincing argument made for me, but there you have it.

"He's one of us," Sparrow declares. When I meet her concerned gaze, which bounces between Lily and me, it's clear that Lily finally told her about us. I would respect her for trying to defend me as her fiancé's best friend, but I respect her even more for standing with me now.

"Graham is the best!" Rafe yells.

His tone tells me he is still in shock that this is happening, and I'm right there with him. I mean, could this be illegal? Yes. But is Birch Borough a small enough town to make me pay for it even if they really can't (legally) get me out? For sure.

I understand their motivation. They probably think I moved here to come after her when, in actuality, I was trying to find something I had lost. To them, I've hurt someone they remember walking through town with chocolate on her face and picking flowers from their yards as a young girl. I'm the newcomer here.

But I can't tell them the truth without hurting Lily. As the seconds tick by, my idea to move here just seems worse and worse.

Still, I feel a righteous indignation creeping up from inside. I get that they want to protect her. Heck, if a man did double-cross her, I'd run him out of town myself, law and order be darned. But I didn't, and I don't deserve this.

"Lily, I think it's up to you," Gladys speaks again.

"Wait—what?" Lily chokes out the words, wiping frosting from her lips with the back of her hand. She must've started eating a second cupcake.

"Graham. Does he stay, or does he go?" Clark asks, as if this is a real thing people can do—tell good, upstanding citizens to hit the road.

"I don't think I can make that decision right now," Lily says.

Her reply surprises me more than the expression on

Grey's face when I turn around to see if everyone is staring. They are. Everyone in the room is turned toward me, and I feel the weight of their glares. Is this the moment the people retaliate, and I'm left running from the room, chased down by pitchforks?

"You *belong* to this town, Lily," Ollie, the sweet owner of the toy shop, says in front of me.

Once, Lily told me she had visited his shop since she was a little girl. Her first stuffed animal came from there. Ollie used to give her sparkly stickers that she could put on her lunch box. I think I saw a few of them stuck to a journal she was writing in once filled with recipes she was working on.

My attention goes back to Lily. She's not making eye contact with me. Her shoulders are hunched. She's shutting down more and more with each passing second because she knows that my future in Birch Borough does hinge on her.

I feel my shoulders sink. Rafe claps a hand on my back in the way only guy friends seem to do. As much as I usually love anything made by Lily, I'm still chewing the last bite of cupcake, my stomach revolting at the idea of everyone thinking I'm the one who broke someone's heart. And not just anyone's heart: Lily's heart.

I will myself to breathe in and out, my eyes downcast to the crevices on the wooden floor. It was probably installed during the Founding era of American history. Murmurs and a gavel being used mix with my heartbeat and my racing mind. Everything is a blur, but I don't know what I expected. I guess a woman who ran from a relationship with me wouldn't also defend me. Makes sense.

"George, I . . ." Lily says quietly.

I refuse to look at her. My jaw works, calculating how

many seconds it would take for me to cross the room and get out of here. I'm just about to bolt when Lily's arm touches mine. She leaps out of her seat.

"Stop!" she yells. "That's enough. I love you all, but you don't need to defend me like this. Drop your theoretical weapons." She takes a deep breath. "He didn't break my heart."

Everyone freezes; the only sound is the creak of the heater as it cranks somewhat warm air through the grates in the floor.

"He didn't break my heart," she says again, the last syllable vanishing in the air as soon as it's spoken.

My lungs allow full breaths again. I swallow, my attention shifting fully to Lily. I can't quite look up at her. My pride won't allow it, but I can make out the determined set of her shoulders and her wide-legged stance. Sparrow gasps, and Rafe puts his arm around her, his other hand gripping my shoulder in support. This is not how I wanted the truth to come out, and he knows it. But I'm curious to know how much of a revelation she'll allow.

"Then what—" Clark begins.

Annoyed, Lily makes a noise that sounds like a buzzer. Her hand lifts in a signal for *Stop, don't cross the street.*

"But your chemistry . . ." Mrs. Fiore laments.

"His hands!" a woman's voice yells from the edge of the gathering, and I have no idea how her input could be construed as positive or negative.

The buzzer noise resounds from Lily one more time as she directs her open palm toward whoever is coming at her with their reasoning.

It turns out that she is a superhero with the power to

stop people in their tracks. I wouldn't be shocked if fire started coming out of her hands and flaming in whichever direction she finds opposition.

"But the way he looks at you . . ." Grey says behind us.

Lily doesn't stop her, even though I know she hears Grey, as it's clear her words are more observation than a rebuttal. She continues, "Listen here, all of you, before I withhold baked goods and decide not to make any *pains au chocolat* tomorrow." There's a collective gasp about the space. "It's not your business, but I know you love me. So, leave Graham out of it, and trust me when I say . . . he is a good man." The last part was significantly softer but still audible.

The murmurings of the crowd carry through the air before the gavel rings out again.

"Well, with that settled, this meeting is adjourned. See you next month!" Clark shouts, waving his hands toward the door.

At that, everyone files out like nothing about this whole evening was noteworthy. I'm still stuck on Lily defending me while speaking of the one dream I told her I had for my life when we first met. She remembered.

"You okay, man?" Rafe asks. "That was wild."

"I've never seen that happen before in my whole life," Sparrow states with a hint of shock still lacing her words.

Rafe stands. He leans against the chair in front of us, facing me diagonally. "Do you want us to stay with you for a bit? We could go to the tavern?"

I shake my head. Words are still a bit of a problem for me right now.

"Call me if you need me, okay?" Rafe insists.

Once again, I nod. Because that is all I can manage right now.

With another shoulder clap, Sparrow and Rafe extend their goodbyes before making their way toward the door. I hear apologies and, "Welcome to Birch Borough," swirling around me, even though I've already been living here for months.

Lily isn't moving. Her legs stretch in front of her, the tips of her toes pointing toward the ceiling. She is collapsed back like her defense of me took all her energy. It probably did.

"Thank you," I manage without fully looking at her. My dimming resolve and the emotion of it all are too much for me to also feel compelled to give in to my need to care for her.

"If anyone should be run out of this town based on the evidence presented tonight, you know it should be me. You don't want me to explain, and you don't want to do this again, but . . ."

She stands abruptly and starts to gather her purse and the pastry box. The box has a thumb length of chocolate icing smeared across the top, no doubt from her rushing to put the cupcakes into the box. For some reason, this makes me grin, even when I know I shouldn't.

"You're a good man, George. You always were." And with the second confession she's given me this week, Lily vanishes into the night, leaving me sitting with the half-eaten cupcake still in my hand and a trail of crumbs beside me.

Chapter Twelve

Lily

The smell of fried spring rolls hits my nose with a tantalizing burst of toasty fragrance when I'm still a few doorways away from my destination. I've been dreaming of eating at Amara's Sunshine Thai Kitchen for days. Sparrow's Beret is closed for the afternoon, and it feels like the perfect time to satisfy this craving, especially after feeling as if I've been struck by a hangover that has nothing to do with alcohol and everything to do with hoping too much lately.

Determined to fully appreciate this moment to myself and regain a sense of normalcy, I reach for the door handle and swing it open to receive an immediate assault on my senses. I'm greeted with smiles from the owners and their family members. The sound of food being cooked in scalding hot woks hits my ears all the way from the kitchen. The comfort of spices, chilis, and lemongrass mingles in the air. The sight of Graham sitting in the corner feels like a relief until it hits me that he isn't supposed to be there. Clarification: His handsome figure is currently occupying *my* booth like *he* plans to eat dinner there.

As if my presence triggers a silent alarm, Graham's eyes lift to meet mine. I feel the frustrated growl tickle the back of my throat. My body and mind are immediately in conflict. The soles of my shoes cement themselves to the floor while my heart tries to rush me forward. I look like I have stopped mid-motion, a freeze frame of a reel I must've seen before.

Narrowing my eyes, I will my body to move and finally get my feet to walk. Graham stiffens at my approach, his tall frame pressing his spine farther into the back of the booth. If he felt relaxed before, he certainly isn't now.

"This is my booth," I say sharply and without greeting. I hover near the edge of the table. I'm not proud of the catch in my voice at the start of my announcement, but here we are. If we have any chance of being normal with each other again—especially after that nightmare of a town meeting— then we need to get back to fighting. Pretending to be at odds is the only way to protect my heart and avoid crushing him again, especially with all the confessions I seem to be making of late.

His eyebrow lifts. He searches around the booth as if looking for something he can't quite seem to find.

"Funny. I don't see your name on it." Graham has the audacity to grin as he locks gazes with me again. Suddenly, we're in a stare down. "Good to see you again so soon, Lily."

I wish that I didn't love the way his eyes flash with a hint of the playfulness of old or the way that I can't quite articulate why, but it feels like a win every single time I catch him off guard.

When we first met, it was like I had an X-ray machine to see right through him. Despite our breakup, this superpower has never left me. Even in the subtlest of ways, I can still tell which remarks hit his composure at its core. It serves him right for knowing the same about me.

The worst part of running into Graham all over town is that he's still infuriatingly handsome. How I will ever get through the wedding is still a mystery to me.

"Is this now a table for two?" Amara's sweet voice breaks the spell of Graham's staring contest.

He looks between us, his attempt to look casual thwarted by the shake of his hand as he adjusts the silverware. "It seems that I've taken her booth."

Amara's eyes widen as she looks between us. She is the daughter of the couple who own this restaurant. I remember attending her first birthday party. Fast forward to now. She's been away at college but just recently decided to come back to Birch Borough. I've missed her.

Crossing my arms, I give her a smile that sets her at ease. "Ah, yes. This is her booth."

I stifle a laugh as Graham's eyes widen. Without making eye contact, he shifts to the edge of the seat before I feel a crack in my heart. Because this is Graham. He fights for what he wants. I may have teased him about not playing fair, but when it comes down to it, he is fair in every way. Of course, he will move if he thinks he's in the wrong. Even when things inconvenience him, if it doesn't hurt him, he does the right thing. And he does it willingly.

"Stop," I insist.

Graham awkwardly shifts forward then leans back. His hands brace on the table to leverage him up in the uncomfortable position.

"Sit, George," I continue with a grin. "We're adults."

Cautiously, he looks at me. His eyes shift to Amara, who gives him a nod.

"Besides," I continue, "it's not like we've never shared a meal before."

At this, his eyes flash, and I know the exact memory he's thinking of . . . the one in which we got takeout from an Italian restaurant in LA and tried to recreate the scene from *Lady & The Tramp*. Let's just say we didn't end up eating much pasta. We gave it a few tries, and then it turned out we were much more interested in sharing kisses than cold Italian food.

He clears his throat. I was right. *Got him.*

"Of course," he says quietly, his blue eyes laser-focused on me. "We're adults."

The room feels infinitely warmer, like I've just taken a bite of the spiciest curry.

"Lily, are you okay?" Amara asks as I feel the flush breaking out across my skin.

"Fine. Just warm. Ran here."

Graham looks at my shoes, which are high-top wedge sneakers that are as clean as the day I bought them. I have a thing with my shoes not looking scuffed or messed up, so he knows it's a lie. But it's not one directed toward him, so he smiles. The side of his mouth infuriatingly reveals a dimple I've tried to forget and couldn't.

He hums but doesn't say anything as I slide into the seat across from him. Even though we aren't saying much aloud, there's still so much being communicated in the silent current of air between us. I feel like a white flag has been raised. We're sharing the same air and the same booth, and for now, that's enough.

Amara walks back and forth with menus and water glasses, even though she knows exactly what I'm going to order.

"Do you know what you'd like?" she asks Graham after she and I exchange a nod. She knows it's the usual for me.

"Did you want to order first?" he asks me.

"I just did."

"You just what?"

I shrug. "Ordered. I just ordered."

"When?"

"The head nod, George." He bristles at my tone. "You must've missed it."

He shakes his head before turning toward Amara with a calm expression I know he doesn't feel.

"I'll take the Massaman curry, please." He smiles.

Immediately, I know it's sincere, but it's not the smile he gives to me. Correction: The smile he gave to me. I haven't seen that smile in years. Lately, I've observed a thin veil of it creeping back in. It's like something is a little off with it, though, as if someone has aligned a photo over an old image and hasn't matched it up quite right. I can't tell him how much I miss his old smile.

It's weird that we can sometimes be jealous of a memory. We want so badly to relive it that we're almost irritated at our old selves for not recognizing the last time we'd ever see something so we could commit it fully to memory.

"And do you want it spicy?"

I realize Amara is still taking Graham's order. I try to hold back a smile of my own. "Oh, he doesn't do spicy, do ya, George?"

The look he gives me could melt the silverware between us. "Oh, I can handle some heat."

I swallow, my throat suddenly closing, even though there is plenty of air.

"I'm sorry. Is your name George?" Amara asks him, confused as to how she got it wrong.

"No! No," Graham replies quickly, motioning with his hands toward me. "She just seems to have trouble calling me by my real name."

"It's true," I interject and talk myself into looking directly at him again. "So, here's the deal, George . . . there are five spice levels for the food here. A rating system just for Birch Borough that Amara and I brainstormed. I enforce them, of course." I hold up my hand and start listing off the levels with each finger. "One, weakling. Two, recreant. Three, respectable. Four, confident. Five, brave. I've only gotten to a four, and trust me, it has taken me years."

"Are those really the levels?" He turns to Amara, who simply points to a sign near the front door spelling out exactly what I just said, including an asterisk at the bottom that instructs diners to take it up with Lily (me) if they have a problem.

"Noted," he says. "Ok, well . . ." He looks at me, his nose scrunching in a delightful (I mean, in a terrible and couldn't-be-worse) way. "Good thing I feel brave today."

My mouth drops open in shock.

"Are you sure?" Amara says in a tone of wonder. "Only my family and Liam ever eat at that spice level."

He gives her a pleasant look, as if he's about to go on a vacation and not about to get a plate of food that could easily destroy his insides.

"George, even I have to draw the line here," I start to protest.

"I'm fine, Lily." He pauses, his light eyes filled with intention. "I've never been a coward."

One point: Graham.

My jaw tightens at the reference to our past, but I push it away. I have heard those exact words before, delivered once, just moments before he kissed me into oblivion. Graham seems to be playing a game where he says things intended to take us back to the moments I've tried to forget. It's grating on me, and I wonder if my games are having the same effect on him.

"So, *George* . . ." I emphasize the nickname I've given him in a singsong voice. Amara walks away with the unused menus. "Here's a challenge for you. Why are you here alone tonight?"

"Pass." He answers so quickly I don't think I even had time to blink.

"You don't get a pass." Lifting the water glass to my mouth, I take a sip. His eyes watch the movement. He clears his throat and shifts in his seat.

One point: Lily.

"Okay, fine. This isn't a challenge," I continue when he doesn't speak.

"Isn't it?" he replies, his voice rich and deep.

Just as I know I've challenged him in every interaction lately, I know this is another. I've made this man run the gauntlet since fate reunited us in this little town. Though, I must admit, I'm still waiting to be convinced this isn't all an elaborate setup to throw me off my game just before Ashton appears. Whether I'm being punked by the universe or not, for some reason deep within, I keep making Graham meet my demands. I keep pushing him, perhaps only to prove to myself that he's still here. I should play my hand carefully. I pushed him a little too hard a couple of years ago. And he didn't follow me . . . until now.

"If you want to turn this into a challenge, here's a question for you. Lily, why won't you use my name?" he continues when I don't reply. The words fall on my ears so casually, as if hearing them doesn't shoot a sharp dart of pain through my ribs.

"I've used your name."

"You haven't said it since the day I moved here, by the moving truck. Why?"

I shift on the seat, debating whether or not to rush out the door. I'll text Amara that I'll pick up the food later.

When I don't reply, Graham says a single word. It goes straight to my heart. "Please."

I take another sip of water. The condensation slips around my fingers and causes me to question if I have a grip on the glass—or this conversation.

"I've called you *George* since we first met." I'm going to try to avoid this question for my own peace of mind.

"And then you didn't."

"And now I do."

I say the last words with a firm finality. What I don't explain is that the difference is whether I can call him mine. When I could, he was Graham. And when I couldn't, it was safer for my heart to go back to pretending I didn't love the way he used to bury his face in my neck as he hugged me, the scratch of his beard across my skin the evidence of how close he tried to get. Now, there's more than a table in the chasm between us.

"Since I called a pass to your question, it looks like I owe you a challenge. What's it going to be?" Graham's hands are occupied with the fabric napkin he's pulled up from his lap. The top peeks over the table as he fiddles with the corner without looking at me.

I swallow back the emotion in my throat and attempt to put a smug look on my face. "You're right. I did challenge you. So, since you've asked for it, I dare you to eat at least three bites of the molten lava you're about to get put in front of you. I think you'll find it a worthy challenge if you can make it through the first bite."

"Hm, I'll accept. Don't think I've forgotten that you still haven't answered my challenge question to you," he says as the food is delivered to our table.

The anticipation of comfort food prevents (or saves) me from replying. The bowls are steaming, and my eyes are already watering from the spice that hovers in the air between us. Even Graham clears his throat. Amara brings two more glasses of ice water and a small ceramic bowl of coconut milk ice cream.

"To help with the spice," she tells him, an apologetic look on her face before she rushes away. Even she doesn't want to witness the meltdown about to happen.

I wrap my noodles around a pair of chopsticks, bracing myself for the heat I know is coming. My first bite is everything I've hoped for—sweet, sour, tangy, spicy goodness. Graham tracks my movements before he clears his throat and picks up a pair of chopsticks too.

I glance up, prepared to see him suffer, and suddenly, we're locked in another stare down. I let the noodles slide from my chopsticks as he picks up a bite from the bowl before him. He doesn't break eye contact. Show-off. Because of course he can use them skillfully too.

I throw the handle end of my chopsticks on the table, pointing them in the air like I am about to conduct a symphony or throw them like darts. My eyes widen as I see him open his mouth. I'm already feeling for him. He can't say I didn't warn him.

Slowly, with almost methodical precision, he takes a big bite. Mesmerized, I watch him, waiting for any sign of him internally combusting from the amount of heat I know was in that bite.

His eyes water as he chews. My gaze catches on his lips, which I know are now covered in a level of spice that would bring me to my knees. As if they are a heat indicator, his eyes change shades of blue, his chest calmly rising and falling with his breath. With a soft clearing of his throat, Graham swallows. I feel my lips part with a sense of admiration. He's not even sweating.

My chopsticks clatter to the table, and I shake my head. "When did you . . .? How are you . . .?"

He picks up another heaping bite of rice and curry and opens his mouth, the scruff on his face catching the light from overhead and casting his jaw into a surreal glow. I think I'm hallucinating.

I try to brush a piece of my hair from my face—the one that continuously seems to enjoy sliding out of my ponytail. I jump back when Graham's hand slides a bobby pin across the table. And not just any bobby pin. The curved ones that I like. Startled, my eyes flash up to his, but he continues eating as if he didn't just have a bobby pin that I know for a fact he doesn't use waiting in the confines of his suit pocket.

"So, Lily," he says after swallowing the bite. He hasn't even touched his glass of water. "Are you in love with me yet?" His voice is light, but I hear the challenge in his tone.

"Don't ask me that." He knows I'm not allowed to lie. And yet, I'm not willing to admit the truth. "Besides, we both know I like to keep you humble."

We lean in closer to each other across the table, our gaze flaring with a daring heat. I break etiquette protocol to have my elbows on the table for leverage. Graham matches my movements. Forgetting the food between us, I realize this is the fire I was worried about when I made the decision to eat with him. I wouldn't be surprised if I combust after this moment. As our eyes lock, my heartbeat accelerates, and my mouth goes dry. I lick my lips and watch his eyes darken as they track the movement.

Sharply, I inhale. It seems to break the spell, the sound kicking his gaze back to his food. Graham clears his throat. Only then does he reach for his water, downing the whole glass before setting it back on the table with a clink.

And gosh, if there isn't something tantalizing about a person you think you know surprising you. It's not even the halftime mark for our challenges yet. At this rate, I'm not sure I'll make it to the wedding with a win.

Chapter Thirteen

Graham

My mind is still reeling from Lily's confession at the Town Hall meeting a few nights ago. She thinks I am a good man. I don't know why I needed to know what she thought of me, but deep in my bones, I did.

I've spent the whole day trying to work through my inbox and decide the next steps in my career. Since Rafe made me his manager, I've had a chance to breathe and figure out what I want to do with my life. I've saved up enough to live comfortably for a while, but I know I will need a challenge soon. I like to feel like I'm winning. And while Rafe's career and his creative happiness show me that I'm doing what he's wanted me to do, managing one artist—and an easygoing one at that—feels like a piece of cake (not the kind that Lily makes) compared to previously falling asleep at my desk as I worked so late into the night.

Turns out, I like sound booths and studios much more than I ever loved a cubicle or courtroom, no matter how good I was at my job. The sense of finding justice in protecting Rafe's creativity (while also using my legal expertise to bring restitution for songs that were once stolen from him) and maybe serving more artists in the future is satisfying in a way I couldn't have predicted. It's also helped to have a bit more time to wander and pretend I'm on some sort of sabbatical. Sure, after the wedding, we'll work a bit harder to get him more tour dates if he'd like, but he's been so happy songwriting that this different style of life has me considering getting us a property in Nashville to save on hotel bills.

My current daily distraction is recruiting various people from town to go to Sparrow's Beret for me. Even though I was just there for the cake tasting, I'm still not sure I'm welcome to be a frequent patron. So, about once a day, I have someone run in and bring me something baked by Lily and a cappuccino. I know when Lily makes the coffee by the handwriting on the cup. Having something—no matter how small—that she made nearby is the best distraction while I work to figure out my future.

Today, I'm extra distracted by the fact that my mouth is still burning from the meal we shared yesterday. The curry was delicious but just as hot as I remember from visits to Thailand. Since I woke up this morning, I've eaten bread and milk, trying to cool the heat. I'm about to kindly beg Amara for some more coconut ice cream after I stop at the gift shop for a Mother's Day gift for my mom. I'm planning to pick up a box of maple candy for her and some wild Maine blueberry jam.

I'm almost at the entrance when my phone rings. I pull it from my pocket casually. I half expect it to be Evan. The sound engineer in Nashville promised me news on the production progress of Rafe's new single no later than this afternoon. A smile frames my face, but it drops quickly.

The call is from Lily.

My phone vibrates insistently. There's no way Lily is really trying to call me. This call is either a prank or one of her challenges. Nothing good can come of giving in to her. Still, I slide my finger across the screen to answer.

"Lily?"

"George! I need you!" her voice yells into my ear through the phone.

I stop midstep, barely preventing myself from knocking into an outdoor table piled high with sale items in front of Elsa's Golden Finds. I freeze on the sidewalk, my hand poised to pull open the door. I've been to this gift shop a few times. They sell everything from confections to personalized keychains and postcards.

Lily's announcement that she needs me would usually send me into a fit of happiness that could break my persona of being a grown man. Either she's lost her senses and is ready to confess her love, or she's about to throw things. While I hope it's the former, I'm not naive enough to let my mind wander. Sparrow and Rafe left for Nashville yesterday. I know something is wrong because there's no way Lily's first action after their departure would be to tell me she needs me. She wouldn't do it now, not like this.

"George! Are you there?" The urgent pitch of her voice snaps me from my thoughts.

"Lily, what's wrong? Are you hurt?" I hear the sound of pans banging and clashing in the background and also a noise that sounds like running water.

She doesn't answer my question. "Just get here—the bakery—now!"

Abruptly, the line is cut off. I veer course and rush toward the shop. I'm practically running through the street, my loafers slapping the pavement with sharp, steady thuds.

Grey waves at me through the window of her bookstore, but by the time I wave back, I'm already past the storefront. I'm a man on a mission. If Lily calls, I'm running to rescue her. My girl needs me.

When I arrive at the café, I find it locked. I tap on the window like a bird trying to get in. At first, the glare from the sunlight on the glass keeps me from seeing much of anything beyond the door. When I press my face into the glass, it takes all of two seconds to see that inside is pure mayhem.

Lily's arms are flailing. At my insistent tapping, she rushes toward me. Within seconds, she's at the door. She unlocks it for me to enter, beckoning me inside. For a second, I wish this was the sweet scene when Rachel and Ross from *Friends* have their moment. I'm quickly brought back to reality as Lily pulls me into the bakery, her grip like a vise on my arm.

Espresso covers the floor. I'm talking about a river of dark liquid. It pours from the front of the espresso machine, sliding across the cream-colored counters, finding freedom as it trails around the register and drips onto the floor. The stream is rapidly rushing toward the front door, where I stand speechless. However this caffeine got loose, it now looks like a map of a national park.

"Lily?" I ask incredulously, looking at her in disbelief.

Her hair is disheveled, her ponytail at half-mast. With wild eyes, she turns to me, almost pleading.

"It won't stop!" She's yelling, her movements frantic.

First, I wonder how on earth it got to this point, and second, why can't she just turn it off? I eye the mess before us skeptically.

"And don't you dare tell me to just turn it off, because I've tried over and over again!"

Here's to Lily still knowing what I'm thinking without having to tell her.

"Okay, well, I . . ." My words halt as I try to assess the best solution. I'm not sure whether it would be better to let the river of espresso flow out the front door or keep it inside to protect unsuspecting passersby. I opt to open the door a crack. We watch as the coffee pools at the threshold before making a tiny trail near my shoes and flowing out onto the front step.

"Be free," I whisper, propping open the door with its stop and hustling over to a distressed Lily.

She barely even looks at me as her hands flail wildly. Melted chocolate covers her forearms.

"This is my nightmare," she says.

Her eyes lift to mine. The look of defeat on her face makes me want to hold her in my arms. I wish I could try to help her remember that, for a brief time, I was her safe space. Whenever I'm in Lily's presence, it's difficult not to get lost in the memories of us or ask her why she left. I told her we couldn't do this again, so it's no wonder she doesn't think I'd want to rescue her. Little does she know I would rescue her a thousand times over, no matter the cost. My loyalty to her should surprise me, but it doesn't. She's been mine since we met.

The coffee machine keeps grinding, the canister of beans above the espresso chamber shifting, their level lowering quickly.

"Okay, first things first." Grabbing a bowl, I stick it under the espresso dripping from the nozzle.

"I should've done that!" Lily exclaims, and I try not to

laugh. "I blame the amount of coffee—I think I'm buzzed from the caffeine without actually drinking it. Is that possible?"

I smile as I grab the canister of espresso beans and carefully lift it off the top of the machine. Grabbing a to-go cup, I scoop out as many beans as possible, both to save them and because, at some point, it has got to stop brewing.

Lily's only response is an exasperated groan. "Should've done that too," she confesses over the sound of the machine.

Finally, I look for the cord, ready to yank it out of the wall and end this mess. Quickly, I discover the reason Lily couldn't unplug the machine. The cord is threaded through a hole drilled into the counter to hide it from customers. I jiggle the handle. The cabinet is locked.

I raise an eyebrow, and she shakes her head.

"Right." She puts her hands on her hips. "If you think I've known this whole time where the key is and just happened to 'forget,' you've got another thing coming. I'm pretty sure Rory buried it somewhere, and I've never had to get into the cabinet before."

I notice a piece of forged metal in her hair and lean in for a closer look. Yep. Just as I suspected. A bobby pin. Possibly the one I gave her from the restaurant.

Before she can yell at me, I tug it gently from the top of her hair and try not to get distracted as a few golden blonde pieces fall forward across her face. Clearing my throat, I kneel on the floor in front of the cabinet and do my best to pick the lock.

"Rory's dad made those," she says, pointing to the cabinet.

I can read between the lines. What she isn't saying is that I'd best be sure I don't break anything since they're one of a kind and can't be remade.

"Got it," I grunt.

For a moment, I think I have the lock, but then I don't. A drizzle of brewed espresso with a trace of what could've been perfect crema pools around my knees, staining my carefully creased trousers. I'm not even concerned about the damage to the clothes. Although I love the smell of coffee, this is *my* nightmare: being alone in a room with Lily, where I'm unable to do anything but pretend I'm not trying to combust from the desire to hold her again. I'd let the espresso river run a little bit longer just to pull her into my arms and hear her say, "Graham, I need you" again. Heck, she can even call me George.

After several more seconds of struggling, I finally hear a click, and the cabinet door swings open.

"Oh, thank God!" Lily exclaims before she rushes in beside me. Her movement isn't aggressive, but the surprise of her approach is enough to knock me off balance. I feel the warmth before it registers in my brain. I've landed on the floor, the seat of my pants already soaked through with espresso. Thankfully, the trail to the floor cooled it down, but I feel like I'm going to smell like coffee for the rest of my life after this experience.

Lily may be right about getting buzzed from caffeine contact because I swear my eyes feel a little jittery, and my heart is racing. My reaction surely has nothing to do with the nearness of this woman who turns my world upside down in every possible way. She climbs halfway into the cabinet, reaching forward with uncharacteristic urgency.

"Got it!" She emerges. The cord is hanging from Lily's hand, her face plastered with a triumphant grin before shifting to a look of horror. "Oh no, oh no, oh no," she says, standing above me.

I can now confirm she is just as pretty from this angle as when I tower above her.

"I—you're—soaked!" Hand towels are thrown at me, the paper towels having long surrendered to the espresso machine and its madness.

"Lily, what happened here?"

She runs her fingers through her hair, having no idea she is also smearing chocolate across her forehead. Her forearm is thrown across her forehead like she is a Regency heroine collapsing on the couch in a fit of fainting.

"I was trying to clean the machine after today's afternoon rush, and the button . . . stuck! Pouring . . . nonstop! I thought that machine was alive, and I'd entered a portal to a coffee-powered dimension, and this was the villain. I don't know what I did to offend it, but it clearly has it out for me!"

I'm listening, trying not to let amusement show on my face. I've always controlled my reaction around Lily because I care for her. From the beginning of our relationship, I understood—almost instinctively—that she seems to struggle with feeling that she's the only one not measuring up. It's wild to me that she could think that, given both her incredible talent and how I feel about her, but it has always been clear that laughing *at* her is the conclusion she draws before she realizes you're laughing *with* her.

"I say we take that machine down," I reply with conviction.

I stand, and it is the most uncomfortable feeling I've ever experienced in my life. Coffee drips through my dress pants, running in little rivulets down my legs. I shudder. "Well, this is horrible," I mutter.

"Oh gosh, what have I done?"

It's then that Lily looks deeply at me, her grey eyes reflecting the beauty found in an overcast day. There is a hint of purple at the edges of her pupils, the hope of spring coming alive at the end of winter.

"George," she begins, "thank you."

My eyebrows arch up, the vulnerability in her eyes evident. "Don't mention it."

Lily takes a step closer to me. Before I can process what's happening, my hand reaches out to push a piece of her hair that has fallen back into place behind her ear. I've dreamed of feeling her silky hair between my fingers again so many times since she pushed me away . . . I just never thought there would be such a powerful aroma of coffee when I finally had my chance.

The scent is so strong my eyes want to water. What is even stronger is the urge I have to reach into the pastry case and grab a handful of brown butter biscotti to dip into a fresh cup. But the strongest of it all is the pull I feel toward Lily.

My hand goes rogue, gently wiping some of the chocolate off her forehead before it trails down the side of her face to cradle one side of her jaw in my palm.

"I don't know why I can't seem to let you go. Lord knows I've tried," I say softly, my voice cracking.

Lily responds by slowly raising her hand and placing it above my own. I inhale sharply, the sound loud to my ears as Lily closes her eyes and ever so slightly leans her head into my palm. Her movement is so nuanced I almost miss it.

I am leaning my head toward her a bit when I'm hit with the force of her eyes flying open, her gaze instantly connecting with mine. The only sound in the bakery is our breathing as we both lean in. My free hand clenches to restrain myself from pulling her closer. The other, I will not to shake as it caresses her jaw.

After all we've been through, is this the moment I get to kiss her again?

"Yoohoo! Lily!"

Gladys' voice breaks through the trance we are in. Lily's eyes widen. Immediately, a flash of emotion rushes through me, and I feel as if I could cry as I see the frost cover over any spark of new life between us once more.

"Have you seen the latest post I sent you about the men with glasses drinking coffee? They are my latest obsession! Art at its finest."

The door creaks as she pushes it open. With a little jump over the currents of coffee still escaping to party in the town square, Gladys enters, oblivious to the mess. Her eyes lock on us.

"What's going on in here?" she says with delight, eyeing Lily and me with a look so expressive I know I now have a lot to worry about.

And she hasn't even seen the state of my pants. Too late. I see her eyes shift to my trousers. She shakes her head, swiftly opening her phone to take a picture or record—I'm not sure which.

"Honey, this is some act of chivalry, let me tell you," she says under her breath.

Lily jumps away from me. "Ah!" she yells, running to the back kitchen. Pots bang loudly. I'm pretty sure I hear a few utensils thrown, and something that smells like burned caramel makes its way through the air as she pushes through the swinging doors and steps toward me.

"I burned the croissants." Her despair is evident, her face crinkling with regret.

Normally, this would only be a laughable offense, but the look on her face tells me there is more to this than baked goods. Lily is excellent at her job. She co-owns the bakery, and there's no way she would ever do anything to let Sparrow down.

"If you wanted him to burn your croissants, all you had to do was ask him, lovely," Gladys chirps softly as she walks to the front door with a smile. She pops open an umbrella as soon as she hits the sidewalk, even though there hasn't been any rain all day.

"I don't even know what that means, but I feel like I need to tell you that is something I would never ask of you," Lily says. She closes her eyes and takes a breath. I can barely hear her mumbling but make out the words, "Something else . . . maybe."

"What?" I blurt out. My pants may be drenched, and I have no idea how I'll ever be able to walk home without my picture appearing on a poster board at the next Town Hall meeting, but I desperately want to know what else Lily would ask of me.

As if on cue, a torrent of rain—much like the river of espresso we just stopped—pours from the sky, the force and sound of the sudden drops ricocheting off the pavement. Maybe Gladys is this town's fairy godmother. I wouldn't be shocked if she was at this point.

"Well, I guess I'm waiting this storm out," I remark, staring at my pants and wishing that this wasn't going to be the last impression I leave on Lily today.

The wind howls beyond the windows, whirling through the street and sending the café chairs on the little patio outside toppling. While it was set for spring weather, the tiny pellets of frozen rain tell me it was wishful thinking. I'd forgotten this level of cold after being in LA. One can only hope I won't still need a winter jacket for the wedding. Together, we rush out to bring each one in. I attempt to grab two at a time as Lily assists beside me. We manage to get all the patio furniture indoors, getting completely drenched in the process.

"I'm no longer worried about the coffee," I laugh, looking down, the stain of espresso on my pants barely visible.

"The weather was nicer earlier, I thought . . ." she muses with a sigh. "Disaster upon disaster today."

She's throwing hand towels at me from the kitchen. Silently, we wipe the furniture down. My eyes try their best not to focus on the drops of water that seem to fall from the ends of her hair every few seconds.

As we finish drying the furniture, Lily begins to shiver, even with the now-soaked hoodie she threw on before we bolted outside. Her arms wrap around her waist just as the lights flicker. She winces, her nose scrunching in disbelief.

"No, no, no," she grumbles. Once, she told me she hates storms, that the sound of a storm is the one thing that frustrates her more than anything else . . . besides people who make idiotic decisions.

"Do you have a change of clothes here?" I ask.

She shakes her head.

"I'd say we could go to my place, but—"

"My place is closer," she counters.

"Right. I'll walk you and then head back . . ." I almost say *home*, but I can't seem to make myself when I know it will only feel like home if she is mine.

The moment feels like we're nearing the edge of something. I hate that I'm holding on to each precious second I can get with her, but if I'm going to spend time with anyone, I'll choose Lily every time. With the wedding only weeks away, the time we have together—once again—is running out.

Lily stops me by taking a step closer. "Please, I . . . don't want to be alone."

"You have friends, though." I'm pushing her, but she promised to tell the truth. "Ivy? Grey?"

"Yes, I do. But I . . ."

The stricken expression on her face crushes me. It's the same look as when she used to ask me not to leave, and we'd end up kissing for another thirty minutes. The thing about Lily that I'm sure most people don't know is that once she lets you in, you're fully in. She used to want my affection. She was the one who held tightly to my shirt when I started to pull away. She was the one who buried her face in my neck to smell me, hoping I didn't notice.

So, maybe it isn't so wild to hope she'll seek my comfort again. Our best friends may be out of town, but she is surrounded by countless people and other friends who would quickly come to her side.

I can't help but reflect, though, that when Lily needed help today, she called for me. Tonight, she doesn't want to be alone in the spring storm. And truth be told, neither do I.

Chapter Fourteen

Lily

The storm rages as we rush into the shelter of my apartment. Water seeps through my clothes and causes a shiver to run up and down my spine. I'm soaked from this late-April rainfall. I feel the chill seeping into my bones and question whether I'll ever know what it is to be warm again.

The tiny entryway is crowded as the two of us stand just inside the door, our breathing heavy from the effort to get here. I kick off my soaked tennis shoes and click on a small lamp. When I dare to peek at Graham, the glow reflects off his skin. In the dimness, his hair appears a few shades darker. Tiny drops fall from the perfectly trimmed, arched ends that graze his forehead.

He removes his loafers and a pair of discreet socks, both of which are probably ruined, either by my espresso river or the torrential downpour we just ran through. He places them on the mat by the door, sucking in a breath when he steps on the cold floor. He tries to shake out the chill too, his nose reddened while his hands look frigid. I have the urge to wrap my own cold hands around them to see if I can restore their warmth.

I can't explain why I offered him shelter in my home, except the idea of being alone while knowing he could have been with me wasn't acceptable tonight.

"I'm sorry," he says, his shoulders hunching as water drips to the hardwood floor below him. "I'm not trying to ruin your place."

The vulnerability in his eyes sets me on edge. I could cry from the emotion of it all. Even after he rescued me tonight, staying with me at the bakery, scrubbing the tile on his hands and knees, and cleaning coffee grounds from the crevices of the espresso bar, he's still unsure around me. He doesn't realize that I couldn't care less about the floor.

This moment feels like a picture of our relationship. I invite him in from the cold, and he does the same for me, only for our disappointing history to give him pause, questioning himself and us and whether he has the right to love me completely.

I step closer to him, my body shaking like a new leaf flipping in a storm. "Don't apologize." That's all I can get out.

He nods. I realize I need to clean up the puddle of water we're creating near the front door. A sudden uptick in the intensity of the howling wind causes both of us to look toward the windows. The rain pelts the windowpanes, echoing off the tin grooves on the awning of my building. I usually find the sound of rain comforting, but tonight, every single drop resounds like a drumbeat throughout my apartment.

My apartment!

I freeze, realizing this is the first time Graham has ever

seen my space. Rapidly, I look around, taking in what he must be seeing with fresh eyes. There are Bohemian touches here and there—a mismatch of things I've found over the years at thrift stores and crafts I've handmade. Featured on a side table is a glass candy jar filled with chocolates. A treasure chest sits in the corner near my well-loved couch, blankets cascading out of it. Technically, I live in a studio, but it has a weird layout that separates the living spaces and makes them seem like rooms. There's even a tiny hallway in the unit.

In short, it's charming. In long, my home could be an acquired taste.

Slowly, I turn to Graham, squinting a bit in case I catch a disapproving look from him. Instead, I find him taking everything in with a soft smile on his face. Only when his eyebrow quirks up at the sight of the fireplace do I realize we're still standing here, freezing. We need to dry off and warm up before we catch a cold.

"Whatever you see, no judgment, please," I say quickly, tiptoeing to the hall closet. I don't know why I think moving gingerly will ensure I don't get more water than necessary on my floors, but I do it anyway. It's like running faster in the rain . . . don't we still get soaked because we catch more raindrops?

Grabbing the biggest towels I can find (the ones without any embarrassing makeup stains or cartoon characters), I am returning to the spot I left Graham when I stop in my tracks. My doorway is empty. He's gone. I start to inhale sharply just as I catch movement to my left. Graham is kneeling in front of the fireplace and is starting a fire.

He looks up hesitantly, and I nod at him in approval. I

watch as he adds a few more pieces of old newspaper I collect for this purpose. He peeks at the headlines along the way.

"I like the news," Graham states simply, as if I didn't remember. He rises and stops in front of me. A few drops of water from his hair are trailing down the side of his neck. I'm shocked by my sudden urge to wipe them away and ensure he's wrapped in a blanket with a steaming cup of tea immediately.

Instead, I extend a folded towel. "You should go get warm—change—I don't have any clothes that would fit you, of course."

He nods. I'm delighted to see a piece of his hair starting to curl at the end. My mind conjures up Mr. Darcy (the Colin Firth version of *Pride and Prejudice,* please) when he walks up from swimming in the lake at Pemberley. That scene marked me for life. Oh, what it could mean to see a man's clothes soaked through by the elements.

I have to say, Graham looks even better than Colin when he and Elizabeth run into each other unexpectedly on the lawn. A few buttons of his dress shirt are open, a hint of his chest hair nestled within the makeshift V-neck. Those blue eyes are soft and tentative. Graham's expression is taking me back to the night he told me he loved me. There are so many moments to remember that I had tucked away for a rainy day. Today feels like that day.

As I rapidly descend into fight-or-flight mode, I remember I do have something my guest might be able to wear.

"Wait!" I rush toward my washing machine and pull out a few random items from the laundry cupboard. It's makeshift at best, but it might work.

I hold out the items as if they're the answer to all the problems between us.

"A sweatshirt Rafe left here at Thanksgiving. I've never given it back, but don't worry, Rory said I could keep it. Boston Celtics sweatpants that will be way too short in the legs and too wide in the waist, but they're my dad's. And a t-shirt that is mine but way oversized."

And then I hold up the prize. "And socks. They're somewhat . . . fuzzy."

I'm still shaking a little, the fire reminding my body how much of a chill we still need to work through.

"Are these supposed to be croissants?" Graham says incredulously.

"Oui," I affirm, trying to hold back a laugh.

His eyes are intense. They darken before moving to my lips and just as quickly flash up again.

"You change first," he says. The sound of the rain just outside of the walls punctuates his words. "I should probably get home, anyway."

"You can't!" The words fall out before I think them through.

His eyes squint like he's gotten a new clue in a case and is ready to follow it until the end. The weather seems ready to support my protest as the lights flicker ominously. I live in an old apartment, and while we're usually pretty safe from the fury of severe thunderstorms and snowstorms, every once in a while, the wind will be strong enough to knock out the power for a few hours.

"I don't like storms," I say.

"Then I'll stay," he replies softly.

Nodding, I rush to the bathroom. I close the door behind me and lock it, not because I'm afraid of Graham, but because my mind isn't ready to admit how his words eased an ache in my chest.

Less than an hour later, Graham and I are sitting on the couch with steaming cups of tea warming our hands. The sound of the dryer heating Graham's freshly washed clothes is now mixing with the beat of the rain, which hasn't lessened. As expected, the sweatpants that were still in my cupboard from the last time my father happened to be at my apartment are way too short and rest several inches above Graham's ankles. I'm distracted by the space between the hem of the pants and the top of his foot, but I can't seem to figure out why.

It's weird seeing him in my shirt. Thankfully, I found one that represented my deep love for putting my frame into a t-shirt it can absolutely swim in. Oversized clothes are paying off. His light hair is almost see-through in the light of the fire. If I had a choice, I don't know if I would reach out to touch his hair or the cozy, fuzzy socks he is wearing first. The scene is all so domestic I almost don't recognize myself or the fact that I'm enjoying it.

I'm wrapped up in fleece-lined leggings (you don't get through New England winters without them) and an oversized sweatshirt that says *BU* for Boston University. Graham's eyes widened when I walked back into the room wearing his alma mater. I didn't attend BU, but after I met Graham and found out he had gone there, I didn't question my sanity for adding it to my online cart and wearing it as much as possible. My excuse is that it's cozy. It has nothing to do with the fact that it reminds me of him. It's unfortunate that tonight, of all nights, my other sweatshirts just happen to be in the wash. (At least, that's what I tell him. To make it true, I threw the rest of them in the hamper so I could wear my favorite one).

My phone battery is getting low, but I pull up Liam's social media account. Earlier, he messaged me to check out a new guest on his latest reel. Despite staring at the screen, I can't process what I'm seeing. Graham is in an apron, his dress shirt rolled up at the sleeves, his hair and beard meticulously styled. He is glazing carrots in a skillet while simultaneously flipping parmesan-crusted potatoes on a sheet pan. The cat, A-cat-pella, sits on a stool next to him with a tiny chef's hat, eyes tracking his every movement. He lets out a meow of approval, and Graham smiles in the video. *He smiles.*

I'm feeling warmer than I did during the heat wave last summer. I clear my throat. Graham looks over my shoulder, nerves radiating off him.

I need to do something to clear the attraction growing by the second, and I find I don't want to.

"Well, there you have it, A-cat-pella. Dinner and a movie," on-screen Graham says. Liam appears beside him as he tentatively sets a plate of food in front of him. The video has been edited, and Graham's apron is now stained.

"Wait. What is on your apron?" I'm so close to laughing, but I know I can't.

At the town meeting, I challenged Graham to insert himself into a video with Liam's social-media-star pet. How he managed to win over A-cat-pella, Liam's beloved cat (his name is a nod to Liam's love for music), is beyond me. That cat has more opinions than people who choose between Jess or Dean (I'm Team Jess, always).

"Well, there was roast chicken on the menu, so I hope it's jus."

At this, I do laugh. Because of course Graham would use the fanciest word for a type of sauce.

"You're hanging out with Rafe too much," I mutter.

I am rewarded with Graham's chuckle. The sound is so low it's almost smoky—like dancing embers, so close to flirting with the fire. If he would let himself laugh fully, I remember it to be a beautiful thing.

Except, as the video loops again, I'm mesmerized at Graham's chuckle when A-cat-pella first hops up beside him. And, apparently, so are the other over one hundred thousand viewers who've seen it, no doubt mostly women— who must be swooning at the sight of Graham in the kitchen. Liam already gets so many DMs he has had to put a disclaimer that he doesn't read them on his profile. I'm certain he's gotten an influx of people who want to know who Graham is. Graham has never wanted to be famous, but based on the comments, there are plenty of women who would be happy to make him their world. My stomach clenches before a spark lights. Because they don't know him. But I do—*did. Actually,* no. I still do.

I like the reel and let my thumbs have at it to leave a comment, reading it aloud as I type. "Looks like A-cat-pella just got a new sous chef."

I don't say it out loud when I add, *If you think he's good in your kitchen, you should see him in his own.*

Let's hope Liam doesn't check the handle too closely. I

close with, "Hashtag hot men cooking."

"You think I'm hot?"

I sputter, realizing my blunder, and silently wish that he won't check out my full comment later. "No—I mean, maybe you were before, but . . . you've aged. So, you know, hot man in past tense. But that wouldn't make a good hashtag. Besides, this comment is specifically for Gladys to track since she follows all those accounts. Not that she hasn't seen your guest appearance already. The other day, she sent me a post featuring a shirtless man, and the message said, 'Long-haired men are my theme for the day.'"

Graham does laugh at this. The sound feels like the pure joy of taking a sip of hot chocolate when the whipped cream hasn't melted yet.

"You should laugh more often," I tease.

"You were the one I laughed the most with." His voice is quiet, but the effect is loud.

"Stop it," I manage, taking the last sip of my now-lukewarm tea. It has steeped too long. Though the sweet honey offsets the bitterness in my mouth, it's still an additional reminder of what I've ruined.

"Stop what?"

"Stop acting like I'm the sun and the moon in your world."

He pauses, his hand gripping his mug of tea a little more tightly. "But what if you are?"

"What?" My eyes flick up to his. I see determination written into his jaw and the set of his shoulders.

"What if you are?" he repeats slowly, his voice low and deep, enunciating each word without a hint of condescension. It's a question posed with possibility, as if perhaps a new theory of the world exists that I've been missing entirely. "What if you are those things to me?"

Tears burn the back of my throat. I don't know how he can see me in this way, even after all this time. The hope that springs up almost hurts.

"I don't know how to act in ways that are untrue to who I am," he says matter-of-factly, as if a truly authentic human is not one of the rarest sorts of humans to exist. "So, if that's who you are to me, that's how I must behave. I won't embarrass you. I won't push you. But don't ask me to look at you or speak to you in ways that conflict with my character."

I nod. The words are hard to pull out of my vocal cords, like melted sugar being forced into a shape when the air is cooling all around it. "I guess I owe you that much." I hate the quiet tone of my voice.

"You owe me nothing." Graham returns my nod with an incline of his head. He is already standing and walking toward the kitchen with long strides.

I don't know if I've ever been confronted with a more truthful moment—a moment in which I'm not allowed to contradict someone's feelings because they are entirely their own. Before I can dig deeper into the emotion stirring within me, he's back with a napkin full of brownie cookies.

"I found them on the counter. May I have some?"

I nod, not willing to tell him I made them for him anyway. After all, I make everything for him.

"I'm going to brew some more tea." I stand, stretching out my hand to grab his mug for a refill. He sets it gently in my palm, and a flare of heat warms my insides. Even though I'm burning up inside because of his proximity, my hands and feet haven't gotten the memo yet.

I've made it to the doorway of the kitchen when the lights flicker, and I freeze. A few seconds later, they go completely out. Instantly, I'm surrounded by darkness. In an attempt to move toward the cabinet next to the sink with the candles, my foot catches on the edge of the kitchen mat. I release a yell, feeling myself falling before I fully realize what's happening. I try to brace myself for impact, but my hands are holding the mugs. A sharp pain shoots through my right hand as my knees hit the floor. Thankfully, I don't hit my head.

"Lily!" Graham yells. I hear him shuffle toward me and recognize the sound of a hand brushing along the wall for guidance.

I'm moaning lightly, trying to feel where I am. There's at least one piece of ceramic in the pad of my palm. Graham moves cautiously. He pauses, the sound of his breathing heightened in the darkness.

"I'm okay," I moan. There's a sharp pain in my right hand, but I don't sense anything broken.

"Are you hurt?"

I know that I am. "A little."

"Okay, let me help you," he says. "I'm reaching my hand toward you. Grab it if you can so I don't hurt you more in trying to find you."

I hold out my left hand. The lights should power on just from the electricity that sparks between us as soon as our hands connect. I pull him a little closer as he helps me to my feet. One of his arms wraps protectively around my waist.

"Watch your feet." My voice is breathy from the shock

of his touch and the darkness all around us. "Something is broken."

"I think the socks will protect me," he replies dryly, a hint of humor at the edges.

The sound of the rain is a symphony. It lulls me toward him. I inhale sharply when I feel the ridge of his hip as it bumps against my own.

"Lily?"

"Yes?" I reply, not daring to move an inch until we figure out where we are in the space.

"We need to wrap your hand." His tone is scratchy, the words caught in his throat on the way out.

"Yes, of course." My heart races, my chest rising and falling with shallow breaths. I'm praying that he can't feel my pulse jumping with the sensation of his warm fingers wrapped around my wrist.

"Stay close," I say. I feel something inside breaking at how much I wish I could say those words to him and have them be true.

I extend my good hand—the one not wrapped up in Graham's—and feel for the drawer near the fridge that holds my lighter. Pulling it open, I rummage around to find it. I keep shuffling along to the cabinet near the sink, reaching under to pull out the candles I've stored there.

The clatter of the glass on the counter and the sound of our breathing mix with the storm outside. Even though I'm now bleeding, I'm relieved not to be alone. I'm painfully aware of all the times I've cringed in my bed and waited for storms to pass, wishing I had someone to distract me. It's probably the last thing people would expect of me. I'm confident in so much but terrified of storms. I think I remember mentioning my fear to Graham once.

"I can't . . . Will you . . .?" It's shallow, but it feels like such a small thing to ask for his help when I know all that has been shattered between us. But I feel the slick smear of blood on my palm and know we need to act quickly.

"I'll help you," he finishes for me. He releases me for a moment. I instantly miss his touch. I hear the click of the lighter, and then the spark of fire casts a glow across his features. He works quickly to light the candles I've haphazardly set on the counter. With each new light, a fresh part of his face is illuminated more clearly, and another grows darker in the shadows, accentuating the features that have been carved into my dreams.

My eyes start to burn, and I wish I could take the wasted years back. Every moment without him. The pain I've put him through. The pain I've put myself through. There's so much regret, and I'm drowning in it. And here he is, still willing to help me see in the dark.

"I'll need some bandages."

"Hall closet," I direct as he takes a candle and walks off, a tiny circle of light surrounding his every step.

He is back in a flash. Gently, Graham pulls me toward the living room, guiding me to the couch. His hands, so generous and kind, trace my palm, busily cleaning my wound. A much smaller piece of ceramic than I imagined is sticking out of my hand. Graham does his best to distract me.

Concern is etched into his furrowed brow. I really can't focus on my hand, as afraid of blood as I am. (I have several phobias, clearly.) I do my best to direct my attention to the man in front of me. Shamelessly, I take him in, mesmerized by the boldness of his features, the grace in his movements, and the riveted way he gives me his attention, masterfully taking care of me in the process.

My eyes fill up against my will. It is only when I feel the pads of his fingers tracing the edge of my hand to tuck in the end of the bandage he's applied that I allow a tear to fall. I hope he doesn't catch sight of my emotion this time.

"I don't think it needs stitches," Graham says softly. The richness of his voice creates a canopy of safety and want between my ribs. "It's wider than it is deep."

"That's . . . good." I work to keep my voice steady.

He nods, not breaking our connection yet. Before I can process what's happening, Graham's hand gently cups my face. He wipes the one tear that escaped. A few moments later, the edge of his thumb leaves a trail of heat as he stands and moves toward the fireplace, preparing to stoke the fire for us both.

Chapter Fifteen

Graham

I look toward the hearth below the crackling fire as if it holds the answers to all my problems. Like a siren in a storm, I followed Lily home. Now, I fear I may not recover. I can't imagine how much more this woman could wreck me, but seeing her first cold and crying and now bleeding and hurt makes my mind race and my heart feel as if it could break.

When I bandaged her hand, I could feel the way she studied me, taking in my features. I almost wanted to ask if I reminded her of the man she fell in love with long ago. I wish the qualities in my nature I know she used to treasure would trigger her to tell me the truth about what happened between us.

I may not be willing to get my heart broken again, but that doesn't mean I don't want to know why it ended. I accept that our love is a lost cause. I can't help but hope that maybe this one moment in which I get to wrap her up in my affection is God's kindness in giving me another chance to take care of her. Perhaps I can show her that I'm truly not mad at her. Maybe she'll see the void in me that has been cold and empty since she left.

"Are you still cold?" Lily asks. I turn to face her, surprised to hear her say anything that could be construed as caring about my well-being.

The firelight reveals the sight of her sitting with her shoulders hunched forward, her hand wrapped with a large bandage. Her usually strong demeanor is frail, fraying at the edges. I steel my jaw with the effort of preventing myself from moving closer to touch her. Touching her face was one thing, but I know she won't let me wrap my arms around her to hold her closely while the storm rages.

Shaking my head, I move toward the opposite end of the couch. We continue to stare into the illuminated hearth together.

Her hair glows in the flickering flames. The shimmer creates a halo around her head. Her ponytail flips at the ends. She tries to pull it down with one hand, but the band gets snagged in her hair on the way out. I've only seen Lily's hair down around her shoulders once, and the sight about did me in. She winces when the band pulls at her hair. Before I can think too much of it, I'm beside her.

"Let me," I say, the gritty quality in my voice like the crackling wood in the fire as it turns to ash.

She turns toward me. With wide eyes, she searches me, no doubt looking for any traps or ulterior motives. But my defenses are down, shattered. I have nothing except the intense need to feel her hair between my fingers again, even if it isn't in the way I once had hoped.

Finally, she nods lightly. She throws down a small decorative pillow on the circle of carpet beneath our feet.

Slipping to the floor, she leans forward so her spine is aligned between my knees. As she arches, her long hair trails down her back.

I force my hands to stop shaking. As one hand cups the bottom of her deflated ponytail, I use my other hand to slide the band from her hair as gently as possible. For a moment, I revel at the rapid increase in her breathing at my touch.

I extend the band over her right shoulder, allowing it to glide softly over the creamy patch of skin peeking out of the top of her sweatshirt—a Boston University sweatshirt, my alma mater, nonetheless. I take note that her fingers don't pull away when we touch in the exchange.

Clenching my jaw, I move my neck side to side to try to rid myself of some of the tension.

"Do you—do you need a brush?" she asks softly, the vulnerability in her voice sending a flash of heat through my chest.

"I don't think we'll need it." My reply comes out husky and deep.

She nods lightly. I count to ten to convince myself not to forget this moment as I simultaneously will my hands to stay steady.

Before I overthink what I'm about to do, I trail my fingers through her hair, starting at the bottom. Inch by inch, I run my fingers slowly and softly through her pale golden strands, gently working out any knots I find, moving my way up with precision.

Her breathing slows in response. When I reach the base of her neck, a shiver is all the evidence I need that she is as affected by this moment as I am.

I sense that her reaction is an honest one, and it reminds

me how much I've wanted to care for her since the moment we met.

Lightly, I massage her scalp, pushing my fingers through the silky sections, watching it flow like golden water through my hands. When I hit a tangle or a piece still heavy with water from the storm, I do my best to patiently sift through it all until her hair flows down her back, smooth and combed with my own two hands.

At some point in the process, Lily relaxes in a way that causes her to angle back toward me. Her neck tilts to the side under my hands, losing its stiffness.

I hear a sniffle. I know she's got more emotion caught up in that mind and heart of hers, but I keep moving. Instead of saying anything that might embarrass her, I carefully part her hair into three sections and begin to braid it.

Piece by piece, I intertwine the strands to create a long braid. As I near the end, the hollow in her lower back dips inward. I will time to stand still.

Before I can ask, the hair band appears over her right shoulder. I reach for it without releasing the ends I've gathered in my other hand. As our fingertips brush, Lily grasps the ends of mine with the lightest pressure. It feels as if her hand is hugging mine. I return the gesture before tying up the braid, content that my work seems to suit her. I've never seen Lily in a braid. The fact that she didn't protest the choice I made for her seems like a small victory.

"My hand hurts," she says. "I'm going to grab some ointment."

She pushes herself off the floor with her uninjured hand. Grabbing a flickering candle, she disappears toward the bathroom. I've always loved the sway of her ponytail in the air as she walks, but something in the bounce of the braid against her back immediately swirls a new level of appreciation across my mind.

When she returns, a shy smile appears on her face. "Where did you learn to braid hair?"

A flush crosses my cheeks. I steel myself and decide not to be embarrassed by something that is a part of who I am.

"Uh . . . my mother has pretty bad arthritis. It started when I was in college. I learned in case I ever needed to help her with something she couldn't manage anymore."

Without a word, she simply nods and moves to sit near me on the couch. Rather than pull away, she leans a bit closer to me. I'm mesmerized as her head angles backward, and she shifts to look at me.

"Do you like weddings?" she asks in a thoughtful tone.

"I—I like them," I answer. "Although, it's been . . . harder lately to picture my own."

Her head nods, her eyes turning up toward the ceiling. "I know what you mean."

Immediately, I feel what we're both picturing but not saying aloud. I bought a ring for her. I wanted a wedding of our own. Once, I would have given everything to know she was the one who would be waiting for me at the altar.

"You still want your own?" she continues. Casually, as if this is the most commonplace conversation, her hand draws patterns on the couch. The other palm rests face up on the seat, the bandage angled toward the fire.

"I—I do." Her eyes flash up to mine, and I'm caught in their lavender-grey glimmer.

"Hm," she hums. "Then, I hope—" her voice catches. "I hope that you get to know what it's like one day."

My heart drops. It is as if she is wishing me well, with no hint of animosity between us. But I also hear what she's not saying: There is no way she's included in my future plans, no matter how much I want her to be.

A flash of light in my eyes wakes me. I shift stiffly, a groan escaping as I try to sit up but feel a heavy blanket draped over my chest and legs. At some point last night, I fell asleep on the floor after a series of card games with Lily. As I drifted off sleepily, I watched her looking toward the fading firelight. She was angelic, our theoretical fighting gloves off and tossed aside. Last night, there was a new openness in her demeanor that made me melt back into imagining what could've been.

At some point, I closed my eyes. I must have been lulled by the warmth of the fire and the comfort of knowing Lily and I were in the same space again. I haven't slept that well in ages.

Forcing my eyes open, I take in the ceiling. It is grey in the morning light, with the candles burned low and the fire long extinguished.

The smell of something floral stirs me. I register the pressure of a ribcage pushing against my own and hear soft breathing. Lily.

She's pressing against me, her body stretched out, chin tipped up toward mine. She looks as if she was watching me sleep when she drifted off herself.

Did she know what she was doing? How did this even happen?

A blanket is spread over me. It isn't covering her,

though, and I realize she must've covered me up with it and then ended up beside me. I hope I kept her warm enough, even though the side of her arm is chilled. Her bandaged hand is across my stomach. Her braid trails over the edge of my arm. I feel the curve of her waist under my hand because of course I would instinctively hold onto her, even when I didn't consciously mean to do it.

My heart beats faster. I force myself to keep it steady so as not to disturb her. I will wake her up soon because I know it's better if I don't let her feel uncomfortable that she settled beside me.

But for a moment, I let myself study her, taking in the freckles dusting her cheeks, the beauty mark sitting softly on the inside edge of her nose, the way her lips hold a soft pink that looks like she's wearing a hint of lipstick when I know very well she's not wearing anything at all.

This—here—is everything I've ever wanted.

I may have challenged Lily not to fall in love with me— the words a shield of armor to protect myself rather than an actual bet—but I realize now I was just as much challenging myself not to fall in love with her again. And the truth is, I know full well that I never stopped loving her.

If this were the nineteenth century, she would be my Elizabeth, and I would be her Mr. Darcy. I wasn't kidding when I told her I wasn't the Wickham of our story. She miscast me from the start.

At this moment, as she hums softly in her sleep, I resolve to do everything I can to show her that I'm still in this. I may not understand what is happening between us, but sometimes, that's what love is. Not understanding everything and still moving forward. Proving that the fear of rejection doesn't mean we call it quits.

Peace between us is going to start with not embarrassing her for something she probably didn't mean to do. So, I turn my head to the side, shut my eyes, and rustle my hand enough to gently nudge her awake. Lily inhales deeply, with a sigh that causes a smile to threaten to break through on my face. I know the moment she realizes where she is.

A slight jump. A sharp inhale. A shuffle to stand.

And then, without a word, I feel the edges of her fingers in my hair. The unexpected contact nearly startles me into giving my pretense of sleeping away. I will myself to be completely still and keep my breathing steady, even though I want to lean into her touch.

"I'm so sorry, Graham," she whispers, "for all of it."

The words bring emotion to the back of my throat. I've needed to hear them for years. I'm a few seconds from opening my eyes when I feel the soft brush of her lips against the side of my temple. They are gone an instant later, and I question whether I imagined it.

But the tingling of my skin and the moisture pooling under my closed eyes tell my heart and mind that I didn't imagine it at all.

Chapter Sixteen

Lily

Today is one of those days in which the always cozy—though somewhat unhinged—town of Birch Borough officially loses it.

Bake Fest kicks off today. It's a town-wide event. Everyone turns out to watch the contestants face off in a battle worthy of the greatest baking shows in history. While participants include people who wishfully dream of being on *The Great British Baking Show* (or *The Great British Bake Off*, in Great Britain) but have never baked a cake in their lives, we also have those who have taken on baking as a serious hobby, plus local pastry chefs who could use more publicity.

It's one of those rare days in our small New England town in which, as much as we care about each other, everyone is out for themselves. Our baking battles are savage. The townspeople get downright territorial over their blueberry scones and lemon pound cakes.

Bake Fest happens in two rounds. One round must include chocolate, but it can't be used in both. Personally, I wish the judges would add another round so I can at least assess if I have the stamina to compete on one of my favorite television baking shows. Because you never know what the future holds. If Graham can be talent-scouted for a movie role, I can certainly find myself being filmed in a culinary showdown.

The winner receives more than just a plate, though it's not much. The judges present a plate with the official Bake Fest logo, the year it was won, and a twenty-five-dollar gift card to Ted's Pet Shoppe, which is unfortunate because I don't have a pet.

I've won several times over the years. If I win again, I almost might want to get a dog. I don't think I'd do well with a fish, for some reason. As much as I love animals (and marine life), I don't think I could handle beady little eyes that don't respond.

When I've won in the past, I usually picked someone in town with a pet and said, "Go nuts!" This year, I've already decided to give the gift card to my favorite waitress, Lucy, for her cat. Liam's cat already has sponsorships and enough food gifted for the next few years that it's like he won a lifetime supply of Rice-a-Roni on *The Price is Right*.

I've been training for Bake Fest my whole life. When Harold, our town clerk, stands at the front of the flower-covered pavilion and yells, "Let the baking begin!" what ensues is a rush of pure adrenaline fueled by sugar. The view is beautiful since it is near the river, but the makeshift cooking stations are pure mayhem.

I love it. I've been competing in Bake Fest since I was eligible the year I turned sixteen.

Sparrow isn't into it. She likes to sample everything, of course, but she always says she wants to enjoy baking for others. She has enough to worry about at our bakery, and she doesn't need another thing to keep her up at night. Meanwhile, I've been slowly crushing my way through all the hopes and dreams of the other contestants each and every year. Most years, I haven't won, but I still show up and expect to annihilate the competition. It seems like the only thing I've known how to quit was Graham.

While I could demolish everyone with my chocolate cake recipe every year, I was banned from ever making it again when I was seventeen. Someone asked to buy it from me, and good ol' Harold thought it was gambling. He didn't want to go to jail since I was underage. I've tried to repeal the ban several times but to no avail. The Bake Fest council takes it so seriously that at the top of the application is now written, *No chocolate cakes allowed*, as if verbally banning me from competing with it is not enough.

This year, I'm making fluffernutter cookies. Yes, that's right—peanut butter cookies with a thick swirl of homemade marshmallow crème. They are divine. I've been perfecting the recipe for months. While Sparrow is known for her croissants and macarons, I am known for my chocolate creations and decadent cookies. I like to crush things on top of my cookie creations just to see how they will taste. (Things like espresso beans, not crickets—I don't care if they're good protein.)

Swiftly, I gather my ingredients. I am trying to play it cool because I know that Graham just walked over to join Sparrow and Rafe. Our friends are back from Nashville and watching nearby, stretched out on a blanket in the grass with a picnic basket between them. They are spreading out cheese and wine (as if we needed a reminder that they're

French). Graham is sitting with them, of course.

I shake off the distraction of his handsome face in my peripheral vision. Focusing all my energy on each baking step, I begin measuring my sugar and flour and getting everything sorted.

In typical fashion, before I know it, thirty minutes have flown by. There is flour all over my apron and sticky marshmallow fluff woven through the ends of my hair. A blob of peanut butter somehow landed a few feet from me in the grass, and a squirrel is now going to town on it. *You're welcome, buddy.*

Bless Sparrow. She knows when I'm in the zone. It is no surprise that when my cookies slide into the little makeshift oven at my bake station, she appears beside me. Rafe and Graham trail not far behind her.

I sneak a glance at Graham when he nears. When I find him looking at me, I give him a little nod. It's all I can manage without completely losing my focus.

I'm still reeling from him sleeping over on my apartment floor the other night. I remember the lights coming on and the rain slowing down to almost nothing before we fell asleep. There was no panicked moment, wondering what to do with only one bed available. Before it even got to that, we fell asleep in each other's arms. Well, I woke up in his, but I hope he didn't notice.

We exchanged an awkward goodbye as Graham walked out with the fuzzy croissant socks tucked into his dress shoes after I insisted he keep them. We haven't talked about that night since. But when I saw him crossing the street yesterday, I waved. I lifted my hand in greeting, a shy smile on my face.

In the last few days, something has shifted for us. I don't think either one of us knows what to do with this new dynamic yet.

And while my palm is still sore and my heart still tender, I'm trying my best to get it together.

"Did you hear from them today, Lils?" Sparrow asks quietly, a furrow in her brow. By "them," I know she's referring to my parents. But if they didn't call me on my birthday because they were training new doctors for one of their clinics, there's no reason for me to expect a call before the humble Bake Fest.

I shake my head, a hint of melancholy overshadowing my usual spunk. I should be used to being overlooked by them by now. What I do feels so small compared to what they accomplish each day, changing the trajectory of lives, often saving them. Still, it stings. What if I have inherited their indifference, their dedication to their passions at the expense of those they love? A fresh wave of guilt hits, followed by the determination to remember why I know I'm not cut out to love someone like he would deserve. The proof can be found by looking over at Graham and letting it sink in how much I'd fail if given another chance, no matter how much I've wanted one. The truth is a necessary punch to my gut.

"So, whatcha makin' for round one this year?" Sparrow interrupts my downward spiral by changing the subject. I send her a grateful grin. Only she can ask me about my baking and get away with a smile from me instead of an eye roll.

"Fluffernutter cookies," I reply. I lift my eyes to Graham, who looks as if he just caught sight of Gladys when she decides it's seventies day and wears bell bottoms and a flower crown in her hair. What a hero that gal is.

"George?" I say in his direction. "Something offensive about the cookie I'm making?"

At this, Graham shakes himself out of a stupor and clears his throat. "No, not at all."

"Is this that peanut-butter-and-marshmallow thing that is common here?" Rafe asks, taking a bite of one of the maple croissants Sparrow packed from the shop.

I grin at the smile he flashes Sparrow while he bites into it, like he just can't help but look at her no matter what he is doing. I mean, the man sings for her, for crying out loud. You'd think she'd combust from all the affection, but in truth, I've never seen her so happy. The sentiment shoots discomfort throughout my chest, and I rub the spot to try to massage it away.

"Yes, it is," Graham answers before Sparrow can reply.

At first, I think he jumps in because, after all, the man lives for questions and riddles and attempting to make sense of the world around him.

But then, he continues, "They're my favorite. I grew up on those sandwiches."

I freeze. His gaze flits over to me for the last bit, and my hands instantly tense as I try to make sense of this sophisticated man eating the humble (but incredible) fluffernutter sandwich. I know he experienced a rough few years when his father left. My whole class knew they sustained me during my senior year of high school . . . and that makes sense to me, but Graham? The man with the perfectly creased pants? I can't fathom it.

"That can't be true," I mutter under my breath.

His eyes remain focused on mine as he replies, "I assure you that it is."

"Well, I can't wait to try these cookies," Rafe says with a smile.

Sparrow wishes me luck, and she and Rafe turn toward their picnic area. As Graham pivots to follow them, I find myself murmuring, "I didn't know."

He looks back at me. His face catches the light, transforming his eyes into a deep pool of blue water. "There are a lot of things you didn't know." He's in motion but pauses to say, "Oh, and I'm sorry your parents didn't call you. You deserve to know how valuable you are. In what you think are the small things and the big things. Even when you doubt it."

I'm left staring in his wake until I jump at the sound of the buzzer.

Round one was a breeze. My fluffernutter cookies knocked the socks off the judges, so much so that their feet should be feeling cold right about now.

I'm confident I can win this contest again with my second-round recipe. I'll be using homemade crunchy shelled eggs—the pretty pastel ones with a sweet coating— and integrating them into brownies. The dessert is decadent. It's sweet. And it's my favorite thing to make around Easter. The holiday may have already passed, but the spirit of it is still going strong in Birch Borough.

It's a good thing too, because I may have gone a bit overboard with my candy-making a couple of weeks ago. There are approximately two hundred chocolate bunnies left that I need to distribute before my landlord realizes the chocolate scent in my studio apartment isn't a room freshener.

The scent of burned sugar carries on the light breeze, and I search the stations for the culprit. I nearly cackle when I see a ruined pan fly through the air, landing with a thud on the grass. One down.

I am in the process of stirring the batter, thinking of all the ways I will celebrate (or gloat) my victory, when the air around me suddenly begins to buzz with intensity. I know that feeling. Graham.

I spare a few precious seconds of concentration to lift my head. Sure enough, he's a few yards from my station, leaning against a tree, and just . . . watching. Not in a creepy way, of course—he doesn't have it in him. No, he's staring at me as if he remembers exactly how much he loves sweets and how much I used to love making them for him.

I drag my attention away and back to my task. After scraping the bowl with a spatula and filling the baking pan with the batter, I chop up the chocolates and arrange them across the top so they sink in, but only just. Since they are so sweet, the trick is to add dark chocolate and decrease the sugar in your brownie batter just a bit for the perfect balance.

I look up to meet Graham's eyes again, wishing I could decipher him. The fluffernutter thing isn't sitting right. I know he had a rough time growing up and started working when it was close to illegal, but the look in his eye when the sandwiches were mentioned tells me that—true to his character—there is a weight in his past that he tried to shield me from when we were together. I guess it's hard to see people clearly when we're sure we already know the full story.

With a start, I realize the stand mixer has been spinning nonstop for the past several minutes while I've been distracted by Graham's presence.

"Argh!" I growl into the air as I check my egg whites. Completely deflated. I throw the batter bowl down and look up to find Graham again, but he's gone.

Pulling off the mixing bowl and beginning again with a clean one from our table of supplies, I start over.

Minutes fly by, and it's only when I'm cutting into the brownies and using a piping bag to create little meringue flowers across the top that I feel the relief of creating something I love. Plus, I get to use a torch to brown the meringues, which is excellent.

Sparrow and Rafe are standing up and cheering as the crowd counts down the dwindling time left in the competition.

"Three, two, one!" our host yells into the air, and applause and laughter ring out.

Our town reporter is circling, ready to go in for the kill of the story of small-town New England residents out-baking each other. If they wanted drama, they got it. I'm pretty sure we've had one injury (non-fatal), three burned desserts (fatal to cakes, at least), and four hundred ways that Graham has taken over my mind (verdict: unsure).

After bringing our second round of desserts to the judges' table, I wait with hands clasped behind my back. It takes ages for everyone to get judged. A line of us arrange ourselves in a makeshift formation. There's trash-talking (mostly from Gladys, who isn't even participating) but mainly laughter. I keep to myself for the most part. After all, I came here to win.

Perhaps I didn't realize it before, but my inner challenger is telling me I have to win this year of all years. Graham has traveled all over the world, sampling the best of foods. And here I am, in this humble baking competition. I've never been ashamed of what I do, but I promised him I would go on adventures when I left LA. I declared my dream to see the world and never made good on it. *I have to make good on it.*

Harold walks to the makeshift podium near the pavilion decorated with old-timey banners and balloons whirling their way toward the powder-blue sky. A microphone appears. "Right, well, let's hear from our judges."

Liam walks around with a boom box, playing music I know must be crushing his soul. He's an artist forced to play from the monstrosity of official Bake Fest music that is decades old. What I think must be a cassette tape whirs within the machine. He sets it on the ground with more force than I've ever seen him use and pulls a harmonica from the back of his jeans. *A. Harmonica.*

He starts to play it, the tin-sounding music fading against his talented rhythm, the boom box forgotten in a heap that will most likely show up in the consignment shop around the corner by tomorrow. I hold back a laugh as Harold tries to figure out where the music is coming from.

"Judith Wilkins." Her name is announced, and Judith walks up to the judges' table, her hands shaking a bit as they play with the greying hair twisted in a knot at the top of her neck.

The names just keep coming, a dozen contestants in all, before they finally get to me. "Lily Thomas."

I take a breath and do a little hop toward the front like I lost my dignity when my name was called. An amused laugh rustles through the crowd. Honestly, I'm not paid nearly enough for the entertainment I bring to this town.

Liam changes the tune to "Baby" by the Biebs—you haven't lived until you've heard it on a harmonica—and I hang my head in defeat. Most of the demographic collected here today won't recognize the song, but it still makes me laugh.

The judges are doing their thing. Harold has moved to the end of the table and is eating like his life depends on it. I swear he scrapes his fork enough times that I want to tell him to just lick the plate and put us out of our misery before he decides he's done.

I turn around, telling myself it's to see Sparrow and Rafe cheering me on. But my heart warms when I spot Graham at the front of the spectators. He seems to be hanging on every word, brow furrowed, carefully watching the judges' expressions, because of course he is. He's taking in every movement, every word, and he's making assessments and calculations of my odds of winning.

I feel my heart leap a little. Something about him living here in Birch Borough is unraveling the walls I've built bit by bit. I thought I was reacting to his proximity, but I'm not.

I see Graham starting to belong. He has a secret handshake with the Andrews kids now. Gladys looks at him like he's her nephew, no longer just a handsome man to trick into being in her somewhat scandalous calendar. I'm unraveling because my heart warms when he shows up for town events. It's not because Graham doesn't think there's anything better than Birch Borough. He's lived across the country and defended plenty of celebrities before Rafe (who is kind of a celebrity in his own right due to his family's French fashion house). It's because he chooses to be present in these moments. Usually, he's all calculations and wanting to know the facts, but here, he's right where he is, taking everything in without pretense every time you see him.

He catches my eye. I flash him a grin, not even caring to make a witty comeback or trying to tear him down. Somewhere in me, I know I need to stop digging up what has taken me so long to plant. I have to stop trying to be on the apps, swiping right (or left), when the love of my life is here.

Maybe I can learn a thing or two from being more in the moment like Graham. After all, it was thinking too much of the future that caused me to run from what we had in the first place. It was never him, and it was nothing he did. I can blame the surprise of the ring all I want, but he didn't read our relationship wrong. It wasn't too fast. I was the one who didn't stand up again when I was brought to the mat by my fear.

The energy that crackles between us is alive and well. It's so strong that I don't hear my name mentioned. I only turn when Graham nods and looks behind me, a smile overtaking his face. I shake myself out of my trance and finally become aware of the clapping all around me. I hear the cheers in the crowd from Sparrow and Rafe.

"That a girl!"

Without even turning around, I know the compliment came from Graham. I'm convinced I could pick the man's voice out of a crowd, even in the middle of a Boston sports game.

"Lily Thomas, please claim your prize!"

I walk to the front of the crowd, relief hitting my shoulders and tears threatening to spill. I brush them away with the back of my hand and walk up to the podium to grab my gift card and plate. This year, a little egg is painted in the corner of the logo. It is almost as if they knew this was my year to win another one of these humble prizes.

I nod my thanks and hop down the stairs, heading immediately toward my station before I'm bombarded by more people. I'm hoping to avoid the town journalists, but there's no luck of that. I'm pulled in for a photo for an article for *The Seacoast Gazette*, our local magazine publication. A group of those wild youth (or, as Schmidt from *New Girl* would say, "*youths*") clamors around. They are really darlings but just want to take unflattering selfies with me to post on their social channels.

It's only when it's five or thirty minutes later that I finally make it back to my station to stash my prizes in a large tote and pull out a container from the supply shelf.

"Ahh! Lils, you did it!"

My smile is genuine as I start hacking at the leftover brownies and dishing them up to my friends, even Liam. Graham stands off to the side, silently observing with a soft smile on his face. He's not looking at me, but still, he looks happy.

While my friends—well, our friends, since Graham has been making them with or without me—talk about Liam's harmonica solo, I move toward Graham. He's positioned near the edge of the table, so I walk backward, smiling and hoping that no one notices my attempt to be subtle.

"Well done, Lils. I'm happy for you."

I pivot to face him in surprise. He still isn't looking at me.

"And you didn't sabotage me once," I reply. The twitch in his jaw gives his amusement away. "I made you something," I continue softly.

At this, he does turn. The sun casts such a striking shadow on the curve of his cheek that I want to draw it. I'm not an artist, but if I had to guess, that shadow is the perfect angle to touch him. The palm of my hand would fit just right. There's something poetic about the sun doing it for me. Instead of reaching for him, I hand him a small container.

He clears his throat, taking it from my hands and cracking open the corner to smell what's inside—not look, smell. Always searching for the answers and taking nothing at face value. "Peanut butter. And marshmallow."

I smile, adjusting my face quickly. I peek over at the river as I fight to keep my expression from being anything but neutral. "Fluffernutter cookies."

"You made me fluffernutter cookies?"

"No, I made them for the competition, as you know. But there were some left to share."

"And you're giving them to me." His tone says it is more of a statement than a question. "Why?"

I dare to step a bit closer to him. Our shoulders brush, a hint of the scent of peanut butter still swirling around us.

"Why would you do this?" he asks again. There is an urgency in his voice that makes me turn toward him. The urge I usually feel to push his buttons dissolves when his icy blue eyes catch the sunlight.

I shrug, as if the truth isn't gutting me first of all, but also because of the effect it is having on him. Graham is the one who used to wish I'd say what I'm about to. "Because," I say softly, "they're important to you."

He hums and holds the container a bit closer.

I push myself to make sure he hears me now, hoping he is ready for me to say what has been weighing on me lately. "Thank you for staying with me the other night. I hate storms."

"I know."

"Of course, oh wise one," I reply with a grin. "The man who remembers everything and can't seem to forget a thing about me." I wring my hands together behind my back. At the moment, I feel more in tune with him than I expected. I'm waiting to push off the edge of whatever we are by his response.

"I wouldn't want to. I never wanted to change you."

I swallow. "I know."

"Good."

"Still . . ." I begin.

"Still what?" His voice is unmistakably gritty when he rotates to face me again, as if the next words I say must be held extra close between us.

My eyes trail upward from the center of his chest over each of the buttons on his dress shirt, catching on his trimmed beard and full mouth before they lift to meet his gaze. The subtle widening of his eyes tells me he's surprised I'm intentionally looking at him. I know I have something to give him.

"You make me want to soften," I murmur.

It's the closest we're going to get to a confession of my

feelings. At first, I'm not sure what his response will be. But Graham's eyes reflect instant relief. He clears his throat and opens the container I've given him. A cookie emerges, looking small in his large hand. He takes a big bite, and a grin lifts the side of his face with the enjoyment of something I made. And I know that, in this moment, my words are enough.

Chapter Seventeen

Lily

I feel ridiculous. As I walk across the green toward Town Hall and the center of town, I question all my life choices. I've anticipated this night for months, but I'm beginning to have my doubts that it will turn out to be what I've envisioned in my head. When I ordered my dress for the first annual Regency Ball in Birch Borough, I was elated. I fought with the powers that be for months in the hope that I could persuade them to let us create more culture around here. I want to buy dresses I can wear at a ball and see men in great coats. Long before Sparrow and Rafe announced their wedding, *this* was the event of the season.

If I couldn't magically transport myself back to bygone days of men throwing their gloves down to challenge one another to a duel and women having fainting spells, then Lord knows I was going to find a way to recreate it. Halloween is a bust when it comes to dressing up as if we still ride in carriages, because no one takes it seriously. It remains to be seen how seriously they take it tonight.

Unlike Halloween and every other day, except for my occasional lapses in judgment, tonight, I'm not wearing black. Instead, I'm wearing a vintage dress the color of lilacs in bloom. The shimmering fabric almost looks blue when it hits the right lighting, reminding me of a flower raising its head to greet a clear spring day. To complete the effect, a pair of creamy satin gloves whisper just past my elbows. I've gone all out tonight, and I expect my fellow townspeople to have done the same.

It's not that this town is unfamiliar with dressing up, with our historical reenactments and all sorts of events that require a form of costume, anything from celebrating *The Great Gatsby* to our Christmas parade. It's just that the one thing I did not calculate was how devastating a certain *someone* is going to look if he appears at this event tonight. I know he is bound to since he seems to test me in every way with his presence.

I'm determined not to let one infuriatingly handsome man ruin my fun. The Regency Ball is set to be *the* event of the season. It's finally my moment to step into the movies and television series I love so much and get my mind off Graham. Anything to get my mind off Graham Winnings.

At least my dress is making a good effort. However, I already think I might smell a bit like someone wore this outfit on stage one too many times without a good dry cleaning. The online reviews for the costume store where I found my ensemble warned that they were old. There were no refunds allowed since my dress made an appearance in a show with someone somehow related to an actress who once played Elizabeth Bennet in London, so I guess I can't complain too much. It was a lot harder to find authentic clothing than I imagined. Still, I'm hoping that walking outside in the fresh air (while I attempt not to think of Graham and his fresh-air smell) won't hurt. I'm still reeling from the satisfied look on Graham's face when he ate nearly a half dozen cookies I gave him at Bake Fest before he wandered home. These past few weeks have been full of wedding planning and final details, mixed with my excitement for this event, so I haven't had time to properly process what happened that day.

I pause for a moment on the lawn. While the vintage shoes that go with the dress are surprisingly comfortable, they are thin. With the spring rain we've had recently, I'm worried about getting mud on them. I'll be the talk of the town if I show up to the ball I organized with muddy dancing shoes. I laugh at myself for thinking I would fit in perfectly on my favorite show, *The Man is a Rake*. The show is alarming, it's borderline outlandish, and the men who feature as guests should be studied for their ability to raise a woman's temperature, evoking a sudden need to fan themselves. I can relate.

Silently, I applaud some of our locals for wearing garb that would qualify them to be extras in a historical drama as they make their way down the street toward Town Hall. I'm still lingering, amused at the sight, when I feel a bit of wetness soaking through my shoe. Is there anything worse than having your feet wet unintentionally?

"Are you kidding me right now?" I mutter, the stay—or version of a corset for this era—suddenly feeling much too tight. Oh, why did I ever think I'd be happier living in a Regency novel?

If I'd just kept walking, I would have had my answer to

that burning question. When I look up and see Graham moving across the square near the gazebo, I know exactly why my daydreams have been filled since girlhood with visions of men striding across a misty lawn while the dew clings to blades of grass. My mouth goes dry as I track his movement. I feel my jaw drop, but I'm too impressed at the sight of him to care. He's wearing a cravat, people—those incredibly attractive precursors of neckties—and a dark blue coat that has tails. *It. Has. Tails.* High leather boots fit his calves like a glove. Speaking of gloves, I see a pair tucked into one of his coat pockets. Rather than being perfectly styled, his hair is shifting in the balmy evening air, and I swear I can already smell the scent of his beard oil and the wildflowers in his hand.

The closer he gets, the more I want to cry. The man really should come with a warning label for my heart. Forget Darcy crossing a field—this is Graham only crossing the street in my hometown, and I can't understand how this is real life.

He looks like a dream. I try my hardest to breathe normally while also feeling very grateful that I chose to make the ball a Regency theme, meaning I don't have a fake piece of whalebone digging into my ribs right now. It's hard enough to stay upright. I can still feel his hands in my hair as he braided it weeks ago. The memory sends a wave of heat to my cheeks, climbing up my neck like ivy on a wall.

When he gets within a few feet of me, I notice the infuriatingly attractive grin on his face. He knows how affected I am by him. Honestly, how could I not be? Suddenly, I understand why women carried smelling salts back in the day. If a man who looked like Graham came across my path almost two hundred years ago, I would've had trouble functioning too.

Here's the truth of it: One of the most unrealistic things in all those made-for-television movies (or any movie, really) is not when the main actress has a tool for a boyfriend. It's when she's close to the more attractive guy who is clearly into her, and she doesn't marry him immediately. How is that travesty even a choice? I'm one to talk. I'm already living that nightmare.

A gust of wind sends Graham's smell closer to me (because of course it does). He does, in fact, smell like clean laundry and the sweet scent of open pastures as he always does. It's madness.

He holds the flowers in his hand toward me, and I feel my eyes widen.

"For you, my lady." He takes a slight bow, the top of his hair shifting once again with the movement. My stomach flips. It's more than butterfly wings—it's the feeling of something buried in the ground coming back to life.

"They're wildflowers," I say. I could smack my forehead for how intelligent that line was. When I'm finally placed in a Regency setting, the first thing I do is state the obvious. Perfect.

He hums in amusement. *Hums.* "They are indeed."

"Stop that immediately," I gasp.

"Stop what, exactly?"

"Speaking like Darcy!"

Graham remains undeterred. His eyes sparkle. "Hm, I see we're going to act a bit uncivil today, are we? Even after we've already had our interlude during the rain. Don't worry. My feelings won't be puffed or my wishes unchanged, although I did think you wouldn't be as taciturn on a day you are meant to be incandescent."

I lift myself in my satin flats so I stand a little taller. "I think you're just adding a bunch of words together to make it sound like you're auditioning for an Austen TV movie. And I am *not* uncivil, and . . . thank you?" I drag my eyes away so I can stop staring at his handsome face, focusing instead on the people walking down the street. I have to distract myself from the way my fingers are begging to touch Graham.

As I observe the costumes many townspeople are wearing, I'm thrilled to see so much enthusiasm, but the sight of them makes me want to stop them and ask what they were reading or thinking of when the notice of tonight's Regency Ball landed on our town website. I'm pretty sure Andrew, our town pharmacist, is dressed as a pirate. But with Graham beside me, I suddenly don't care if tonight doesn't ring as historically accurate as I hoped.

Standing a short distance away, Graham clears his throat, the flowers still extended.

"Why did you even get these for me? And don't you still need to find a plus-one for the wedding?" I cringe immediately at the sharpness of my tone. I don't mean it, but I don't know what to do with the surge of emotions this man stirs in me.

"There's time," he replies. There really isn't with Rafe and Sparrow's wedding almost upon us. My heart leaps, but I push the feeling away. If he doesn't want to talk about it, then I gladly won't. "And I may have spoken too soon," Graham continues.

His words make my heart race and hope at the same

time. "You didn't get lilies," I state the obvious again.

"You're allergic."

I can't help but grin. "Yes, but people still buy them because of my name. They don't usually remember—"

"I remember." That's all he says before turning toward the event hall and holding out his arm for me to wrap my hand through.

"George, I . . ." I can't seem to finish the sentence, but I slide my hand into the crook of his arm. It's warm and strong beneath my palm.

"For Sparrow and Rafe," he says. Graham's gaze is distant, his eyes squinting. "Can't have it look like the wedding party is at odds now, can we?"

Rather than reply, I pretend to be riveted by a little boy who is struggling to keep his socks pulled up across the way. My thoughts dance to a dangerous rhythm. He's right, of course. And what I know Graham senses, that few others realize, is that I don't bristle because I'm angry or trying to be a grump. I just don't know how to fit into what society terms as normal. And it's exhausting trying to be what everyone wants me to be.

Hence, why I tend to give too much of my time and free pastries to locals who may have read Austen in grade school and agree that a Regency-themed party is a chance to test out a British accent.

Graham and I step forward together. As we cross the street and count down the shops along the way, Town Hall looms closer and closer. Its open double doors allow warm, golden light to spill onto the green. In a deviation from the authenticity of the night, Cricket (not her real name . . . I think) snaps photos of all the guests as they enter. No doubt the mayor will use them for the next fundraising campaign as evidence of how cultured we all are. I stumble over my vintage shoes, thinking of having to see Graham next to me in photos other than the ones I've been preparing myself to endure after the wedding.

"You guys look great!" Cricket yells, waving her hand in our direction.

My face flushes with the compliment. It's strange when people who know me see me with Graham, especially when his memories feel like a hidden treasure chest in the ocean of my heart. I wonder what they think of us together. While I used to think it would be a disaster for anyone to think I'm tied down—given the comments and speculations that would ensue when Lily Anne Thomas settles down—their glances tonight only make me pull back my shoulders with pride. Even if I'm only on his arm for tonight, I'm proud to be seen with Graham. If anything, the strange feelings I'm experiencing have very little to do with anyone's reaction . . . except my own.

We pause in front of Town Hall, waiting for a group of ball attendees to pose for a photo before proceeding inside. The exuberant notes of the string quartet drift out to us, carried on the soft spring night air.

"I dare you to take a photo with me," Graham murmurs, his voice husky in my ear. I whip my head to face him. He arches his eyebrows in a silent challenge.

Despite my determination to maintain my cool around this man, I can't help but let a grin break out across my face. If he thinks he can out-dare me in my own game, he's got another thing coming. "Oh, you've got yourself a challenge, good sir. The question is, tonight, are you a gentleman or a rake?" I reply in a low tone.

He laughs, the sound a warm rumble that echoes all the way to my toes. I nod resolutely and try not to collapse with happiness when his warm hand passes gently across my lower back. Graham's other hand wraps around my own in a take on a modern-day prom pose. I imagine it looks more like those vintage-style, sketched photos where we appear far more important than we are, but I'll take it.

"Smiling or not smiling?" I grind out between my teeth as we move forward to take our places in front of the photo backdrop of a majestic English manor and gardens that could easily grace the cover of *Pride and Prejudice*. As Cricket readies the camera, my face moves from grimacing to resting Regency face—whatever that is (confused . . . confused is what it is).

"Smiling," Graham replies without hesitation. "When I'm this close to you, how could it be otherwise?"

Internally, I blackout. The camera clicks in my ear, and I hear people milling about in the background, but my body is frozen until Graham gently nudges me forward. A low chuckle escapes him again, the sound sending the wild impulse to rip off my gloves and toss them in the nearest trash can coursing through me. This man's forearms (and his laugh) could cause a woman's gloves to spontaneously disintegrate. I'm not sure if I can force myself to go the whole night without touching him for real. Lifting my chin higher, I take a deep breath, trying to ignore the tingling sensation that still lingers where his hand just rested on my lower back.

The next couple moves into place behind us. As we pass Cricket, I lean over and whisper in her ear, "Send me a rough cut of that, will you?"

She winks. I applaud myself for snapping out of it enough to secure evidence of the moment that just unfolded between us. No one will ever know what sweet words Graham whispered in my ear except for me.

When we reach the wide steps leading up to the entrance, I take in the fabric banner signs hanging above the door. Hand-painted calligraphy welcomes us to a festive spring dance and Regency Ball celebration. We hear the party first. The music from the string quartet carries beyond the ballroom. When Graham and I enter the hall, my spirits are already in the mood to dance. We step through the large, wooden doors, and my breath catches. It's too much to take in. What was once a boring judicial room has been completely transformed, and goodness if I don't tear up at how perfectly it all came together. It's like a scene right out of my dreams.

Everyone has embraced the spirit of it. Ladies and gents from a bygone era mill about the room, drinking punch and laughing while they converse together. Gosh, if I don't love this town even more for showing up today and giving it their all because I care about it. Everyone knew the Regency Ball was my passion project when I proposed it last year. But as soon as Sparrow's wedding was announced, and I stepped away to give her my full attention, the Music and Arts Committee promised they'd take care of all the details. And take care of them, they did.

Candles and some magic of dim and romantic lighting cast a golden glow throughout the room. Cream linen-covered tables piled high with scrumptious desserts are tucked into the corners. Wooden chairs and benches line the perimeter of the dance floor for the people who don't feel like dancing but want to be part of the festivities. Front and center on the stage of the hall, which also serves as a theater sometimes, is a band. Liam is playing the cello as a group of his friends, all in costume, play classical-era minuets and concertos that make my heart very happy.

I catch sight of Gladys lingering near the punch table. She seems to have gladly taken on the look of what I imagine must be Mrs. Bennet. I let out a delighted laugh that carries across the room. When she spots me, her eyes widen. She gives us a nod of approval before whirling in a spinning dance move that causes her dress to float about her legs, a few drops of punch spilling onto the wooden floor.

"Is she going to be okay over there?" Graham remarks, catching sight of her with a hint of amusement in his voice.

"Oh, yes. She'll be right as torrential rain."

"I don't think that's the saying . . ." Graham trails off.

"Trust me. It is now."

When Gladys winks and moves her eyebrows while simultaneously looking Graham up and down, I flash her what I hope is an affectionate grin mixed with a bit of horror.

"There you are!"

I hear Sparrow before I see her. Turning to greet her, the smile that overtakes my face is genuine. Despite her dark hair, she's the picture of what I imagine Jane Bennet to be— namely, the most gorgeous person in the room with the amiable and handsome Rafe right behind her. When he's comfortable and carefree—as he is around Sparrow—he makes the most perfect Bingley. I don't know how I missed such a resemblance before.

"You two look positively brilliant!" I exclaim in a British

accent I've been quietly perfecting my whole life.

"First rate," Graham interjects next to me in a posh accent.

"What's that you say?" I raise my eyebrows in mock confusion. "Quite the Cockney accent this one." He could audition to play British royalty tomorrow. But the furrow in his brow is satisfying.

"Is this where we start to say words like 'dashing' and 'incandescent'?" Rafe asks with a smile. He doesn't need to playact a character as his charming, native French accent slips through more and more each day.

"Oh, I already tried that," Graham replies with a laugh.

Lightly, I pat his arm. He hasn't let me go yet. "He's finally ready to audition for a Hallmark movie."

Graham's exasperated sigh is delightful.

"You can use words like that if you'd like. Or you could just speak French. It was just as romantic back then," Sparrow murmurs to Rafe, a serene smile on her lips that almost makes me want to stick my head in the punch bowl just to get a break from the continuous love fest for a minute.

"Oh, and those flowers, Lils," Sparrow begins. I clench the stems of the bouquet a little tighter. "You love wildflowers."

Graham's arm stiffens briefly as I blush. Instead of pulling away as I expect him to, his free hand comes to rest on my own. It feels like home.

"Will you two be dancing?" Rafe asks.

My reply gets stuck in my throat. For all appearances, it looks as though Graham and I are planning to give each other the first dance of the night.

Searching for a distraction, my gaze wanders. I feel an unspoken pressure and tension hovering in the air as I decide what to do. At this point, dancing with Graham feels as if it will stitch something between us that will never be undone.

"Lily, I feel like this should qualify as one of your challenges," Rafe continues after a pause. I'd yell about the fact that he knows about my little bet with Graham, but of course he would. "I mean, unless you're scared," Rafe teases.

Lifting my chin in the air as high as it will go, I level Rafe with a glare. Graham chuckles but has the decency to hide it behind a very fake cough. Sparrow does the best-friend thing so well. Immediately, she changes course by stating how much she loves the costumes, and isn't the music great, and something about Rafe asking Liam to play the cello at their wedding.

Saved by her distraction, I glance around the room and lock eyes with Edgar. Though I'm still taking my weekly boxing lesson, I've been avoiding the hours I know for sure he's in the gym. Things ended between us long ago, and we're still friends, but things have felt different lately. I must admit, though, that Edgar looks great in his suit and tailored coat. There is a cravat around his neck, but something about it doesn't hold the same thrill as it does when I see it tucked against Graham's costume.

Edgar looks between Graham and me. He takes a step toward us when I swear he's pushed three feet off course as Gladys crashes into him. It's an intentional collision. I nearly gasp as I see her loop him smoothly onto the dance floor. His eyes catch mine again as she pulls him away. With a slight limp, he twirls her around. She's shameless, and I love her for it.

The crowd gathers and begins to clap. I tune everything out when I hear the opening notes of one of my favorite pieces of music begin to play. I know this dance. I've memorized it. And while I know the committee sent dance instructions and Georgian-era music examples in the town's spring newsletter in preparation for tonight's ball, I can say with certainty that I'll be the only person nerdy enough to have practiced this dance on my own since 2005.

I so badly want to dance it and can think of only one partner who could possibly keep up. The very man who—if I'm calculating correctly since he revealed it when we met— has read the book sixteen (now, eighteen) times and has watched the movie just as much. But asking him feels like an impossible task.

As if he senses my distress, Graham stands a bit taller and relaxes his shoulders. Sparrow and Rafe are already on the dance floor, moving in what is more like a slow dance than a true, lively Regency dance (which is not surprising with those two).

"George, I'd like to challenge you to perform a proper English country dance. If you dare . . ." Tilting my head, I flash my gaze upward, hoping he can't read how badly I'm longing to jump into the crowd of moving couples on the floor.

"And how do you expect me to stick to your 'no touching' rule while we dance, Lily?" he questions me gravely, his downward glance reminding me of the absence of my gloves, which are well on their way to being gone and buried forever by now.

I flush. "I'll allow it for dancing purposes only. After all, the townspeople of Birch Borough have come here to experience a night of culture, beauty, and charm. They clearly need us." I wave my hand and nod as if I'm a royal gracing the ball with my presence and not as if this moment means everything to me.

I realize how much I want to see Graham dance, but though I know he's seen the movies and read the books, I can't imagine he will know the period dances as I do. I feel a buzz of excitement while he visibly considers my proposal. This moment might be the chance I've been looking for to leave him in the dust of our mutual battle for Birch Borough. So far, Graham has met and exceeded my expectations as I've challenged him to tasks that I thought his reserved and dignified nature would hesitate to do. If I have any hope of winning and convincing him to move, it's clear I need to up the ante, even though crushing him in the competition sounds less and less satisfying.

He turns to me. "Challenge accepted. And Lily"—he hesitates for a fraction of a second—"it would truly be a pleasure."

The rasp of his voice as he says my name shoots a thrill down my spine. I suck in a breath. As much as I may regret it later, I don't want to miss this moment. The books and films I love finally feel within reach. With Graham beside me, tonight will live in my memory as more of a fairy tale of old than a reminder that, though he is standing within my reach, our future isn't what it could have been. And I already miss him.

Chapter Eighteen

Graham

As she tilts her chin upward, I try not to react when Lily makes eye contact with me. She nods slowly. I hold myself as still as possible to let my words take effect. I need a minute to process too. I'm still getting used to Lily not treating me with hostility. More and more, she is allowing me to see the thoughtfulness behind her eyes, looking at me without hesitation, of her own accord, even when we aren't bickering. It feels like a gift.

And now, I may have the chance to dance with her. As much as I love to dance, this is one thing we never did in LA. My heart drops when she turns away abruptly. But she is only handing the wildflower bouquet I brought her to Anna, who is overseeing the dessert table.

When Lily turns back to me, I see the playful hint of a smile across her face. She's radiant, and it takes my breath away. I see now that I've never truly appreciated Regency-era fashion to the level I should have. The lilac-colored dress skims the length of her willowy frame, whispering of the curves beneath. Her hair is swept up, a few curls escaping to graze her neck. I could swear she had a pair of gloves earlier, but only the soft, bare skin of her arms awaits my fingertips now.

"Let's see what you've got."

Little does she know I'm thanking my lucky stars for all the dance training I received as a kid. When I received the links for the dance instructions in the Birch Borough newsletter, I recognized them immediately. At my request, Liam sent me some music I could use to practice. Once I was certain I had the correct cadence, I got to work. Are my legs still sore from trying to figure out the steps until the early hours of this morning? Yes. Is it worth it as I observe Lily's tentative enthusiasm? Absolutely.

Tucking her hand through my arm again, I lead her to the dance floor. I swear the world grows quiet despite the buzz and hum of the crowded room. As I take my place opposite Lily, intensity echoes in my bones. It was all coming to this: the moment we met in the movie theater, the loving, the fighting, the heartbreak. We were always going to end up here . . . somehow.

I don't believe we've ever lived other lives, but if I did, as she grips my hands, and we take our first tentative steps—and I attempt to execute the steps perfectly and command my lungs to breathe—I could imagine we've done all this before, many times in many lifetimes.

The movement overtakes me, steps that are both familiar and brand-new imprinting themselves on my memory. As the magic weaves between us, I almost miss the way that everyone else seems to clear the dance floor. The music seems to match the rhythm of my heart, and I know I will never forget the warmth of Lily's hands. Even when the tips of our fingers barely touch, I still feel her everywhere. Her eyes seem to deepen and take on a new glow as we sway and spin across the floor in a timeless expression of human connection. I could become addicted to this feeling. I sense that Lily feels it too. Say what she will about planning to run me out of town, this is the definition of romance.

Without uttering a word, we've yet said so much that when the music finishes, we stay locked in an eternal gaze. People clap around us, slapping me on the back, but I'm mesmerized. Lily has always been achingly attractive, but at this moment, I see a new depth to her beauty. She was made for the soft, feminine costume of a nineteenth-century maiden, her signature ponytail replaced with an updo. For once, she isn't wearing black, and I feel as if I'm seeing a full-color motion picture—rather than a black-and-white film—for the first time. She chose to dance with me, even though we've hurt each other deeply. She may have used her words to hurt me, but I hurt her with my silence, however justified it was.

After the briefest pause, another song starts to play. It's a lively one. Seeing Edgar stuck on a bench, Gladys' arms wrapped like a vise around his, I realize she has essentially freed up Lily's dance card for the evening. And I'm ready to fill it. I extend my hand to her, letting a mischievous expression peek through my face, and without a word, Lily reaches forward and places her palm in mine. Her silence surprises me. Momentarily, I wonder if her willingness to dance with me is just another way she is plotting to throw me off my game, but before I can analyze it too much, the music sweeps us away.

It's only several dances later, when I step away to fetch us some drinks, that I allow the depth of this night—which is punctuated by some otherworldly effect caused by either lighting or fate—to sink in. Lily waits across the hall. I approach her, cups of punch in my hands and the feeling of my coattails moving gently behind me. When she lifts her face to mine, I picture a different life with her with a sudden rush of clarity. Perhaps, had we lived in another time or place, we would've been ready to fight for each other, disarming ourselves on the dance floor while sipping fragrantly spiked punch (my money is on Gladys as the culprit).

I extend a cup to Lily in a *cheers* gesture and take a sip. Immediately, I'm sputtering. Lily's laughter rings out. Her form goes blurry from the tears in my eyes as she tries to decipher what could have possibly been put in the punch to make it taste so much like either medicine or moonshine.

Something tugs within my heart. Throughout this evening, through her laughter, her intentional touches, and the question in her eyes each time they meet mine, it's like an invisible knot has once again been tied tightly between us. Fate loosened it once, but now it feels as if it is becoming stronger than ever. From the brightness in her gaze, I wonder if she senses the same. I take a step closer, and she tracks my every move.

"More dancing, George?" Her challenge is presented with a smile.

The heat in her expression, familiar yet new, threatens to cause my knees to buckle. "Indeed."

I can do this. I can do this. Silently, my brain chants to my limbs. I move forward to meet her as she moves too, and we both stop in the middle. I'll always meet her halfway if she'll let me.

Rather than speak, I extend my hand. She takes it. For a moment, I allow myself to enjoy the feeling of our hands clasped together. She lets me lead her toward the other couples taking up their dancing position once more. It's not normal for Lily to let someone else lead. I'm in awe that she trusts me enough to allow me to take charge for a while. Maybe the fatigue of being apart, if it feels anything like mine, has crept into her bones too.

A waltz begins, more modern in style and a little slower. Lily echoes my uncertainty about the forced (though I'm looking forward to it) proximity as she looks up at me. Silently, our hearts seem to connect as they have all night. In truth, I've hardly been able to look away from her. I know enough about classical ballroom etiquette to remember that the partners don't always look at each other. Lily didn't get the memo. She's staring at me so intensely that it causes my spine to both strengthen and soften at the same time.

Our hands arch together, intertwining. Somehow, my other hand has already traveled to the lower part of her rib cage. I'm being cautious, realizing that we're leaving the romanticism of Regency and traveling to the present, and there will be less propriety and more questions. To my relief, Lily chooses to break some of the ice by reaching for my hand, sliding it farther down her waist, and stepping closer to me.

I search her face with a gaze I expect to be a look of wonder mixed with hope. My brow is furrowed as I question this move. If I didn't know her as well as I do, I'd think she is playing me, trying to trick me into failing her challenge. But I know she's not. I recognize that, from this moment on, everything I feel isn't going back into neat little boxes. Together, we've blown them to bits when she stepped forward and let herself fully exist within my orbit . . . in public. Tonight, she's not with me because we accidentally fell asleep in the same room during a spring storm. She's not here because she needs my help. And it's not because someone forced us to be civil. We both want to be here.

It's only been a few seconds. We've only missed one turn around the room, but it feels like we've existed in this space for years. Because that is the truth. We've missed our turn time and time again. She changed the music on me. She told me to dance it alone. And I listened, instead of realizing that, when she ran from me, it was her misguided way of protecting me.

"Let's keep dancing," Lily says, the words almost a question hovering in the air between us.

I nod. Slowly, I guide us into an elegant waltz. I'm trying to be a gentleman, gently leading her across the floor, steering us smoothly around other couples—some of whom are also dancing, some who cheer, and some who merely gape in our direction—as we no doubt look like we just stepped out of a movie about a star-crossed royal couple with all the odds stacked against them until fate intervenes and gives them a chance to work it out on the dance floor.

Driven by instinct, my feet take over. Even though I miss a few steps, my strength and determination try to cover us each time. The more Lily trusts me to lead, the more I feel myself easing out of any lingering stiffness. I can't keep the smile off my face as we continue to spin. I glance about the room, spotting ahead of us so we don't crash into anyone.

When the music stops, I catch Lily staring at me. With what feels like a caress, her eyes meet mine. A grin lifts the corner of her mouth. I'm mesmerized. For a moment, the world is nothing but light. The more she smiles, the more I know that I'm the one who put it there, and clarity steals softly into my heart.

She's been trying to do all of it on her own. I've been trying to prove my love, but the emotion might as well be engraved in stone between us.

As the music swells again, we dance. The people clap and laugh. I never expected so many people in Birch Borough to attempt to follow along with the steps they don't know, joining in the festivities. It appears that the Regency Ball is a success. Hours pass before we start to wind down. Lily looks breathless but happy.

"Do I win this one?" I ask over the noise of the room, a hint of mischief in my tone.

"You can't 'win' one; you can only complete it," she replies, and her voice is warm and light.

"Well, then . . ." I grin. Does she notice how often I seamlessly insert previous moments and phrases I've said to her into our conversations? She must.

"However, you've passed," Lily concedes, allowing me a small sense of victory. Not because she admitted it, but because she said something similar when I brought her to a new ice cream place in LA, and she dared me to try an exotic new flavor I'd never had. That flavor is now my favorite.

Lily remembers as much as I do, I realize.

My hand runs through my hair. My heartbeat is a

racehorse trying to figure out which lane to run in order to win. I know Lily is sorry for what happened between us. I'm sorry too. I don't want our history to compel her to push me away for moments lost and missed opportunities.

If none of us ever forgive, if we hold back our love every time someone makes a mistake—even the big ones—I don't know how we could claim to love one another at all. And love each other, she and I did. I'm not asking Lily to give her heart to me fully. I know it may take time for us to meet on the bridge of love again, but I'll be there when she is ready. I'll ask her gently to let me love her, every time. And I will always be there when she needs me, even if she never asks.

In one of our final dances, when I slow and spin her, drawing her closer, I lose my train of thought completely. Scanning her face, my gaze lands on her lips. Her head tilts, tipping to one side like she is extending both a question and an invitation. I'm ready to tell her why something happening between us could be a bad idea, but I find that I don't want to.

We're moving so slowly that I'm convinced ice has frozen on a summer day faster than the passage of this moment. She has the audacity to lick her lips. I track the movement, suddenly desperate to remember what it felt like to let myself love her. Her breath hitches in response. She moves another inch closer, her head tilting. One of my hands grips her waist, the feeling of the silky fabric beneath my fingers enough to hold onto when this moment passes.

The music continues to play as the world disappears. I can't wait to finally do what I've wanted to do since I last saw her. In the middle of the crowd, I incline my head down to hers. Our lips barely brush. When the edge of her mouth and her breath greet my cheek, the touch sends delightful tingles across the side of my face, shocking my system. The feeling is an explosive current that causes me to rear back with wide eyes. Once again, we are standing on ground that is familiar and yet new. The fear of diving in just for her to leave me again is overwhelming. Theoretically, it punches me in the face, and I'm hit with a wave of emotion I didn't see coming.

"I . . . can't," I say. I hear the grit of pain in my voice. It surprises me to find my actions and heart so at odds.

"Right. Of course." Immediately, Lily releases me, her face flushed.

I catch the moment she realizes we lost our senses. She looks about the hall, and her face shows relief that people have continued to dance. The world didn't stop because of the scene we just shared. The fact that she doesn't look me in the eye again tells me just how much I sabotaged our moment. Once again, my knee-jerk reaction is to retreat. As much as I love Lily, I'm still unsure if I can trust her. There's too much unspoken history between us.

She wraps her arms around her waist. I take it as my cue. The music is suddenly too loud, the lights too dim, and the fury in my heart too wild. I give her a nod and walk out of the room, the scent of love and loss lingering heavily in my wake.

I'd tell my younger self that another rejection wouldn't nearly be as painful as the knowledge that Lily doesn't believe I'll run after her again and again. Somewhere deep within me, I think this must be a core part of what it is to be human. We live in fear of something we both want and need so desperately. Occasionally, that fear overtakes us, and we wonder what life would've been like if it hadn't.

When I'm older, the sound of the music mixed with her laughter is the memory I'll pull from. The way she felt in my arms tonight is the storyline that makes me want to freeze time. I make it just outside the building, my hands threading through my hair, pulling at the edges until I'm not sure they'll exist after this moment.

"Stupid, so stupid," I mutter. Unbidden tears spring up to sting my eyes.

"You okay, man?" Suddenly, Rafe is beside me.

The feeling of loss—this time caused by my own hands—nearly chokes me. I reach for him, and he opens his arms to hug me tightly, as if I'm a brother who is holding too much emotion to process on his own.

"I'm losing it, man," I manage to get out. "I don't know what's up or down. I—I love her so much. And I can't . . . I can't . . ."

I don't even need to finish the sentence. Rafe leans back. He pushes away to look me in the eyes, never lifting his hands from my shoulders.

"You're the best man I know," he replies. His next words gut me to the core. "You're not alone."

I wipe my eyes, willing the emotion down. I'm not one to make a scene, but the emotion of it all has been just at the surface, trying to break through my skin for weeks. It's more than Lily. It's what Lily reveals. She shows me how much I've always feared being disposable, desperately avoiding a feeling of uselessness. I know that I can't help but be all in when I make up my mind. And the disappointment kills me every time. First, with my father. And now, with her.

Rafe nods. Together, we walk around the corner of the

brick building, the sound of music and laughter spilling out into the night, uncontainable within the walls.

"You held her," he states simply.

"I did."

"That's a start. And you danced with her."

I nod in reply, focusing on the shadowy, moonlit birch trees in the distance—the namesake of this town—to give me a sense of grounding. "It felt like we've danced a thousand times before."

Rafe mirrors my choice to gaze out into the distance. "I know what it's like to hold the woman you love in your arms and not know how things will end up. I don't think it's something a man recovers from. It's not something we can forget."

"That's the problem right there," I reply with a sigh, already pointing my shoes toward what now feels as if it is only my temporary home. "I never could forget. And I wouldn't want to."

Chapter Nineteen

Graham

"What are we doing here?" I mutter, pulling open the door and stepping into the gym. I spot her immediately on the other side of the room.

Already, my breathing is ragged from the sight of Lily in a white tank top and black athletic shorts. I thought she was kidding when she texted me this morning to challenge me to a boxing match at In the Ring.

Got another challenge for ya, George, her text said. *If you're not too scared. Or you can forfeit this challenge and take the hit. There are some nice apartments in Portsmouth.*

Not completing a challenge is out of the question. Not with the wedding fast approaching. Lily knows she can't literally force me to leave town. But what will happen when she realizes her plan to drive me so crazy that I move of my own accord doesn't work? Now, I'm wondering if this is her way of forcing us to duke out our differences once and for all.

We haven't seen each other much of late. I've even found myself missing her ridiculous challenges. After the fluffernutter cookie incident, I thought she was softening toward me. But after the night we almost kissed while we danced at the Regency Ball, we now seem to be avoiding each other at all costs.

Walking toward a small bench in the corner of the gym, I drop my bag with a little more force than necessary. At the sound of the thud it makes, Lily pivots toward me. A smirk flashes across her pretty face. The look tempts me to kiss her for the reminder she just gave to my heart that I haven't lost all of myself after all.

"George, you made it," she says.

I should be frightened at her tone—a little giddy tinged with a sense of adventure—but my muscles clench in anticipation instead.

"Warm up," she instructs.

I unzip my hoodie, carefully laying it over my gym bag. Glancing up discreetly, I watch Lily watching me in the mirror. She doesn't realize that I can see her, so I take an extra moment to arrange and fold the sleeves of the sweatshirt. Her eyes take on a dreamy quality, as if she's doing a math equation, and my arms and shoulders hold all the answers.

Interesting.

It would have been smarter not to show up today. I don't trust myself not to pull her close and whisper all the things that feel as if they could climb out of my skin when I'm around her. I want to let the burn of her kiss sear me right through and push away my fear. I want to wrap her up in forgiveness and love for the rest of my life.

But that's the problem. I'm drowning in a one-sided love that will always be more empty than full until she chooses to admit what she has felt all along. I need more than an explanation; I need action. I know she has something in her system that haunts her about our time together.

Everything I feel radiating from her might as well be worth nothing if she can't admit it to my face. I know she won't be making a confession of love for me today. The second I walked through the door and saw her expression, I knew I was in for it. Still, I'll admit that the satisfying thud of her gloves as they meet the weight of the punching bag again and again while her ponytail bounces behind her is distracting and wildly attractive.

I've never pictured her in this environment, even with her snarky hints that she's capable of taking someone down on the mat. I've heard her telling other people that she's happier than ever now that she's getting her aggression out. But I've yet to see her in action. As I watch her now, it's clear that, despite my presence, Lily is focused on maximizing each and every punch. Her gloves land hard on the bag, rattling it in its foundation. I don't know whether to applaud Edgar for his training or flat out level him to the ground (or try to).

I'm not a violent man by any stretch of the imagination, but I feel the instant bristle toward anything (or anyone) that has taken me away from her over the past few years.

In short, I'm in for it today.

My approach startles Lily. She knocks into the bag, and it swings back a bit, lightly hitting her in return before she's steady again on her feet. I'd laugh, but there's nothing funny about what's about to go down in this space.

Edgar—who has a good bit of weight and muscle on me,

might I add—walks out from the direction of the lockers just then, and Lily gives him a wave. Instantly, I want to add him to the list of men I'd level, if necessary.

"Hey, Edgar," she calls.

He flashes her a grin, and it's confirmed that I hate him. "Hey, Lils," Edgar replies with an easy familiarity. He casts a cool glance my way and gives me a brief nod before returning his attention to her. My hands clench into fists. It shouldn't surprise me, given how gloriously sharp and fiery Lily can be, that another man might be interested in her. Of course he wants to stay on her good side.

Rolling back my shoulders, I try to muster the confidence of a man who was asked to be here today. I'm not just some out-of-towner who hasn't ever worked out. I work out every day. Surely, today's challenge should be more than manageable—I think.

Lily pulls the Velcro tighter on her gloves. She's gearing up to go into battle, and while the punching bag is her current target, I wonder if her aggression toward the bag is about me.

I approach gingerly, my hands working to adjust the boxing gloves I pulled out of my bag. Are they brand-new? Yes. Did I buy them specifically so that Lily couldn't hassle me about borrowing a pair? Also, yes.

She motions to the second punching bag a few feet away and continues to hit one of them. At the moment, this may be a warm-up, but the stiffness in her limbs tells me she's been waiting for this conversation for a long time.

"So," I try to begin casually, "when exactly did you take up boxing?"

She huffs out a laugh and picks up the pace of her

punches. If I don't start soon, she's going to be exhausted before I even warm up. I catch her glance over at me, her eyes doing a quick scan from my hair to the mat and then back as she continues punching like the bag personally offends her.

"I'm pretending these are filled with chocolates, and if I hit them hard enough, they'll fly out like they're shooting from a confetti cannon," she replies in all seriousness. "And I started taking lessons a couple of years ago."

Interesting. The timeline checks out for when she left my life.

"Well, I've heard that exercise can increase endorphins," I say. The sound of her gloves hitting the bag is the only response. "Help the immune system." Punch. "Lessen one's anxiety." Punch. *Punch.*

Truthfully, that's why I started an intentional fitness plan after we broke up. But she doesn't need to know that tidbit. "So, did you ever go exploring around the world like we . . ." I stop with an awkward pause. "Correction, *you* planned?"

Where did that come from? I punch the bag in front of me just to do something with my hands. The force of the bag connecting with my glove brings me a measure of relief. My last comment made me wince. Now, I think I may need to install one of these in my apartment or get a membership here if this is as therapeutic as I feel like it could be.

"No. I had other things come up. But I explore in other ways too," Lily replies to my question forcefully, the reverberation of each punch accentuating different parts of her words.

"So do I," I pant, trying to keep up with her. My muscles are warm, loosening with each passing minute. I feel the sweat across my forehead, my arms straining at the exertion.

Being in the same space as Lily sends my mind reeling. I wasn't kidding when I said I wanted to get her in the ring, but her determination to excel is my undoing. She sets her sights on something and goes for it, no questions asked. It hurts to realize that, in the end, she failed to do that for me.

"And now, you keep Rafe out of trouble." She pauses, wiping the sides of her eyes with the back of her arm. The gloves look oversized on her, as if she got her hand stuck in something far too big but doesn't mind that she got caught.

I reply with an easy smile and walk to where she stands. "He's my best friend. I like protecting him." I give the bag between us a quick jab, facing her, my own side of the gym abandoned. "Besides, he makes it easy. Especially because he is in love."

Lily pauses a bit too long at the word. It hovers between us, and I freeze, staring into her deep eyes. She uses the break in my defenses to land a punch on the bag that knocks me back an inch. I know it's only because I was distracted, but I let her take the win just the same.

We seem to have moved beyond the warm-up into full workout territory. She picks up the pace so much that I look over at Edgar for an indication of what to do. Is this even safe?

Her jabs at the bag end abruptly. Without a word, she hops into the ring in the center of the space—the boxing elephant in the room—and gives a jerk of her head to motion for me to follow. The slight give from the padding of the floor canvas takes some adjustment as it absorbs more than the shock of our movements. Lily taps my gloves before lifting her own up to chin height. She starts to throw punches just as my brain catches up with her intention to strike my hands through my gloves.

As the sound of her jabs reverberates throughout the space, Edgar glances up. He shrugs and goes back to typing on his computer. The fact that he knows her enough to know this isn't abnormal makes me swing back in time to receive a punch from Lily so hard that I almost stumble backward from the force. Meanwhile, Lily's arms are moving like tiny machines.

"How are you doing this?" I yell over the noise, not even trying to hide both my concern and appreciation of her tenacity.

Hesitantly, I step toward her again, hoping it's not my face she has pictured each time she's practiced this little exercise. Ensuring that all my best bits, besides my face, are hidden, I look around my gloves cautiously.

"That's not." Grunt. "The point." Punch.

My heart is racing so quickly I think it might punch out of my chest. She gives an additional grunt, hitting my right glove again, this time with enough force that it stings and almost knocks her out on the rebound. The strength she has is otherworldly.

Lily motions with her gloved hands. "Can you help? Stay steady for me, please?"

"How often are you here, beating the crap out of something?" I reply. I'm panting, my sweat dripping to the floor.

"I told you. If I'm not loving you . . ." she begins then pauses abruptly.

"You took up boxing," I state, no emotion in my voice. *This* is why I've been bothered by the whole situation. Once, she jokingly remarked that if she weren't loving me, she'd be boxing. And here she is. "Boxing or loving me, right?"

I really don't think I want an answer, but sometimes I think I romanticize what we had. She doesn't spare me a glance but pulls her bottom lip between her teeth, the light sheen of sweat on her causing the shorter tendrils of her hair to stick to the sides of her face and the curve of her neck. I swallow. Lily goes back to punching, but I've had enough. It's time to lay the truth bare.

"Why did you walk away, Lily?" The question is spoken in a low tone, but she hears it anyway. She freezes, gloves pressed together.

"Because I'm a mess," she replies tensely.

"Not true. And not enough." I shake my head. By some stroke of good fortune, the gym is empty, except for Edgar, and he's now talking quietly on the phone across the room. "I need a reason. Please give me a reason."

I'm practically begging, but my analytical brain has repeated the day she left me so many times that I need some relief before I go mad. I need someone to give me another angle, another way to see why our relationship failed. I think she's the only person who can.

"You did nothing wrong," Lily insists.

I shake my head again.

"Is that still not enough?" she counters with fire in her eyes. They're turning a darker shade of grey as my words hit a nerve. I won't let her get off quite so easy. Not after all this time. I'm not seeking these answers to hurt her. I'm seeking them to give us both a chance to move on.

I pin her with my gaze. "You can't apologize for the wreckage without telling me the cause." I'm breathing heavily, and I hate it. "Were we . . . too much?" She shakes her head. "Too fast?"

Again, a head shake.

"Too slow?" My brain struggles as it tries to compute what's happening.

Tears brim in Lily's eyes, but there's no hostility. If I had to guess, I'd think the expression on her face looks like fear. But that's impossible. How could my seemingly fearless, brave, spitfire of a woman be afraid of me? I release a sigh.

"Too . . . afraid?"

Her eyes flash upward. I know I've found the thread of truth. My mind races as my stomach fills with dread.

"Of me?" Instantly, I deflate, my hands dropping to my sides. "Did I do something?"

I feel as if I could vomit just thinking of a woman being afraid of me. I've witnessed that dynamic in my mother's relationships with men. I vowed never to allow fear to be something a woman associates with me.

"No," Lily hastens to assure me. "No."

She brushes tears from her eyes, and I want to take her in my arms. But it's not the moment. Not until we get to the bottom of it all.

"Not of you." Her shoulders tremble as she shifts her frame from side to side.

I sense there's so much more going on that she isn't saying, but I can't do anything without the truth. We're stuck in a holding pattern. While I had called the time of death on our relationship a couple of years ago, being thrown together with her these past couple of months almost makes me believe in us again. When I held her the night of the Regency Ball—when I nearly kissed her—it made me feel as if I were coming out of hibernation.

Her answer now causes pain to shoot throughout my heart and my limbs. I know what it's like when Lily confides in me, the look in her eyes when she's fully with me, and the feeling of her body melting into mine when she's in my arms. She ran in fear once, and then I repeated the mistake at the ball. I'm terrified to admit, even to myself, that I wish I hadn't chucked the engagement ring I once purchased to offer her.

Now, I see what I didn't see before. Lily is wearing herself out. Framed by her furrowed brow, dark circles hover under her eyes. Seeing her in pain, knowing she's been afraid of . . . something that I triggered, gives me the courage to make this the last time. Our friends are getting married, and this battle between tension and hope has gone on long enough.

"Lily, I'm gonna call it. You win."

"What? No." Without realizing it, she reaches for me like she did that day at the moving truck. While all I've ever wanted since I turned down her explanation was for her to need me in her life again like she did long ago, this isn't how I want it to occur.

I nod my head in affirmation. "I used to pride myself on my winning streak in the courtroom, but I think this may be a case I'll never resolve. If you're not ready to tell me why you felt it best to walk away from what we had, I'm finally—really—okay with it."

To be clear, I'm not okay with it, but Lily's well-being will always be more important than my own. It must be.

"What about our challenges?"

I feel myself sink a bit. I've fallen for this tiny town. I

can see myself living here long term. But I've never *not* fallen for the woman before me even more. I know things can't continue this way. Something has to change for us both.

"I'll look for a new place soon. Maybe Liam or someone in town will want my current space. It's a nice apartment."

She wraps her arms around herself and stares out the back window. It has a glimpse of the river rushing by us, upset and high from a recent spring storm.

"It's okay, Lily," I continue. "Let's just leave it here. Because I'm . . . tired." I turn away from her to hide the emotion I feel creeping across my face. I duck to slink through the ropes and down from the platform when her voice cuts through the sharp air.

"No!"

I freeze in my tracks.

"Don't you *dare*, George!" Her jump from the ring and the sound of her footsteps hurry to follow. She pops up in front of me, cheeks red from emotion. "We shook on it!"

"It wasn't a binding contract."

"It was to me." Her eyes flare.

"Lily, we can't keep doing this. Do you understand that? Can you respect that?" I see when the thrill of the fight hits her system.

She lifts her chin in defiance. "We almost kissed."

A figurative punch hits my stomach. "We . . . yes, okay?"

"And then you ran away."

"I didn't—okay yes, but I only walked out quickly . . ." There's something else she isn't adding. With everything that has already been exposed, I let it slide.

"You're not quitting, George. We still have the wedding to get through . . . so this isn't over." She says the last part of the sentence with extra force, her voice a hoarse whisper as Edgar strides over to the main part of the gym, carrying his laptop in one hand.

I stuff down the hope that sparks in my heart, releasing an unamused laugh instead. She's got me again. "Fine, but Lily? This is the last time."

She glances over at Edgar and then to my chest, never making eye contact and no doubt trying to assess just how much he can hear of our conversation. "Look, you wanna say I messed up? Say it. I know I did."

A drop of sweat falls from the side of her forehead and blends in with a tear that slips out. She goes to brush it with the back of her hand but can't quite catch it from the awkwardness of the gloves. "And I'm paying for it. But you messed up too."

Before I can overthink it, I rip off my gloves and throw them to the floor. My hand lifts to cup the side of her jaw. I use my thumb to wipe away the rogue tear. She doesn't fight me, the grey in her eyes overtaking any lavender edges.

"Lily, what are you talking about?" My eyes scan hers, and I watch as she squeezes them shut, another tear slipping out at the edges. She hates to cry, which is how I know this goes soul deep.

"I'm just so . . . mad."

The world keeps spinning, but I'm reeling in my own universe. The force of her words pushes me back as if I just went from zero to eighty on a roller coaster. Not that I've been on many of those. But the one time, yeah, that's similar to this feeling. Rather than follow up on what she just said, she goes back to punching the bag with more force than before.

"Sweetheart, you're going to hurt yourself if you keep doing that."

"Edgar!" Lily yells, pulling us out of the moment. He pokes his head around his computer screen precariously hovering on the edge of a fallen punching bag that I'm pretty sure he uses as a makeshift desk. "I need five."

Somehow, Edgar knows what this means and is fine enough with it to walk toward the rear changing room and disappear. I turn back to her, refusing to let this moment pass if I finally have a trail of the truth to follow.

"Why are you mad?" I reach for her.

She evades my touch, turning her face away so that all I can see is the rise and fall of her shoulders.

"Lily, why are you mad?"

"Because . . . you . . . you *know* I lied!" She spins to face me, the force of her fiery and yet heartbroken attention enough to drop like a rock in my stomach. "You let me tell you all that crap, and you didn't even call me on it. You just let me say it, and you walked away. You didn't even fight for me."

The tension in my shoulders intensifies at an unnerving rate. While I'd never yell at Lily, I'm instantly furious. I didn't go after her? I let her go?

"Are you hearing yourself?" I ask quietly. "I wanted to spend the rest of my life with you. And you walked away. You did that, Lily. And call me irrational, but you wanted me to fight for you? Would you fight for someone who told you they didn't want you?"

Tears are streaming down her face now. I know there's nothing I can do to wipe them away, not as emotion chokes me up too.

"I still wanted you, even though I clearly see it's too late." She moves toward her things piled against the wall. "Oh, and kissing you? Yeah, I never stopped wanting to do that either."

Rather than stay here and talk it out, rather than verbally sparring with me or proving her theory incorrect by grabbing and kissing me, she grabs her bag, hands still in those oversized gloves. Without even putting on a jacket, she leaves, the thud of the door reiterating her choice.

The excuse for a door opens. Edgar sticks his head out, looking from me to the empty gym. "Is she gone?"

I move toward my bag, my limbs numb as I pick up my hoodie and pull it over my head, trying to piece together how her words have reframed my past in a matter of minutes.

"Yeah, Edgar. She's gone."

I use the cloth and spray to wipe down the punching bags. Edgar politely watches my every move. Maybe he isn't such a bad guy after all. As my jealousy dissipates and the toll of what went down here sinks in, I have an overwhelming desire to go home. Picking up my gloves from the floor, I pause at the sight of a folded piece of paper discarded on the mat where Lily stood.

Reaching for it, I open it to find what looks to be a list of sorts.

1. Finish Rory's gift.

2. Learn a French phrase for D'Artagnan.

3. Tell G the truth. (Or forgive G.)

Out of all the things that happened today, she's already checked one off the list. And if my dreams have been any indication, we'll need to do the same for each other more than once.

Chapter Twenty

Lily

My skin is still itchy from the Regency-era costume I wore last week, which, in retrospect, was probably quite dusty. At least, that's the excuse I give myself to explain why I keep fidgeting in the car and avoiding eye contact with the man driving it. I keep telling myself that the racing of my heart and the swooping sensation in my stomach have nothing to do with Graham and the memories of his face so close to mine while we danced, proving that while the night was a dream, the outfit sure wasn't.

That evening, I leaned into the feelings and the romance of it all. Under the dim and moody lighting, it wasn't hard to admit to myself that my feelings for Graham had deepened despite our time apart. When he held me close as we waltzed across the floor, it seemed as if, perhaps, he was feeling what I was too, just a little.

Acknowledging my feelings also ripped open a new wound—one that I'm not sure how to mend. (The unpleasant feeling in the pit of my stomach may also be the punch I managed to drink that night. I still don't know what was in it, even days later.)

The Regency Ball was disorienting, that's all. I see why women used to faint all the time. The influence of the music, the food, the dancing, and the men in great coats—they can change a girl. And knowing what Graham looks like in a cravat has now made this feeling of misplaced faith in what we could be stick like glue to my hands and my heart.

My discombobulation has nothing to do with the man that I once loved and lost choosing to linger beside me the entire night. Graham and I were in sync just like before until we nearly kissed under the twinkling lights of the dance floor. I could both see and sense the emotion breaking through his usually calm demeanor. I don't blame him for leaving. And now, we're stuck with each other once again.

"Don't worry. It's vegan," Graham breaks the silence abruptly, distracting me from my thoughts.

"I'm sorry?"

"The seats. You keep rubbing the dashboard like it will grant you three wishes, but you're unsure if you should accept it. I thought I would put your mind at ease and let you know it's synthetic leather."

"Why would you . . .?" It makes sense that Graham is conscious that I'm a vegetarian. I'm not vegan but avoid materials like real leather. He once joked that I fit right in with the LA crowd, but I never expected him to remember such a detail. I try not to listen to the little murmurings in my heart that whisper he bought the car for us. "How long have you had this car?"

With his hand on the shifter (because of course he can

drive a stick shift), he risks a glance over at me when we're stopped at the light. Birch Borough doesn't have many stoplights, mostly stop signs, and this is the last pause before we cruise out of town.

"Two years . . . about."

"I see."

He nods, enough said between us that we both know he purchased it after our fallout. Something in my chest aches a bit at the idea that he has lived for a time without me. It doesn't seem right. After we discovered each other's existence, it seems incredibly unjust to have spent any time apart, even in light of our mistakes or the lingering reality of what could've been.

Add to that sadness the awkward truth that poured out of me at the boxing studio. I don't know what came over me. I blame the confined space and lack of oxygen. And the endorphins brought on by getting into the ring to spar with Graham. Maybe I was dehydrated. All I know now is that my nerves are frayed, and having to spend the evening with Graham isn't helping. My nerves feel like live wires ready to blow the circuit breaker of my fears. He called me earlier to ask for my help on a wedding-related duty. Apparently, Sparrow asked us to help her with a last-minute wedding task that couldn't be put off any longer. As the maid of honor, I'm not about to renege on my duties just because I have uncomfortable feelings for the best man.

So, I pretend to be fascinated by his car, just to avoid having to make actual conversation for a little bit longer. Graham's car is what dreams are made of. The seats feel like literal flower petals. They're so soft and smooth. It's a weird description for a car, but accurate.

"Ugh, this car positively purrs," I exclaim.

Graham lets out a laugh. "Don't tell A-cat-pella that."

"I wouldn't dream of it."

His hands clench the shifter, deftly switching gears. Suddenly, I'm rethinking the calendar idea Gladys set aside for firemen this year. Let's try devastatingly attractive guys driving cars instead. Maybe it will add some balance back into the world from all those car selfies on the "those that must not be named" dating apps. Actually, I'm not sure that the unattached hearts in our poor town could take the stimulation if the glimpse I have now is any indication of the effect such photos could have on viewers. They may be interested in more than the days of the week.

Discreetly, I study Graham's profile. The beard is bearding today. His hair swoops perfectly away from his forehead. He's perfectly groomed in a blue suit that echoes the color of his eyes, the picture-perfect model of a man he's always been. That's one thing about Graham. He was perfect then, and he's perfect now. The ache in my chest intensifies.

"Did you find a plus-one?" I cringe immediately after blurting out the question. I don't know why I asked. I don't really want to know.

"No."

"Interesting."

"What's interesting?"

"Uh, nothing." Which isn't true. Thinking about Graham choosing someone besides me in my town to take as a date to the wedding is positively maddening. I don't know how I'll ever look at the woman the same after he picks one. As much as I love them, something in me hopes it's not Ivy or Grey. Because their goodness would be proof that I'm not the person who is best for Graham. Besides, seeing them together would be a whole carnival of awkwardness. I need to change the subject before I burst. "So, where are we going exactly?"

"We're going to an estate a few towns over. There's a wildflower field there and—"

"And you're looking for potential photo opportunities."

He nods, glancing at me briefly, the barely setting sun hitting his eyes in a way that brings out the golden tints in their blue depths more than any other lighting. The man is made for the golden hour. I've never forgotten his eyes, but it's like I'm seeing them again for the first time.

"Rafe and Sparrow haven't seen each other much lately—well, not as much as they'd like," he says with a grin. "So, I volunteered us."

I nod. He doesn't comment, even though he didn't see my response. The weight of what could have been tries to overwhelm me. Being with Graham feels like the cheerfulness of tulips poking through the ground despite a cloudy sky full of rain overhead. The truth is, even though he is the brightness and beauty I've been missing in my life, I know that hope is fragile and easily crushed.

Graham continues, filling the silence. "The estate's owners, the Campbells, have lived here for generations. It's rumored that in the 1940s, or maybe '50s—I can't remember now, to be honest—anyway, the newlywed groom planted wildflowers for his bride in honor of their wedding day. He said he wanted her to see their love blossom every spring."

"That's nice."

Graham's charming grin in my direction catches me off guard. "I'm not sure how true it is, given how people make up stories all the time. Liam mentioned it to me, and since he's pretty much the town historian, given his family's history here, you'll have to ask him for the full story. But yeah, it's a nice thought."

"I will."

He's so handsome, his hands resting easily on the steering wheel and gear shift, the sun shining through the windshield and bringing out the golden highlights of his hair, that I can't help but smile in return.

We drive in silence the rest of the way. When we arrive at the estate, Graham steps out of the car and rushes toward my door, but I step out before he can reach me. He takes a few steps forward then turns back to me. His arm swings out behind him as if it is for me to take before thinking better of it. He clears his throat and slides his hand into his pocket so seamlessly that I almost think I misinterpreted it. But then I catch the sudden hint of color in his cheeks and the tightness in his throat. Inwardly, I can't help but feel pleased that I know all the nervous tics he does when he's uncomfortable.

We follow the signs around the property that point to *Wildflower Lane*. It is actually a field, and as we walk together in the idyllic setting, my nerves grow more than I'd care to admit. After avoiding the most uncomfortable topics in the car, I feel them sprouting into weeds between us. We have so much to discuss, and I wonder how long he is going to let me keep avoiding it. Graham and I still haven't brought all the truth to light.

"I was told just to take a look when I called. Do you think we need to meet anyone?" Graham asks. His voice echoes behind him, carried on the wind.

It rushes past my ears but no more so than my heartbeat,

which has picked up its pace since we arrived. Something about the crystal blue sky and the white fluffy clouds, a light jacket on after a harsh winter, and the man in front of me, who is leading the way as if he's walked this path a dozen times and not like this is his first time wandering over it, sends my heart soaring.

His dress pants now have the slightest bit of dirt starting to power up the hems. The sight makes me like him even more. He'd rather be himself and dirty his clothes than dress down and not feel as comfortable as we trek through the brush toward our destination.

I'm nearly about to attempt a text to Sparrow to be sure this is truly what she wants for photos filled with wedding bliss when we round a grove of trees and reach a clearing.

My breath breaks its rhythm as I discover the most gorgeous field I've ever seen in person. It's nothing fancy. It truly is a field, with trees around the edges and a patch of wildflowers the size of half a football field in the middle. The patch of grass we're standing on walks right up to a wall of flowers. There is a small alcove just big enough for people to stand in while the earth looks like an upside-down smile.

I don't know how it is possible I've never been here before. I've lived nearby my whole life. At first glance, the flowers appear to be mostly yellow. But when you look closer at them, you begin to see that the colors woven throughout are rich shades of pink and red, purple and blue, with even some hints of white. It's stunning. But the meadow is not Sparrow's aesthetic.

"Huh," I muse, walking toward the little alcove in the flowers, trying to immerse myself in as much of this experience as possible.

Graham follows me—his presence not unwelcome—and when I'm close enough, I lean over to catch the sweet scent of wildness meeting beauty.

"As much as I'm loving this scene that would surely thrill the legendary Bob Ross, this isn't our friends' vibe," I remark.

"No, it's more . . ." Graham doesn't say it, but we both know the end of that sentence. It's more *us*.

When I turn toward Graham, his eyes are closed, his face tipped up to the sun. The wind blows the top of his hair in a mesmerizing pattern, spinning some gilded threads throughout the light brown. As much as I miss the sight of his blue eyes, it's at this moment that I see Graham not as he is now but as he could be. *He and I.*

Maybe it's the dark grey dress pants and the white button-up shirt he's wearing, rolled up at the elbows and perfectly tailored, but my throat starts to close at the mental image of Graham and me in front of a pastor in the middle of this field. The wind in our hair, nature all around us, hard edges meeting softness.

I feel hesitant, but I move toward him anyway, the feeling that we're the only two people in the world propelling me forward. My hand reaches out to grab his wrist, which hangs loosely at his side. His eyes flash open. He turns to me immediately with a question in his eyes. Rotating it toward me, he turns up his palm in an invitation. This time, without hesitation, I slide my hand over his and thread our fingers together.

"Lily, what are we doing?" There is a question wrapped all around and in that statement, from the tone of his voice to the look in his eyes.

"I wish I knew."

He releases a hum of contemplation. "You do know that, as much as it meant to us . . . I'm not Darcy. You're not Lizzie."

"Then who are we?" I whisper.

"We're Graham and Lily. We always have been." He starts to pull away.

I pull him back toward me, refusing to let his hand go now that it's threaded through mine. "It's stunning here, and I . . . I want to feel it all."

His jaw shifts. "What do you want to feel?"

"Everything. You. This."

"You have a funny way of showing it."

I wince a little at his words because he's right. If someone could win an award for mixed signals, I would be the unequivocal world champion.

"Are we going to talk about it yet?"

I shake my head, unwilling to ruin the memory of this field and this moment with the things that have haunted me. His brow furrows, eyes wandering over my face, reading my features, searching for something I don't know he'll find. "Why are you looking at me like that?"

He steps a bit closer, the space between us blurring. The edge of his thumb traces the top of my eyebrow and the plane of my cheekbone, sending tingles throughout my face. His thumb lingers near the top of my lips. The weight of it meeting gravity causes it to slide down and caress my bottom lip, parting it from its mate. I've never wanted anything more than to be stuck in this moment with him for the rest of my life. A moment frozen in time, where he's looking at me like he's remembering what we used to be, and his eyes have picked up a light that could be interpreted as reflecting *more* than what we've been.

"You know what I've been wondering?" he says softly, the hand not tied to my own sliding down again. The edge of his thumb now maps a route from my jaw to my neck. He continues until he traces an inch of my collarbone, his hand slowly gliding to wrap around the back of my neck.

"What?" I whisper, my body leaning into his through some invisible force. Or perhaps the years of heartache that are trying to heal compel me toward him.

"I've been wondering if you still taste like chocolate." The intensity of his expression meeting the slight grin pulling at the corners of his mouth tells me he has, indeed, been wondering this.

Of all the good fortune, I actually did eat a chocolate bar before he picked me up. So, I know I won't disappoint him. That must be why, instead of running away or making a joke, I match his grin. "I think you should find out."

His eyes darken, their various blue tones meeting vats of dark chocolate as his face hovers over me. My chin tilts up to welcome whatever he's willing to give me with his kiss. If it's like anything we've shared before, I'm about to be lathered with his affection.

With my free hand, I reach up and cup his face, the delightful feeling of his short beard soft beneath my palm. He used to put on beard oil to make it even more smooth to the touch. When my palm glides across his jawline, I smile because I know this about him. And it hasn't changed.

"What are you waiting for?" I murmur.

The scent of his skin is already filling my senses, the anticipation of kissing him again almost more than I think I can bear.

"We've gotten close to this before. What if this is a dream?" The edge in his voice calls up emotions I've pressed down to the surface.

Under the warmth of the sun and amidst the swaying of the wildflowers surrounding us, it's easy to slip into the hazy, dreamlike quality this moment is creating. Still, I can't assure him this is real if I'm overwhelmed too. All I know is that I need him. And I don't want to wake up either.

"Then you better make it a good one," I whisper.

His breath hitches. I catch a glimpse of his eyes closing before his lips crash into mine. He's not a man unsure or confused as to how best to love me in this moment. He's a man who knows exactly how to undo me. He's determined to figure out if all his theories and past research remain true.

This is what I've been missing: a man with the courage to pour out his heart with each press and pull of his lips, with each touch of his hands. He's not taking. He's giving. And this is the difference between Graham and every other man I've allowed to get close to me. He gives me life with his love and doesn't wear me thin. When I see him clearly, I don't question my worth. I don't feel like I'm too much.

In Graham's arms, I'm adored exactly as I am, and feeling this truth has me pulling him closer. I'm unable to think clearly, though I still sense the fog of loneliness clearing from my mind. The scratch of his beard across my cheek is a match. It's a fire warming your bones after being in the rain. It's lightning coming back to finish what it started.

I run my fingers through his hair. The light groan he makes causes me to melt toward the earth. My muscles relax, my frame taking a break from the pressure to feel strong. He holds me up, not bothered in the least that he's making me dizzy with his attention.

Graham is all intensity, not taking a second for granted. When he releases our hands to pull me closer, never once pausing his kisses, his fingertips trace the length of my spine, trailing across my dress like a circuit board turning on after a power outage.

I match his energy, my disappointment in myself for letting him go finally taking a backseat to my desire for him to know me again. To remember how much I used to love undoing him too. We shift and move with each other as if we never lost a moment. I slide my hands to wrap around his neck, pulling him even closer. I can't get enough of him. If I taste like chocolate, he adds a hint of caramel—my second favorite kind of confection.

Minutes or hours pass, and I'm lost in him. We're wildflowers dancing in the wind, thrown beside each other, trying to thrive. Like seeds that have sprung up and missed the sun, only finally to take their place in the light, we make each other blossom.

When we break apart, breath short and hearts racing, I run the back of my hand over his beard. I flash him a grin and stretch up to press a kiss to his cheek. Graham still hasn't opened his eyes, so I outline his cheekbone in soft kisses, trailing to the soft spot beneath his ear, until I'm planting kisses down the side of his neck, his skin warm beneath my lips. It's pure bliss, like wrapping your lips around a ceramic mug full of steaming hot tea.

"Lily," he says, his voice gravelly and rich with love.

I lean my forehead on his chest to catch my breath. His

head comes to rest on my own. One of his hands cradles my head close to him as I turn my cheek to look toward the field of wildflowers and the grass waving in varying shades of green in the wind.

"I know I questioned if this was a dream. But the truth is, I've been sleepwalking without you." His voice hitches, a raspiness in it that wasn't there before. "Thank you for waking me up."

Chapter Twenty-One

Graham

When I awaken the next morning, I can still remember the taste of melted chocolate, caramel, and flakes of sea salt between our lips. The sun hits my eyes and reminds me that the storm has passed. The thought of her eating candy right before I picked her up to drive out to the wildflower field makes a smile cross my face. Of course she was. The woman is the chocolate queen, always with bite-sized bits of chocolate wrapped haphazardly and thrown into pockets, purses, and anywhere else she can store them.

When we were together those weeks in LA, I'd find the shiny wrappers sticking out in odd places, like she was a human disco ball of chocolate. I always had the urge to go on a treasure hunt to find them, and it was a challenge to force my analytical brain to tune out the desire whenever I hugged her. Suddenly, there would be a crackling sound coming from her clothes, and a wrapper—sometimes filled with chocolate, sometimes empty—would pop out of hiding. We'd laugh that I was at the scene of the crime for continuous confectionary murders.

Rolling onto my side, I slide up in bed and lean my back against the headboard. Swiping a hand over my face, I gift myself another thirty seconds of visualizing our encounter and committing it to memory. Will I ever forget how the ends of her hair danced merrily around her face, the scent of wildflowers swirling around us, or the vividness of her bright pink lips against the cloudy sky? When her eyes met mine, what once felt hollow was somehow filled.

I'm reveling in the memory all over again—a smile beaming on my face—when my phone pings on the bedside table. Though I shouldn't let my hopes rise, my heart beats faster. Kissing her in the field of wildflowers convinced me that all sorts of things may be possible. I never thought we'd kiss again, and here we are. On the drive back, neither of us talked about it much—or at all—but just the fact that it happened must be a good sign.

Reaching for my phone, I rub my eyes to better grasp what I see. It's a group message that includes Sparrow and Rafe.

Sparrow: Graham, I'm so sorry to ask, but is there any way you can check on Lily?

Rafe: I'm sure he'd love to check on her . . .

Instantly, my throat goes dry.

Sparrow: Something isn't right. I'm covering the café this morning, but she texted me, and none of it made sense. Then, when I called her, she said she kissed you and hung up.

Rafe: My man, you kissed Lily? Does this mean you're staying in Birch Borough for good?

I feel like I'm going to be sick but force my emotions back in check. Lily may be a wild card, but she isn't the type to ever hang up on her friend. Rafe, however, is going to mysteriously need new guitar strings the next time I see him.

While I'm not certain what I'm signing up for, my feet are already on the floor. I type a hasty response to the group as I rush to gather some clothes.

Graham: Will be there in ten. I'll send an update.

Sparrow hearts the message, and I toss the phone on the bathroom counter. After taking one of the fastest showers of my life, I berate myself for almost putting my pants on backward. I avoid eye contact with myself—a man who can pass the bar but can't get his arm through his shirt without almost punching a hole through the fabric.

"Calm down, calm down," I mutter. Lily isn't far away. Unsure of what I'll be walking into, I slide into my shoes, grab my keys, and barely manage to throw a protein bar into my jacket pocket before I'm out the door.

Since Lily's studio is only a few streets away from my apartment, I'm already calculating that it should take me less than two minutes to drive there, including the starting of my car. Turns out, I'm there in less than one.

In my haste, I almost leave the car in neutral when I exit. Quickly throwing it into park, I nearly trip on the way to her building's front door. Thankfully, because I was here when we escaped the storm, I know where she lives in the non-creepiest way possible. As I enter the building, a door flies open on the first floor. An older man with intense round glasses and a long cardigan wrapped around his shoulders steps out, pieces of his greying hair sticking out in every direction.

"Can I help you?" His question comes across as more inquisitive than threatening.

"I'm looking for Lily," I reply. "And you are?"

He bristles a bit, clearly offended that I don't know him. *Should I?*

"I'm her landlord, Mr. Crumbs. That lady is always up to shenanigans." He shakes his finger.

His grim tone brings out an involuntary laugh from my chest. To cover my faux pas, I nod as if this accusation is a truly serious issue instead of acknowledging how distracted I am by his last name. Impatiently, I look away and spot a chocolate wrapper on the edge of a stair tread leading up to Lily's door. I don't know whether to keep it or commit myself for study.

"If you find that amusing, then you two deserve each other," Mr. Crumb says. He turns around and slams his door.

Relieved to be back on mission, I rush up the stairs two at a time and knock on her door with the backs of my knuckles.

"Lily, honey." I surprise myself with the term of endearment that just slips out. If I wasn't so worried about her, I'd be thinking about the way I'm hoping and wondering if she'll look at me again today like she used to.

From inside her apartment, I hear what sounds like a crash. I'm about to break down the door when it flies open, revealing Lily slightly hunched with her hair wrapped in a bun on the very top of her head. It appears alarmingly like a bird's nest, and I take in the sight before registering the rest of her ensemble: a black sweatshirt that reads *Tell it to the judge*, joggers (black, of course), and a look in her eye that immediately tells me what's wrong. She's sick.

"Stuffed up. Shivering. All of this!" she mutters, using

a hand to signal around her face. She reaches into her pocket and grabs a tissue.

Right at this moment, it occurs to me that I've never seen Lily sick. She's always been so formidable, unable to *not* be ready for battle. I hear her let out a little whimper—she's clearly not fully realizing who I am at this moment. Or she doesn't care because her defenses are down. Or perhaps she recognizes that I'm the closest thing to hope.

She turns from me without a word, her feet shuffling in slippers that are light pink and covered in chocolates. Of course they are. While I suspect that Lily thinks she's moving quickly away from me, it's really a pathetic shuffle. She stops halfway to her couch and looks longingly at the kitchen. If she were fully aware of my presence in her current state, I'd be embarrassed at how quickly I'm behind her, my hands hovering just beside her ribs in case she starts to sway.

"What do you need?" They're the only words that escape my mouth, though I could say more. While I wish her answer would be me, I mean more along the lines of medicine and picking up soup from the diner.

She makes a squeaking sound. Her little noises are quickly shattering my resolve not to pick her up and bring her to the couch myself. Her energy seems spent, the floor appears to be lava, and she can't seem to get away from the safety of where she stands.

As gently as I can, I put an arm around her shoulder and guide her toward the couch. I nearly forget to breathe when she places her head on my shoulder. But that isn't where she lands. Immediately, she shifts her face so it's turned toward my neck. She nuzzles against my skin. I tell myself she doesn't mean to be so vulnerable. The heat radiating from her tells me there's a fever involved, but I use the gesture as permission to scoop her up into my arms.

"Do you want the couch or your bed?" I whisper, not sure if her head is pounding.

She points to the couch, and I set her down as gently as possible. Lifting her head with the palm of my hand, I support her neck and shift a cushion underneath. Not good enough.

"Hold on," I mutter. As I move away, I keep my eyes on her until the last possible second, when my vision is cut off by the wall—you know, just architectural conventions separating me from her—and rush to her bedroom. It takes me a solid ten seconds to muster the courage to step over the threshold, but my woman is sick. She needs more than a couch cushion. Spotting the fluffy pillows on her bed paired with an eccentric quilt that I decidedly ignore, along with the lingering smell of what must be her body wash or perfume, I'm back by her side a few moments later.

"What are you doing?" Lily mumbles, her nose scrunched in pain.

"Taking care of you." Gently, I lift her head again to replace the pillow.

"This was my dream," she whispers.

I'm going to need more time to process those words. Hastily, I text Lucy and ask her to have an order of vegetable noodle soup ready. I send an SOS to Liam—the most solid guy I know, practically a fixture in Birch Borough, and someone I now consider a good friend—a request to grab some tissues, lozenges, and medicine from the general store. I also ask him to order a vat of ice cream from Bette's for me to pick up. I text Sparrow to tell her that I found Lily, she's sick, and I'm not leaving her. My phone pings with a reply immediately.

Sparrow: Thank you for taking care of her. She couldn't have anyone better.

My mind races. If I had to guess, this is the equivalent of having Sparrow's blessing. The phone pings again, and I scan the message before pausing to read it again.

Rafe: Just remember: Lily once told me I could change the ending. Rooting for you both.

I put the phone down, my hands shaking.

"Lily, honey," I begin, that word slipping again through my filter. "I need to pick up some things for you. Can you . . .?"

I'm cut off by another faint sound as she shifts to try to get more comfortable. Before I can think any more about it, I text Liam again to ask if he can bring everything here. I'll transfer money to him later. I tell him to get an extra ice cream for himself. With Lily in this state, there is no way I'm letting her out of my sight right now.

A few hours later, I think I'm wearing an actual hole in Lily's floor. There is at least some newly evident wear on her area rug. It's been hours since I first arrived. My t-shirt is wrinkled. I've called a local doctor, Sparrow and Rafe, and even put in a call to Gladys. Liam dropped off the items hours ago. God bless him. I hugged him from the relief of finally having something in my hands that may help her feel better.

After giving her a dose of medicine and pain reliever and making her a cup of tea to soothe her throat, Lily fell asleep again. I've been waiting for her to wake up. How have I kept myself entertained? I haven't. Books on her shelves that would normally be enjoyable to read? Lackluster. A whole library of Regency television shows, including multiple seasons of her favorite show, *The Man is a Rake*? Not today. Anything other than trying not to stare at Lily in an unsettling way while she rests? Unacceptable. The way her face looks like an angel's while she sleeps? Devastating.

Eventually, I flip through the pages of a newly released novel. But the quiet atmosphere causes my brain to wander, playing with an idea I've had for a while. I end up charting out the path to creating an LLC to provide pro bono or low-cost services in the area for local artists and musicians. When Rafe gets married, he won't need me quite as much for the next few months. Something about being near Lily makes me think of the future again. I find a notebook on the side table and a pencil with a chunky eraser that says *Write Me* and get to work. The pencil flies across the pages, and I realize I haven't created or dreamed like this in ages.

"Graham?"

Her whisper hits me right in my core. I look at Lily, immediately regretting that I was finally so focused on what I was doing that I missed the moment she opened her eyes. My pulse quickens, and I remember one very important truth: Lily only called me by my real name when we were together.

"How are you feeling?" I ask, tossing the items I've been using to the floor by my feet.

"Everything hurts," she admits.

My hands find her feet. They have been nestled under my thigh while she slept (her doing), and I rub them through her fuzzy socks.

"But better," she adds.

"I'm sorry." My words are quiet. The sentence feels like a loaded statement, full of everything we've yet to say to each other, but I think Lily might be too sick to notice.

She looks toward the table and the box of rosemary crackers precariously hanging near the edge closest to her. "Those are my favorite."

I nod.

"You got me my favorite crackers?" Lily is all practical, her voice void of emotion.

"I did."

"You're taking care of me."

"I am."

"Why?"

My hands pause. I look at her, caught up in the way her grey eyes expand their lavender edges as the fairy lights she has hung throughout her apartment illuminate them with hope.

"Because you needed me to."

I expect her to huff or give me a snarky quip, but she doesn't reply. After yesterday's kiss in the wildflower field, I'm not sure where we stand, and while I would love to say that we're past everything we've been through, I don't know if it's true. As much as I've wanted a different ending to our story, my mind doesn't let me forget that it's entirely possible Lily may bolt again. But I'm not a casual guy. I can't do short term. And with Lily, nothing short of forever will ever be enough.

"I told you that was my dream." Her eyes suddenly widen with the realization.

"You did."

"No plus-ones!" she blurts out.

"What do you mean?" With gentle pressure, my hands tighten around her shins in what is hopefully a comforting move. She curls deeper into the couch and stretches more of her legs onto me, so I think it must be.

"No plus-ones," she repeats.

"Does that mean I lose your game?" My breath hitches. The question hovers in the silent air for a few seconds. What I'm really asking her is if she wants to be here with me. Are we done pretending we'd rather fight than kiss each other whenever we'd like?

Her voice is soft, and her eyes are downcast when she replies, "I think you've already more than met anything I could ask of you."

"What do you mean?" I need her to explain. I don't want to leave anything in the dark between us.

She waves her hands to indicate the space between us. "Best man. Maid of honor. Who has time to add another human to that dynamic? At best, we'd dance with them. At worst, we'd leave them in the dust while we are celebrating our best friends."

I nod, a hint of a smile trembling at the edges of my lips. "So, I don't lose?"

"No." She shakes her head, all business. "You can't lose because the challenge is technically fulfilled. Isn't that how it goes? Best man, maid of honor. I mean, if you're single. You *are* still single, aren't you? Oh, I really should've asked you that yesterday . . ."

Lily's eyes finally lift, and the intensity in them causes what feels like a blush to creep up my neck.

"Jury is still out on that," I reply, and she gasps. I laugh and squeeze her foot. "Honey, you think I would kiss you like that if I wasn't free?"

Before she starts thinking that my rush to care for her today is just a way for me to cement myself more into her life, I hasten to add, "You don't need to decide our status right now."

Lifting herself briefly, she slumps back into the side of the couch, which is cradling her bones if the way she curls into it with a sigh is any indication.

"Graham, I need to tell you something." Her voice is soft again.

I shut my eyes and focus on my breathing, willing my body to relax no matter what she may say next.

"Wait—why are *you* sorry?"

So, she does remember the statement I was hoping she'd forget, even if I did say it within the last five minutes.

"I won't apologize for yesterday, if that's what you're asking." I rub the arches of her feet again, needing something to do with my hands. When I slow, she wiggles her feet as if she wants more of my touch but is unsure if she should ask for it. Our hesitant push and pull feels like a metaphor for what we've been to each other for the last two years.

"I didn't mean it," she whispers. "In LA. I didn't mean it. I was . . . scared."

I consider my words carefully before replying. "Love is scary, Lily. It's not a sure thing—clearly. But you have to commit to it. You have to lean into it despite the fear of the unknown. I respected what you wanted and stayed away when you told me this was a one-sided love in LA. I did what you told me to do when I moved to town. I loved you enough to be committed to your wishes even if there was no hope for us. I'm sorry if that made you feel that I didn't fight for you."

She clears her throat, the slow blink of her eyelids a sign that she won't be awake much longer. I feel an urge to get out everything I've wanted to say while I can. I open my mouth to speak again but am cut off from the intent by the crumbling of her smaller frame. Her strong demeanor has been brought down by a virus and honesty. Her eyes glisten with a sudden sheen. I see the tears pooling at the edges. One trails along the side of her cheek, gravity pulling it more quickly toward the crack in the couch cushions from the angle of her face against it.

No response feels worthy of the vulnerability she is allowing me to see without saying a word. Instead, I grip the tops of her shins and massage them gently, hopefully showing her that I hear her. I'm here for her. The rise and fall of her chest while she breathes is as when someone cries, the silent kind until her breath hitches involuntarily. Unable to stop myself, I lean forward, sliding my hands underneath her shoulder blades to scoop her up.

Without hesitation, she nuzzles into my neck and shifts to wrap her arms around me. I lean back against the couch. She curls up with her face close to my heart, her ribcage supported by my arm on one side while the other wraps around the side of her face, my fingertips caressing the edge of her hair. Her cheekbone presses into my palm. I want to memorize the ridge of it and the softness of her skin.

Knowing her head hurts, I start to massage the back of her neck. An energy pulses through me. If I don't move, I fear I'll crack fully. The damp flood of tears through my new t-shirt and her sniffles tell me that she's doing it enough for the both of us right now. There are two parts to Lily's mind that I've observed—the one she shares with others and the one she only shares with me when she feels safe. The part she shares when her defenses have been disarmed. It seems as if she has to fight with herself before she lets herself be free. Lately, I've gotten a glimpse of how she could love me again. I remember how she liked to be held when she worried about leaving LA and felt lost. At the time, she told me she felt secure in my arms. I can only hope she still feels the same.

Only when she's sound asleep, her breathing soft, her body flush against mine, do I let myself inhale deeply. The warmth of her wraps around me. It reaches the places of my heart I forgot had grown cold. Without her, it seems as if I don't just forget how to make a fire. I forget that the flame exists at all.

Chapter Twenty-Two

Lily

I awaken to the sound of soft piano music and the smell of a fresh meadow. My eyes flutter against my closed lids. It's so serene that I would think it was a dream. It hits me that, for only the second time in two years, I didn't dream of Graham while I slept.

When I shift over, despite the dull ache in my head, I realize that I didn't dream of him because I didn't need to. He's beside me again, and I marvel that the only other time he has escaped my dreams was the night he protected me from the storm by staying with me until it passed. Here he is, caring for me again. I'm still too weak to get up, so I allow myself a moment to take all of him in as he rests at the end of my couch, my feet stretched across his lap. If I had to guess, as the subtle glow of light frames the edges of my room-darkening curtains, it's dawn.

Graham's hair is slightly mussed, like he couldn't help but run his fingers through it. His head leans back, angled toward me. His brow is relaxed with not a hint of the angst I've seen on him lately. His forearms are exposed, lengthening from under his now-wrinkled navy t-shirt.

In the dim light, I take the opportunity to study him. My eyes catch on each handsome feature of his face. I trace the full lips that kissed me less than thirty-six hours ago and memorize each line of the hands that have held and cared for me so well. There is a hint of a vegetable soup stain across the top of his chest. I flung my spoon toward him (truly on accident—this time), and the remnants are still evident, as if even my soup just wanted to be closer to him. I honestly don't blame it.

Graham is exceptional. I've never met a man who's just so . . . sure and steadfast. He never wavers and doesn't make anyone feel less about themselves. He's the type of man who—if you have him—makes you want to explain to the world that you know he's too good to be true while also assuring them that he is everything he seems to be and more.

The only time I've seen his steady demeanor nearly crack was at the Regency Ball. The sight almost broke my heart all over again. I've been so unclear with my intentions. Sparrow tried to tell me. Even as he has existed around me and beside me these past several months, I feel so gutted that I've lost even more time with him. He has been right next to me, but because of my own pain, I've kept him at a distance.

While I'm praying that he doesn't catch whichever virus I have, I reach over and tenderly wrap a hand around his strong forearm. There is just enough light peeking through to allow me to keep studying him and remember the things that make him so uniquely . . . him. His inquisitive mind plays out in the lines on his forehead and between his brows. His determination for justice presents itself in the clenching of his jaw. His kindness lives in his smile. His passion and love for me echo on his lips, his adoration and devotion lingering in his eyes. I've seen it all before, and yet, it feels so new.

The haze of sickness is still lingering at the edges of my fuzzy brain. My strength feels like it has been taken and exchanged for crystal-clear clarity. Perhaps for the first time, I think I could settle into this kind of love. Loving Graham wouldn't lead me to become less of myself. He may soften my edges, but he also strengthens my spirit. With him, I believe I could finally allow myself to relax and rest, holding onto the man I've wanted all along. I don't know why we sometimes forbid ourselves from the very things we most desire. Against all reasoning, we talk ourselves out of love. Or worse, we tell ourselves the lie that we don't deserve it, convincing ourselves falsely that there's something about us that will be better off by pushing love away before it pushes us to the end of ourselves.

Graham is all elegance and confidence, the perfect combination of intensity meeting restrained passion . . . except when he happens to let out that passion with me. It's no mystery why Birch Borough has been slowly falling in love with him—why I'm in love with him. I don't know how I ever managed to stay away from him for this long.

If I had known all it would take for me to finally recognize what my heart desires was to fall ill and allow him to take care of me, I would've hung out with the kids in town more often. Distributing residual Easter bunnies to the germ-infested daycare the other day is most likely where I caught the bug.

The congestion in my head and the urge to cough remind me that I'm still sick. As I shift a bit on the couch cushion, I realize how much my bones and joints are protesting from a day of being sick. It's unfortunate to be stuck inside since we're knee-deep in late spring, and the weather is lovely.

I feel my latent aggression looming as I contemplate what comes next. Just because I know I can love Graham again doesn't take that part of me away. If anything, I'm more determined to use the angst deep within me to finally fight for the good things. For the right things. To fight for him.

My uncomfortable movements alert him that I'm awake. He sits up, pushing the heels of his hands into his eyes and yawning in a way that I shouldn't find as adorable as I do.

"Sorry, honey," he says in a sleepy voice. His piercing eyes meet mine in the inky light. "Do you need anything? How do you feel?"

Lord, help me. I am melting.

His hand moves across my shin, gently giving it a press. He seems unable to keep himself from showering me with affection now that we have a new memory of words spoken between us that are for our good and not our demise. I grin even as shyness creeps in and causes more of a blush to creep into my cheeks than usual.

"I feel like a train ran over me and then decided it was going the wrong direction and ran over me again," I say in reply to his question.

He doesn't flinch at my response. "I'll get the pain reliever."

Before he's able to move, his phone rings. I nod for him

to get it and reach behind me to switch on the lamp. The sudden flood of light causes me to wince.

"Hey, Mom," Graham says as a smile breaks across his face.

"Hey, S'mores," she replies.

In a panicked rush, Graham tries to take it off speakerphone, but he isn't fast enough. He's *so* going to pay for this.

"S'mores," I whisper with a giddy surge.

"You're on speakerphone, Mom," he says with a tight voice, his cheeks turning a delicious shade of pink.

"I'm so sorry, S'm—I mean to say, *Graham*." Her voice is so kind and warm that it triggers a sense of homesickness within me immediately.

"When I was a kid," Graham starts to explain the nickname in a quiet tone, the edge of his face shifting in my direction, "I loved s'mores so much that my mom thought her term of endearment was amusing since my name is paired with the crackers they're eaten on."

"He was all sweetness and melted chocolate," his mom says affectionately from the speaker.

I watch with delight as he hangs his head in defeat, a fresh rush of redness creeping down his neck. I've never seen him so embarrassed, and it's doing weird things to my head and my stomach. Must be the sickness. Still, I can't help but let out a delighted little laugh. His admission gives me so much ammunition.

"Who's with you, love?"

"Oh, my . . ." His eyes widen as he searches my face. "Um. Just a . . . someone special." He gives the slightest shake of his head, clearly frustrated to be caught off guard.

I know that his mom definitely knows who I am and how he feels—or rather *felt*—about me.

"Someone special? Graham David Winnings."

Silently, I mouth his full name and start to ponder where I want to tattoo his name on some weird part of my body just to embarrass him even more.

"I'm with Lily, Mom," he states with more assurance this time.

I twirl the end of my unkempt ponytail between my hands. Her reply is swift.

"Lily. *The* Lily?"

The way Graham stares at me makes me at an uncommon loss for words. I open my mouth to reply but can't seem to speak. He switches it off speakerphone and gives me a slight nod before standing and pacing beside the couch.

"So, Mom, are you okay? What's going on? You're off speakerphone, by the way."

A tightness works through my chest.

"Dinner." His tone is incredulous as he peeks over at me. "Next Thursday." His hand is now rubbing the back of his neck. "Yes, I know it's soon, but with the wedding . . ." She cuts him off, and what ensues is a bunch of humming and assuring her before his eyes fully catch mine. "Okay, I'll ask her."

He clicks the phone over. "Mom, you're on speaker again."

Her voice comes through, pleasant and friendly. "Oh, good. Lily, I would love for you to attend Graham's birthday dinner. Would you want to come?"

I just took a poorly timed sip of my water. I sputter as it

chokes me. Peeking up at Graham, I see the tightness in his jaw, the subtle shifting of his head, and the light tapping of his foot. I don't want to make things unnecessarily harder for him anymore . . . unless it's clearly just for fun.

"I'll be there," I cough out.

"She'll be there," he repeats firmly, a hint of a smile teasing his mouth into what looks like relief.

The fact that he was worried about me refusing is enough to make me want to do better at putting action to my affection. He takes the phone off speaker again. I don't miss the tensing of his shoulders as he sits beside me, reaching for my legs without making eye contact. His hands are warm and send comfort throughout my limbs. Who knew a tiny movement could do so much?

He looks like a throwback to the high school guys I would crush on in middle school. I use the fact that he can't move much once I've trapped him with my legs across his lap to commit him to memory. And it makes me wish that we had known each other back then. High school sweethearts sound nice, but that's not what we were. I don't even know what we've been.

Still, seeing his full and brilliant smile break through as he chats with his mom, I grin. His happiness is my happiness, and his sadness is too. That realization sends me reeling.

"Yeah, Mom. She's worth it."

Graham's voice pulls me back into my living room. The intensity of his gaze in my direction leaves no question that he is referring to me. He says it even when he knows what it means to wait for someone to love him back and be disappointed. They hang up, and he stands, already moving toward the hall closet.

"Pain medicine," he says over his shoulder. "I didn't forget. And as for my birthday dinner, Mom won't take no for an answer."

I nearly laugh at the ridiculousness of it all, unable to contain my joy that I have my person back. It's one thing to have a best friend who handles your havoc, but it's another thing when it's a person you want to spend your life with. It means so much more when it's the one you want to exchange vows with, and you want to commit every moment to ensuring they're beside you for as long as earthly possible.

Oh, my lands. I want to spend the rest of my life with Graham.

The realization hits me hard as Graham walks back from the hallway. For the first time, I notice his pants, a pair of grey joggers that fit tightly across his muscular legs and stop deliciously at the bend of his ankle. I didn't know I was attracted to ankles until right at this moment. The memory of my discomfort when he wore sweatpants before creeps into my brain. There is something about the end of his pants meeting his ankles and bare feet that causes my lingering fever to climb much more quickly than medically possible.

"I need you to cover your feet." I sit up and wince, shielding my eyes from that area of his body. "And your ankles too."

I'm looking at the wall, but I can see him slowing his stride, those bare feet creeping closer.

"Lily, I hear you say a lot of things, and mostly, I understand your language, but this one has me stumped."

Cautiously, he moves closer to the couch, medicine in hand. The sight of his approaching feet again sends another flash of heat blazing through me. I'm actually sweating now.

"Don't come any closer! Put on some socks!" I scrunch my nose.

"Do I smell? I can't smell. My feet never smell," he states, as if he's not human.

"Ha!" I laugh in an unhinged way then clasp my hand over my mouth as I remember that my throat still feels sore. I also continue to have an unfortunately clear view of his ankles.

Let the record show that I will forever blame the fever for my reaction. I feel my nose scrunch again as I fan my face, silently willing him to sit so those ankles and feet will be out of sight. I also miss touching him, and I'll be able to reach him from the couch cushion.

"Lils, are you attracted to my feet?" Finally, Graham sits. I ignore his question, thinking I'm out of danger, until I look over to see his foot propped up on his knee, like a sitting figure four.

"Not your feet!"

His smirk is maddening. He actually has the audacity to smirk at me in my distress.

"Your ankles," I mutter.

"My what?"

"You heard me."

He laughs, a rich reverberation filled with depth and a hint of spice—basically, a chai latte wrapped up in a sound. "Of all the things, this is what's doing it for you?"

Proudly, he assesses his shapely ankles. The medicine is held out to me in his palm.

"It's the fever," I protest, greedily grabbing the pills from his hand and taking them with the huge glass of water he put beside me. I didn't even think I owned a cup this big, but he has managed to find a vat to hold water in. I'll never be dehydrated again. "So, what happens now?"

Looking at me thoughtfully, he runs a hand through his hair. The top is so startlingly unruly for him that I feel proud, knowing what it means for me to see him like this, slightly unpolished and disheveled.

"And where did you get those pants?" I pause to breathe because I'm still stuck at the mental bus stop of inexplicable feelings. I've seen him in something other than dress pants only three times before today. *Three!* Once when we went to the carnival in our pre-challenge era (what I'm affectionately calling the time before he showed up in Birch Borough), once for the storm in our modern-day challenge era, and once at In the Ring. This makes the fourth.

"I own them," he states without explanation. "And I think that what happens next is that we are . . ." he trails off, reaching for my hand. We meet in the middle of the couch, my fingers intertwining with his, my palm vibrating with the thrill of it. "This. I think that we are *this*."

Nodding, I lean my head onto the cushion, focusing on the warmth I find in his eyes. We're *this*. And I want this.

"I also think . . ." he begins, reaching for the remote. Turning on the TV, I watch in delight as he navigates to my recorded programming and clicks on my favorite show. "I'll make you more soup when you want it. I'll get you hot tea and cold ice cream, depending on what you want to soothe your throat, and I'll sit here and suffer through this mayhem." Though he says it with a straight face, his eyes narrow as he scrolls down the list of episodes as if he's searching for a specific one.

Satisfied with a selection, he leans back, his frame melting into the back of the couch, his hand still in mine. The theme music for *The Man is a Rake* plays through the air, and tears brim in my eyes.

"You watch this show?"

He swings his head toward me dramatically. "I don't know what you mean."

"You picked an episode," I insist, using our clasped hands to point toward the screen. "You know this show."

"I plead the fifth."

"You picked the one with the rake who reformed and left city life to go after his girl in a small town. It's us! You. Watch. This. Show."

He laughs, its perfection coating the air between me and catapulting a smile onto my face. Being sick bites, but being sick with Graham? Not bad at all.

"Oh, also, I forgot to ask," I continue. "Are you going to be sick because you've been with me all day? Do you have to leave?"

In another dramatic gesture (which he seems to be full of today, and I'm enjoying way too much), he grunts and reaches for my legs as if they're too far out of reach. Catching the hint, I scoot closer and swing my legs up until they are tucked across his lap. My head rests on his shoulder.

His strong hands—their heat creeping through my own pair of sweats—are the best warmers I've ever experienced in my life. Instantly, I settle in, nestling into his neck.

"I think that's as close as you can get," he says with a smile in his voice.

"I'm testing that theory," I reply, my eyelids already heavy with sleep.

He answers my earlier question. "No, I won't get sick because I took a bunch of immunity shots already, and I don't think my body will let me go down. I want to take care of you too much."

"That's sweet," I manage. His kindness finally settles into my system, allowing me to fully feel his presence as our synchronized heartbeats get reacquainted with each other.

His voice continues softly in my ear. "And no. I don't want to leave. If I had my way, I'd never be out of your sight again—even if my ankles must be."

I grin and curl my free arm up to my chest, the other still safely entwined with his. The sounds of the TV dim, even as the beat of his heart becomes stronger. I feel him nuzzle into the top of my head, his lips lightly kissing my forehead.

"Sleep, honey. I've got you."

And I know he does. It's why I know that, even in my fevered state, there will be no nightmares tonight.

Chapter Twenty-Three

Lily

Chamomile is everywhere. My favorite flower sticks out in cheerful clusters all around me. I've gathered some into vases and have set them out around the bakery and café. This morning, I noticed bunches and bunches of the pretty flowers surrounding the café steps. Seeing them makes my heart happy. I wear a ton of black clothes, and there's something so satisfying about chamomile's tiny, creamy, white petals sticking out of a bouquet in my arms. I also love the smell, earthy with a hint of sweetness. Currently, I wish it was in tea form because I could use a bit of a sedative right now as my thoughts are consumed with everything Graham.

It turns out that love does not always make you immune from viruses. Graham started to feel sick the next day. Thankfully, Sparrow and Rafe have been in town, and we're still a couple of weeks away from the wedding. It was easier for me to get better and head to his place to bring him care packages, sitting with him while we binged our favorite show. (I say *ours* because, eventually, he admitted in his fevered state that he has been watching it religiously since we met.)

As I wander around the café, arranging the freshly picked flower stems, the overhead bell rings. I look up with a smile that instantly freezes. Graham is here. His eyes are wide, tentatively taking everything in. While he has been here before for the cake tasting and once to rescue me from a runaway espresso machine, this is the first time he has come in without an invitation.

"You're here."

He nods, and the entire space seems to go quiet. Sparrow rushes in from the back kitchen with a tray full of macarons. She pushes them toward me, trying to give me something to hold before she thinks better of it. I know I should be mentally prepared for this monumental moment, but I'm not.

"Don't want you to jump him," she mutters before placing them on the counter. "Graham, welcome! It's so good to have you here, and I'm glad you're feeling better. Have a seat at the counter. Rafe usually sits over there," she continues cheerily, pointing to the soft white countertops and an empty stool.

He moves toward them.

"Coffee?" she asks sweetly.

Meanwhile, I stand like a statue in the middle of the floor, my mind positively combusting at the idea of Graham willfully entering this place and seeing it for what it is. I wonder what he thinks. Is it less glamorous than he imagined, now that he's about to really take it in, and we're not at odds? Or is he glad he managed to avoid the woman with her feet currently frozen to the floor in her natural habitat for so long?

As these thoughts race wildly through my mind, I spot a

fresh bunch of chamomile sticking out of his suit jacket's pocket. My eyes light up and meet his, and it is then that I see a grin deep enough to reveal a dimple gracing his mouth.

As his voice blurs under the pulse in my ears, I think Graham agrees to have a coffee.

"Lily, will you make a cappuccino? For the man who cared for you while you were on death's door last week? Please?" Sparrow is pinching my side and shoving a cup into my hands.

If I wasn't having so much trouble with the degree Graham has caught me off guard, the comical scene would make me laugh.

"Chamomile," I declare, finally coming to my senses and doing my best not to notice the tips of his hair sticking up everywhere after he must've just run his hand through it. My heart does the thing where it starts to make a scene within my ribs, and I have to will it to calm the heck down.

Miraculously, I make a cappuccino on sheer willpower and manage to place it on a saucer and in front of him with a hand that is only slightly shaky. Per usual, he's wearing a button-up shirt tucked into suit pants. If I could see his feet under the counter, I know they would be dressed in Italian leather shoes. I know his suits cost more than my monthly rent, and as much as I want to hate the expenditure, I can't. I don't, and I can admit that. I love the stylish way Graham dresses.

When neither of us speaks, Sparrow breaks the silence with her joyful chatter. "Graham, we found all these lovely bunches of chamomile flowers growing outside the shop door this morning. Lily was thrilled, of course . . . well, not of course." She pauses awkwardly.

"It is her favorite after all."

He says it so casually, not at all like the little comment just broke through to another part of my heart that has been boarded up over the last two years. I feel the countdown clock to my implosion from his nearness begin in my bones.

"It is," Sparrow exclaims, a hint of delight in her tone.

No doubt, this scenario is more confusing to her than enlightening. Inwardly, I vow to do something extremely nice for her soon to show her how much I appreciate her friendship. No one handles my messy, roller-coaster emotional situations with such grace and dignity.

"It's a bunny." Graham stares at the top of his cappuccino.

I nod. My latte-slash-cappuccino art has finally progressed from unintentionally indecent figures and blobs to identifiable objects.

"I thought you banned them from your existence until next Easter."

"Oh, I did. But I'm not the one drinking it."

"This is good," Graham says, taking a sip.

The deliciousness of the moment unfolding before me creeps into my consciousness. I would guess he means the coffee, but from the intensity of his gaze, the ceramic cup tiny in his muscular hand, I can't be sure.

The bet I challenged him to weeks ago hovers in my mind. I don't want to call an abrupt end to our game for fear of what it could mean for our budding relationship renewal. I like challenging Graham and seeing how far he'll let me push the limits of his dignified, steady demeanor. Making him squirm while he rises to the occasion is immensely attractive. Will our feelings for each other fade without a circumstantial tie to pull us closer together?

As we grow closer to the date that we will officially be beyond our friends' wedding, this is *something* that has been ours, and I don't want to let it go. And because I'm the queen of awkwardness when it comes to him, I yell the first thing that comes to my mind.

"Eclairs!"

Sparrow looks at me like I've lost it, and Graham raises a single eyebrow. "You're making them?" he asks with more diplomacy and dignity than I expected, to be honest.

"Yes! Right now. Sparrow, are you okay here?"

"Yes, of course," she replies hesitantly. "I'm just going to finalize the order for the Rochester wedding. I'm good here. Do you want me to put those in water?" She motions toward the bouquet of chamomile that threatens to be squished if I hold it any longer.

I forgot about the handful before I got into this stare down.

"Yes, please. When I'm done . . . we feast on the eclairs!"

We just added the pastries to the menu, but that's beside the point as I rush to the kitchen. I'm doing my best not to think about what it would mean for Graham to stay in Birch Borough. If his future isn't with me, I don't know how I'll move through it. My nature, the way I process feelings and words, makes me want to run to the mountains. And I don't even hike. I'm considering taking it up—much like I did boxing—when Graham reaches for my hand as I pull out a set of pans. Gently, he lifts it to his lips. Just when I think he's going to kiss the back of it, he turns my palm so his mouth meets the base of my wrist, his lips warm and soft against my skin. I clear my throat, a smile blossoming on my face as he grabs my apron.

We settle in. He unbuttons his shirt, rolling up his sleeves to his elbows. I act as though I'm immune to the sight of it, even while my throat constricts with awareness of him. Even when we were at odds with each other, he never raised his voice to me. He has never called me a name or made me feel like I'm an unacceptable human. He's always steady, cautious, and curious, qualities which make it all so much more puzzling that he wants to be with me.

At times, I know I irk him. I poke when I shouldn't and prod when I need to quit. I give sharp retorts and like to be ornery. I wear black to his mostly blue. I've always had what I needed, and he's been working since the day he could—even before it was fully legal. He calls his mother every morning, and I'm lucky if I get to check in with my parents once a quarter. It's honestly a bit of a miracle that we ignited with the sparks we had. But ignite like a blazing fire, we did.

"So, are we still challenging each other?"

I see the tentative expression in his eyes. The question hovers between us of whether I still want him out of this town or if he is welcome to stay. I'm not confused about how I feel about him, but I'm still unsure that I'll be able to love him fully and in the way he deserves.

"We're not past the wedding yet," I reply shakily. "Perhaps we can just see . . .?" Wildly, I motion toward the ingredients I've been throwing in a pile on the counter between us.

The smirk playing on his face transforms into a gorgeous smile. "Then let's do this," he declares, all assuredness and joy.

His eyes flash with a bit of heat meeting amusement. Looking at him, I feel growing excitement for a game we haven't even begun. He looks at me, not a hint of anything besides happiness on his face. He doesn't act like our arrangement is absurd or abnormal. That's one of the things I've always loved best about him. Graham never attempts to talk me out of my antics. He just goes along with them. He'll call me out on my crap and tell me if he doesn't want to do something, but he is always so clear about his boundaries that I can't ever get mad.

Anticipation flows through my system. I'm like a wheel of possibilities, and a sudden realization hits me. Graham is the one who elevates what I think I'm capable of. He makes me want to do irrational things like change the shape of my eyebrows or wear something that's not . . . black. Ha! Joke's on him. I'll always want to wear black. I allow only colored accessories and one colored clothing item a month into my wardrobe.

Graham turns to face me and slowly takes off his watch. At this, the blush surges on my cheeks. Graham is clocking every part of my face right now, his eyes trailing the path of embarrassment taking over. The heat of his stare isn't helping. His expression is subtle—and if I remember him at all, with a hint of something like desire at the edges—which triggers memories of us standing in the wildflower field . . . and of him taking care of me . . . and of me taking care of him . . . and of the chamomile sprig this morning. I try to quiet the war within me and attempt to quell the trigger response that itches to categorize him as a nemesis all in a vain effort to fortify my heart. All I can think about is the smear of chocolate icing that hovered at the corner of his mouth at the cake tasting . . . and the feeling of his soothing hands on my shins . . . and those scandalous ankles.

"By the way, tomorrow night is my birthday dinner. It's with my mom and uncle."

I hear the hesitancy in Graham's tone, and I ache to go back to the days when there wasn't ever a hint of it. "I'll be there."

He nods, his shoulders shifting down a touch despite my reassurance. As I will myself to maintain eye contact, the challenge in his eyes mixes with a hint of something like skepticism for what I'll say next. I hate that he still has a reason to doubt me.

"One day, I hope you'll call me Graham again," he says as he studies the butter I'll need to melt over the stove, even though I'm already melted from the blue in his eyes that I want to get lost in. "Because I think that's how you feel about me. And I think you know how I feel about you."

My breath catches as he walks backward with a smile, his head tilted away as he rearranges the bunch of chamomile in his suit pocket.

"Oh, and even if you're tempted to, don't ever go easy on me, Lily."

With that, he smoothly turns on his heels toward the front of the store and walks through the swinging door. I peek through the tiny round window, and my mouth falls open as he has the audacity to start laughing with Sparrow. A *pain au chocolat* is handed to him on a plate with a smile. A few minutes later, he's behind the counter, washing his hands. In disbelief, I watch him put macarons into the case, each one looking tiny in his large hands as he gently stacks them on their trays, his smile strong and bold. He appears far too comfortable, and as much as I enjoy the sight of it, the pain of panic grips me. In a short span, I went from wanting to drive him out of town to wanting to do whatever it takes to keep him here. And I may know just how to do it.

Another point: Graham.

Chapter Twenty-Four

Graham

I think you should know this is more than alarming," Lily whispers. Her eyes catch on the view as we stand outside the old North Church in Portsmouth.

An art crawl is being featured along the streets tonight. Lily has always said she wants to fill her life with more art, so I thought this would be a great way to do it. My mom loves art as well, so it is a win-win.

"Meeting my family or being with me?" I look down at her with a smile.

"Neither. I am talking about the sheer number of people I'm seeing right now who should be on a sitcom and not casually walking through their lives as if they don't belong on television."

We took the day to explore the quaint neighboring city of Portsmouth. All afternoon, I've watched Lily's blonde ponytail swaying through antiquated streets, coffee shops, and tiny shops filled with trinkets. She stops every few feet to look around her, like this old city is somehow new.

Now, we're lingering under a tree with new green leaves,

waiting for my mom and uncle to meet us for my birthday dinner. The sound of a violin and a trumpet mix somewhere from opposite directions. The music, the fresh air, the faint scent of the ocean on the breeze—all of it reminds me why I wanted to move here in the first place. There's magic in the small towns scattered across New England. It feels as if I've come home but discovered something I never have before in the process.

"Thank you for being here," I say, cataloging in memory the glow of Lily's hair in the just-setting sunlight. Even though I know to expect it now, I'm still surprised every time I see it. I reach out to her, and she wraps her arm around mine. I'm still getting used to the fact that I can touch her and hold her and not have her respond with hostility.

"You're welcome," she replies softly. Tonight, she is wearing a black, short-sleeved dress that whispers deliciously around her frame. It's the stuff of madness, with what I think is called eyelet lace and satin ribbon accentuating her waist. Despite the extravagance, the dress is also so very her, clothing the color of a silky raven mixed with elegance and femininity. She's the element of dreams, this one.

True to her word, Lily agreed to meet my mom for the first time tonight—at my birthday celebration, of all days. We're moving from kissing again to sharing birthdays. While it could be uncomfortable, given our fragile state as we move back into the realm of a romantic relationship, it feels like Lily should've always been by my side. Meeting my family is part of the script of our love story, and we finally get to move to the next scene together.

"You'll get used to them," I continue. "You're used to dealing with all sorts of people at the café. If you can handle customer service, you can handle my mom. Fair warning: She's going to want to adopt you."

She looks at me as if she doesn't quite believe what I'm saying but truly wants to. She smirks. "So, are you issuing any other challenges this evening?"

I say the first thing that comes to mind. "I challenge you to never leave my side."

"For the duration of this dinner, you mean?" She swallows.

I decide to let her think that was my intention when, in truth, I meant forever. I quickly think to reassure her. "It's just my mom and my uncle tonight, the two most important people in my life—not including Rafe, of course."

Until you, I almost add. She hums her acknowledgment, the tone indicating that she's aware of the addendums made since we were officially together. Because the most important person in my life used to be her. I want her to know she holds that place in my heart again, especially because it's my birthday. I'm not sure if Lily remembers that I once told her my wish was for her to be with me for every birthday. It feels monumentally important that she's with me today. It's the first time my wish has come true.

I'm not a sentimental guy, except toward the people I love, but my birthday is another reminder of why I'm committed to being a man of my word and being known as a good man. While it's wonderful to have the people we love show up at the major moments of our lives, we also feel and sense the ones who should be there but aren't. That's a different kind of grief. Every year, I'm grateful for my mom while also seeing a missing space that should be reserved for my dad, which has been empty since I was eleven years old. Having Lily tucked into my side feels like someone long absent from my life making their way back to me.

"S'mores!"

I hear her joyful voice before I see her. I cringe a bit at the nickname, but I can't be too upset when I see Lily's delight. Turning, I see my mother and my uncle descending upon us, my mother's eyes already lighting up at the sight of Lily. My mother is hesitant—cautious, even—but the joy in her face shines brighter than her hesitation. My uncle is already looking at us like we're one of his construction projects. He's searching for the soft spots that could need some reinforcement. He knows what happened between Lily and me two years ago, so it's only natural for him to be surprised that we're here together.

I take charge of the introductions right away. "Lily, this is my Uncle John and my mother, Wendy."

"So nice to meet you, Uncle John, and you, Mrs. Winnings," Lily says with a sincere grin, stretching out her slender hand. She does a double-take and studies my mom's face, taking in the long, grey braid draping over her shoulder. "Wait—*you're* Mrs. Winnings?"

"Oh, please, call me Wendy," my mother protests immediately with a soft smile.

"You know each other?" I ask as a fresh layer of nerves works through my system.

"Uhh—yes," Lily starts. "Well, she's been to the café. You're the woman who told Rafe to ask Sparrow out last year, aren't you?"

"Good memory. Great croissants, by the way. But I think you'd be more interested to know that I especially loved the *pain au chocolat*."

"Thank you! They happen to be my favorite as well." Lily's full smile breaks out across her face.

Five seconds later, her eyes take on a devious sheen, and my stomach drops at the sight. Knowing Lily, she came ready to play and find any opportunity to tease me. Meanwhile, I'm still reeling from the discovery that the two most important women in my life have any sort of history at all.

Lily flashes me a pointed glance. "Wendy, I have it on good authority that you have some incriminating evidence on this gentleman beside me. I'm going to need to hear it as soon as possible. Never mind that he's your son. And Uncle John, if you have anything to add, please do. It's my mission in life to take him down a few pegs."

My mother has the audacity to look delighted. She laughs. "Well, what would you like to know, dear? I can tell you a story about the time, as a little boy, when he walked around in nothing but his tiny white underwear and cowboy boots. Or perhaps you could use the story about his unusual habit of lining up his stuffed animals and toy soldiers like they were in a court of law and he was the judge?"

I'm already mortified, my mouth dropping open at how quickly I was demolished by my own dear mother. Lily's laughter is loud and unrestrained.

"I already love this woman," she says, wiping the edges of her eyes. "You're my hero." She turns from me to face my mother, and I can't argue with that statement.

"Mine too." I give my mother a look, and the look she sends me in reply lets me know she's happy, which is good. I must be showing signs of healing, because she's not looking at me with as much worry as she's shown the last two years.

I try to hustle our little group along before my mother blurts out any more embarrassing childhood anecdotes. "Well, let's go. I made reservations."

We walk around the corner toward the outskirts of the city, where a charming row of shops and restaurants hugs the edge of the port. The view is a glimpse of a calm bit of ocean meeting a brigade of small boats. A bridge rises in the distance.

The evening is unseasonably warm for late spring. My mother and Lily brought jackets, so we agree to sit outside, the setting sun pleasant as the hostess leads us to our seats.

We peruse the menu and place our orders. I wrap my arm around Lily and revel in the way she responds by leaning into my side. I realize how much more relaxed she is outside of Birch Borough, an attractive glimmer of freedom and fun gracing her face, her laughter quick, and her hand warm intertwined with mine. While I wish things were the same all the time, it's nice to get a glimpse of this hope of what we could be again.

"Okay, please do tell me more." Lily leans toward my mother, her head propped on one hand as if she has all the time in the world to uncover incriminating evidence that I'm a flawed human being as well.

"Well, I'll just say, dear, that Graham has certainly had his moments. But he's always lived with such conviction, intent on making the best choices. He's made mistakes, to be sure, but when he put his mind to something as a young man, there was no way you would ever talk him out of his resolve. His stubbornness was almost to a fault."

Lily stiffens beside me. When a faint memory of telling her, "I choose you," on a studio tour in Burbank surfaces, I want to hide under the table. I'm not ashamed of saying the words, but I am getting tired of the looks of pity on people's faces, particularly people who know our history. Looks like the one I'm currently getting from my uncle.

"Yes, he is very determined," Lily affirms. There's no need to insert an addendum, but she does. "From what I know of him, of course." Changing the subject quickly, she inclines toward my uncle. "How about you, Uncle John? Or should I not call you that?"

He grunts in agreement, as is typical for him, but a smile plays at the edge of his mouth, which is noticeably contrary to his usually gruff nature. Of course Uncle John would like her immediately.

"This one here," he starts, pointing to me with a look that makes me dread what he is going to say, "well, he used to want to go feed the ducks on the little pond behind my house. He wanted to feed them bread and all that before we knew it wasn't healthy for them."

I grip the edge of the table, my knuckles whitening, but I realize it will be of no use to interject. In fact, any reaction from me will probably only add to Lily's interest.

"Anyway, Graham went to feed them and saw one he really liked. He went to go after it—only it wasn't a duck. It was a swan."

"Wait," Lily says with such energy it's like someone just told her she has a chance to win the lottery. "Oh, please, please, please tell me it's a Jess from *Gilmore Girls* situation, and the mama swan attacked him."

My uncle laughs. He *laughs*. "I don't know who Jess is or

whatever you just said, but the thing attacked him and got him good. I'm pretty sure he still has a scar somewhere behind—"

Desperately, I interrupt. "I got attacked by a swan. End of story. And just like Jess, I stand by my claim that the swan was at fault for false representation!"

"This is too good!" Lily practically squeals, her hand slapping the table with gumption.

My face flaming, I will it to calm down as I also catalog the delightful sound of Lily's continuous giggle. To get her to laugh, apparently, all I have to do is keep feeding her stories that cast me in a less-than-stellar light. Noted.

"So, *Graham*," my mother emphasizes the word, thankfully not using my nickname again. "Have you found a house yet?"

And this is the moment where my water is suddenly the only thing I can focus on.

"What does she mean . . .?" Lily trails off.

"He's looking for a new house so Wendy can take the apartment he's got," my uncle unhelpfully informs her.

"Oh, yes—I—of course," Lily responds, although she had no idea this was my plan.

Two weeks ago, at a questionable hour of the morning, amidst the blurry haze of yet-to-be-had caffeine, I made a deal with my mother for her to move into my apartment in Birch Borough while I find another place to live. Moving to another town may have been mentioned. Unsure of what the future held for Lily and me, my apartment in Birch Borough suddenly felt like too much. I knew my mother would appreciate it, and it's a good place for her to be in this phase of her life.

Oblivious to our discomfort, my mother continues, "And the work? Did you set up the LLC for your new legal firm?"

Lily inhales sharply. My heart sinks. I should've prepared my mother for this evening, but I was so consumed with spending the day with Lily, so tentatively hopeful about what has been unfolding between us, that I didn't want to scare her away. It may be too late.

"New legal firm?" Lily breathes out.

My mother's expression of confusion is enough to nearly break me. It's not her fault I've had trouble finding the words.

"Uhh—yes," I begin in reply to her, "I did."

"Legal firm?" Lily says again.

"Pro bono work in the intellectual property law field. I want to help other artists in the area—or rather, everywhere, truly."

"But you're moving?"

"Yes."

At this, Lily grabs the edge of my suit jacket and pulls me up. "Will you excuse us?"

"Why, of course, dear . . ." my mother begins, but it's too late. Lily is already dragging me away toward a secluded corner of the patio. We need to get better at not abandoning tables and finding places to discuss important matters. First, the diner, and now this.

"What is happening?" Lily asks, her eyes wide and brow furrowed.

My hand is running through my hair before I can help it. Now, I recognize that it looks like I've been withholding information from her when, truthfully, I was only trying to protect myself. It's still not a good look.

"Why didn't you tell me?

My hesitation gives me away.

"Right." Lily's voice is thick with emotion, her lip between her teeth with worry.

"I didn't say I was leaving Birch Borough, but with Rafe getting married and the extra space opening up, I wanted my mom to take my apartment. It's on the first floor, so it's a good fit for her at this phase of life." I clear my throat. "At the time, it felt like moving would be a win for you too."

Lily lifts her chin, the bottom of her jaw quivering. "So, all of these challenges . . .?" She trails off. "And where will you go?"

I don't answer because my heart hopes the answer is obvious. I've only ever wanted to be with her. Anywhere with her. "I've been looking in Nashville."

"You've been looking in . . ." she repeats, her rib cage rising and falling rapidly. "And the new law firm?"

I sigh. "I've been thinking for some time about a way I can use my experience to help local artists and musicians, the ones who can't afford legal action after having their intellectual property violated or stolen, who don't have people to fight for them to get the best recording deals, or someone to review their contracts. I hope I can help others like I've helped Rafe."

She nods slowly and turns to walk back to the table where Mom and Uncle John are waiting politely in front of our just-delivered plates.

"Lily, please. Are we . . . okay?" I reach for her.

She fidgets with her dress, and I know there's more to her reaction, more that we'll need to figure out together.

"It's your birthday dinner, not the time to talk about your new potential address," Lily states matter-of-factly. "But, G, this isn't over."

My heart leaps when her hand stretches out for mine. I take it, and we walk back to rejoin my family. As we settle in and conversation and laughter take over the table again, I'm flooded with relief. In the back of my mind, though, I feel as if I am still waiting for the floor to give out from under me.

"All this stuff should be banned," Lily exclaims, a look of horror on her face as she picks up various flavored chip bags as we move through the grocery store. Because this is a small town, they're closing in ten minutes, and Lily is taking her sweet time. From the looks the cashier is throwing our way from the register, I wonder if my date is doing it on purpose.

Dinner was enjoyable, but my mind was racing after our rushed conversation in the corner. When Lily went to the bathroom, I called off any plans my mother had for dessert and singing "Happy Birthday." I wasn't feeling festive anymore with the weight of the impending decisions ahead of me. We managed to see a bit of the art displayed, but we left after an exhibition of self-portraits that left me more confused than inspired.

Afterward, not wanting to leave her with unspoken words still hovering between us, we ended up back in Birch Borough for a riveting evening finale of picking up items we both need for the week. By the time we leave the store, we're practically pushed through the front door as it locks behind us.

"Sheesh," Lily mutters. She looks at me. It's the first time she has looked at me in a while, her eyes seeming to wander everywhere but my face . . . again. I hate it.

She motions for me to follow her down the street, and minutes later, I find us at the back door of Sparrow's Beret. Lily unlocks it and ushers us in, only turning on a few lights to keep it dim.

Moving to the industrial refrigerator on the wall, she pulls out a pastry box and sets it on the counter between us. Candles are taped to the top. She pulls them off, grabbing a lighter from a nearby shelf.

"Open it," she instructs with a grin.

And when I do, there, in all its glory, sits a cake. From the smell of it, there's peanut butter and marshmallow and some sort of chocolate hidden inside.

"You remembered," I say softly. "It's perfect."

Her eyes shine at the compliment, and I see her gaze finally flit to my mouth. She lights the candles, and I let the light of the flame captivate my vision.

"Before you make a wish," Lily begins, "I know why you didn't tell me."

"Lily, I was going to—"

"No, it's okay." With gentle pressure, her hand alights on my arm, a sad smile lining the edges of her lips. "You need to believe that I won't do what I've done to you before. And I don't blame you."

She's right, of course. We're rebuilding our trust, but as much as I love her, I don't know how I could ever live without her again.

The only words I can get out are, "I hope we figure it out." Because I want this relationship to work, but trust takes time. She slips her hand into my palm, and I hold it tightly.

"Okay, make a wish before the place burns down, or the wax gets into the icing." She shudders with a laugh.

When I close my eyes, all I see and feel is Lily's presence surrounding me. Every word, every moment adds up to this. I'm content to hold her in my arms. Getting old with her would be a privilege. She sparks in me the desire to be open and to dream a little more. When I'm with her, I don't want to take life so seriously. I know I could happily love her for the rest of my life, even when it hurts.

As I have done each birthday for the past two years, I wish for us. Then I open my eyes and blow out the candles. As the faint whiff of smoke drifts to the ceiling, its lingering scent singeing my nose, I look at Lily. There's an expression on her face I've never seen before.

She is the first to break the silence. "I don't want you to leave. That feels like something you should know."

I swallow, the truth of her words settling into my heart.

She continues, "Graham, I know you won't know what this means yet. But it's not lost."

"What isn't?" I can't help asking the question. I'm not yet willing to ask if she meant to use my actual name or if it slipped in just for tonight.

"Possibly everything," she replies.

When she withdraws her hand from mine, I miss it instantly. She walks to a shelf where forks and plates are stored. She has only taken a few steps before she peeks back over her shoulder, a soft smile on her face.

"Oh, and happy birthday."

Chapter Twenty-Five

Lily

Next week, our two dearest friends in the world, Sparrow and Rafe, get married. And the decision for what happens next between Graham and me is mine.

We haven't kissed again since before I was sick. I've wanted to (oh, how I've wanted to), but I know that Graham and I are on the edge of fully diving in. Last night, Sparrow and Rafe grabbed a pizza from Lorenzo's, and we all sat around one of our tables at the café and ate and played card games. Graham brought a bottle of wine, being the perfect guest that he is. We drank it in our ceramic latte cups and finished the meal off with broken pastries that were within their date but unsellable. It was perfect. And I'm terrified.

Today, while Sparrow picks up our lunch order of dumplings and ramen before we start an afternoon of making macarons, the little bit of sun warms my face and sends a flush of heat to my limbs—or maybe that's from the residual memories of Graham's kiss. My phone rings, and the warmth is doused with a chill. It's a video call from my parents. This is why I've feared it's always going to be winter in my heart. I start to thaw, only to get stuck back in the muddy ground of my own fears. I'm like the groundhog that predicts six more weeks of winter every time.

Their call isn't great timing, but it's going to have to work. My "Maid of Honor" sweatshirt (black, of course) that I've been wearing like a uniform lately seems to take up most of the screen when I accept the call. It glitches at first, and then my parents' faces come into view. Sometimes, I compare my life to theirs and wonder if I'll ever travel across the world with someone I love. Could I ever fully commit and trust that someone sees me as someone they could spend the rest of their life with when I haven't been sure how to get along with myself most days?

"Lily, honey! It's good to see you!" My mom's face takes up most of the screen. The angle is awkward and so true to her that it makes me ache a little. I get some of my fire from her, along with my love for chocolate, no doubt.

"Janet, I can't see her." That would be my dad, dressed like a man perpetually on a golf course or someone who didn't get the memo about not wearing high white socks and khaki shorts. I still love them so much it's laughable. I still want their approval, even when the sting of being overlooked at times is strong.

"That's because your face isn't over here."

"How can my face be over 'here' if your face is all that's there?"

Oh, yeah, and if I inherited some of my qualities from my mom, I can't deny the pure nonsense I've gotten from my dad. It's a beautiful thing.

"Lily, who's that behind you?"

By the alarm in my parents' eyes—a squint from my dad

and a widened expression from my mom—I know instantly that Graham has arrived. The humming in my system is only further confirmation.

"Hello!" My mom says the word much too loudly.

Before I can warn him, Graham is at my back, the warmth of him seeping into my shoulder blades. He politely yet distractingly leans over my shoulder to get a better look at my phone, aka the meeting of my two worlds that I will never hear the end of for as long as I live.

"And you are . . .?" My mother asks the question with far too much of a delighted tone.

Graham clears his throat.

"You're Graham," my dad says, beating him to it.

My cheeks flush, because my parents have absolutely seen pictures of the man whose scent is searing my senses. I could be skipping through a freaking meadow with the way it reminds me of moments in a wildflower field, or nights looking out at the ocean, or movie theaters and rolled-up shirt sleeves.

"Yes, sir, I am." Graham's voice sounds like the river as it moves over rocks, rich and full of strength.

"And you are . . . her friend?" my mom asks, and I nearly break my face from trying to hold back my eye roll.

"Well, actually, we're—"

"Friends! Just friends, people." I force a grin onto my lips, but it's fake.

"Friends?" Graham grits out between clenched teeth.

I feel his stare, the weight of everything between us sinking to my feet. I swallow, my hand shaking now. And because Graham is the decent human he is, he reaches out and holds my hand to keep the phone steady. I honestly don't know how anyone can deserve him.

Despite my declaration, we're now embracing like lovers. He is wrapped around me so that we fit into the phone frame, but I sense the sudden miles between us. I did that. My knee-jerk reaction was to cover our relationship again to try to keep what we are safe, but I'm wondering what he would've said if I hadn't cut him off.

"Well, that's lovely." My mom is anything but convinced as her brows furrow.

My dad gives a small shake of his head. The words that linger in the unspoken space between us are that they both know I'm the problem here too. They've seen enough of my escapades and emotional avoidance to know that, by calling Graham a *friend*, I just messed up. Again.

"Yes, your daughter is the most passionate person I've ever met. It's admirable."

My eyes widen, and emotion crowds my lungs.

"I really must run, but it was so nice to meet you. I've heard only good things. If your daughter is anything like you, I know you're wonderful people," Graham continues, and with that, he's walking a short distance away to give me my privacy.

"Take care," my dad says while I observe my mom wiping what might be a tear from her eye.

"Oh, he's something," she whispers as the hollowness from where Graham just stood sways me backward.

"Sure is."

"Don't crush him like you did last time, if you know what's good for you." Her tone is laced with tenderness, but her eyes hold a warning. I've seen that look before on the occasions they wanted me to settle down and not embarrass them, like the incident with my shirt being inside out at the school pageant in fourth grade.

"Are we going to talk about it?" My father sighs.

I grit my teeth. "So, Rory's wedding! Do you want me to call you in? I'll be standing at the front, but someone here will do it, of course."

My dad gives me a look, but my mom is all excitement as I shift the topic of conversation. "Yes. Oh, I can't believe sweet Rory is getting married. We wanted to be there, but with the flights and the time zones and the clinics set up here . . . She does know we wanted to be there, right? Does she know we wanted to be there?"

I let out a much-needed grimace. "Yes, she knows."

"Oh, Thomases!"

I turn to see Rafe walking toward me, a French muffin in his hand (the ones with cinnamon and sugar that he and Sparrow have created even more of a demand for at our little shop), smiling like he can't believe living in this town is his life.

"D'Artagnan! Or should I say *groom*?"

Rafe smiles his easy smile. I turn the phone over to him so he can catch up with my parents for a minute while I catch my breath. He met them once in person over New Year's, and now they've adopted him as one of their own. It makes sense since Sparrow is practically their daughter too. It's weird to see my parents show them more affection than they do me. I still haven't processed how I feel about that.

I'm lost in my thoughts over Graham's reaction. He's now talking easily with Ollie on the sidewalk. Ollie is demonstrating a flying airplane contraption. Graham has his back turned to me. I don't blame him. He looks uncomfortable, hands shoved in his pockets. My heart melts a little more. The question is whether I'm going to text him, throw rocks at his window, or carry a giant boom box over my head to try to convince him to forgive me. With a single call from my parents, my plan to win him over fell into the pits. Yes, I panicked, but that can't be my excuse anymore. Except for not telling me right away about his potential upcoming move, he's given me no reason to doubt him. And I think I'm finally mad enough at my fear to refuse to allow it to keep me from him anymore.

I bite my nails, not caring enough to give my voice or energy to the bird-watching group gathering outside the café with binoculars and sun hats. Normally, I'd have a feast of quips for them. I'm just not in the mood.

I peek through the window to check on the pastry case and realize that the cream cheese brownies I made are almost sold out. It's not even our afternoon rush yet. "You know what? I can't be mad at those greedy little chocolate nutcases," I mutter to myself.

Willing myself to gather the strength to start melting more chocolate for a fresh batch before the macaron madness begins, I see that Rafe ended the phone call. By my parents' lack of closure or goodbye, they knew I'd be in the middle of a meltdown after what I said to Graham. I'll attempt to call them back next week.

"Sparrow will be over in a minute. She's learning to make homemade spring rolls," Rafe laughs easily.

"Of course she is. She picks up dumplings and then ends up in the kitchen. Sounds about right." I shrug.

Rafe opens the door for me as we walk inside Sparrow's

Beret, the aroma of coffee and baked goods as familiar as my sarcasm.

"You're being hard on him. I wish I knew why," Rafe says on an exhale, taking a stool as I move behind the counter. The sound is cathartic because I need to breathe out fully and can't seem to manage it these days. He takes a bite of a French muffin, having somehow swiped another one without me noticing. The cinnamon sugar sprinkles to the counter. He wipes it with one hand, and I lean my elbows onto the smooth surface, trying to figure out how to allow more honesty to blossom between us. We've been through a lot, Rafe and me. And the fact that he fought so hard for my best friend tells me everything I need to know about how much I can trust him. And he's just a really decent (although goofy) human.

Out of the corner of my eye, I see a mini chocolate bar sliding across the counter. I grin as hints of sunlight through the windows reflect off its shiny wrapper. I take it, unable to resist the call of chocolate, and Rafe knows it. Unwrapping it, I take a tiny bite, willing it to last longer. I think I'm going to need it.

"More chocolate for more information." Rafe's smile is evident in his voice.

A laugh escapes me, and it cinches my ribs together in a way that's a bit painful. The last time I truly laughed was with Graham, the night before, when he nuzzled into my neck and told me how much he missed me over bites of his birthday cake. Because, yeah, Graham is a nuzzling king.

Rafe shifts beside me, his arms casually resting on top of the counter, his guitar-playing, calloused hands moving gently, as if he'd rather be playing the piano or making music than talking right now. It's one of his nervous tics. I almost appreciate it, knowing that he is making an effort to check on me.

"Listen, D'Artagnan," I begin, a sniff echoing between us as I hold back the emotions threatening to appear at any moment. "Don't worry about me. It's Graham you should be worrying about."

I catch Rafe watching the front door, where Graham is now talking to Gladys. Rafe's brow furrows.

"Do you think he needs rescuing?" I ask.

"Nah. It's best he learns how to handle Gladys sooner rather than later."

"True." I shrug. "Hey, did you know about Nashville?"

Turning so my hip can lean against the counter, I face him but not before shoving the rest of the mini chocolate bar into my mouth. If he's annoyed, he doesn't show it. But that's Rafe. And I almost envy Graham for having Rafe as a friend before me.

"Yes, but it might not be permanent. Sounds like a good business decision. He can rent it out when I'm not there, or when he visits, we will all save on hotels. We have a lot coming up later this year. I wouldn't worry too much about it."

"While his mother lives in his apartment? So, where's he gonna live, D'Artagnan?"

"I thought you wanted him out."

I huff, and Rafe hums, fresh crumbs from the muffin littering the counter while he sways back and forth, wrestling with his thoughts.

"Let it out," I warn with a snarky smile.

A determined look crosses his face. "If you can stop

being stubborn for a minute, you'll realize that Graham living in town is a gift."

"A gift?"

"You hurt him. I know. And I'm not minimizing that. But he's *here*." He gestures toward the window where Gladys is now measuring his shoulders with tailor's tape. He is either going to end up in a play or posing for one of her next portraits. In short, he's doomed.

"For now," I mutter.

"And if you think for a second that you don't deserve to love or to be forgiven, then you're not letting yourself be human. We all make mistakes. We all hurt. We all want love, Lily. And you have it. Right in front of you."

At this, I glance back at Graham through the window, who still (rightfully) has concern etched across his face. He begins to unbutton the sleeves of his shirt. I watch in fascination as he rolls them up, one after the other, so quickly and efficiently that it's over before I can register that those arms want to hold me . . . and I've kept them at arm's length.

"You should realize that you've won, even if he stays in town." Rafe partially sings the last words.

"What on earth do you mean? If he leaves, I lose him again. If he stays, I need to figure out how to trust myself enough to love him well. I don't know, D'Artagnan. I think I'm okay and that I can move on, but then I'm alone, and I'm tempering chocolate, or adjusting my ponytail, or—I don't know—trying to fall asleep for the hundredth night in a row, and the deepest parts of me whisper that a memory of him will never be enough."

I wrap my arms around my waist, trying to process how

tears have slipped out.

"Because you love him."

"He's infuriating," I counter.

"He's your spark. One that you shouldn't let burn out. Got it?" Rafe asks.

I nod because he's right. I stand a little taller. "Got it."

"*C'est beau ca.* Now, what are you going to do about it?" There's a bit of a spark in Rafe's eyes, and I think about all the times I poked him last year—grilling him about his intentions with Sparrow, never letting him off the hook for a second. Graham is more than a friend to me, and everyone knows it.

I laugh lightly, the levity welcomed in my stormy heart. "Well, D'Artagnan . . . I'm going to try to make it right. Again. Think I can do that?"

He must sense my actual question: *Is there still enough forgiveness for me?* "Of course you can," he says easily.

"How can you be so sure?" I need to know.

Rafe gives me his signature grin. His scarred eyebrow lifts subtly. "Because you're Lily. And that will always be enough for him."

Chapter Twenty-Six

Graham

I'm sitting at a high-top table in Aesop's Tavern, watching Rafe chat with Lily. She's holding what looks to be a piece of chocolate in one hand. It flails about as she wildly demonstrates whatever she's talking to him about. All I know is that he's laughing incredulously, and she's got tears streaming down her face from laughing so much. The chocolate is being destroyed as they speak. I'm not jealous of Rafe, even though I wish she felt comfortable enough to be that carefree with me right now. I'm just sad that it's not me.

We're all at the tavern after a long day. Rafe and I worked through his upcoming tour schedule this afternoon, setting up performances at a few venues. We also scheduled some meetings we need to have the next time we are in Nashville. The warm feeling of this place pushes me to lean in to enjoy it despite the headache threatening to take me out for the past few hours.

"Penny for your thoughts."

Sparrow's voice pulls me from my focus on Rafe and

Lily, and I force a smile. She is wearing a lovely cream dress that looks like satin and flat shoes with bows on the toes. Even though I don't feel a bit attracted to her, she looks beautiful.

"I've never seen him this happy." I gesture toward Rafe, who's still laughing with Lily like they've discovered a new level of hilarity that didn't exist before. I can feel Sparrow studying me, her eyes following my gaze, which is forever stuck on Lily.

"Thank you for being such a good friend to him," she says sweetly. "He hasn't had many people he can trust."

Looking at Rafe now, it's clear he has found his home with Sparrow and been welcomed into Birch Borough. I had hoped to find my home here too. But given Lily's latest *friend* comment and her lack of protest over my potential move to Nashville, I'm curious to see how this is going to end. My eyes catch on her again because they can't seem to do otherwise.

"She looks beautiful, doesn't she?" Sparrow remarks quietly.

Before I can think too much about it, I hear myself respond, "Always." I slide one thumb around the top of my glass. My other hand rests on the wooden table beneath it.

"So, are we ever going to talk about the fact that you asked me out on a train platform, of all places?"

I wince and let out a laugh. "Not my best moment, I'll admit." I'm surprised when Sparrow stifles a laugh too. "Although," I continue, "to be fair, you did pretend to ignore me with earphones that weren't even connected to your phone."

She laughs again. At least she hasn't held our awkward

initial meeting against me. I've been wondering. On the contrary, Sparrow has done nothing but make me feel welcome since I arrived. I straighten in my seat, mustering the courage to tell her what I've been meaning to say for some time.

"Just so you know, I don't normally ask women out like that," I start. I turn to face her, and even though she's taller than Lily, I still have to tilt my chin down to meet her gaze. "Actually, that was the first time I truly tried asking anyone out since . . ." I look at Lily instinctively.

As I watch her, she unwraps the chocolate in her hand and sticks it into her mouth. I love how much she loves eating sweets . . . and how they linger on her lips. I let out an unamused laugh. Chocolate may now be ruined for me for life, yet somehow, Lily finds a way to keep enjoying it. I'm not sure she could survive without it.

"You don't have to tell me," Sparrow says kindly.

With sadness, I grin and clear my throat. "I want to, though. I know you're not in the dark about us anymore."

Sparrow shrugs. "Soon after things happened between you too, I fell into a deep pit of grief as my father's health declined. It makes sense she didn't tell me right away. She's an open book when it comes to her thoughts unless they're rooted in fear or love. And it feels like whatever she had with you was deep enough that she became a vault and forgot the combination."

I turn back toward the table, the revelation knocking me in the gut. The impact of knowing that, while I thought we were making progress, Lily didn't own up to anything more than friendly feelings in front of her parents makes me hunch over a little, my hopes dashed on the rocks. Focusing again on Sparrow, I find the words I've wanted to tell her for months.

"I'm sorry that I asked you out," I say sincerely. "Not because you aren't a wonderful person but because of the awkwardness of it all." I hope she hears the sincerity in my voice. If I could rewind our first meeting, I would. "I convinced myself that even if it was impossible to feel for anyone what I felt for Lily, I had to try to move on anyway. Don't we have to try?" The question is one that has been haunting me for a long time. Shifting my weight, I take a sip of the whiskey and set it down a little too forcefully.

"Graham." Sparrow's hand rests gently on my shoulder. When I turn, her eyes are filled with compassion. "Do you love Lily?"

Her eyes are so sincere that I find myself willing to say the words that have been on repeat in my mind for the past two years. "I love her more than anything."

"Hmm," Sparrow hums, her eyes filled with heaviness.

"I'm sorry about all the awkwardness between her and me. You can trust that I'll be completely professional during your wedding. I care about Rafe . . . and you." I allow a playful grin back on my face.

Sparrow gives me a look that I can't read. "The thing about being friends—and you are a friend to me now, Graham—is that you shouldn't have to be professional. But I appreciate what you're saying."

"So, we're good?" I ask after a beat of silence between us.

"We're good," she replies with a smile before her eyes go wide at something happening behind me.

Before I can turn around, I hear Gladys yell, "Let's go, Hallmark Hot G!"

"How do you know about that?" I call out to her

incredulously. Already, I'm moving, trying to escape.

Suddenly, her hands are pressing on my back. She must have superhuman strength because she pushes me toward another high-top table with such force that my shoes slide across the floor. Sparrow laughs, and I will Gladys' hands to stay on my back and not wander farther down.

Jumping in front of me, she hands me a plastic container filled with what looks like two cakes stuck together with cream filling, like the cake version of a chocolate sandwich cookie.

"It's a whoopie pie! A New England classic!"

My eyebrows shoot up, and I want to disappear into the floor immediately. I know she's harmless, but this is not how I imagined the evening going. I know Lily must be enjoying this spectacle too much, but when I look around to find her, Rafe is now talking to Liam by the piano, and Lily is nowhere to be seen.

Gladys leans closer and speaks in a conspiratory tone. "Listen, I need to tell you something about your girl."

"I'm not certain she would appreciate you calling her that." The hint of bitterness in my voice is highly detectable.

"Oh, she's as stubborn as they come, that one. Wild child. Free spirit. She's been wrestling with the world since she could talk. She wants to go on adventures but can't seem to figure out how to get out of her own way."

I nod, absorbing every single one of these words that give new insight into the relationship that has been wrecking my sleep for years.

"Her heart is softer than most," she adds like it's a secret.

"I don't disagree with you."

Gladys' hand gently touches my arm. The gesture is

uncharacteristic for her. But when I stop to notice the way she's always supporting other women in this town, it isn't such a surprise.

"She regrets it," she informs me.

I search her face for any hint of amusement or jest. She's serious. Her eyes are weighted with worry as her hand lightly taps mine.

"If I had to guess, she's sick with it. And regret can make a person hard. It can also make them angry. But really, who is it they are angry at?"

"I thought it was me."

Gladys nods lightly. "Ahh, that would make sense. But when you make a mistake—"

"She thinks she made a mistake?" The words are out before I can stop them, hope rising in my chest with a fierceness I've never allowed myself to feel before. Hope comes in levels, and sometimes it's enough to push you over the edge into action.

"Dear, you're a smart man. You've done well for yourself and probably worked yourself to the bone on more than one occasion."

Her keen insight makes me feel strangely emotional toward someone who once asked me to help her raise money to repair the gazebo by posing in suspenders . . . without a shirt.

I shake my head to wrestle it out of the image of that declined request. Unfortunately, I didn't get out of making an appearance at one of her upcoming group art classes in the park. Rafe laughed for two minutes straight when he heard what I agreed to do.

Gladys continues, "I know about the business.

Nashville. The apartment for your mom."

"How did you . . .?" And then I give up because I honestly don't think I want to know.

"As I was saying, sometimes, when we make a mistake, the person we can't seem to forgive is ourselves. And it can be a hard thing when you can't escape yourself."

"I think *I* may have made a mistake." I sigh, knowing full well that I did make a mistake, and this isn't news. "Gladys, I . . . when I first moved to town and saw her after all that time, I told her I couldn't do it again, the back and forth, the push and pull between us. I didn't think my heart could do it." I'm reeling at the unexpected honesty between us, and I'm trying to hold it together. "I didn't tell her my plans."

"Hmm. Good thing I have a key to the newspaper office."

"What?" Her cryptic message makes me wonder if I'm now an accessory to a crime or a world event. It's a toss-up question—one that she doesn't answer.

"Let me know if you need it. Regardless, the townspeople seem to be coming around to your presence."

The way she says it, I know there's more to the story. "I never did find out who submitted my name to the vote at the town meeting."

"Didn't you? Strange." The tone of her voice is a clear sign that nothing about this conversation tonight *wasn't* premeditated. And I'm more impressed with her by the minute. No wonder Lily says that Gladys is her hero.

"Why would you do that?" My fingers grip the table, willing the answer to be a good one, even though I know that's not how it works.

"I admit to nothing, dear. But someone had to drive your

girl to admit what she's always known. You're good for her. And nobody gets to mess with you . . . well, besides her."

Suddenly, Lily appears beside me, a to-go drink in her hand. My guess is that it's a chai latte. Gladys winks as she hurries away.

Once, Lily told me that she feels as if people keep trying to get her to tame her personality down or rein it in. But maybe Birch Borough is exactly what she needs to maintain that feisty spirit, especially if Gladys' support is any indication. I don't want to quench her fire. I just want her to let me be warmed by it.

She lifts the cup to her rosy lips, and I lick my own before catching myself. Our eyes meet, and I feel the weight of our connection as it punches me in the gut. I'm punched every time I'm in her presence. MMA fighters have nothing on what it feels like for someone to hold your heart in their hands, even though you don't remember giving them permission. Maybe she's a con artist.

I have a burning interest in those lips of hers. Right now, they may be pressed against a compostable lid, but there have been moments they have brushed against my own.

"What?" she asks.

"I'm sorry I didn't tell you, Lily." I look at the floor, not wanting to see her intense gaze focused on me for a minute. I need to think straight. "You were right."

"Say it again?" She crosses her arms with a smirk, her cup lightly hovering beside her elbow.

I shake my head and push down a grin of my own. "I was scared. I didn't know if you still wanted me here or if you would change your mind."

"I understand. We're messy. Complicated. Challenging."

She shrugs, but there's some heart behind it.

I wince because she isn't wrong.

"And yet, still I dream of you," she says.

I take in the strong set of her jaw, the lavender flecks in her eyes being overtaken by the grey, the light illuminating part of her face as she stares forward. She doesn't dare look at me after uttering those words, but I hungrily take all of her in.

How can a woman be so feisty yet so adorable? She is wearing a cropped sweater and wide-leg jeans, all in black. She paired the look with white sneakers. The effect is utterly charming and all Lily.

"Is that honest enough for you?" Her bottom lip quivers, and my chest tightens.

If I assumed she was about to run, I was wrong. Maybe I was wrong about a lot of things. Because we can have the facts, the ones we create stories from, but we forget that other stories are present too. Facts don't always hold all the truth. I should know this better than anyone, yet I've been so caught up in my emotions and trying to make sense of it all that I forgot to remember the truth.

Lily left. Fact. Lily never contacted me again. Fact. I moved to Birch Borough. Fact. I accepted a series of challenges from Lily. Fact. I could move again and find a new address. Fact. We both don't know how to live without the other. Truth.

"I just don't think it's enough," Lily says.

And *that's* enough for my heart to sink. After all this time, we're back to her being so sure and then uncertain just the same. I turn away, convinced that if I keep looking at her, I'll do something stupid like digging for more of the truth and tearing us apart in the process.

Excavating heartache is a risky business. And I'm just not in the mood to push further tonight. But I know that her words confirm what she feels for me. They are now filed in the recesses of my mind. Soon, they'll come to the surface again, either in a dream or the next time I eat chocolate cake.

"Well, then," I grind the words out, "there's nothing I can do to convince you. And I need to think."

If I walk down this road with her again, I'm never getting off it. I want to walk it with her more than anything, but my fight-or-flight response is screaming at me with the need to clear my head. My heart is all over the place tonight.

Lily swallows and nods, her skin turning a paler color than before. "No. Gosh, I just keep messing this up, don't I? Don't you have a manual or something? I can't seem to tell you . . . to make you feel . . ." Her voice trails off.

The sinking feeling in my stomach urges me not to keep waiting. *I need Lily to be sure.*

I couldn't have guessed that this was the place where Lily and I would end up. If you told me this was how our story was written, I would've bet my whole savings account that it could never be, that we wouldn't have gotten a second chance, or that we would've ended up eloping, surrounded by flowers and a preacher who doesn't understand why we can't even wait one more second to call each other *mine*.

But here we are. Sometimes, the truth truly does get swallowed in facts. Maybe my next challenge needs to be finding out more of the truth.

"Hey, are you good?" Rafe asks, coming up behind me

and placing his arm on my shoulder.

"I'm sorry," I begin, trying to avoid eye contact with Lily before more emotion surfaces. "I'm happy for you, but I also feel like I'm losing . . ."

I can't finish the sentence. My jaw clenches, awareness of all the things that should have been shooting through my neck, and I force down the emotion.

"It's okay, man. I understand." Rafe glances between Lily and me, and it's clear that he does. He understands what's between us, and I feel the shame of it creeping up my spine. "I'll see you at our place?" Rafe carefully watches me, his scarred eyebrow arched.

I know that I must be the best man possible, even when I'm in pain. If it was any other night and he wasn't so distracted and elated to be marrying Sparrow, I think he would notice the minor changes in my appearance and the way my foot taps the wooden floor impatiently. But he doesn't. It's Lily who will be left with the unraveling when he leaves.

As soon as Rafe disappears, Lily's piercing grey eyes go right to my soul. I can see hers too, fighting to keep it civil between us. I know what it has to be: It's either an all-in *I love you* from both of us, or it's nothing at all.

"George, I . . ."

There she goes, not using my name again. I've hoped for a sign to show me she's not ready to call it. I wasn't expecting it to be like this, but I take note of the undertone of her voice. For a moment, we're back at the movie theater two years ago, with enough hope between us to leap into love without having to first know the ending. We're Graham and Lily, with honesty and confessions of love between us. So much honesty. We're slightly younger versions of ourselves with my hands in her hair and my heart in her hands. We're not *this*.

I shake my head.

"You win," I say softly. "No arguments this time. No retractions. My—" I start, voice cracking, "my best friend . . . is getting married." A deep breath. "And I will be there for him. For them."

Lily nods, her eyes focusing on a spot on my chest and not my face, as if we haven't covered more ground than this before. It's back to a formality I once tried to uphold and preemptively ripped to shreds the second I thought she was truly choosing to come back to me.

"Oh, and I heard back about Nashville. It's perfect, actually. For Rafe . . . and his career . . . I can make it work. A win-win."

"Okay," she whispers.

My breathing turns shallow. We've reached the part of the fight where one of us must choose to stay down. And again, it's me.

"No more challenges," I declare.

Lily shuts her eyes. It's a moment I never want to remember, even though I know it will be a constant replay now.

"No more challenges," she repeats, her tone matching the emptiness I feel.

As if I just can't help but say something—have the final word to try to wrap up what we've been—I step back and struggle to get the words out. "I was happy."

Lily's sharp inhale makes me want to return to her, but I don't. I must move forward with the knowledge that there are only a few more scheduled events to endure. And then our friends will be married, and I'll be leaving, a hollow version of the man I once was but still finding ways to see the beauty. How many people know what it means to love someone so completely? I may not have run after her the first time, thinking that my distance honored her will, but I've loved her every second I've known her. And in a world that shifts like water through my hands, time seems to find ways to leak out without me wishing for it. I know I will never find it within myself to regret a single moment of the time we've spent together.

As I step out into the spring air, the chill at the edges of it elevating my senses, I let the sound of the nearby river calm my nerves. The lights from the restaurants along the path cause tiny orbits to hover over the surface, illuminating some of the rocks the water crashes over on this side of town. Music carries into the air, and laughter evaporates into the inky sky. A train whistle once again greets me in the distance and reminds me of how far I've come.

While my neck muscles are tightly coiled, and my stomach feels unsettled from the emotion of this evening, I also feel immensely proud. I've been fighting so hard for others to believe that I'm a good man that I didn't realize I was always really trying to convince myself. But trying to be one doesn't make me one.

It's having the courage to love someone else in a way that I wish I had been loved all along. It's being okay with not having my love returned and yet not treating her any differently. I don't have to always feel useful. I am able to not always have the answers yet still choose to believe that, when it comes to love—while it hasn't been what I've hoped for quite yet—I haven't been overlooked. Besides, I'd rather love Lily with my whole heart than know I've withheld anything that I am from her. And for that, at least, I can find no fault.

Chapter Twenty-Seven

Lily

We're back at the church, waiting for Pastor Wilfred to continue leading us through the pretend ceremony before the real one begins tomorrow. My feet are killing me, and I'm questioning all my life choices, especially the ones pertaining to a certain unforgettable man. Pastor Wilfred's talk of love and marriage feels like warmth melting through a frozen part of my heart. It stings a little.

He moves to the front of the church, acting like it's his stand-up hour. I love him. He has known me since I was a baby, but the joke about Eve being the apple of Adam's eye can only be told so many times (actually, it should never be said in the first place). His speech is starting to drone on and on about what will happen on Sunday. Choir members are leaving from the practice that began just before we got in, which is fitting since I'm ready to sing a song of lament.

It will be a small wedding party, with only Graham and me at the altar next to the happy couple. The rest of the town will show up as attendees, so I'll have no other buffer till then, the reality of which is making me antsy.

Liam is strumming his guitar on the stage, waiting for the rehearsal to officially start. Ivy is probably at her studio choreographing the dance for the summer festival. Even Grey, who would usually show up to cheer on Sparrow and Rafe, is at her bookstore, wrapping up the party favors.

While the bride and groom would've chosen a larger wedding party, Rafe doesn't have brothers or other best friends in town. Maybe Liam would've stepped in as a groomsman, but then, who would play the music for the ceremony? Besides himself, I suspect Rafe only trusts Liam to do it. So, here we are . . . one quaint wedding party consisting of two fated lovers and two exes. What a dream team.

Except, when I'm being honest with myself, my insides tell me this could've all been so different. If I hadn't run away—if I had just stayed that night on the beach and been open with Graham—I would now have more than an engagement ring. Something whispers within me that we would've been married by now. And Sparrow would've been my maid of honor, and I wouldn't be looking at Graham with more longing than I know what to do with.

My gaze shifts to where he sits quietly in the front row, his arm over the back of the wooden pew. I've put myself a few rows behind him so I can drink in the sight of him for all I'm worth. It's here, with the fresh evening glow filtering through the stained glass windows as the spring air swirls and bounces through the open doorway, that I'm permitting myself to do the thing I told myself I never would. I'm pulling back the curtain of our time together and allowing myself to feel the things I've denied all along. In the process, I'm dismantling all the lies.

The lie that I didn't love him as much as he loved me. The lie that I didn't love the way his fingers twirled through my hair. The lie that I haven't dreamed of him beside me in the morning instead of the ghost of him when I awaken.

A warm, late-spring shower begins. The sound of the raindrops on the roof sends a chill through my spine as I remember the feeling of walking with Graham in the rain. His thumbs traced my cheekbones as they cradled my face. I can still recall the color of his eyes during the spring storm. I remember how he kissed me while we stood among the wildflowers, as if I was the last thing he ever wanted to touch. And I remember the look on his face in Portsmouth when he told me he planned to release his apartment and move to Nashville as I wished.

As Sparrow and Rafe stand up and face each other at the front of the church, I feel tears spring to my eyes. This is it. After the wedding, comes the end of Graham's time in Birch Borough. Desperation rises in me. I'm stunned to realize, as much as I've fought with him, I'm not ready to say goodbye. I was never ready to say goodbye to him. I just haven't been able to find the words to express what he means to me. And Graham needs words. They're the evidence that reinforces the assurance he needs in order to move forward with anything or anyone—including us.

Shakily, I stand to my feet. I come around the pew toward Sparrow and see Graham lifting his glasses to wipe one of his eyes with the back of his hand. He's wearing his glasses. Frames I haven't seen before. He hardly wears them, only when his eyes are tired. They tell me he hasn't been sleeping much either.

"Okay, let's practice you two coming up the aisle before

the bride," Pastor Wilfred says, his index finger indicating Graham and me.

Without a word, I hastily make my way toward the exit, feeling Graham following closely behind.

When we reach the outer doors, I shake out my hands and prepare to touch the man who is about to walk me down the aisle. He extends his elbow, not looking at me or saying a word.

As happy as we are for our friends, this is excruciating. *Will I let myself be Graham's first choice?*

The thought shocks me, and my mind begins to race. The truth hits me. Graham has shown me that he'll choose me every time, yet I haven't known how to believe it. Perhaps I don't need a different kind of love. Perhaps it is less that I'm not strong enough than it is that I need to trust Graham is a man of his word.

With a new perspective, I slide my hand up and into the crook of his arm, willing my touch to be as light as possible, barely resting on him yet feeling it all. Forcing a smile for Sparrow's sake, we begin to walk down the aisle. Liam plays the cello, the sound echoing off the walls and coursing through me, urging me to ask Graham if we could ever recover what was lost between us.

By the time we arrive at the pulpit, my heart is racing. We part, and I miss the warm pressure of his arm. Of all the things I didn't count on, I can assure you the worst one is seeing Graham across from me. He isn't making eye contact and isn't looking at me at all. But I'm looking at him. I'm watching his genuine happiness for our friends. I'm watching as he tilts his head to listen to their vows like they are the life-changing words they truly are. And I'm watching him stare at the ring as if it's something of his own he once lost. I suppose he did.

Sparrow and Rafe wipe tears from their eyes as Pastor Wilfred speaks. It may only be a prelude to their day, but emotions are high. I wipe my eyes as I think of the parents Sparrow lost. They should be here for her too.

I'm lucky she has loved me so deeply and hasn't given up on me, even though I've been giving up on myself for longer than I care to admit. They kiss sweetly. Rafe hugs her so fiercely yet gently that it nearly makes me want to look away. Perhaps loving each other like that belongs on display in a museum or should be protected by reverent privacy.

Pastor Wilfred releases them, and they walk down the aisle hand in hand. Rafe throws his arm over his head in victory as they reach the outer doors, and I grin. They're just so darn happy. And they deserve it all. And Graham deserves it all.

He holds out his arm to me again, still not meeting my eyes. We walk toward the exit together. When we're halfway down the aisle, I turn to him, knowing that if I don't get this out now, I may not have the chance.

"You're really leaving?" I ask.

"It's what you wanted," he replies, a distant, passive expression on his face.

"When . . . when will you go?"

Finally, his gaze meets mine for the first time with a flash. I'm knocked back from the fierceness in its depth. It strikes me that the warmth his eyes used to hold for me is now nothing more than a barely flickering light.

"Don't worry about it."

As much as I don't deserve his trust, and even though

his tone is gentle, fear tries to claw its way out. I feel the urge to snap back rising in my throat, but I restrain it.

Graham tilts his head, sadness in his eyes. "As you've said, this was always a one-sided love.

The words have barely met the air, and I despise myself for the outcome. "I'm sorry—no, it wasn't . . ." I'm about to say the word *true* when he shakes his head.

"I said don't worry about it."

Graham races down the length of the aisle with quick strides. I slink after him, willing there to be a chance to make this right. I've had so many chances to make things right between us, and I've wasted each of them.

"Graham," I plead.

To my relief, he stops and turns back to me slowly. His eyes are full of questions and filled to the brim with trepidation. I also wonder if I detect something that looks a lot like hope.

"I know how this all started, and I know that I've fought with you every single moment since we met here again. I was terrified. I'm not—"

"Lily, I don't— I can't—" he whispers with obvious pain. His jaw is clenched, and his blue eyes quickly turn stormy. "There's no need."

And I realize he thinks I'm going to do it again. He thinks I'm going to run and not look back. If he reaches for me again, he assumes I'm going to turn him away. And I won't. Because even if my parents never love me in the way that I crave, I can choose to be loved by Graham. At my core, I may not have felt chosen over my parents' patients and dreams—or really by anyone except my best friends— but the man in front of me is *my* dream. Instead of trying to protect him from my love, which I believed was delicate, I realize at this moment that choosing Graham is also choosing myself. It's acknowledging that Graham is the one I want, and letting myself love him freely means I'm giving myself permission to be loved freely too.

"No," I declare with as much frustration as I can express while my heart breaks all over again. "Listen to me!"

He's moving now, out of the church and down a garden path at rapid speed. His shoulders are tense, the very tips of his hair pulled back from his hasty walk. This time, I'm the one reaching for him. Trying to keep up, I nearly topple over in the wedges I insisted upon wearing today. I'm regretting my fashion choice but am committed to following through with what's about to unfold. He needs to know. He must know.

"Wait, you rake!"

At my raised voice, Graham stops abruptly. I nearly crash into his back from the momentum. He doesn't turn around but looks over his shoulder, eyeing me with his peripheral vision.

"You heard me," I say.

He faces me, frustration pulsing off his frame, hitting me full force with its intensity. I take a deep breath to steady myself. I'm more than attracted to this side of him, but I realize I need to focus on the moment. He laughs mirthlessly.

I know what he is thinking. Even now, when we're at a crossroads together, I would have to do one more thing to provoke him.

Chapter Twenty-Eight

Graham

et me get this straight."

My voice comes out calmer than I feel. Lily stands
in front of me, an earnest expression on her face. She's not
going to let me leave until we have this conversation. Since
we're essentially trapped at this rehearsal together, there's no
point in outrunning her.

I continue, "So, we meet. I fall in love with you. We say
we love each other. We make plans. I want to marry you. I
buy a ring. And then, you see said ring and run away without
a word. No, not a word. You tell me everything I thought
we felt for each other was one-sided. Oh, and then, just to
further confuse things, you never reach out to me again. Not
even for the box of stuff you left behind that I still packed
and took with me across the country like an idiot in love
because throwing it away felt like throwing you away."

Tears are streaming down Lily's face now, but she nods.

"Let's continue." I begin to pace, deliberately avoiding
looking into her eyes because I never could stand to see her
cry. Whatever troubles Lily endures, I always want to fix

them, to hold her until the world is right again. She used to let me. She's *been* letting me . . . which makes me more determined to finally speak the words I've wanted to say for a long time.

"I can't get you out of my head or my heart. You told me the little town you lived in was a dreamy and darling place to call home—albeit sometimes unhinged—but a place to mend a broken heart. In case you haven't guessed it, that is why I showed up in Birch Borough in the first place."

I wring my hands and crack my neck. It's emotional, laying out all the evidence for my case against her in real time. For once, she doesn't speak, letting me pour out my heart without interruption.

"During your parting shot to me, you promised me that you were leaving the country. You weren't going to stick around, you said. I believed you. Again. And I moved into an apartment here. Why? Because I like to blow my life apart, apparently."

My hands rise to loosen my tie. I work on the buttons of my shirt to roll up my sleeves.

"Graham . . ." Lily whispers. She can't seem to get out the words. My chest is hollow, with the harsh facts spread out before us. I can't take them back or will myself to stop. I'm aware of the internal alarm going off in my head, warning me that I should've stopped a few hundred words ago, but I keep pacing, the truth tumbling from my lips.

"Fast forward. Our best friends—of course fate would connect us for life somehow—are getting married. I'm in this wedding with you. And I have to watch you . . ." I pause, emotion clogging my throat.

The tears slip down her face, the drops soaking the top of her linen dress.

I gather myself and go on, "I have to see you. And talk to you. Through some magic, I got to kiss you in what must've been a portal to a dream world. I get to have you near me again. Yet, even when it feels like things are working, I know what I've already lost every single time."

Her breath hitches. I clear my throat. I'm still not done.

"Still, knowing all this, I let you challenge me for my future in this town. I agreed to your terms. I fulfilled your demands. I put my whole life on the line again. Every step of the way, I warned myself not to fall for you, not to dare bare my soul just for you to crush it again.

"I thought we were on the brink of something. Everything I had buried started to break through the dead soil in my life. I thought my heart found the strength to beat again. It was as if my real heart was merely going through the motions of keeping me alive until you came back to me.

"And then you ask me if I'm leaving before we walk down the aisle—and I remind you . . . that you . . . you once said—I can't even say it out loud because it feels like poison and a weird excuse for what we are to each other. So, I give my mom the apartment. I give you what you want. And now . . . you call *me* a rake?"

"You wouldn't stop walking!" The frustration in her voice is like a poker, prodding the coals between us to keep the fire burning.

"Why should I stop, Lily? I'm genuinely asking . . . why?"

"Because I . . . I . . ." she starts, but the words get stuck in her throat.

"And a *rake*? Really? I've done everything in my life with

the goal of being an honorable man. I'm not perfect, but I'm not that, and I . . ." I trail off.

"It's my favorite show," she says, her jaw lifting minutely, defying me to call her on this truth.

"I know."

"I watch it over and over."

I sigh. "I know."

"I can't live without it. I don't want to do life without it."

I wince. "Okay . . ." I shake my head and hold my hands to the side, my body language practically begging Lily to fast-forward through the painful parts of whatever is ahead.

"And I can't live without you. I don't want to live this life without you."

Her passionate words catch me off guard. I did not expect them. For the first time tonight, I allow myself to search every feature of her face, looking for anything to prove them false. There's nothing. She really means it. And deep in my gut, I know it's true.

She's staring at me so intently that I couldn't move if I wanted to. I feel the sigh escape my lips before I've thought it through. I'm tired of pretending that I've ever been anything but hers.

"Lily, this had better be the last time . . ." I plead.

"It is. Because I can't pretend that you aren't everything I've ever wanted and that I've been too terrified to admit it. And because I love you," she says with her signature smirk. Fresh tears fall down her face through the smile.

They match my own. I couldn't hold it together right now if I tried. Slowly, pulled together by the invisible force that exists between us, we meet in the middle. I take her in fully. The glow of the church's interior lights filters through the windows, carving a journey from the crown of her head to the tips of her hair. Her piercing grey eyes are now clouded by the glare catching off my rain-specked reading glasses.

"Graham." Her voice catches, my name sweet on her lips. "Graham, I love you so much that I don't know where you end and I begin. Even if I can't be your first choice, after all we've been through, you're mine. And I'll choose you every time. With all my heart, I choose you."

Hungrily, I take her in, the ache settling deep in my stomach. She moves her hand and does what I've been hoping she'd do again: touch me without giving an excuse for it. Her fingers stroke the edge of my jaw, and she lightly rubs the back of her hand over my beard. The sensation causes my lips to part.

"You're wearing your glasses," she marvels, a hint of wonder in her voice.

I haven't worn them in front of her since LA. I nod, my reaction taking a few seconds to catch up with her words.

"It's a miracle you can see out of these things." Her voice is soft and low. Despite her tear-streaked cheeks, she moves her hands upward with confidence to gently remove them from my face. She uses the side of her dress to wipe them clean before she pauses, a blush creeping up her cheeks. When she hands them back to me, there's a subtle caving in of her shoulders, a hesitation, a shyness I've never before noticed. I'm caught in a state of wonder at the realization.

Though my instinct has always been to care for her, to feed her, and to make sure she's okay through all the ups and downs, Lily has struggled to show her tenderness ever since we reunited. She's always so strong, seemingly unbothered by the opinions of others.

But this, seeing her vulnerability and weakness in this moment . . . *She really does love me.*

I choose my words carefully, wanting to speak with intention. "As much as I'm for this turn of events for us, I don't want to rush you. There has been a lot of emotion this season. So, I'm going to give you until the wedding. My feelings for you are what they were in LA. What they've always been. So, tell me how you feel after our friends get married. Until then, I'm still yours."

I fold and place the glasses in my jacket's inner pocket, the one over my heart. Without them, there's no barrier between her gorgeous eyes and mine, and it turns me inside out. I just want her to be mine again.

"It's up to you what happens next. I mean that."

She reaches for me, her hand lightly grasping my wrist and then sliding down—slowly and gently—until our fingers are intertwined. Without breaking eye contact, she shifts her weight so she's leaning closer as music from the back of the church begins to play softly. Its heady notes whirl romance all around us.

When I use my free hand to reach for her, she freezes. This moment in time could be placed over the moment when she once rejected me in perfect synchronicity. The reenactment has haunted me for two years—the moment when I reached for her, and she backed away.

Except, this time is different because she leans in. The edges of my fingers wrap around her shoulders. I feel the brush of the ribbon around her waist. I haven't even commented on the wedges she's wearing tonight, but I love them. I love her. I tug her closer to me as she wrestles with a grin.

"Lily, I never . . . I never could pretend you're not the sun and moon of my world," I admit.

My hand slides up her waist, over her elbow, and up her arm before it lands at the curve of her neck. I pull her to me and place a tender kiss on her forehead. Her skin is soft beneath my lips, and I exhale heavily.

"Graham." Her eyes lock on mine as she leans back. I watch them swirl into a pool of affection as she passes them over my face before halting at my mouth. "Hit me with your best shot," she challenges.

She's barely finished the words before I feel her lips pressed to mine. Instantly, the weight of them transforms me from someone with a broken heart into someone who knows what it means to have everything that was missing returned to me and then some.

The warmth of her touch sends me reeling. Liquid heat moves throughout my body. Her arms wrap around my neck as I release her mouth just long enough to trail soft, lingering kisses down the side of her neck. The scruff of my beard slides against her smooth skin as I move my way back up the path I created, and she shivers. Gently, I nuzzle my face into the spot beneath her ear and feel her breath hitch. The edges of her ponytail are calling to me. With one hand clasped around her waist, I lift my free hand to gently weave through her ponytail, twisting the golden strands around my fingers. Knowing she's near me—that she wants me near her—is a sensation that leaves me feeling steady and exhilarated at the same time.

When she leans back again to look into my face, I will

her to really and truly hear me. Once hostile, her eyes have given way to a wave of love.

"You're it for me. Got it?" I say, the gritty quality of my voice revealing my affection. "I love you, Lily. And I'll choose you first every time."

Her eyes glisten with tears, and I feel a few of my own trailing down my face and catching in my beard. Slowly, she lifts her hand to wipe some of them away with the back of her hand. The gentleness of it all is a contradiction to the fire still in her eyes.

"Sounds like a challenge," she declares with a grin.

I know without a doubt that my heart is finally in her hands for good.

Chapter Twenty-Nine

Lily

"Let's blow this popsicle stand!" I yell the words, the feeling of freedom within my hands.

It's the feeling of three of my dearest friends in Birch Borough—Sparrow, Ivy, and Grey—deciding that we're going to make Sparrow's wedding day the best day ever. My heart is light. My man (my man!) has been texting me our favorite quotes from *The Man is a Rake* all morning, and I'm ready to sing like those little birds that have been screeching outside my window each day. For once, they didn't annoy me this morning.

We just left Train Car Diner after a special breakfast complete with pancakes dressed in wedding gowns due to the whipped cream piled on top. After stopping at Angie's Pies to grab a box of desserts and coffees, we head to the church, where Sparrow will make the final preparations for her wedding day. The spring air is cool at the edges this morning, promising warmth when the sun has more time to shine.

Leisel is going to meet us to finish Sparrow's hair and

makeup. Gladys promised she'd come by to give Sparrow something "old" (whatever that means). Cricket is meeting us to take behind-the-scenes photos of us all getting ready. While Ivy and Grey aren't officially in the wedding party due to the limited number of groomsmen, they're here with us for the morning.

While we planned to have a wild extravaganza for Sparrow's last night before getting married, the truth is, none of us know how to stay out much past eight at night. Everything in town closes early. Sparrow and I know all too well what it means to occasionally have to temper chocolate or make yet another batch of croissants before others have hit the brew button on their coffee pots. Grey has incredibly late nights, but it's because she reads until she's convinced herself that one more chapter truly will be the end of her. And Ivy has been on a set sleep schedule since high school for optimum dance training and performance. She has never relinquished the habit.

So, last night, we ended up at Ivy's dance studio, huddled on the floor with blankets spread out, surrounded by wall barres and memories. Ivy keeps the studio strung with twinkle lights, and they added to the cozy ambiance as we reminisced about the days when we all took lessons together as kids. Even considering the updates Ivy has made, the studio is still the place where my underwear ended up sticking out from my leotard and halfway down my thigh (I have pictures to prove it). I was traumatized to know that when your hands don't look graceful, they can be called *spider hands*.

I only lasted in dance lessons until the spring recital, when I went rogue and started doing my own rendition of break dance moves. I didn't even know what I was doing, and I blame *High School Musical* (the original, thank you very much) for the delusional idea of what can happen on a stage. Needless to say, I was kicked out of class. Grey lasted one more year until she sat in the middle of the stage, pulled a book from behind her, and began to read during practice.

Ivy and Sparrow were the only ones to stay with it. Sparrow danced until she was injured in her senior year of high school. Ivy went away for a bit, did a stint with a company in New York City, and then moved back to Birch Borough to open her dance studio. She's owned it for five years or so now, and it's clear to everyone around her that this is what she was meant to do with her life. This is her life calling, even when I see the familiar hint of sadness around her eyes and hear the way she jokes about dating apps but without giving her full smile. Sparrow is the only one of us who has found her person so far—correction, *was* the only person. I know there's more to Ivy's story than she lets on.

"Lily, tell me," Ivy begins this morning as we unload our makeup and supplies in a room at the back of the church. "How do you feel not being single anymore? I mean, now I'm going to have to find someone else to suffer through the dating apps with." She gives a frustrated growl, but she is smiling. We all cringe.

"I don't envy you the struggle, my dear. That's for sure."

"You've fought well. I'm glad you made it through to the other side."

I nod as she and I clink our champagne glasses. We've earned the celebration after enduring so many men and their mostly questionable choices for putting the best version of themselves on their dating profiles. Ivy is not yet in the clear, but I have hope for her.

"Grey, you're not going to join Ivy on the apps?" I stuff my face with a cracker and French Brie from our makeshift charcuterie board.

Her cheeks tinge a light shade of pink at the question. "No, I don't think those are for me."

Ivy and Grey exchange a look that I note.

"Wait—what was that?" I ask, attempting to cover my mouth while still chewing.

"Honestly, Lils. Leave Grey be," Sparrow whispers, always trying to be the peacemaker.

I swallow and point frantically, like I've just discovered a new way of applying nail polish that doesn't involve fumes and a fan. "They shared a look!"

"I have a better question." Sparrow redirects the conversation, aware that I'm oh-so-close to embarrassing myself and my friends. "Tell us more about who you're bringing to my wedding."

The smile on her face tells me that she's asking because there *is* someone, and Grey has RSVP'd accordingly. She'd never call her out if it weren't true.

"Boston."

"You're bringing a city to Rory's wedding?" I ask skeptically, my eyebrows trying to meet my hairline, hoping she sees amusement on my face rather than an actual question. "Is he just your friend, or do you love him endlessly?" I'm clearly unable to keep the conversation light.

Grey's skin shifts shades of red like a color-changing lava lamp. "I—" she begins, "I mean, I've known him since summer camp in sixth grade—literary camp."

"Let's get lit!" I mutter. Thankfully, she doesn't hear it. Ivy stifles a laugh.

"I've seen him every year since . . . I mean, so, I love him, but . . . I mean, besides all of you, he's my best friend." Grey shrugs her shoulders as if that wasn't the most awkward explanation for a male friend that I've heard in a while.

"That sounds lovely," Sparrow exclaims, giving me a look that tells me to quit before I get deep into trouble with these people I love.

I turn back to Ivy instead, riveted by the turn this conversation is taking. "And who are you taking as your wedding date, Ivy?"

Her eyes widen as she takes the biggest bite of a brownie that I've ever seen.

"Ives, have you even met the man you're taking?" I grin, using my nickname for Ivy—the one I'm not sure she loves but she knows she's going to get anyway.

In reply, she nods and then stuffs the rest of the brownie into her mouth. If she's hoping we move on without asking her any more questions, I want to give her an award.

"Okaaay," I drag out the word.

She swallows, a hint of chocolate crumbs thrown in the air as she rubs her hands together. "It's not worth dancing about," Ivy says in her deep and sultry voice.

I've always been so jealous of her voice, which naturally sounds like the real-life equivalent of a bowl of rocky road ice cream. All elegance and grace, she's everything sweet with this gritty, gorgeous speaking voice. How I wish it didn't make mine sound like a chipmunk in comparison.

"Besides, you have a gorgeous man who is in love with you. A man who happens to be best friends with your best friend's fiancé. A man who knows how to *dance*, Lily. Do you know what I would give for a man who loves me and can also dance with me? I mean, honestly."

"But I—" I begin before she puts up her hand. Now I can understand how she wrangles all those tiny dancers in each and every class with such grace. She's got the heart of an angel and the discipline to whip little terrors into shape.

"Besides, Graham may look like a billionaire, but something tells me he kisses like a rake."

My mouth drops open in both surprise and delight at her statement.

"Knew it," she concludes, her nose scrunched, fist lifting in a subtle pump of victory.

"Ladies!" Rafe's voice carries through from the other side of the door.

I fight the urge to grin at Sparrow's instant blush. It makes sense that they couldn't keep away from each other for the entire day. She most definitely sent him a sneaky picture of the charcuterie board. The man is French after all. He can't avoid wine and cheese even if he wants to.

"Stand back, D'Artagnan!" I yell toward the door. "Can't be getting any bad luck over here—I don't need those vibes!" He chuckles audibly as I mutter, "Graham and I have been through enough."

I know Rafe has been spending the hours leading up to the ceremony with Graham, which means he's somewhere nearby too. The train whistle sounds throughout the space from the nearby station, and Sparrow looks at me with a grin before looking at the door.

"Hear that, Sugar?" Rafe croons with a smile in his voice, no doubt thinking of how they first saw each other on a moving train. "That's all the good luck we need."

Gracefully, Ivy rises, her feet naturally turned out, dance training evident in every move. She glides closer to the door. "And is your Hallmark-worthy friend with you too?"

A deep chuckle I recognize as Graham's makes me rush to the door.

"Ivy, Grey—you're on Sparrow duty," I say, excitement lacing my voice. "Close your eyes, Rafe!"

With that, I'm through the door and standing in the hallway. Rafe is startled by my sudden appearance, but Graham gives me a smoldering look hot enough to cook the pancakes we ate this morning.

Pulling away my attention, Rafe hands me an envelope with his handwriting on the front. It's addressed to *Sugar*. I nod to him, already knowing he wants me to give it to Sparrow.

"I will," I assure him without being asked. In an uncharacteristic move, I throw my arms around Rafe and hug him. I hug him because he loves my friend so well and because he cares for the man I love so much. And I've come to love him as a close friend too.

"Thanks, Lils," Rafe says, his warm return hug comforting. He is so much like how I imagine the brother I always wish I had would be. When he releases me, he looks between Graham and me, giving us a nod. "I'll give you two a minute."

With a wink, he's gone.

It's just Graham and me in the tiny hallway of the stone church. I want to hold him close and never let go. I'm in my trusty "Maid of Honor" sweatshirt and jeans, but he looks at me as if I'm already wearing my silky gown.

"Hi, honey," he says, his voice rasping with the perfect amount of grit.

"Hi, Graham." I use his name with deliberate intention. Graham deserves to never be called George again (although, I'm sure I'll find other terms of endearment for him soon).

Slowly, he tucks his arms behind his back. I've never seen him in the posture before, and it's the stuff dreams are made of. It's maddening and even more so when he shifts his weight to one side so that his other leg is relaxed. Graham's casual pose is the stuff women faint over, to be honest. The draw is the pull of confidence when a man stands as if he is utterly relaxed and without a care in the world while he's at your side. And, of course, at the sight of it, my hormones throw a rager.

I know what it means to see someone you want and not be able to find the words you need to express what you feel. There have been moments when I couldn't find the courage to show him what he meant to me, even when he was right in front of me. There is a dread that hits in the deep of night after you've mulled over your relationship a while and are caught between regret and wondering if you're the only one walking in a haze of your own making while everyone else gets to see their path with clarity. I know what it means to sit across from someone at a dinner table and wish it was someone else. And now, here he is in real life.

I reach for him, my hand alighting on his shoulder. But I pull my hand back, still getting used to the fact that I can touch him anytime I want.

"You all right?" Graham asks, such concern etched into

his brow that it almost makes me want to laugh or cry. I can't decide.

"Hand fell asleep," I reply quickly.

"We touched for two-point-five seconds." His eyebrow arches.

I want to roll my eyes at his smugness—and for his accuracy with time. "I'm warming up."

"Warming up for what exactly?" The hint of playfulness in his tone sends me back to LA. In the memory, we're eating tacos from a food truck and riding the Ferris wheel at the Santa Monica Pier. We're visiting studio sets and attending tapings for some of our favorite shows.

And I realize it's just him and me once again. It's the way I've always wanted it to be. I step forward and wrap my arms up and around his neck, the tips of my fingers grazing the ends of his hair. He closes his eyes and leans his forehead down to mine, expecting me to meet him halfway. Instead, I press gentle kisses at the edges of his mouth, the scent of his beard oil and the promise of tomorrow pulling me closer.

Sharply, he inhales. Without opening his eyes, his hand cups the edge of my jaw. His breath is sweet peppermint, warm and welcoming as his lips hover over mine. Graham brushes them softly, passing agonizingly and deliciously over my own. The electric current between us sends chills down my spine. His arms wrap tightly around my ribs, pulling me closer before he gives me one final kiss, his fingers gently tugging the hair at the base of my neck.

"I'll see you at the altar," he says slowly near the shell of my ear. His voice ruins me for any other words because nothing could mean as much to me. We're not getting married today, but that was everything I needed. A promise of a beautiful future to come.

By the time I gather myself enough to move again, Graham is halfway down the hall, walking back to the room he is hanging out in today with Rafe.

Inhaling, I open the door to the bridal suite to find all three of my friends looking at me with knowing grins. Holding out the card from Rafe to Sparrow is all I can manage, my body still reveling in the cocoon of Graham's affection.

"Okay, Rory." I smile, tears suddenly brimming in my eyes. "Let's get you married."

For today, the fear I've held close for far too long is a memory instead of a companion. I told Graham he makes me want to soften. What he doesn't realize is that his love is also what makes me strong.

Chapter Thirty

Lily

Raphaël, do you take this woman to be your lawfully wedded wife, to have and to hold—"

"Yes, always to hold," Rafe replies.

I wipe a tear from my eyes as Sparrow laughs. I'm annoyed at the bride and groom for being so sweet, but I'm also so happy for them that I can't even be mad about it. They continue their vows. While I try to stay in the moment and commit all this magic to memory so I can chat with Sparrow about it one day, my eyes keep wandering to Graham. Because he is my moment. He's the one that I know I want to share vows with one day too. The thought of standing at the altar with him one day (hopefully sooner rather than later) makes my eyes burn. When the mist clears and I peek over at him, I see that Graham's eyes are filled with tears as well.

Sparrow and Rafe have a way of getting to you. Their love is so pure and so healing for each other that I wouldn't want anything more for my best friend. As I hold Sparrow's bridal bouquet and my own, the heady, floral scent now infusing my thoughts with sweetness, I think about the roses in my hand. Despite their presence, the thorns along their stems never stood a chance of destroying their beauty. I think that's how it is with Graham and me. I've had many thorns that have gotten in our way. In the past, I've wounded him to protect myself, but he saw what was possible all along. Together, maybe we'll be able to remove all the thorns so I can heal more too. Because isn't that love? The ability to go through the mess and hurt each other just for being human, only to remain steadfast in love and choose each other again and again?

When we were together in the bridal suite earlier this morning, Sparrow told me it's up to me to decide what the future holds. She gave me a *koala hug* as we've termed it. (I'm scared of bears, so koala hugs are what we call the alternative). And she's right. Witnessing the fulfillment of her love as she marries Rafe, like the brave and fearless woman she is, makes me want to write my own love story.

Sparrow's vintage wedding gown is so stunning I could squeal just thinking about it. With a deep V-neck and capped sleeves overlaid with lace, it molds to her frame, tapering at the waist and flowing out into a dreamy mix of floor-length tulle and lace. Rafe is in a suit hand-tailored by his father's fashion house. Even though they still haven't reconciled fully, the suit was a nice gesture from his parents. It's a slim-fit suit with a button-up, no tie. Of course, he is wearing a pair of fresh high-top sneakers. He planned to wear loafers, but Sparrow wouldn't have it.

Pastor Wilfred continues, "Sparrow, do you take this man to be your lawfully wedded husband, to have and to hold—"

"I do." Her serene voice speaks with bold surety, her hands clasped in Rafe's.

A soft laugh echoes throughout the church. They're so sure that Pastor Wilfred need not even finish the words. He does it anyway and makes them repeat it, but the scene is so sweet I don't know how to process it. I think if I didn't work with sugar all the time, acclimating me to such a syrupy lovefest, the sight of it would make me ill.

"Sparrow," Rafe begins, "you're my favorite song. If I only get to hold onto one thing in this life, it has to be you. It must be you. If I only get to sing about one thing, it must be our love. Thank you for seeing me. I promise to always save you a dance."

I pull a tissue from the middle of my bouquet, glad that I had the foresight to stuff them in there for these moments. I'm not typically a crier, but the emotion of my life these past few weeks has wrecked me in so many ways.

"Rafe," Sparrow says with a content smile, "I think from the first time I saw your hair sticking out of the back of your baseball cap on that train from Boston, my soul knew. You're my person. God is so kind to have given me you. I know . . . I know my parents would've loved you. You've proven to me that we can have both what we want and what we need in a person. Thank you for loving me so well. You've given me the full kind of love—and I promise I'm fully yours forever."

Now, everyone is a wreck. Sniffling can be heard throughout the stone church, which is covered in flowers and candlelight. Looking around through clouded vision, I see the shiny evidence of tears on faces all over the room.

I'm choking thinking of how Sparrow's dad would have

gleamed with pride watching this—so proud of them both. The bride and groom have both experienced heartache. They knew what was at stake when they fully committed to loving each other. And they both chose each other above all the doubts and fears.

I lift my eyes to look at Graham. His eyes are still brimming with tears, a blink away from falling. If I was close enough, I would catch them when they do.

Sparrow and Rafe exchange their rings while my mind starts to race. Hungrily, I take in the sight of Graham in his suit, his posture perfect, his intensity devastating. I suck in a breath, watching as he pulls something from his pocket and slowly adds it to the boutonniere on his jacket lapel. It's a tiny bunch of chamomile flowers.

Like a veil lifting, I see our future all so clearly. I see myself in a white gown with black trim. Graham is in a suit. (Well, he's almost always in a suit, but a suit on his wedding day? Unprecedented.) I picture nights by the fire, his fingers weaving through my hair. I imagine bowls of soup and babies in our arms. I envision card games and chocolate cake clinging to our lips and our memories. I picture fighting and then making up in ways that cause my bones to ache with need.

When it comes to the rest of our lives? I want all of this with him. The truth, even when I couldn't see it, is that I've wanted this with him all along. And this time, I'm not going to let myself get in the way.

"You may now kiss the bride!" Pastor Wilfred yells, and the church erupts with applause and shouts, the loudest cheers being from Gladys, Ivy, and Grey. I can hear their joy as they celebrate from the front row.

Rafe holds Sparrow like she hung the moon, and their kiss is anything but PG. I almost expect the pastor to need to step in, but he's forced his attention to the ceiling. He looks back toward the happy couple in time to see Rafe holding Sparrow so closely that it's like they've become one heart. I've never seen anyone hold someone like they hold each other—as if they're holding on for dear life while also completely content to never let go. My eyes travel again to Graham. He is clapping and giving some sort of whooping sound that surprises me, coming from his smiling mouth.

When the newlyweds release each other enough to face the back of the church, I hold out the bridal bouquet to Sparrow. Her eyes are loaded with a reflection of so much history and friendship between us. Tears threaten to pour from my eyes again, but I hold them back, nodding to let her know that it's okay. I give her a shooing motion with my head and watch as the newly married couple hustle down the aisle. All the way, Rafe's arm is up in the air like he's on top of the world. And I know he truly is.

I'm watching their exit, but I catch Graham's arm reaching for me from the corner of my eye. His suit creases at his elbow, his arm extended, waiting for me to take it. I look up at him and feel in every way that this moment could've been ours. I believe it still can be. I know if Cricket is catching any of this on camera, what she will capture is the longing I feel for this to be permanent.

"Go on, you two," Pastor Wilfred encourages.

I face the back of the church and try to figure out how I can kiss Graham before we make it down the aisle. When we burst through the exit into the spring air, whose warmth swirls around us with a hint of dusk at the edges, I'm ready for my own forever to begin. In the evening glow, I can feel winter finally relenting, and it feels like love would whisper for us to wake up from the ground covered by frost.

With the newlyweds on the move toward their car, we follow. We'll be heading to Wicked Good Farms to get some pictures before everyone arrives for the reception at the big white barn. The next few hours will be glorious. Still, I know that all night, I'll be holding my heart up with a string still in knots over Graham.

Graham hasn't stopped staring at me. During every photo, whether we are in the shot or not, his intensity breaks my concentration. After my little revelation in church, I'm struggling to maintain my composure.

It was a gorgeous wedding, a beautiful and perfect wedding. But I'd be lying to myself if I didn't admit how much I long to be alone with Graham for a few minutes to show him how much I love him. Finally, at the end of what feels like a thousand clicks of the camera and enough photos taken of us that I'm going to make one of those photo books to ensure I can hold onto all of them, it's time to get ready for the reception.

Sparrow and Rafe huddle close to each other, whispering things that—if I heard them—I probably would need to have my ears cleaned out or extensive therapy to recover from. I feel the countdown clock ticking in my bones. They wander along the path, the distance between us growing. I'm left with no choice. I decide to make a move that I know I won't regret.

"Okay, you! I need to talk to you now." I'm a woman on

a mission, and I can't linger here another moment without laying all our cards out on the table. "I love you, Graham."

He blinks, giving no other expression or emotion. He merely stands on the path . . . blinking.

"And I know people say all this stuff about love and blah, blah, blah," I continue. Of course I'm using words that aren't words to express my love for him on my best friend's wedding day, of all days. "You're my favorite. I did a terrible job of showing you that."

Graham still hasn't moved. If not for the rise and fall of his chest under his suit and the steady blinking, I would think we lost him about thirty seconds ago.

"Fine, you want me to keep going?" I ramble. "When I stood at the altar in church, watching our two best friends declare their love for each other to the world, I saw it. You. Me. Babies. Are you scared yet? Because you should be. Because I'm scared. I'm so scared. Last night and that little display of yours this morning knocked some sense into me, you know? And so did the sight of you in that suit, because . . . wow. But that's for another time." I inhale, trying to catch my breath from the heady rush of words.

"The point is that you're worth everything, Graham. You've always been worth everything. Every doubt and every fear is soothed by your presence. I'm so sorry that you ever had cause to doubt that."

At this point, tears are streaming down my face unbridled. I know my makeup has been shot to sticky streaks. As evidence, I glance down to see a concealer and mascara-tinged droplet stain on the bodice of my dress. I'm going to have to do serious damage control before we enter the barn for the reception.

"And you were right," I whisper. "You're not the

Wickham of this story. You never were. That is who I meant, by the way, when we met in the movie theater. The truth is, you're the Darcy of it all. You make me want to go on those adventures we talked about. I think my heart knew it didn't want to go without you. You make me want to tell my mind to stop warring against what I want. Because you're all that I want."

A pulsing suddenly begins to move through his jaw. I can see the evidence of my words sinking in. His hands clench and unclench. His weight shifts, like he wants to move closer, but something is still holding him back. Finally, his throat clears.

"Lily, I'm only going to ask this one time," he says, his voice gravelly and delicious. "I thought we said what we needed to say last night. I was giving you time to be sure. But this—what you're saying . . . I need it confirmed. You know how my mind works."

I have a suspicion that what he's about to ask me is going to change the trajectory of my life and our lives if my wishes are answered. I take a deep breath and nod, using the back of my hand to dab at the tears streaking my face.

"What do you want?"

"I want you to fight with me," I urge.

The tone of my voice is almost begging him to hear the layers of what I'm trying to say. I don't mean to fight in a violent, unsavory way. I mean, I want him to fight with me like he shows up every time I see him with a fire in his eyes and an unbreakable composure that urges me to unravel him in the best way. When we struggle, I want my body to get a few degrees warmer and my heart to beat faster just from being near him.

"Why on earth would I want to do that?" His brow is

furrowed, his breathing heavy. Graham isn't messing around.

I know all my cards need to go on the table. It's now or never. "Because when you fight with me, it feels like you're fighting for me."

He takes a short step forward, his hands shoved into his pockets, his eyes sparking with a look I know will burn for a lifetime. "Lily," he whispers, a cross between a plea and a prayer.

Already, my eyes are filling again with tears. He pulls one hand from his pocket and extends it toward me. It's all there, just as when I wrestled myself to sleep. The watch wrapped around his wrist, the crinkle of his shirt where it's rolled up to his forearms, the rise and fall of his chest as I wait for his response.

Tilting up my chin, I imagine what it might be like to feel Graham's kiss again after the affection we've witnessed today. I want that affection to grace my life more than anything I've ever wanted. His long strides carry him to me, and Graham's warm hands rise to cradle my face. My eyes close from the sensation.

"Open your eyes, love," he says into the air between us.

I take a ragged breath and open them, staring into piercing blue eyes that never left my soul. Their rims are wet. Tenderly, I try to wipe his tears away with the edge of my hand. There's a soft smile on his face, paired with a lingering look of disbelief.

"You called me 'love,'" I whisper. "Still."

"I did," he says without hesitation.

"Even after all this time . . . you still look at me like I'm somehow made of magic."

"Yes. I believe you are."

"We've lost so much time," I whisper. The weight of my words settles between us. "Are you sure there can be forgiveness for what I did to keep us apart? I couldn't take it if you woke up one day and realized that you can't get over it."

"Lily, I'll never get over it."

My breath catches, his tortured blue eyes tearing me apart.

"Only because I've never gotten over you," he continues. "The past is all part of our story now. We can't change it. We won't forget it, try as we might. There's time lost that we won't get back. But we can love each other with all we have now. We can choose to give grace to each other."

Lifting my hand, I wrap my fingers around the back of his neck, caressing the ends of his hair. I feel it when he relaxes into our embrace. My investigative, protective angel finally trusts that I'm not going anywhere. I know I'll reach for him for the rest of my life.

"At the altar, I . . . I wanted it to be us standing there."

His eyes widen, searching my features. "Sweetheart, I—" he says, and I stop his words with another kiss.

The kiss is urgent, and it's hungry, the weight of it wrapping through my spine like tendrils on a vine. It's the fragrance of tulips in the spring and the creamy look of pastel-colored roses. It's chamomile tea with extra honey. It's the stuff that fairy tales are made of.

His lips move sweetly over mine, savoring, testing, asking me without words if I'm still the woman who remembers the bolt of lightning that struck us both. We have stories to remind ourselves of what's possible. All the tales of old hold an element of universal truth—we want to be loved. We get caught up in our own humanity and stumble over obstacles of our own making. If we're brave enough, we may be able to make it to the other side, holding onto something or someone who looks an awful lot like what we wanted all along.

Maybe I wasn't born at the wrong time after all. My own love story is found not in the past but in the present.

I know this to be true: While Sparrow and Rafe are celebrating their love tonight, so are we.

We part. Graham's fingers lightly caress my collarbone, his thumbs casually turning downward, creating a makeshift heart near my chest.

Finally and truly, our love is made new.

Chapter Thirty-One

Lily

The week following the wedding feels like a dream. While Sparrow and Rafe are away on their honeymoon in Paris, I move around town with a ridiculous smile on my face and hope in my heart that things are truly changing. The love of my life and I are headed toward a new season.

The moment when Rafe and Sparrow Durand—wow, that will take a moment to get used to—entered the white barn on their wedding night, the crowd erupted. The barn was transformed into a reception hall at Wicked Good Farms. The scene was chaos and joy and everything lovely. I don't think I let go of Graham's hand once after our confessions of love before the reception. It turns out that I may love those photos of us after all. Instead of hiding them in my bedside table, I'll be able to hang them on my wall . . . well, maybe *our* wall.

Gladys stood in the corner, yelling something to a group of townspeople that sounded strangely like, "To the calendar!" I'm going to need to ask her about it, but she's been cunningly avoiding me ever since. Not one person was sitting as the newlyweds entered. Everyone celebrated the couple, who may be (or feel like) orphans but who have found their family in this quiet little corner of the world.

As we watched Rafe and Sparrow step on the dance floor for their first dance as a married couple, Graham's arm wrapped around my waist. We stared at the crowd, the warmth of it all overtaking my senses and quieting my fears. Grey danced with her best friend, Boston, whom she definitely wants to be more. Ivy ended up bringing her older brother, Freddie (short for Frederick). That night reminded me of what a gift it is to be a part of this wild group of people. I love their quirks, our history, the way they make me question my life choices, and the love that's evident every day.

Over the past week, Graham hasn't let me out of his sight, and I love it. He seems to need to touch me at all times. I even tried to make chocolate truffles with one hand the other day while my other one held his. It was my idea. Call it a bit obsessive (on my part), but he's become like the best type of name-brand cling wrap.

While he still wears suits each day, I did get him to cave once and go shopping. He now owns a few new V-neck t-shirts and a pair of jeans that he said he may wear for half a day on Saturdays. I don't ever want him to change, but I do want to know that he's comfortable enough not to feel the need to use his clothing as a shield. He even decided—of his own volition, I might add—to wear a baseball hat on occasion. Now, I absolutely see the appeal and why Sparrow wouldn't stop talking about Rafe in one.

Yesterday, at the café, after writing his emails and making his calls for Rafe, and after a rousing card game of

Go Fish with Ollie, I handed Graham a newspaper and watched him settle in as if he was always meant to take up the corner near the counter. I plan to put a barstool on the edge, so he's technically in my space while still being on the side of a customer. I'm not complaining about the distraction it's been to have him linger so closely.

On the Sunday following the wedding, as I walk to Sparrow's Beret, I halt at the sight of a stack of newspapers on our front door. We never get the paper. Bending to pick it up, my eyes catch at the headline of the *Birch Borough Bulletin*: "A Girl Named Lily."

My heart picks up its pace as I plop down on the stoop outside the bakery, not even worrying that my delay could mean we won't have enough croissants for opening. Those flaky buggers are going to have to wait.

I open our newspaper, which consists of no more than a few pages of ads and town shenanigans on a typical day. I freeze at the sight of an article about me written by Graham. The featured photo is one of us at Sparrow and Rafe's wedding. We're staring at each other as if the whole world can be found in each other's eyes. If I didn't feel so happy, I would find it obnoxious. There's a photo of us from two years ago in LA printed right beside it.

"She helped me find the words . . ." I mutter, skimming over it and willing myself to keep reading despite the ginormous tears now streaking down my face. My man has written an entire article—an argument, really—on all the reasons we belong to each other.

I'm laughing as he goes on, with detail upon detail, about all the ways we're perfect together. There are pieces of evidence, statements from townspeople, and even a quote from his mother, stating that as soon as he first mentioned me, she knew his life would be forever changed. He annihilates every argument one could possibly contrive against us, and while it's not Austen, it's better because it's from him. The article is one of the most romantic things I've ever read in my life. Graham systematically disarms every argument I could ever conceive, channeling his skills from the courtroom once more in favor of us loving each other for the rest of our lives.

I pull out my phone and try to call him, but there is no answer. Instead, I run toward his place and bang on the door. Still no answer. The pressure to get back to the café is strong, but I'm determined to see or talk to him before I do anything else. How could I not?

"Hi, honey."

Graham's gravelly voice causes me to turn around. I've been looking over the bridge to the river below, the warmth of spring creeping into my heart. Today's breeze is the type that reminds me that I'm alive and that the cold has truly relinquished its hold for a while in the presence of a new season.

Graham is wearing his new jeans, a t-shirt, and a leather jacket (synthetic leather, of course). It's one he was eyeing at a shop last week. He must've gone back to get it.

"Hi, hot stuff," I reply.

He grins, holding out the to-go cup in his hands. "I made you tea."

"What kind?"

His raised eyebrow sends a spark down my spine. "You have to ask?"

I laugh lightly, the sound a bit foreign to me. My laughter

was hidden during the years without him, but it's breaking free now that there's this ease between us.

"Chamomile," I whisper. I catch his nod as he looks at the river, his jawline etched by the lingering sunrise, still spreading its light across the morning sky. "With honey."

It's things like this that have made me so irreversibly in love with him. What I feel for him has nothing to do with his appearance or words (both heart-melting in their own right) and everything to do with his character.

"With honey," he replies with a bit more confidence than required, but his tone is also on brand with where we're at in life right now—delighted to pick up where we left off while also starting new.

The thing that is not new and has only improved with age is how his presence makes my heart race. While I hid my attraction to him under the guise of anger and resentment for quite some time, the truth was that, without him, my heart ached to be his again.

I lift the paper between us, those pesky tears threatening to spill once more. "I tried calling you."

"Ahh," he says with a sheepish grin. "I thought you could use a physical reminder of my love. You know? In case you ever doubt again."

While the cup of tea warms my hands, he pulls me closer. His strong hands frame my jaw, and his blue eyes, once icy but now thawed with love, rove over my face. Dropping one hand to my shoulder, the other reaches up to wrap itself in my ponytail. Once, twice, three times, his fingers twine in my hair so gently it's almost a whisper, even though I know they are now entirely hidden in my strands. He settles his hand against the base of my neck and kisses me softly on the cheek. The scruff from his beard and the scent of his beard oil blend perfectly with the taste of honey from my last sip of tea. I turn my head into his shoulder, breathing in his fragrance.

"I won't doubt you again," I whisper into the soft skin below his ear, his pulse point greeting my lips. "I won't doubt myself either."

"Hmm," he hums. "That's good."

I lean back to look at his face, warm with affection and sweeter than the milk chocolate I love so dearly. The soft wind blows strands of my hair across my face, and my ponytail now feels disheveled and a bit off balance on my head. He releases it, and I pull down my hair, my fingers rapidly working on the band in a frantic effort to release it without pulling more hair from my head than necessary.

"Wait," Graham says. His arm gently pauses my movements. "Please leave it?"

The hesitancy in his voice tells me this moment means something to him. So, I go still, waiting for him to continue.

"In my dreams," he begins, and I feel my eyes widen, "you never had your hair down." He clears his throat, the edge of a smile working its way to his face.

Cautiously, he reaches out and strokes his hand through my hair, the tips of his fingers causing shivers to break out across my head and down my spine. I almost laugh at how electric his touch feels, but any urge to laugh pauses at the intensity in his eyes. Graham looks as if he's finally experiencing something for the first time that he thought was out of reach.

He pulls back and smiles down at me, the expression so full and glorious that it warms me more than the hot drink ever could. He mirrors my movements as I turn my body to face him, tangibly showing me how much he'll meet me every time.

Graham recently decided to bunk with Liam while his mom takes over his place, and Rafe moved in with Sparrow. The feeling of even more change is in the air. He has completed all the paperwork for his business. Already, as our fellow townspeople make themselves his personal version of strategic marketing, he is lined up to meet a few artists over the next month. Even though he decided to rent a home in Nashville for the times he and Rafe need it, he most likely won't be going anywhere after all. Or he'll find a way to take me with him.

"Ahh!" I yell, almost spilling my tea and scaring the crap out of Graham as he continues his caress of my hair.

"What is it?" There is panic in his voice.

"The croissants!" I take off running toward the bakery, Graham tailing me.

To my relief, he works with me the rest of the morning to help me catch up. I also suspect he wants to stay close to me. I'm not complaining. He's becoming quite an accomplished bakery assistant. The only time we end up being apart all day is when Graham takes a call from some fancy music people while I make more *pains au chocolat* than I've ever made on a Sunday. Once word began to get out that I personally temper the decadent chocolate for the center, they've been more popular than ever. My money is on Graham spreading the word.

Later that evening, after kisses in charming alleyways and saying goodbye for the night so many times I lose count, I enter the front door of my apartment building and find a little white envelope with my name on it peeking up from my jacket's pocket. I recognize the handwriting on it as one thousand percent belonging to Graham.

Running up the staircase, I rush in and close the door of my studio, already out of breath from anticipating what could be inside, and tear open the top—well, not tear . . . Truthfully, I open it gingerly so as not to ruin this paper artifact that I'll probably hang on to for far longer than necessary. Inside, I find a printed ticket to a Boston Red Sox game, the date for . . . tomorrow?

I pull out my phone to text him, but as I turn the envelope over in my hand, a small piece of paper falls to the ground. I stoop to pick it up, my eyes devouring the neat script.

A final challenge, one I hope you will accept. Wear your jersey. Love, G.

Graham knows I have a jersey because he gave it to me. It was one of many gifts he poured out while we basked in the bliss of our six-week romance in LA. I have never gotten rid of it. I couldn't. In light of tomorrow's game, I decide to let it be my one colored clothing item for the month.

Alarms flare inside my head as I throw everything onto the couch and rush to my closet to pull a box from the corner of the top shelf. It's a box with cryptic markings on the side. Little would anyone know that it holds some of my favorite things in the world. I bring the box to my bed, opening it to find items I don't think I would give up for anything, Graham's jersey being one of them.

Draping it over my arm, I return to the couch to find my phone and pull up Graham's number.

Lily: Game on.

Three little dots dance on the screen.

Hot Stuff: Still have your jersey?

I want to tell him I don't just to frustrate him. Instead, my fingers fly over my phone.

Lily: Guess you'll find out.

Silencing the ringer, I toss the phone into my bag. I collapse on the couch, my mind racing with possibilities. I don't know what Graham is playing at. We talked once about seeing a game together. A grin overtakes my face as I pull another item from the box. I study it. When I decide to take it with me to the game tomorrow night too, my heart begins to race. Whatever is in store for us, I'm ready to play ball.

I love the atmosphere in Fenway Park. In the world of Major League Baseball, it's the oldest ballpark, having opened in 1912. There's just nothing like it. From the *Green Monster* wall in left field, a favorite spot for players to measure home runs or grand slams and fun for the fans to sit on, the park is iconic in every way. As you move through the tunnels to get to your seat, you see the old wooden framework, bending a bit into a smile while holding the history of all the games ever played in Fenway Park. I try to catch Red Sox games whenever I can during the warmer months. Tonight, I'm just happy to be here with Lily, knowing she wants me near her. It doesn't matter why we're here as long as we're together.

"Why do you think these workers are just so dang amusing?" She nods toward the men who walk up and down the stadium steps with boxes, coolers, and food warmers on their heads. I know they are full of pretzels, cotton candy, or hot dogs. Watching them work is riveting. I know I couldn't even bench press what they probably lift. At the speed they fly along the rows, up and down on repeat, it's a wonder their calves don't burst through their pants. You can barely see their feet because they move so quickly.

"I need snacks!" Lily yells. She bolts from the seat, her purse swaying behind her as she hops up and runs down the aisle, trying to get someone's attention. Calmly, I raise my hand to one of the men, who holds what appears to be caramel corn. I'm munching on the buttery sweet goodness when Lily returns, her eyes wide and hair a little disheveled.

"How did you . . .?" She points to the caramel corn, shrugs, and then steals a kernel before sitting down without a care in the world.

A question burns in my mind, and I feel like I'm going to burst with the anticipation. The only thing stopping me from blurting it out is the fact that I haven't found a ring worthy of it. Nothing compares to the ring I lost on the beach that night, so I've held back, biding my time. I want to savor each moment we are dating, even though I'm ready to speed it along. I think I could run all the bases with the energy that's pulsing through me right now.

I look over to see Lily holding out a Fenway Frank for me, the name for the iconic hot dogs served at the park (and, for some reason, they do taste better than any other hot dog). It's covered in mustard and relish. She takes the biggest bite of a pretzel she bought for herself. It sticks up from the crook of her arm. The brilliance of the setting sun behind her casts a glow over her high ponytail, making her hair look like pure gold. She's the angel of the ballpark, and I happened to witness it.

A grin plays on her face as she chews, one cheek stuck out in pure joy, a hint of mustard layered on her top lip.

Clumsily, I reach for a napkin and start to hand it to her, but I quickly realize that, with her soda clutched in one hand and her pretzel in the other, she isn't able to wipe her mouth.

"Help!" she squeaks, laughing at this turn of events. I lean forward, folding the napkin and patting the top of her lip ever so gently. The edges of my fingers graze the satin skin of her cheek. I can't tear my eyes away from her lips, a cherry-red stain accentuating their Cupid's bow.

Her eyes widen, no doubt from the intensity I know I'm serving at this moment, but I can't help myself. For a moment, we're back to the time before things went wrong. It's just Lily and me out on the town, living life. My brain and body remember what it feels like to hold her without a care in the world. Vividly, I recall how it felt to kiss her perfect mouth and wait for her feistiness to make an appearance.

Even though we've rekindled our romance in Birch Borough, it hits me differently to know that we're out and about in Boston, in public, and Lily is officially back to being my girl.

She swallows, watching me, her grey eyes deepening as the charcoal embers of twilight around us turn to dusk. I move closer, and at the expression on her face as she tilts it up to me, my knees almost give out. It's a small gesture, but to know she's remembering our moments together means more than I ever thought it would. With a sudden resolve, I decide now is the time for me to do what I came here to do.

"Lily, I—"

Crack. The sound of a bat hitting the ball and screaming toward the stands has us scrambling to avoid getting hit. A teenager with a hoodie starts pumping his fists in the air as the crowd screams and cheers for the home run. Lily raises the hand clutching her soda toward the sky and screams at the top of her lungs. I can't help but laugh between cheers (we are in Boston after all). I beg my heart to remember this feeling forever.

That's the only time I see a score. Soon after the home run scored by the Red Sox, Lily insists she needs soft serve ice cream served in a plastic baseball cap. Even though there's a degree of chilliness in the evening air, it sounds amazing—until it isn't.

We've scored five more runs, and I've missed all of them while waiting in line.

"You'll have plenty of time," Lily said. "Nothing exciting will happen while you're gone."

At this point, should I be anyone else, I would think it's good luck for the Red Sox whenever I leave the stands to get some food.

I may have underestimated the courage I need not to propose we elope tonight. When I finally return to my seat, Lily digs into the chocolate and vanilla swirl ice cream topped with chocolate jimmies (sprinkles to most people who aren't from New England). I'm mesmerized.

If I hadn't already gotten Rafe's encouragement and blessing to ask Lily to marry me when I sent an SOS text to him earlier today, I would be a lot more nervous than I am. Thankfully, being the good friend he is, he didn't mind my invasion of his honeymoon. I'll owe him a case of French wine when he gets back.

The Red Sox are winning, the scoreboard lighting up the night sky as the dusk of a late-summer evening makes its full appearance. When we're in the eighth inning, everyone rises to their feet to join in singing the iconic "Sweet Caroline" blaring through the speakers.

Lily sways and joins the crowd as they chant, a tradition that seems to be something you can't escape in the stadium. All at once, it's like everyone gets the memo to give it their all, and no one minds a bit.

"Sweet Caroline . . . bum-bum-bum."

I'm laughing as Lily is jamming to her own beat, as she often does, singing with such a sweet smile on her face that my knees are wobbly. Emotion creeps up the back of my throat.

This is what I've dreamed of since we met—Lily carefree beside me, happiness in her eyes, ponytail swaying, her smile wide. Her image starts to swim as I wipe my eyes with the back of my hand. It took us a while to get here, but we made it. And I'm just so grateful I've gotten to live this story.

"So good! So good! So good!" the crowd inserts, per tradition, at just the right moments as the song continues.

The crowd is still cheering, yelling, and singing when I feel Lily's hand wrap around my wrist, pulling me to stand beside her. Her skin is silky and smells a bit like the snacks she's been consuming. She wipes a tear from one of my eyes, and my vision clears again.

"Graham," she says, and then she kisses me. Softly and sweetly, she wraps her arms around my neck, pushing onto her toes to show me how much she's glad to be with me, ice cream now abandoned. Out of everyone in the world, she's picked me to be near her. I feel how much she's missed me in that kiss.

Leaning back enough to study her face, I place a light kiss on the edge of her mouth then move to the other side.

She takes a sharp breath, simultaneously melting into me. I laugh. I knew she would remember this scene from a certain movie we both love and draw the correlation.

"A place for fun and dreams," she whispers in an echo of one of the best days of my life. And then Lily shocks me to my core by uttering the words I once never thought I'd hear. "Ask me, Graham."

Looking down between us, I see it. Clasped in her hand is the ring box I thought was lost long ago.

"How did you—? When did you—?" I stare at her in disbelief and wonder.

She wipes the tears falling from her eyes with the backs of her hands. "After that night, I went back and searched for it in the sand. Hands-and-knees type of searching. It took me hours, but I found it. I . . . I just knew it had to be mine."

"Lily . . ." The words in my throat are choked off as I decide I'm not going to finish that little segway of affection until later.

Her eyes sparkle, peering into my own. I'm struck as the light from the stadium creates a kaleidoscope of lavender and grey tones, mixing with the emotions swirling through her eyes.

Without a second thought—without waiting to see if she'll run from our love this time—I switch places with her so that I'm standing in the little concrete aisle. I drop to one knee. I don't need to question if this is the right moment. Her eyes widen, and her expression is a memory I'll cling to for the rest of my life. Instead of fear or heartache in her eyes, I only see hope.

"I could tell you how much you mean to me. I'm not sure you'd believe me," I begin, and she lets out a choked laugh, emotion pouring out from the edges of her eyes.

"You'd probably argue with me about it," I continue, encouraged by the disbelieving smile she's giving me as she bites the bottom of her lip, "and you'll definitely need to cease doing that with your lip if you want me to finish what I started here."

I'm still reeling from the fact that the ring I thought was lost forever—the ring I could never find the perfect replacement for—is now back in my hands. She's back in my hands.

The people next to us seem to catch onto what's happening. Cheers from people who've had too much to drink and those who love a good grand gesture ripple through our section. I register the flash of lights, no doubt because this moment is being recorded. Leave it to us to become a meme or go viral.

I look up at Lily as the breeze plays with the end of her ponytail. Suddenly, I can't continue. That darn ponytail undoes me every time. For all that we've done, for all that we've been through, the emotion is too much. The thought of my love for her is all-consuming. And I realize that if everything in our past is what brought us to this moment— the moment in which I'm vaguely questioning if it's mustard or ice cream that I've stuck my knee into on the concrete floor—then I'd do it a million times over.

"Lily, I—" I manage to get out. Instead of laughing or teasing, Lily does the most surprising thing by kneeling in front of me. We're wedged between the seats, my feet still sticking into the aisle.

"You truly have *the* ring?" I ask. The fact that she's holding it out to me instead of running from it sends fireworks of hope shooting through my heart.

She shakes her head. "You didn't lose it after all. You didn't lose *me* after all."

"You've had it all this time?"

If she thinks I'm upset that she held on to it, she doesn't realize how I've often felt like it was only lost because it wasn't on her finger. That ring has always been meant to be her own.

She hands me the small box, and I open it slowly, lifting it above the seats where a stream of light catches it. Lily extends one hand cautiously, pulling it back, then reaching for it again. I give her a nod to encourage her.

Instead of squealing or yelling as I'm so accustomed to her doing, Lily slides the ring onto her left ring finger. She clutches it, and I know without a shadow of a doubt that the only way it will leave her hand is if someone pries it from her. Softly, she moves her fingers over the top of my forehead, the effect sending a shiver through me. She traces my face, her eyes shining with reflected light. As her hands rest on the sides of my jawline, a look of determination that I've rarely seen etches itself within her features.

"Marry me," she whispers.

Her eyes search mine, exposing all my adoration for her. I pull her toward me, my neck nestling in the curve of her own. I nuzzle in, catching the scent of her as I feel her arms wrap around me. Her touch unleashes something in me, and I start to cry. Relief washes over me that I didn't just win her heart back. I won mine back in the process too.

"Beat you to it," she laughs.

A chuckle escapes me along with the sob. I'm a grown man crying at a ballpark, but I couldn't care less.

The announcer sounds like an otherworldly narrator in a dream that I've had a thousand times. The only way I know it's real is because, this time, I feel Lily's pulse under my fingers. Her cool hands run over the jersey on my back, and the warmth of her breath hovers above my ear.

Leaning back to catch her gaze, I cradle her face between my hands. "I've said it before, but I'll say it again . . . you will always be my first choice. No one ever has or ever will come close to you." I say the words with as much power as I can, my voice catching. "I will never stop fighting for you. Are you with me, honey?"

Her response is a kiss that sears me to my core. Before we can take it too far, people around us cheer. Suddenly, we're laughing, shouts erupting throughout the stadium. When we rise to our feet, Lily wipes her face, and I wipe mine, and we stare at the lavender stone nestled between the glittering diamonds on the vintage ring together. With wide grins, we peek at the scoreboard to see what all the fuss has been about in the stadium and see it: a grand slam.

Chapter Thirty-Three

Lily

Sparrow and Rafe are still on their honeymoon in Paris. I'm trying to keep my crap together over the fact that I've got Graham back in my life (like, really). A fact he's very willing to remind me of every chance he gets. He says it's because we've missed too many kisses during our time apart. He calculated (of course he did) an approximate number of missed opportunities to show his affection. My now-swollen lips and giddy (yes, giddy) heart says: Noted.

Today, Graham and I drove to a wildflower field (yes, another one), this time near a castle. A real-life castle because the wild thing about New England is that you'll find seemingly random castles springing up throughout the region. It's as if people long ago wanted a piece of Europe here for themselves. I love it.

As soon as our plans were made, all I could picture was a dress that caught my eye in All Sewn Up. The gown was hovering in the corner during my bridesmaid dress fitting. I noticed it when Graham was (kindly) helping me out of my dress—which sounds a lot dirtier than it was. Yesterday, I rushed in, purchased it, and spent all night sewing black satin ribbon onto the edges and around the waist to make a wrapped look I'm obsessed with.

There was no way I was going to get married today without a hint of black. That color is my love language.

Of course, Graham already had a tux because he's Graham. I called Pastor Wilfred at five-thirty this morning and asked if he was available to meet us at "the castle" (I sent him the address, don't worry) late this afternoon, just before sunset. I think he thought I was on something, but when I told him Graham and I plan to get married, he was overjoyed.

I also called and begged the people who manage said castle to let us stand outside of it for thirty minutes. I may have bribed them with pastries. The fun thing about our state is that we don't need witnesses to get married, and there is no waiting period before they issue you a marriage license. This morning, when we met for croissants and cake, we stopped at the town clerk's office (I woke him up this morning too, thank you very much), and then Graham kissed me in a way that told me just how much he's willing to be my husband for the rest of my life. I can still feel the delectable scratch of his beard and smell the trace of mint from his beard oil.

I keep having moments where I bite my nails with a smile and nearly squeal. I know Sparrow would want to be here if she could, but I also know there's no way I'm spending another day without being able to call him my husband. She knows me enough to know what this means to me.

My parents were less than thrilled, but it feels like a relief not to feel the weight of it like I once feared. Yesterday afternoon, I called my parents, and before tapping on their contact information to place a video call, Graham gently held my free hand and asked if I was ready to announce my love for him. Little did he realize I was ready to shout it from the rooftops. (Or from the couch of my apartment, which resulted in Mr. Crumbs banging the end of his broom on his ceiling. He was yelling at me to stop my shenanigans, and I was stomping my feet to get him to stop while also telling him where he could send a wedding gift. It wasn't somewhere nice.)

After my liberating call during which Graham was announced as my soon-to-be husband and so much more than a friend, my parents said they'd love to get us monogrammed towels. I didn't even know those still existed. But I remembered they were what my parents always had hanging in their bathroom when I was a young girl, and so I'm choosing to take it as a sign that they know this is the real deal. My parents and I may not ever be what I had hoped, but allowing myself to love Graham is allowing me to dream of him with me for always, believing that we will get to share our lives. And that feels worth celebrating.

Thankfully, Ivy was free when I banged on her door late last night. She stayed with me overnight, gave me the best send-off possible while we ate pizza and chocolate, and even helped me get ready this morning while Grey attended a conference for booksellers. I invited her to come to our ceremony, of course. She said that, while she'd love to, if the whole town isn't in on it, she thinks this should be a sacred moment for Graham and me. She also mentioned that her boyfriend is now a nutcracker . . . as in, since she's already dreaming of the choreography for her studio's Christmas performance, she won't have time for anything else. "Waltz of the Flowers" will be keeping her up from now until New Year's.

As I sat in front of a makeshift mirror propped against one of my walls, and Ivy helped to put my hair into the highest ponytail possible, she asked me, "Do you think we have to search for love, or does love know where to find us?"

I've always loved all versions of *Cinderella*, but when it comes to Graham and me, even though I don't have stepsisters or talk to mice, I recognize that the clock once struck midnight on our time together. And it seemed I loved my shoes too much to have left a slipper behind. Still, he somehow knew where to find me.

Now, as I wait in the middle of a field, my dress clinging sweetly to my curves in the wind, the cool breeze pulsing through the ends of my hair and wrapping me in a hug, I'm finally ready to step into tomorrow with hope.

Sensing his presence, I turn to see Graham walking across the field in his tux, chamomile tucked into his suit pocket like a pocket square. My heart picks up at the determination evident on his face, at the gentle way his eyes caress me, his grin radiant. While a walk across the field from a Regency man is worth swooning over, Graham walking toward me with such affection on his face is worth committing my life to. Because he knows what it is to love me even when I don't know how to receive it. And I love him for it. So much that I could burst.

"Hi, my little wildflower," he says softly when he's close enough.

It's a new nickname, and I immediately decide it's the inspiration for my next tattoo. I think I could have it etched across my ribs and be happy with it always. He pauses as if he doesn't know if he can touch me or if this is all a dream we'll both wake up from in the morning. We've both had enough nightmares apart to want to do everything we can to stay in a dream state for the rest of our days.

"Lily, you're my heart. You've become all of it."

He repeats the words that have stayed with me since LA and now mean everything to me. There may be a hint of a sting hearing the phrase from long ago, but there's no pain this time. He's making things right between us with his words, showing me that everything we've shared has forged something immovable. We've built our own castle, if you will.

"Good," I whisper.

A tear slips down my cheeks as he stands close to me. His arms wrap around my waist to pull me against him. I feel the warmth of his hand through the satin where it rests on my lower back. The texture of his suit against my cheek is soft. He smells like fresh air and a place I can breathe freely until I run out of time. With him, I know that, no matter how life unfolds, no matter where I wander, I have a home to come back to.

"Please, just . . . keep being patient with me?"

I scrunch my nose to hold the emotion at bay as I lift my arms to wrap them around his neck, and he nods. The buttons of his suit jacket push into the fabric near my ribs, yet I pull him even closer still. I never want to let him go. I marvel at the love he holds for me. He's chosen me every time. And I choose him now, forever.

"So, are we really doing this thing?" I whisper into his ear. "Because you're it for me, got it?" I manage to get the words out, and the rightness of them sinks deep.

His beard sends shivers down my spine as he nuzzles into my neck, the warmth of his lips leaving a little trail of fire that descends into my bones. "I do now."

Chapter Thirty-Four

Graham

We eloped!" Lily blurts out, her left hand held up to show off the wedding band we added less than six hours ago, her smile as shiny as the diamond she's now carrying around.

Sparrow's face lights up the phone screen, a look of both shock and excitement crossing her face.

"My man!" I hear Rafe yell in the background with a whoop. He peeks over Sparrow's shoulder in disbelief.

"I know, I know," Lily continues. "It's unbelievable, and I don't want you to hate me because you're still not here—you just *had* to go back to Nashville instead of coming home first. We asked Pastor Wilfred to perform a ceremony in a wildflower field in front of that old castle we've always loved, Sparrow. The reception was pretty spotty up there, and I didn't want to bug you. Also, you're probably wondering if Graham was coerced into this, but I promise he was just as excited to elope as I was. He willingly wanted this."

Rafe and I give each other knowing grins, and I hold back a laugh. Of course Lily feels the need to explain why we decided to get married and make sure no one thinks this was a drunken decision. Impulsive? Yes. Necessary? Also, yes. It was time.

"How can I be mad that I missed it when I'm so happy for you?" Sparrow is nearly squealing with joy.

Both women have tears in their eyes, silently communicating their mutual joy without actually speaking any words.

"Can you believe it?" Lily exclaims.

"This is just the best!" Sparrow replies.

And then they're saying bits of words that make no sense on their own but clearly make sense to them.

"So soon!"

"The ring!"

"Honeymoon later!"

"Not an existential crisis!"

I bite my lip and ping-pong my focus between the two women, hopeful that this conversation is still working in my favor and isn't a secret cry for help.

"I love him more than anyone."

Lily's words stop me in my tracks. The way she's looking up at me tells me everything I've ever wanted to know about love and what it means. My confidence is boosted as I realize that I get to be with Lily every day and night for always. This is more than a dream because I get to hold her and touch her, and I don't need an excuse or a challenge to do it.

It's unnerving to watch the things we weren't sure would ever happen in our lives unfold suddenly. It's going to be Lily and me forever. I used to think if I could just get close enough to her, she'd let me love her. But now, I've realized that sometimes love also means letting go for a bit. That's a way to fight for someone too.

"Okay, so the dress . . . It was this little white thing from the tailor shop. I added black trim, and I thought Graham was going to pass out at the sight of it. I may have done that on purpose."

Lily winks at me, and I'm undone. I knew she wore the open-backed dress to marry me in for a reason. I'm not complaining, but she sure knows how to get under my skin . . . in the worst of ways and the best of ways.

"More than prom?" Sparrow says with a look of shock.

"Oh, way more than prom," Lily laughs, and I feel myself clench.

"What about prom?" I ask, and while they laugh, I text Rafe to tell him I'm done with this, and we need our own call soon.

"Honey, don't worry about it," Lily replies softly. Precariously perched on the edge of the couch, she lifts her chin to me and lets her lips brush my ear. "You've seen way more than anyone else ever has, that's for sure."

My cheeks absolutely burn with the heat that comment creates. Needless to say, Lily's special brand of flirting works for me. I'm saved by my phone vibrating. Lily sees it's Rafe calling, from the goofy picture now flashing on my phone, and gives me a searing kiss.

I groan lightly and answer the phone. "Save me."

Rafe's laugh is enough for me to know there's zero chance he's concerned about my well-being. "Not a chance."

I'm a grinning fool, and we both know it. "If anything, I think I should be mad at you. Holding out on telling me just how good you have it being married to your best friend, who is perhaps also someone who makes you so nuts . . ."

I sneak a look at Lily, who's still cracking up, using her hands to weave a story into the air. Every once in a while, she yells phrases that I don't understand, like, "More than a rake," "Above a hand flex," and, "These mashed potatoes are so creamy." I think I remember the last line being from one of her favorite rom-com movies.

Without missing a beat, I cover the end of the phone and walk quickly toward Lily. "Yes, I'm more than your favorite show. I'm glad you think I've finally reached Darcy status, and I will watch *While You Were Sleeping* with you again."

Lily's ponytail whips around. Her eyes flare. But the expression in them is something that looks like desire and definitely *not* rage.

"Rory, I gotta call you back." Lily ends the call.

I hear the cutoff of what might be, "Understood," from Sparrow before the phone is tossed. I'm riveted by this development and nearly forget who I am, despite hearing Rafe saying something on the phone. His faint voice is cut short by Sparrow yelling, "For the love, hang it up! I don't want to hear—" And the screen goes blank.

It's at this moment that I realize we're alone—in her apartment. *Our* apartment. And Lily is my wife. She seems to come to this realization at the same time. Her face comes positively alive with a grin, her posture becoming playful as she pulls herself up to lean against the back of the couch. She faces me with such a look that I'm nervous the furniture between us is going to burst into flames. And my brilliant thought? Let it burn.

Hours later, when all is quiet outside, the world is starting to move toward sleep, and Lily and I are sitting in our home—a thought I still can't wrap my mind around—and she's curled into me as we watch *Pride & Prejudice* for the millionth time.

"I know we've seen it before," Lily says softly, a hint of vulnerability reaching the edges of her tone. "But it's . . . different now."

I grin and pull her deeper into my side if that's even possible. My hand molds around the edge of her hip and the curve of her waist beneath the pajama short set she's wearing. The color is light blue and (surprisingly) not black, with tiny white hearts on the fabric. I want to trace each one just to show her there's nothing about her that's not important to me. Everything I do for her—from the special bands I picked up for her to help with hair breakage to ensuring she has static spray in her purse for the times her apron that reads *pain of chocolate* sticks to whatever she's wearing each day—I'm determined to make sure she knows how much she is loved. Once, she said I make her want to soften, and while I'll never want to change her, I meant it when I said I hope she at least finds a safe space with me.

And the more she pretends she doesn't need caring for, the more I know that it means something when I do. I've learned she has been waiting to give herself permission to care for me too. She thinks of me in all the loud and quiet ways, from the pastries she makes to the time she spends running her fingers through my hair before we fall asleep.

I'm not sure how we got here. Some of it feels like a blur between waking up and letting myself dream. But just the chance to hold her for the rest of my life and know she has filled what used to be hollow is enough.

Elephants!" I yell into the dry air, the bright red earth an indication of how far from home we truly are. But when I turn to see Graham, his hair blowing in the wind as we ride on top of a Land Rover speeding down the African plain on safari, the smile on his face tells me I've taken my home with me on this trip.

Maybe that's the difference between what I thought my parents had and what I wanted to have all that time. It took me ages to realize that the greatest thing we can accomplish is to live a life of love. The ultimate bucket list item is to make someone our first choice. So, I don't need to be afraid of being limited or unable to care for him the way he needs because, somehow, love gives you the ability to be more than the person you are on your own.

The sparrow tattoo on my wrist peeks out as I extend my arm to point out a baby elephant that has just appeared from the brush. I grin, knowing how proud Sparrow is of me for letting love in and (for once in my life) using my spitfire spirit for something worthwhile and not internally destructive.

"C'mon, honey," Graham says, affection dripping off his words. He places his hand on top of mine—the one gripping one of the bars of the open-sided vehicle so we don't fly off—and rubs small circles with his thumb over my knuckles. The shiver it gives me has nothing to do with the adventure we're on and everything to do with the person I'm with.

Far in the distance, at the top of a hill, the silhouettes of trees blend with the silhouettes of giraffes. The pattern is almost one I could weave on a design, and I want to try to figure out how to make what I'm seeing into latte art one day. We've seen rhinos and a cheetah too.

Just yesterday, we went on a Nile River cruise, with crocodiles lurking just under the surface and larger-than-life hippos growling and breaking through the water with their giant mouths and teeth open to the sky. They're honestly terrifying animals, and I was incredibly grateful to be in the middle of a large boat. The truth is, I still held my breath anytime we drifted past one and plastered myself to Graham's side (not that he minded).

We decided late last night, while we were tucked away in our room at the lodge after eating our fill of delicious food and wine, that we'd go on at least one adventure each year for the rest of our lives. Let's face it. Our whole life will be an adventure, given the chemistry between us, which is always waiting to explode. But while I used to fear it, I now crave it because I know that spark creates something magical when each of our elements comes together. Much like the recipes and experiments I make with chocolate and baked goods, being with Graham is like inventing something new with the same elements every time. How could one possibly grow bored of that?

Deep in my soul, I know, while I still ache for the time we missed, there's an appreciation for him that I'm not sure I would've had if we didn't go through heartache with each other and come out on the other side. There's a certain strength in our relationship that I know is immovable because we wounded each other and then found the courage to heal together.

We know how much it hurts to fight *with* each other, so we fight *for* each other. And that has made all the difference.

It's not perfect. There are days I still want to throw things because I get caught up in my own head, wanting my own way. Yet, Graham is ever-present—steady, sure, and willing to investigate everything possible to bring a smile to my face. Since we've been married, I've found several ways to bring a smile to his face that are just too much fun.

On some days, I still feel the weight of my actions, including how I rejected him and the day he found me again. I almost can't believe that we ended up in the life we get to live together now. How kind is God to have given me someone who will (literally) go to the end of the world with me? Someone who will let me be free while keeping me safe?

Graham treasures me. He loves me. And as I take in the gold wedding band around his finger—classy and timeless, just like him—I'm in awe that I get to love him back for the rest of my life.

Graham

If you ever meet someone named Lily, hold onto them with everything you have. This is what I've learned in the course of my life. We all have thorns, and sometimes the ones you love need help removing them before they're able to be held. But it's worth the wrestle.

Lily is sitting on the balcony, overlooking the animal reserve below. In the week we've been in Africa, we've occasionally woken up to giraffes looking in through the windows on the third floor or the sound of hyenas whooping in the distance. It's been an adventure that I know we'll never forget.

I stir in our bed and sit up, watching as Lily fidgets with the lens of the camera, working to bring something she sees into focus. Her glowing blonde hair is in a long braid down her back, legs curled up beneath her. A once-steaming mug of coffee is abandoned beside her, along with a half-eaten pastry. As I lean forward a little more, I catch the shiny wrapper of what used to be a chocolate bar lightly fluttering in the wind. I chuckle to myself and rise.

She senses I'm awake and turns to face me, her eyes lighting up as a smile breaks over her face. I hope she always looks at me like this. Gently removing the strap from around her neck and setting it on the chair, she rushes to the sliding glass door.

I'm already waiting on the other side when it cracks open, the sound of bird calls in the nearby trees breaking through the air that crackles with energy between us. Moving toward me slowly, as if she's trying to find someone in their natural habitat, she gives me a grin that weakens my knees.

"Hi." She smiles as my eyes rove over her face. I'm exploring every detail I can, always trying to track the ways she looks different to me in each segment of the day.

"Hi, little wildflower," I respond, chronicling the new details I'm finding today. The sunlight makes the edges of her lavender-grey eyes a little darker, freckles are starting to appear on her cheeks and the tip of her nose because of the sunlight we've been enjoying this past week, and a speck of melted chocolate lingers near her top lip.

"What?" she asks.

My breath hitches when her eyes snag on my mouth. My insides are on fire, and it's all I can do not to take her in my arms and show her all the ways I will treasure her for the rest of my life. Then I realize I actually can do just that. After years of holding back and trying to rid myself of my love for her, I'm free to pour out my affection on her and feel her heart opening more to me each day. It's a miracle I didn't dare to hope for.

I bend down to pick her up and hold her in my arms. The surprise of it all sends a squeal from her mouth and a laugh into the morning mood. She's still sassy, she still holds her own, and she still yells her opinions into the world. But she has also softened with me in such a way that *my* Lily, the one who fought with me every step of the way before now, is now battling for me too. She's positively radiant.

Her arms tighten around my neck, and her fingers gently brush through the back of my hair. I'm practically purring like the wild cats that I'm sure we'll see later today when I feel the air charge to another level.

"Graham."

My eyes meet hers, the love she has for me as clear as the cloudless blue sky. I furrow my brow, waiting for her to ask or tell me what's on her mind.

"I need to tell you something," she whispers, her eyes scanning my features. I'm still holding her close, unwilling to put her down yet unless she asks me to.

"What do you want to tell me?"

I walk us over to the bed and gently place her on the edge. I kneel in front of her to stay at eye level. Her gaze flares with heat, and my heartbeat quickens as she begins to run her hands over my face, slowly and carefully, like she's tempering chocolate and wants to know how my features are designed.

This is love, the ability to let myself be open before her, nothing hidden, and allow her to be the same with me. It's the ability to forget the wrongs between us and still choose each other, still protect each other. And to do it all with joy because it's my joy to love her. Love permits me to be the one she holds onto despite her independence, knowing that, while she doesn't need me to be able to do all the incredible things that have yet to unfold in her life, she wants me beside her with her whole heart.

"Are you trying to figure out how to replicate my face, or what's going on here?" I tease, delighting in the smile forming on her face.

"I have to make sure you're really you. Ever since we've gotten here, you've turned even more into a mush." She's grinning, and I know she loves how much I care for her and prioritize her in everything I do.

Soon, I'll need to go on some music tours with Rafe. I won't be in town every moment like I have been. So, while we've been away, I've already been searching for houses in Birch Borough that Lily may love. I want it to be a surprise when I find the right one, and I've already arranged for Ivy to take over Lily's apartment since it's so close to the dance studio, when a deal goes through.

After we eloped, the town quickly rallied to show their support. It looks like the only thing I needed to earn their welcome was to have Lily's full approval, not just in words but in actions. Although, I have to say that Gladys and Lucy seem to have been on my side from the start.

They told me they had to know I was worthy of their girl, worthy of standing beside her as her husband. And with every part of me, I know I proved just that. We don't always win the battles we face, but in this instance, we won.

"I have to tell you . . ." Lily continues, the feeling of her fingers caressing my face bringing me back to the moment, "I truly love you, Graham."

Lily runs her fingers through the edges of my beard, and I know that's my sign to kiss her like it's our first time and like it could be our last. Her passion for everything in life makes me want to remember these moments and live like we're mad with love for each other because, it turns out, we are.

I lean closer to her, my hands pressing into the bed on either side of her hips. I watch as her gaze, heavy with love, drops to my mouth. Slowly, ever so carefully, I feather my lips over hers, breathing her in and taking my time. I feel her impatience gathering, but she waits, ready to meet me for what we know will be a storm of love to get lost in for a while.

"Lily?" I whisper, the scent of sweet chocolate on her breath a tease.

"Yes, Graham?" she replies.

Even now, I'm still not always used to hearing her say my real name, so I treasure it every time she does. It proves to me that we're so much closer than I ever hoped we could be again.

"Don't play fair with me."

Her eyes spark, and her mouth is on mine again before I can take another breath. All may be fair in love and war, but fighting for someone you love is a whole lot more satisfying. For the rest of our lives, I'll never stop fighting for Lily in every way she'll let me.

She breaks the intensity to tease the edges of my smile, her silky lips breathing fire into my bones and mind. I move to capture her sassy grin, but before I can—with one arm wrapped around my neck and the other around my back— she pulls back enough to hum between us, "You know I love a good challenge."

Lily (again)

Over the summer, I feel like I'm soaring. The goodness Graham adds to my life reminds me that there are still people in this world who know what it means to love someone more than themselves.

There are moments of intense passion and—yes— irritation (I think I'll always love riling him up a bit). In all the moments, I tell him that I love him. He tells me that he knows.

We adventure around the world, from sheep farms in England to vineyards in Italy. We eat Thai food in Bangkok and pretzels in Germany. We even go to Paris to see what all the fuss is about. (It turns out it's more than great.)

Everything feels perfect because Graham is beside me. I always use his real name and invent new ways to be incredibly vocal about how much I love him and am his girl. After long days in which I'm covered in chocolate and flour, sometimes with Graham baking beside me, we collapse into each other and hold on even tighter. We watch *Pride & Prejudice,* and he reads me excerpts of the novel at night, sometimes right before I fall asleep.

I hoard each memory of his hands cradling my face or braiding my hair, knowing that, at any moment, he will kiss me like it's the first time and the last. I've never felt so thoroughly adored. He loves me with an intensity that tells me he'll always care for me and keep me close. I'm reminded that he has always found me beautiful. And I believe him.

And each night, when sleep hovers around us and vulnerability softens us both, I remember how far we've come. Our love is like lightning, continuously pulsing through our frames and pulling us deeper into love. We share more chocolate bars than we can count, and when I see my ring—the one that made it through the tempest with us—I do my best not to tear up each time.

Because I have Graham's whole heart. And he has mine.

Acknowledgments

For you, dear reader. Thank you for finding my second book and for taking a moment to read this part too. I hope you've found words that stay with you awhile. I wrote this book in a very challenging season, when I wrestled with doubt, loneliness, and the pressure life can sometimes bring. This book brought healing in unexpected ways. And, while I was certain this book would end up shorter than *I Love You in French*, it ended up being much, much longer. Lily and Graham had more to say, and I'm so glad I listened. They were complicated and feisty and beautiful and pulled on pieces of my heart that I didn't know existed. I will always treasure their story, so thank you for trusting me enough to read it.

Britt, we've done it again. You've loved Lily and Graham so well, and I have felt your support through every text, email, and edit along the way. You are a gift, and I appreciate you so much. Thank you for really seeing me and what I'm trying to say and creating space for me to trust you with my stories. Let's work together for many more, shall we?

Jenn, it's a gift to have your excellence added to my writing journey. Thank you once again for your patience and understanding and for your overwhelming kindness. I'm so grateful.

Erica, thank you times two because I wouldn't have had ILYIF without you! Your encouragement and support have meant so much to me. Thank you for doing what I couldn't and for ensuring my books are lovely for readers to move through.

Hailey, thank you for your encouragement and support and for being the very first alpha/beta/all the things reader I've ever had but, more importantly, for being my friend. Your comments have made me both laugh and cry, and trusting you with this story was invaluable–thank you for loving Lily and Graham in their unpolished state and for being with me on this novel-writing journey. I still can hardly believe that I used to get lost in your gorgeous books (and still do) and can now tell you so in real life. #teamtrentforlife

Philly Fam (and Elijah, Ashlee, A, & Z), thank you for believing that writing books is simply a part of my life and for believing that my stories are important (and for treating me as though my writing is far more well known than it currently is!). You are the cheering section I've needed. (And Kirby, I hope this one still makes you want to read another chapter.)

Alyssa, I still can't get over that I get to have your gorgeous art on (and in) another book. You capture my characters and then exceed my dreams with how they show up in the world. I still don't know how you perfectly knew who Graham needed to be with his gentleness and kind eyes. Thank you for your friendship and for making beautiful things to surround my stories.

Tay, can you believe we've done this twice? Having you as my friend and someone I can depend on to see my books make it to the finish line means the world. You have been a source of comfort and encouragement and remind me that everything is going to be OK. I'm so grateful.

Jen Grisanti, thank you for knowing what I'm capable of and always calling me to rise to it. You pull the parts of stories out of me that I need the courage to find, and it's been one of the best gifts. Thank you for your support and belief–I will always be grateful.

Liz, I hope this book is long enough for you! Thank you for reminding me why I do my best to keep writing the love stories that keep me up at night.

To the friends who have supported my writing and send me texts or messages to encourage me to keep going–I appreciate you.

Derek and Leah, I will still think of you with each book I write.

Mama, thank you for listening when I needed to talk through how Lily and Graham were wrestling with me and why I couldn't let go of their story. Your support means so much, and I love you.

To the beautiful readers who leave me comments, reviews, or message me to tell me you're excited about anything I'm writing: I hope I never get over it. I've held these characters so close to my heart, that to share them with you and know that they also move you in any way feels like one of the biggest gifts of my life. Thank you for your support. I feel it all.

And, once again, I couldn't close this book without giving thanks to my Creator–these dreams You've put in me to write have given me a determination to create and have brought a fulfillment that I didn't know was possible. Keep my heart soft.

ABOUT SARA NORTH

Sara North is a New England native who often dreams of Paris. While books held her heart first, Sara's training included writing and story development for both film and television scripts and fueled her desire to create with heart.

With a passion to cheer on creatives and writers across art forms and industries, Sara recognizes the power of stories to bring healing, hope, and happiness. When she's not writing books to build a dream on, her loves include 90s rom-coms, Old Hollywood films, Hallmark Christmas movies, beloved sitcoms, music to match her mood, café hopping, baking, eating chocolate, and celebrating all things fall.

AuthorSaraNorth.com | @AuthorSaraNorth